Rav

"Superb character   world,
with a detective s   into the
storyline. Marshall Ryan Maresca impressed me with *The
Thorn of Dentonhill*, but *A Murder of Mages* has secured
me as a fan."   —*Fresh Fiction*

"*A Murder of Mages* was another hit for me, a fantastic
read from a new talent whose star continues to be on the
rise."   —Bibliosanctum

"Books like this are just fun to read."
                                    —The Tenacious Reader

"*[A Murder of Mages]* is the perfect combination of urban
fantasy, magic, and mystery."
                                    —Kings River Life Magazine

"Marshall Ryan Maresca has done it again. After introducing readers to Maradaine through the eyes of criminals in
The Thorn of Dentonhill, he focuses now on the constabulary, the ones catching the criminals, in *A Murder of
Mages*.... Another rollicking adventure of magic and
mayhem."   —The Qwillery

"Maresca's debut is smart, fast, and engaging fantasy crime
in the mold of Brent Weeks and Harry Harrison. Just
perfect."
—Kat Richardson, national bestselling author of *Revenant*

"Fantasy adventure readers, especially fans of spell-wielding
students, will enjoy these lively characters and their high-
energy story."   —*Publishers Weekly*

DAW Books presents the
novels of Marshall Ryan Maresca:

Maradaine:
THE THORN OF DENTONHILL
THE ALCHEMY OF CHAOS
THE IMPOSTERS OF AVENTIL

*

Maradaine Constabulary:
A MURDER OF MAGES
AN IMPORT OF INTRIGUE
A PARLIAMENT OF BODIES*

*

Streets of Maradaine:
THE HOLVER ALLEY CREW
LADY HENTERMAN'S WARDROBE

*

Maradaine Elite:
THE WAY OF THE SHIELD*

*Coming soon from DAW

MARSHALL RYAN MARESCA

LADY HENTERMAN'S WARDROBE

A Streets of Maradaine Novel

DAW BOOKS, INC.

DONALD A. WOLLHEIM, FOUNDER

375 Hudson Street, New York, NY 10014

ELIZABETH R. WOLLHEIM
SHEILA E. GILBERT
PUBLISHERS

www.dawbooks.com

First Printing, March 2018
1 2 3 4 5 6 7 8 9

DAW TRADEMARK REGISTERED
U.S. PAT. AND TM. OFF. AND FOREIGN COUNTRIES
—MARCA REGISTRADA
HECHO EN U.S.A.
        PRINTED IN THE U.S.A.

Acknowledgments

Several years ago, I got an email from my friend and beta-reader Miriam Robinson Gould. She had just read the draft of *The Holver Alley Crew*, and I had told her my plans for the second book of that series. Her response was simple: "I will not be pleased until I have book two in my hands."

Miriam, it's in your hands now.

Miriam has been a first reader for me for years now, and she and Kevin Jewell have been invaluable for all the books, including this one.

Of course, I'm grateful for the help and support of so many people. Novel writing is a marathon, and you need your trainers, coaches, and folks with water on the sidelines to make it through.

In addition to Miriam and Kevin, there's a whole community of writers whom I rely on, including Stina Leicht and Amanda Downum at the top of the list. There's my agent, Mike Kabongo. My editor, Sheila Gilbert (ahem: Hugo-winning Best Editor Sheila Gilbert), and everyone else at DAW and Penguin Random House: Betsy, Josh, Katie, Kayleigh, Alexis, and several more whose work is so behind the scenes I don't even see it.

Then, there's Dan Fawcett—the man who's added more to Maradaine, and especially to Asti & Verci, than I could ever calculate.

Further thanks are owed to my parents, Nancy and Louis, my mother-in-law, Kateri, and my son, Nicholas.

And highest and first in my heart, my wife Deidre. None of this, absolutely none, would have come about without her. She's the north star by which I can always navigate my way.

LADY HENTERMAN'S WARDROBE

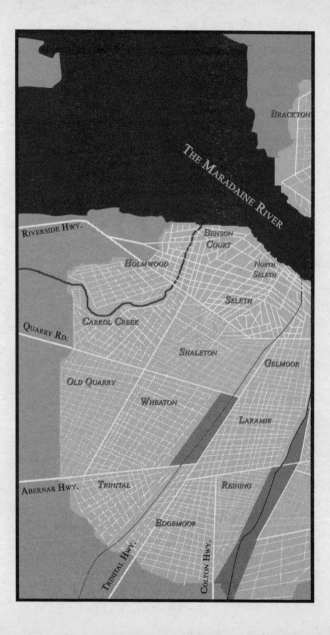

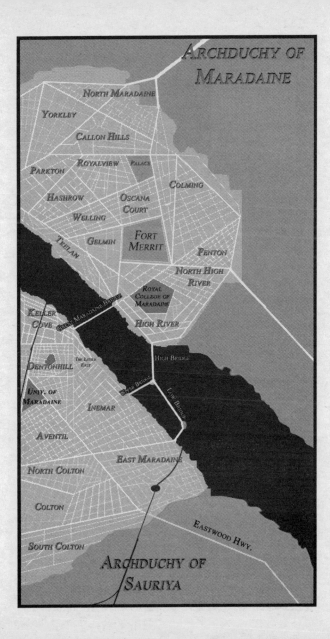

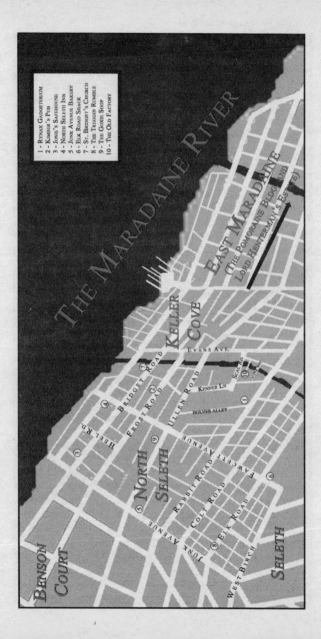

1 - Rynax Gadgeterium
2 - Kimber's Pub
3 - Josh's Safehouse
4 - Ninth Seleth Inn
5 - Junk Avenue Bakery
6 - Elk Road Shack
7 - St. Bridget's Church
8 - The Trisoon Rumble
9 - The Gixie Shop
10 - The Old Factory

THE MARADAINE RIVER

EAST MARADAINE
(THE POMORAINE BRIDGE AND
LORD HENTERMAN'S ESTATE)

KELLER
COVE

EVANS AVE.

SCALORD

BRIDGE ROAD

HEEL RD.

FROST ROAD

ULLEN ROAD

KINNER LN.

HOLVER ALLEY

NORTH
SELETH

FAWELL AVENUE

RABBIT ROAD

JUNK AVENUE

COLT ROAD

ELK ROAD

WEST BIRCH

BENSON
COURT

SELETH

Chapter 1

THERE WAS NOTHING A thief liked more than a boring, predictable person. Especially when that person was in charge of the security for the place he wanted to break into.

Asti Rynax had spent ten days trailing a man named Nel Pitter, and several more before studying him. In those days he had learned absolutely everything there was to know about the man, which was very little indeed. Pitter worked nights, so he slept during the day. His apartment was a second-floor flat in a whitestone in the tony southern end of Promenade in Inemar, which he shared with three other men. All four men in that apartment worked as security guards for the Pomoraine Building, in different shifts. Most of the residents of that whitestone worked at the Pomoraine. Asti imagined housing was part of the wage, as there was no way a security guard would otherwise be able to afford such an apartment, even shared with three others. The Pomoraine took care of its employees.

The Pomoraine was a seven-story office building, the absolute pinnacle of modern architectural grandeur on the south side of the city. It towered over its namesake street, just one block east of Lowbridge. Perfectly situated where the money of East Maradaine met the commerce of Inemar. It housed offices for trading houses, speculators, and merchant moguls.

And, most importantly, the legal offices of Colevar and Associates.

All of the men who lived in that apartment, including Pitter, were incredibly regular in their schedules. Asti had watched all of them, learning their habits. He had determined there was no viable moment of opportunity where he could count on the apartment being unoccupied, or everyone inside being asleep. Breaking into the apartment wasn't an option. But Asti had already dismissed that, since Pitter's usual activities made him an excellent mark for a different kind of run.

He had explained it to the rest of the crew before they had prepared for the play.

"Pitter sleeps during the day, and wakes up at five bells in the afternoon each day. Helene can confirm." Helene Kesser had scouted him through her scope from the opposite roof.

"Literally, the bells of Saint Ollickar wake him up. Not the three or the four. Just the five," Helene had said. "It's creepy."

"Wakes up at five, hits the water closet, gets dressed. Always with pressed shirt and polished boots. Presses and polishes himself, every day."

Asti had seen Pitter come out each day, right at six bells, looking as crisp as the vegetables in his sister-in-law's garden. He would stride down to Low Bridge Street, arriving at The Gentle Shepherd for dinner. Or breakfast in Pitter's case. His meal was always the same—half a roast chicken dressed with pickled onions, cabbage soup, soft cheese and mustard, and a soft cider.

"Each night the same?" Asti's brother Verci had asked. "You're sure of that?"

"Not that the menu at The Gentle Shepherd offers much option," Asti said. "But that's his place. No change. Which makes him perfect."

Asti sat in the back corner of The Gentle Shepherd at six bells, slowly nursing his own soft cider. Not what he'd normally choose, but tonight was a run, so it was best to stay sharp.

The rest of the crew were in position. The only one he could see right now was Helene, dressed like a laundry girl. She had been disguised with Pilsen Gin's ministrations, so her rich brunette locks were hidden under a mousy brown wig and gray kerchief. No one from the North Seleth neighborhood would recognize her. She even wore a set of spectacles—fake lenses—and sat at another table with her nose in a book.

That was the other thing their observation of Pitter had yielded—the man was a reader. His evening meal was taken while reading. When he wasn't walking his patrol of the Pomoraine, he was reading. He read while eating his other meal at sunrise, and for another hour before going to sleep at exactly nine bells in the morning.

Helene was reading—or pretending to read—*The Shores of New Fencal*, the war novel that Pitter had been working on in the past two days of observation. She had balked at the idea of actually reading it herself. "I had enough of schooling when I ditched school."

"You don't curl up with pennyhearts every night in your bed?"

"You need to not be thinking about my bed and what happens there, Asti Rynax."

So Asti had read it that morning and briefed her on it, or at least the first five chapters. Enough so she could fake her way. It was a serviceable enough adventure book, set during the early days of the Island War, though it was based on fantastical ideas about a squadron of Druth soldiers holding against an entire Poasian company. Under normal circumstances, Asti would probably enjoy reading it. But this was a job. They had had to get to Pitter. Pitter would get them the Pomoraine, the Pomoraine would get them Colevar and Associates.

Colevar and Associates would get them the client who had paid to burn down Holver Alley so they could force out the residents and buy up the land.

Pitter came in, right on time, his book tucked under his arm. He sat down at the same table he always sat at—right in Asti's line of sight, and right where Helene could move in on him. He gave a signal to the proprietor, who knew him well enough to simply nod back in reply. In a moment, Pitter's cider was delivered, and he was deep into his own copy of *The Shores of New Fencal*.

Almer Cort came in a few steps behind Pitter, taking a place at a far table. His job was simple, at least this part. He had to follow Pitter from his apartment to The Gentle Shepherd, and give signal if anything was wrong. Cort ordered wine and bread, which meant everything was going fine.

That gave Helene her cue. She reached from her seat over to Pitter's table.

"I'm sorry," she said, talking through her nose. It was slightly painful to Asti's ears—Pilsen hadn't given her much instruction on accents or voices, and she insisted on using one for this job. It was not in her skillset. "I couldn't help but notice." She held up her book to him.

"Oh, yes," Pitter said. "How far are you?"

"Chapter five," she said. "You?"

"Nine," he said. He was a bit standoffish, like he wanted to get back to his reading. Helene wasn't going to quite let that happen. She moved herself, book and cider, to his table and sat down.

"I'm just loving it so far," she said, putting one hand on his arm. "I mean, it's the first one of this author that I've read, but it's thrilling!"

Pitter put his book down and locked eyes with Helene. Which, of course he would. Even in the dowdy disguise, she was a good-looking woman, and she had already shown a mutual interest. Now she just had to keep him.

"I've been following this writer for a bit now," Pitter said. "He started out doing serials in—do you read the *Sword Pulps*?"

"No," Helene said. "But I want to know about them."

She scratched her ear, to cue the next step. Mila was in place for that, watching through the window of The Gentle Shepherd from the street.

Mila Kendish wasn't in disguise, other than wearing a similar laundry girl outfit. She came into the Shepherd and went straight for Helene and Pitter.

"Cassie," she said to Helene. That was the name they chose when they worked out this bit. "What are you doing? You were supposed to come home an hour ago!"

"I'm having a perfectly lovely conversation with a fellow imaginative soul," Helene said.

"This steve?" Mila said, prodding at Pitter.

"Who are you?" Pitter asked.

"She's my baby sister," Helene said. "And she's annoying."

"You shouldn't—" Mila started, her hands giving a signal to Asti and Helene. She had Pitter's keys.

"Go home yourself, Sera," Helene said. "I'll get there when I get there."

"Gerry won't—"

"Not your problem."

"Fine." Mila rolled her eyes and stomped off. Perfect performance. "But I ain't gonna lie for you!" She went out.

"Ignore her," Helene said. "Tell me more about this writer's other work."

Pitter launched into a description while his meal arrived. That, and Helene, should keep him suitably distracted while Mila ran the keys to Verci and Win Greenfield, sequestered in a back alley flop a block away. Win could make an imprint of the keys in a matter of minutes.

That was all the easy part.

Helene kept up her end of the conversation while Pitter went on, eating and drinking the whole while. She was engaging, and he was engaged.

Asti had to admit, he was pretty impressed with her here. He had always known her to be a crack shot with the crossbow. Three months ago, that's all anyone thought of her, and no one wanted to bring her in on a job. Her attitude had given her and her cousin a bad reputation, and several folks on the street couldn't stand working with her. But Asti had known her since he had been out of swaddling, and knew she could be better, do more. She just needed a reason.

Getting the folks who burned down the alley, killed her grandmother, that had given her a damn good reason.

Mila was in the window, nodding. Now she just had to get the keys back in his pocket. Time for the big move.

Asti gave a nod to Almer, who loudly ordered a cider

from the barman. That let Helene know what was coming. She signaled to the barman for another round of cider herself.

Mila came running in, faking she was out of breath. "I told you—" She heaved. "I told you he wouldn't—"

"Shove off," Helene said, getting up.

"Gerry asked where you were, and I said I wouldn't lie for you!"

"You told him?"

"I told you—"

"Cassie!" A giant brute of a man came into The Gentle Shepherd. "Gerry," or rather Helene's cousin Julien, also disguised by Pilsen.

"Why can't you let me be!" Helene cried as Julien stormed over.

"What do you think you're doing?" Julien slammed a massive fist on the table, rattling the plates and knocking over the ciders.

"Who is he?" Pitter asked.

"Her husband," Mila said, cowering near Pitter. "Blazes of a temper."

"Husband?"

"And who are you?" Julien snarled at Pitter.

Pitter held up his hands, open wide. "Hey, she just came over to talk about the book. I didn't . . . I just talked about books."

Helene got on her feet, moving in close to Pitter. "He likes books. He's interested in those things. Unlike *some* people."

Mila had clutched onto Pitter. "The last time she did this—"

"Last time?" Pitter asked. "You make a habit of this, you slan?"

Helene gasped, and then slapped him.

That was off script. A bit worrisome, but Mila had already gotten his keys back into his pocket. That girl had incredible hands; she could steal a feather from a bird mid-flight.

"Well then," Pitter said. He turned to Julien. "Sir, I'm sorry for any inappropriate appearance. I had no untoward intention to your wife, and wish no quarrel with you."

"Cassie," Julien grunted. "Get home."

Helene stormed out of The Gentle Shepherd, inventing new invectives and curses as she left. Mila followed after her.

"Enjoy your dinner," Julien said, and stalked off.

Pitter huffed in discontent and sat back down. Taking a moment to situate himself back to his meal, he again started eating and reading, drinking the cider he had presumed the barman brought when the old one had spilled.

He hadn't noticed Almer was the one who had delivered the new mug.

"It won't taste any different," Almer had said. "The stuff I'm slipping him pretty much tastes like cider anyway. The only difference is, an hour after he drinks it, he won't be able to get out of the water closet."

Asti had been on the receiving end of a few of Almer's apothecarial nightmares, and he didn't doubt that Pitter would be in for a horrible night.

With Pitter out of commission, and copies of his keys, they were all set to get into the offices of Colevar and Associates. After a month of planning, tonight was the night.

Verci Rynax's fingers twitched while he watched Win Greenfield work. He wasn't quite sure what Win was doing, but he understood just enough to be frustrated. He knew making things and taking them apart, and that included how locks worked. In his prime, he could jimmy or jam most locks in a few minutes, or find some way around them.

But he didn't know locks and keys like Win did. The man had them in his very heart. And with the death of his wife and daughters in the Holver Alley fire, it was pretty much the only thing Win had in his heart. So Win worked in silence while Verci watched over his shoulder, trying in vain to figure out exactly what Win's intentions were. It also didn't help that Win's hands were shaking, and his whole head was covered in nervous sweat.

"Is your plan to cut copies of the guard's keys?" Verci asked after watching in a complete loss. Win didn't seem to have cutting tools at all. He had rings and rings of keys, and the soft clay prints he had made of Mister Pitter's keys in the brief moments Mila had allowed them to do it. Win looked like he was completely out of sorts, grabbing keys, looking at them, slamming them down on the table. Win didn't speak, save muttering a few curses under his breath.

Verci wasn't able to help Win, and he was just going to have to deal with that and wait.

This was the annoying thing about the way Asti liked to work. Asti loved milking out the watching, stalking and planning, being downright languorous in figuring out how to pull a job. But then when it came to do the job, then everything was in a rush, having to move like perfect gears.

And when the gears didn't mesh quite right, it always seemed to be up to Verci to be the lubricant to make it all work.

Tonight was no exception. Asti had come up with a glorious gambit—Verci admitted Asti could be proud of the plan—to copy a guard's keys to the Pomoraine Building and put that guard out of commission for the night. An excellent way to give them a window to break in, dig through their files, and find out exactly what they knew about who hired Mendel Tyne to burn down the alley.

Except Asti's plan meant it all had to happen in one night, and they'd only have the keys in hand for a few moments.

Win was confident he could do what Asti needed, but Win wasn't like Asti or Verci or the rest of the crew. At his center, Win was an honest tradesman. He used to work keys and locks legitimately, shop with a sign out front. He didn't think in terms of the gig night. He thought about making copies of keys with all his tools, at a proper workbench, like the one they had at the safehouse.

The safehouse was back in North Seleth. Here, where Inemar butted up against East Maradaine, they only had a backroom flop over a pub called The Thundering. A pub with a stupid name, Verci thought—but it was the easiest place they could find a room to work in that Mila could run to from The Gentle Shepherd and back again in a matter of minutes. In the room over The Thundering, Win only had the equipment he could easily bring in with him without raising too many eyebrows from the proprietress.

Two men holed up in a back room, with a young girl occasionally running in and out, already raised that woman's eyebrows quite a bit.

"I can't cut new keys here, of course," Win said. "But you don't want a perfect key."

"I think I would," Verci said. "That would be rather useful."

"Useful for getting into the places that a guard is allowed," Win said. He looked at the imprints he made again, and pushed two away.

"What's wrong with those?" Verci asked.

"Those two have nothing to do with the Pomoraine. One is for his apartment, and the other ... some other personal need. Maybe a basement or building key for the apartment building. Point is, they're a totally different style, less complicated. These are the Pomoraine locks." He indicated the three imprints in front of him.

"More complicated?" Verci asked. That didn't sound good.

"Gloriously so, but in similar ways. Which is part of the challenge here." He pointed to two of them. "These are the important ones, at least for Mister Pitter's job. They showed more wear when I saw them. But also, they're only some minute variations to their cuts."

"What does that mean?"

"Ah!" Win said. "It means—well, this is what I think, at least. Each of these keys probably only opens one lock. And they won't open each other's locks."

"Yes, I understand the basic principles behind keys, Win," Verci said.

"But the way they are designed, the similarities, makes me think there is a key that would open both locks. And maybe many others in the building."

"A master key."

"A master key," Win repeated. "Now, the question is, which of my dummy keys can I file down to match them? And knowing what I know about these keys, can I make a master key for you to use? Especially one that would get you—"

"Into rooms Pitter isn't allowed into," Verci finished, seeing where Win was going with it.

"So where are we at?" Asti had come into the flop.

"Working on it," Win said. He selected one of his dummy keys and started filing. "Going to be a bit."

"A bit is fine," Asti said. "We're all white flags so far."

"So Mila did the slip-back?"

"Clean as a fresh shave. And Pitter drank the concoction. I watched until he took down every drop and went off to work."

"So what's our window?"

"Almer says he'll be stuck in the water closet for the night, starting in about an hour. The question is how much pride he has."

"What does that have to do with it?" Win asked.

Verci understood. "The prouder he is, the longer it'll take for him to admit that he's sick and needs someone to cover his watch. So the gap in the watch stands until he gives in. What's your gauge of that, brother?"

Asti screwed his face in thought. "I think it'll take him at least an hour, maybe an hour and a half."

"That leaves us less time than I'd like."

"Anything short of 'all night' is less time than you'd like."

"Yes," Verci said. "I would love the whole night, without a single guard in the whole building. That won't happen. Even with Pitter making a hole, there'll still be at least four on duty, presuming we didn't miss something in our watch."

"I don't think I did. Did you, brother?"

Verci knew Asti was just ribbing him, he didn't really think he had been negligent in his scout. But he was trying to get Verci to agree to the plan he had originally had. The one Verci didn't want to do.

"You're still thinking we're gonna have to top-and-bottom this, aren't we?" Verci asked.

"I told you that ten days ago," Asti said. "And every day since then."

"I didn't like it on any of those days, and I don't like it now," Verci said. "But you're right. Time's too short, and we don't know what we're looking for."

"What does this mean?" Win asked.

Asti sighed. "A top-and-bottom—"

"I understand that, Asti," Win snapped. "Someone goes in ground level, someone goes in on the roof. Really, the little codes between the two of you are not anywhere near as clever or impenetrable as you seem to think."

Asti looked abashed. "Didn't want to presume . . ."

"I meant," Win continued, "what does this mean you'll need from me? The plan involved me making a key set for Verci to take in from the ground floor. Has that changed?"

Asti chuckled nervously. "Yeah, Win, that's changed. Verci's going in from the top, and I'm going in on the bottom. Problem is, I'm not much of a locksmith . . ."

Chapter 2

ASTI ADMITTED BRINGING WIN along on the run in the Colevar offices was less than ideal. Win was great with his hands, one of the best lockmen he had ever seen. Came with being a straight businessman. But Win was also ten years older than Asti and Verci, not an experienced fighter or strong runner. Asti had noticed his knee quivered a bit when he walked. It might go out on him in a sustained run. He had little business being in on a run that was hot with guards.

But Asti needed a lockman with him on the bottom side of the top-and-bottom. Mostly because he was terrible with locks. Verci, on the top side, was a strong enough lockman that, with the keys Win cut for him, he'd be able to work his way through. So it was Verci up top, Asti on bottom with Win.

Which meant if things turned left, Asti had to make pulling Win out his top priority.

The Pomoraine was a large building, so it had several soft points of entry. Main doors, of course, were locked at this hour. One guard was in place in the entryway. This was not Pitter's position; it was going to stay manned all night. Any entry on the first floor was going to have to be mouse quiet and soft as slippers.

That was not Asti's specialty. But if they were caught, putting the guard down quickly and quietly was.

The back alleys around the Pomoraine offered other options. There were service doors along the back and sides, but those were designed to only be opened from the inside. There was no latch, no pull, no lock. A prybar and some muscle could probably pop those doors, but not quietly.

The sun had set, and even though this part of the city had oil lamps all along the street and a cadre of efficient lamplighters, Asti found it easy to slip into a darkened alley with Win. It helped that they were both dressed as respectable tradesmen. In East Maradaine, people didn't expect ruffians, and they didn't look for them.

Working clothes were in Asti's satchel, along with his weapons and Win's keys and tools.

"So, the loading dock in the carriage hold," Win said nervously. "That's where we're going?"

Asti would normally snap at the idle chatter while on a gig, but he knew this was far enough out of Win's comfort that he forgave it silently.

They reached the gate of the carriage hold. This had no guard on duty, and from Asti's scouting the past few nights, the guards only made periodic checks throughout the evening. No reason to waste much time on it: it was a heavy barn door with a large bolt lock. A person would have to be crazy to try to break in through there.

Which, fortunately, Asti Rynax was.

"Clever design," Win said as he looked at the bolt lock. "Two separate keyholes, and I think they need to be turned together. If I just had to straight crack it, it would be an hour, or more. And that's just to get at the bolting mechanism."

"This is the part where you should say, 'But, fortunately,'" Asti said as he changed into his dark slacks and coat.

"But, fortunately, we have the masters I built off of Mister Pitter's keys," Win said. He started inserting things into the keyholes. "And I'll need your hands in a moment."

"Let me know what I can do," Asti said. He strapped on the belt of knives he wore for any gig. His father's belt, his father's knives. Damn good knives, sharp ones that kept their edge well. That was what he had left from the old man: a set of knives and a font of ill-gained wisdom on the thief trade.

"All right, hands on each key," Win said. Asti grabbed them while Win pulled out a thin metal rod. He slid that into the crack of the barn doors. "On my mark, turn both together, toward each other."

"That's strange."

"Some people think stranger locks are better locks," Win said. "Most of the time, it's just showing off. Now."

Asti turned the keys, and Win brought up his rod sharply. There was a jarring snap, far louder than Asti would have liked, but the barn door gently swung out.

"Could have been worse," Asti said while Win gathered up his tools. "Now we just have to get inside, and slip up five flights of stairs without any guards seeing us."

They entered into the carriage hold. "Let's shut this," Win said. "If anyone comes checking they won't see anything amiss. And it's simple to open from the inside."

"Great saints, Win," Asti said as Win latched the door shut. "We're going to make a disreputable man out of you."

"Just as long as we get out easy," Win said.

"No worries," Asti said, despite the many worries he was having about that very subject. "Everyone is in place."

"Everyone in place?" Verci asked Helene. She was now out of her washerwoman disguise, her dark black locks hanging over the purple coat and vest she favored for gigs. She was with him, setting up her shooting nest on the roof of the building across the street from the Pomoraine. This was not where Verci wanted to be this evening, but a top-and-bottom was how Asti said they had to play it, so it was what he had to do.

"Far as I can see," she said, eyeing around on the scope of her crossbow. "I've got Kennith in his carriage a block away to the north, parked in front of a fancy pub. He's got Pilsen with him, playing his Tipsy Passenger game. That man puts on a show anywhere."

"Bit too much spectacle," Verci said. "People are going to remember that."

"They'll pay attention to that," Helene said. "And thus not look up at the sky to see you leaping over the street."

"I'm a no-spectacle-at-all kind of thief," Verci said.

"There's a burned-down husk in Keller Cove that says differently," Helene said with a smirk. "Mila's eyes on the ground, right below us."

"Is she selling flowers?" Verci said, looking down over the edge of the roof.

"Asti said that would be inconspicuous. Few actual beggars here, so she had to look like she belonged."

"And Almer and Julien?"

"A block to the south."

"The tea-and-fry shop with the walkway tables," Verci said. "I see them. You're set?"

"I've got eyes, I've got clean shots if I need them, and a hand mirror to check my face painting."

"Helene."

"Let me joke. I know the signals. We all know the signals. You'll be fine."

"All right," he said. He dug into his pack and pulled out the device he'd need. It was a good thing he'd decided to bring it along. Probably because, deep down, he knew that Asti would change the plan and he would to have to do exactly what he was doing. He always packed for contingencies.

Asti knew that. Asti knew he'd be ready for this.

Sometimes he hated the way his brother thought.

"Here," he said, handing the specialized crossbow to Helene. "Load that, and overcrank the crossbow four stops."

"Overcrank of four? I didn't think the Rainmaker could handle that."

He just glared at her, and she nodded and understood. He had built her crossbow, he knew what it could handle. He also loved that she called it "the Rainmaker." She always named her crossbows. He took out his own scope and checked the windows. No guard lamps visible on the sixth floor.

"Aim for the stone outcropping just over the third window from the left edge, second floor from the top."

She struggled with the crank while he clipped a few other devices to his belt, tightened the straps on his pack, and put on the bandolier of darts he had inherited from his father. With that, he was ready to go.

"Damn," Helene said, rubbing her shoulder. "What would happen if I shot a person with four overcranks?"

"Probably take their heart out of their chest," Verci said.

"Or hit someone five blocks away," she said with a wicked grin.

"You think you could make that shot?"

"I think I'd like to try."

"For now, line me up," Verci said. He clipped a cord from his belt onto her bolt. "Take the shot."

She rolled her eyes in the way she did when she flirted with him. Which, he had to admit, made his heart flutter just a little bit.

You're a married man, Verci Rynax.

Without even looking through her scope, she took the shot. The bolt hit dead center where he told her to aim, embedding into the whitestone of the building.

"Nice," he said, tugging on the cord. That sprung the release in the bolt, locking it in place.

"Now?"

He extended a long pole and spiked it into the floor of the roof. Once it was secure, he clipped the other end of the cord to it.

"Now hold that steady while I go."

She raised an eyebrow. "You know I'm not Julie strong."

"It'll hold fine, just keep it steady." He sighed, climbing over the edge of the roof. "It's not like I'm that heavy."

"So you say."

He winked at her—she could stand a bit of heart flutter, herself—and leaped over the edge. Hanging from his belt, he let gravity take him down the line as he flew across the street to the window of the Pomoraine. He landed feet first on the windowsill, and grabbed onto the outcropping.

He glanced down to the street below. No sign from Mila. She was still down there, hawking flowers. So he must not have made any significant noise or spectacle.

Making sure his grip to the side of the building was solid, he looked back over to Helene. She had eyes on him. All good. He unlatched the release on his belt, so he wasn't connected to the cord anymore. Handholds strong. Secure footing. Safe to retract the line.

With hand signals, he gave her a five count, and then pressed the release on the piton-bolt. It sprang out of the wall and flew back across the roof to Helene. She caught it and signaled all was well.

Now if only he could get through the window without leaving any sign of tampering beyond the hole in the stone.

The window was a simple double swing-open, latched from the inside. Easy as anything to pop open. Probably because they would have never guessed someone would be breaking in from six stories up. Verci slipped it open with a slim jimmy tool. Thank the saints for hot Maradaine summers, like the one they were having this year. The folks in these buildings wanted a window that they could get a breeze out of.

Which was a breeze to get into.

Verci was mostly thrilled he didn't have to cut any glass. There was no hiding your work once you did that.

The window led him into a wide hallway, not part of any one office. That was what he had hoped for. Several firms and partnerships had offices in this building, and the individual offices might be lined with janglewires or other traps. But the hallways and stairwells had to be free to move through, for the building staff to do their work.

The last thing he needed was to trip the alarm of some office other than Colevar and Associates. Nothing more embarrassing than being nailed by a mark other than your target.

The hallway had pullcords, which he assumed rang bells at the guards' booth on the first floor. There were also what looked like earhorns built into the wall at regular intervals.

Probably also echoing sound to the booth, so anyone could call for help. Another time Verci would admire the design, but right now it just meant he had to be as silent as anything.

"Oh, sweet saints, how? How? I've never eaten this much!"

That came from behind a door at the end of the hallway. The water closet. Given that Pitter was supposed to patrol this floor and the one below, that was probably him, suffering from Almer's concoction.

Verci did feel some small pity for the man.

But it was also clear Pitter was realizing he was suffering from an unusual malady. There wasn't much time before he would report himself ill, and the hole in patrol would be filled up. Verci went for the stairwell as fast as he could without making noise.

Down one floor to the Colevar offices. The main lobby was surrounded by glass doors, with a darkened seating area inside. Verci could barely make out the individual offices in the hallway beyond.

He went for Win's skeleton key, trying it on the main door. It stuck a bit, but he was able to get the latch to clack open after a moment. A little too long, and a little too loud for his preference, especially with the earhorns. But the door was open, and he slipped inside. Too exposed with the glass door and the open lobby.

Now to find Mister Chell's office. He was the one who worked the sale offers for the burned-out properties on Holver Alley. His name wasn't on the letter to Mendel Tyne—no one's was—but he had to be the one who knew something about it. Whoever wanted the Alley burned, whoever was trying to buy out the properties—Heston Chell knew about it.

Verci was of half a mind to set his office on fire.

He went down the hallway, hoping no guard would come onto the floor while he was digging about. The office doors had nameplates—that helped—but the light was too dim to read them.

Blast and blazes.

Verci dug out the hand lamp from his pack. Clever little

device he whipped up, that could keep the light in a tight beam. Of course, it couldn't hold much oil, and got hot as blazes before too long. Kinks to work out.

He clicked his sparker and lit the lamp, double-checking through the glass door to make sure no one was out there. Still clear, for the moment.

Three office doors down, he found it. Of course it wasn't the big office at the end of the hall. That, presumably, was for Colevar, whoever he was.

Verci tried the door. Locked. He then tried the skeleton key. It moved a little, but it wasn't going to cut it to get this lock.

Back into his pack, he pulled out two lock tools and grease. That should be good enough.

Footsteps coming down the stairwell. Verci covered up the lamp and froze. He was in the shadows, he had closed the main door—

He hadn't fully latched it. If he went back to throw the latch, he would be seen through those glass doors.

The steps came closer down.

And then, "Oh sweet saints, not again." Running, pounding steps away.

"Thank you, sweet saints," Verci said, getting to work on the lock.

Five minutes, he had it open. Far too long. He went into Chell's office and shut the door behind him.

Quick glance about. Window on one wall. A small one, but it had a view of Helene's perch. She was still up there, crouched low and dark. He wouldn't have spotted her if he hadn't known to look.

He opened up the lamp and gave three flashes. One flash came back from her perch.

That was done, no more of that.

Time to start working through Chell's files with whatever time he had left.

Verci had signaled he was in the office. That let Helene breathe easy, at least a little bit. She'd rather he was already back out. It was all taking too long. He should have signaled he was in by the time she counted to two hundred. She was almost at four hundred.

Where were Asti and Win? She had seen no sign of them. Not that she'd be able to see too much from her spot.

She had too many things to look for. Too much damn responsibility. She'd rather just be in a place to shoot, not have to make decisions, not have to signal if there was trouble.

Somehow those Rynax boys had the bright idea that she should be in charge of things while they were inside. A terrible idea.

Follow the routine. Check all the points. She swung her scope over to the right.

Pilsen and Kennith were still at their spot. Pilsen making a scene, but no trouble. And no one paying his chomie driver any mind, so they didn't notice that Kennith was staring right at Helene's perch. Through her scope, he was almost nothing but bright white eyes, burning into her, the rest of his dark features hidden in the night.

They were fine.

She swung over to the left. Julie and Almer at their table. Julie had ordered cheese and bread, and was far too enamored of eating that instead of focusing on her. That was fine, that was why Almer was with him. Almer glanced up after a moment, gave a nod. They were set, and Julien was happy with his cheese. That was about the only thing he needed to be happy some times.

Helene envied her cousin that.

Down on the road beneath her, she set her scope on Mila, working her part on the street, selling flowers. The girl was too clever for her own good. Good hands, good instincts.

"Violets!" Mila yelled out. "Violets of the night, violets for the departed!"

Violets. That was the cue word. Something was wrong.

Helene aimed her scope back at the building. Verci was still in the office, searching around. Through the other windows on his floor, she saw no other movement. She scanned down. Fourth floor clear. Third floor clear.

Second floor. Security guards were on the move, a real active scramble. She had no eyes on Asti or Win, but something must have spooked the guards. They were sweeping each office, going to the stairwells.

"Blazes, blazes, blazes," Helene muttered. Mirror out, she flashed a two-spot to the ground in front of Mila. Acknowledgment, that was all she could give her. Another flash to Kennith and Almer to be at the ready. They might have to run, they might have to help Asti or Verci. She had no idea what to do.

She should never be put in charge of decisions like this.

Sweep the scope back to Verci. No sign of trouble on his floor, yet. But he needed to be warned.

She hit his window with three flashes of her mirror. Danger. Be aware.

Verci didn't notice.

"Blazes, blazes."

Another set of flashes. Verci still didn't notice. He was digging through the office, eyes not on her.

She swept her view down again. Guards were starting to sweep up to the third floor, and others were active on the fourth floor.

And on the second floor, she saw Win in one of the windows, staring hard up at her. She signaled a flash. He returned with some hand signals that made no sense.

Win never learned the blasted hand signals.

"What— I . . . damn it."

If Win was alone in there, that meant Asti was in trouble. Or about to start some.

Win started pointing to his right. Helene followed along to the next window.

Asti in an office, knives drawn. In the shadows, she wouldn't have spotted him if she hadn't . . . blazes, she missed him before. A guard was opening the door to the room he was in. If Asti got into a fight . . . well, Asti would win, there was no doubt, but that would skunk everything.

She swung her aim to the farthest window away from Asti and fired. Glass shattered. New bolt, cranked the crossbow, loaded. Fired again, shattering another window.

Guards were running to those rooms.

She swung her view to Asti. He locked eyes at her when she found him, and nodded. Then he ran toward Win.

Back up to Verci. He was still in the office, still searching through files.

Stupid, pretty Verci.

No time to be subtle. Another bolt loaded, she took aim through that window.

That got Verci's attention. He snapped up to the window. She flashed him the danger signal. He signaled for her to shoot the line to him.

She loaded the line bolt back into her crossbow. She struggled to overcrank it, only able to get it three cranks over. She didn't want to waste any more time, hoping it would be enough. She hitched the line to the bolt, and looked through the scope to find her shot again.

Office window was in her sights. But Verci wasn't in the office anymore.

The place must have had some sort of silent alert trigger. Some way to let the other guards know something was wrong without making a ruckus. Asti had no idea what had triggered them—he and Win hadn't gotten above the second floor yet—but every guard in the building was sweeping the floors. Which meant seven men total, presuming Pitter was still incapacitated.

Asti could send all seven to their graves, but that would make a blazes of a mess. They had almost been caught, and he wouldn't have had any other choice. Until Helene distracted them. Thank the saints for her. He grabbed Win and made for the open stairwell, then changed his mind.

"Win, open up that office," Asti said, pushing Win to the locked door.

"Why this one?" Win asked, fiddling the lock open.

"Because I need it," Asti said. He didn't have time to explain that since the job was skunked, their best course of action—in addition to getting the blazes out of the place— was to hide their target. If the guards thought someone was trying to break into the accounts office of the Faltor Wood and Lumber Company, all the better.

As soon as Win had the door open, Asti went into the office. Quick as he could, he opened up a cabinet, pulled out several papers, strewing some on the floor, and shoved a few more into his coat.

"What is that?" Win whispered when he came back out.

"No idea," Asti said, pulling Win down the stairs.

"Now back to the carriage hold?"

Asti really wished Win would hush up. "No. Service doors."

Service doors couldn't open from the outside, but were easily pushed open from the inside. Send them right back out to the alley. Out and clear.

Asti stopped short before they reached the bottom of the stairs, holding Win back. One of the guards was latching the push bar of the service door.

"That's a special key," Win whispered in Asti's ear. "I don't know if I can—"

Asti put a hand over Win's mouth. He held it just long enough for Win to get the message, and then stepped away. The guard was still turning the latch. Asti slipped down the steps and moved up behind him.

No knives. Too much mess.

Asti jumped up—the guard was a half-foot taller than he was—and wrapped one arm around the man's neck while covering his mouth with the other hand. The man struggled and dropped back from Asti's weight. Asti kept his footing as he hit the ground.

The man tried to swing a fist backward, but Asti twisted out of the way, while holding a tightening grip around the guard's neck. He then delivered a swift kick to the man's knee, forcing him down to the ground.

Now able to hold his weight over the guard, he squeezed tighter while pushing his body onto the back of the man's head. The guard thrashed some more, futilely.

Win came over and grabbed the special key out of the guard's hand and went to work opening the service door.

"Go to sleep," Asti hissed.

The guard finally stopped thrashing, but Asti kept the hold for a few moments longer. He remembered a time in Druth Intelligence when he had been fooled by that trick, and earned a sucker punch to the tenders in return. He wasn't about to repeat that.

That, and the beast in his skull didn't want him to let go. The wild animal, the broken part of his brain, howled to be let off its chain, let it kill this guard and all the rest. Asti wasn't about to let it loose. Not over one guard, when nothing stood between him and the door. He didn't need that. Win didn't need that. Win needed to be taken out of this building.

The guard slumped down and Asti dropped him. Win pushed the door open, and Asti grabbed him by the arm and pulled him out.

"This key is really—"

"Not now, Win," Asti said, dragging him along as they ran down the alley.

"We're going to be seen—"

"Not now, Win."

As they approached the mouth of the alley, a familiar carriage pulled up slowly in front. Familiar, excepted it was mocked up like it was a Mender Company cab.

"Now look here, driver, this is not the way—" Pilsen Gin was in full performance of a drunken, disgruntled passenger. He was leaning out the window, a walking stick in hand, yelling at Kennith in the driver's seat.

"I know where I'm going, sir," Kennith responded.

"I'm sure you do, but what you do not know is where I am going, and that is what matters!" He waved the stick around frantically. Any eyes looking that way would be locked on the stick.

"Now, Win." Asti dove out the alley, rolling under the carriage. Win did the same, but lacking the grace that Verci would have had.

"Now what?" Win asked as they lay under the carriage.

"Runners," Asti said, grabbing the handholds and footholds Kennith had built into the carriage. He pulled himself up so he was hidden from anyone who would happen to look under the carriage.

Win had pulled himself up, but he struggled as he locked his elbows around the hold.

"How long do we have to do this?" he grunted out.

"A few minutes."

"I don't—I'm not that strong—"

"Have to wait until Kennith moves off this street."

"What's he waiting for?"

Asti sighed. What Kennith was most likely waiting for was Verci. Who was probably still in the building.

Chapter 3

VERCI COULDN'T WAIT FOR Helene to send the line. Shattered glass had gotten some attention.

"Fifth floor! Fifth floor!" At least three guards were running up the stairs. He grabbed the files he had found—he hadn't had any chance to look at them—and stuffed them in his bag. He extinguished the lamp and threw it in the bag as well, slipped out of the office, shutting the door so it latched closed.

Not that there was much of anywhere for him to go now. He could hear the guards in the stairwell, hands on the glass windows of the offices. They probably couldn't see him at this angle, down the hallway, but he couldn't count on them not coming in.

Nowhere to go but farther in.

He went for the large office of Mister Colevar. It was farthest away from the lobby doors, out of the line of sight. Plus there was the chance that Colevar was the type of man who had a hiding room or secret escape door. Verci had heard of rich men in top offices doing things like that. If Josie Holt did it as a fence and thief-boss in North Seleth, wouldn't a fancy lawyer in a big office do the same?

The master key opened the door rather easily. Thank

Saint Senea for her small miracles. Verci went in and closed it behind him. He could probably wait out the guards in here, as they would hopefully discover the broken glass in Chell's office, and move on.

Two steps in, the floor panel gave when Verci put his weight on it. Suddenly the whole office was filled with jangling bells.

Stupid, stupid, stupid.

Verci couldn't believe he'd missed something so obvious. He wasn't on his game, not in the slightest.

And there was no chance the guards weren't coming now.

Verci dashed across the room, leaped up on the desk and over to the window, tool in hand. With a quick flip of the wrist, he sprang the latch of the window and pushed it open.

The guards were rushing down the hallway.

He climbed out the window while rummaging through his bag for a rope and a clamp lock. It was a crude way to get out of the building, but he hardly had any other choice. Clamp latched to the windowpane, he tied the rope on and let it drop down. Not quite long enough to reach the ground, but he could make do.

The guards were trying to get the door open, and those damnable jangle bells were still going.

Verci scrambled over the edge and scurried down the rope. As he passed the fourth floor, his shoulders were already screaming at him. He hadn't done anything like this in years.

Third floor. Halfway there. Then all he'd have to do was run like blazes until he got to a place where he could blend in with the crowd. He hadn't heard a whistle call, so the sticks hadn't been brought in yet. He could outrun a few hired guards on open ground.

Second floor. The rope shimmied. Verci looked up. One of the guards was leaning out the window, holding onto the rope. He looked quite vexed, and he turned his attention to the clamp lock.

Verci wasn't worried. He had designed the clamp lock so it would be very hard for someone to release it if they didn't know how it worked. There was almost no way—

The rope suddenly came free, and Verci fell the rest of the way to the alley below. He tried to roll with it, but he wasn't ready. When he hit the ground, he heard a gut-wrenching crack from his leg.

Running like blazes wasn't going to be much of an option.

Mila kept her position on the walkway, hawking her flowers, as she saw the guards running throughout the building, up and down the stairs. She watched while Kennith moved the carriage down the street, and when she saw Asti and Win come out of the alley, she gave Kennith the signal of where to go. The carriage hit the mouth of the alley, and Mister Gin made a bit of a scene so folks on the street would notice him instead of Asti and Win crawling under the carriage.

It all went surprisingly well. She had to admit, when Asti explained the basics of the plan, she had no idea how the blazes it could work. "You'd be amazed what people don't notice," he had told her. "They're mostly in their own business. The average folk on the street won't give a damn, especially if you give them something loud and shiny to pay attention to."

He was right, and Mister Gin's performance was certainly loud and shiny.

She looked back up top for Verci. She didn't spot him, but did see guards on the floor he had been on. She scanned along the length of the building, no sign of him.

"Flowers of the season!" she called out as she quickly walked toward the other end of the building, and the mouth of that alley. She hoped that Mister Gin heard her giving the code for someone in the wind, and managed to follow along.

"Flowers of the season, just half a tick," she called again. She made it down the half a block, and could see into the other alley.

Verci was climbing down a rope on the outside of the building, plain as a wart on Hexie Matlin's face.

"Saints, sinners, and idiots," Mila muttered. If no one on the street had noticed him, the guards up top certainly had.

In an instant, they had undone the clamp lock holding Verci's rope.

As Verci fell, she couldn't help but be annoyed. It had taken her an hour to figure out how to unlock Verci's clamp lock.

Verci hit the ground hard and badly.

"Violets! Fresh flowers of the season, and violets!"

"Turn the carriage around," she heard Mister Gin call out. "I think I need to buy some flowers."

"Oy, he's—" someone called out from high up. Then a grunt. Mila glanced up to see the guard leaning out the window, now slumped over. Helene must have taken care of him. Verci, in the alley, was attempting to pull himself to his feet. She wanted to run over and grab him, but she knew that she had a little too much attention on the street. Mila had to play her part, like Asti and Mister Gin had told her. Draw focus. Keep eyes off the real action.

"You want some flowers, mister?" she called back. "You have a sweetheart to surprise?"

"How about I make you my sweetheart?" Mister Gin said, stumbling over to her. Mila spotted what he was trying to do, if her instincts were right. She took a few more steps over, even though it meant taking her eyes off Verci. She had to pray that Helene would keep him sighted, keep him safe.

Blazes, Helene would snipe every guard in that place to keep Verci safe. Not that she'd admit it.

"You've definitely got a sweet flower I'd like to get my nose in," Mister Gin said. Kennith had the carriage turned around, trundling over to the other alley.

"That's not what I'm selling, and you should be ashamed of yourself for that."

"Who said anything about selling?" He was now in position right by the main doors of the Pomoraine.

"Right, because you probably have no crowns anyway," she said.

"How can you say that, I've got—"

Three guards burst through the doors, the first two crashing into Mister Gin. Mila did her bit by crying out in surprise and getting in the way of the third. He crashed into her, knocking her stock of flowers onto the street. Three guards all stumbled and fought to get back to their feet, with Mister Gin doing his damnedest to hang onto the two of them while acting like he was just drunkenly groping.

"The blazes is your problem?" Mila shouted. "You just crash into—"

"Leave it!" the third guard yelled, running around the corner. "Where'd he go?"

"What?" Mila asked.

Mister Gin was being hauled to his feet by the other two guards. "What the blazes are you doing, old man?"

"There's no need for that language," Mister Gin said, wagging a disapproving finger at the guards. "The saints would not approve."

"Saints don't approve of lechery, either," Mila snarled at him. "Who is paying for my flowers?" She punctuated that by shoving a hard finger into one of the guards' chest.

"What, girl?" he asked. "Where's the scad?"

"He's gone," the third guard said. "Whose carriage is this?"

"It's mine," Mister Gin said, dusting himself off. "A man comes through town for a bit of merriment . . ."

"Shut it, old man. Open this carriage."

"What authority do you have—"

"Oy, chomie!" the third guard—obviously the superior here—shouted at Kennith. "Open your carriage or we'll get the sticks to do it."

"I beg your pardon?" Kennith grumbled out. "Do not presume to speak to me."

"Call in the sticks," the third guard said to the other two. "All of you hold until they get here."

"I will do nothing of the sort," Mister Gin said, heading over to the carriage. "You have no authority to detain me."

"You want to see if we can detain you, old man?" one guard said, getting in close to Gin.

"Oh, yes, let's," Gin said. "Let's see you doing that when the Constabulary come."

"You there!" Mila yelled to a passerby. "Get to a whistlebox! These men wrecked my flowers and are going to beat up an old man!" This was a blazes of a bluff—the last thing Mila wanted was for the Constabulary to actually come.

"We're protecting this place from—"

"Puffed-up popinjays is what you are," Gin said.

"Open up this carriage, chomie," the lead guard said. "Or you'll all find out what we're authorized to do."

"Sticks are our friends, codger," another whispered. "They won't mind if we bruise up an old drunk and his chomie."

"Which one of you is going to pay for my ruined flowers?" Mila shouted, turning to the main guard. "You smashed into me, trampled my goods, and I demand you pay me thirty-five crowns for the lot!"

"Thirty-five crowns?" He shoved Mila right in her face, pushing her to the ground. "Obber, open up the damn carriage. If the chomie gives you trouble, crack his rutting skull."

Whistle calls now pierced the air. Wouldn't be long for the sticks, not in this neighborhood. Obber pushed Mister Gin to his partner, and swaggered over to the carriage. He hesitated a moment at Kennith's glare, but still grabbed hold of the carriage door and opened it.

No one inside.

"Look under!" the leader said. Mila saw a Constabulary horsepatrol riding up the street. She decided this was a fine moment to use the best weapon in her arsenal right now: tears. She let out a horrific wail.

"Nothing under the carriage, boss," Obber said.

"Shut her the blazes up," the boss said. He went over to the horsepatrol. "Evening, Officers."

"What's the situation?" the constable asked, getting off his horse.

"We had a break-in here," the boss said, pointing to the building. "These two interfered with our attempt to apprehend the thief."

"What thief?" Gin asked. "I was just trying to court this pretty girl when these lunks came barreling into me!"

"Aaannd. . . . Tra—tra . . . trampled my flowers!" Mila forced out through her fake sobs. "They ruined me!"

"And broke into my carriage," Kennith added. "Violated my rights, Officer!"

"Oy, oy, everyone just calm down," the constable said. "Where's this thief?"

"He was in the alley, but he's gone."

"Hmm," the constable said, looking down the alleyway. "Nowhere to go but out here, it seems. Yet he got away, you say?"

"He must have!" the boss said.

The constable looked into the open carriage. "But he didn't go in there." He glanced up at Kennith. "This was open when I arrived, it's no violation for me to look inside."

"I know my rights," Kennith growled.

"You're gonna have the right to be pinked up in a cell at the stationhouse if you don't trap your mouth, son," the officer said.

"Who is gonna pay for my flowers?" Mila shouted, hoping the officer would pay more attention to her and less to the carriage.

"That isn't my problem, little girl," the officer said. He glared at the three guards. "Why don't you get back in there, where your authority begins and ends? I'm sure you've got some mess to handle."

"Officer," Mister Gin said, pulling himself away from the guards. "If you have no objection, I'd just like to get in my carriage and head home."

"Hmm," the officer said. "And where is home?"

"Over on Henterfield," Gin said.

"North Colton," the officer said with a nod. "I don't suppose you have any identification on you?"

Gin dug through his pockets, pulling out some papers and loose goldsmith bills. "There you are, Officer. Mister Davian Allarn. Says so right there."

The officer glanced at the papers, grunting. "This is how we're going to settle all this, then. You three, get back in your building."

The guards still hadn't moved.

"If you failed your job and a thief got away, it's not your problem anymore. One of you wants to come to the stationhouse to make a statement, that's just fine. Constabulary will search out your thief." He did not sound like they would actually put much effort into it.

"You, cider-breath, are going to give this twenty-crown note to the flower girl."

"Why would I—"

"Because I said so, and someone should pay for her stock, and you're the one with crowns falling out of your pocket." He took the note from Mister Gin's papers and handed the rest back to him.

"But—"

"And, you, girl, are going to take this twenty crowns and get the blazes out of my sight." He threw the money on the ground at her.

"My stock was worth—" Mister Gin was continuing to argue with the constable, so she trusted his judgment and took her cue from him.

"You're gonna be glad with twenty crowns, and that's that. All of you, get the blazes out of here." He took out his handstick and pointed it at Kennith. "Specially you. Maybe you shouldn't take jobs in this part of town, hmm?"

"Fine, fine," Gin said, getting in the carriage. "It's been a soured night, anyway. Take us home, driver."

Kennith made a noise and snapped his reins, and the carriage started rolling away.

"Girl," the constable said, his attention now on her. "Take your money and get out."

Mila snatched up the note, and made some show of salvaging her tray of flowers, giving the officer one last glare before stalking off.

A block away, Helene came out of an alley and started walking with her.

"That was harrowing," Helene said.

"How long did you watch?" Mila asked as they strolled at a quickened pace.

"Until the stick sent the carriage away."

"Verci made it in?"

"Asti had to carry him, but yes," she said. "That was far too close."

"Let's get back home to the safehouse," Mila said. "I am done with this neighborhood."

The secret compartment under the seats of the carriage had been designed for one person to hide comfortably, or for two people to squeeze in if they had to. For three people to be crammed in there was excruciating, at least for Asti. Especially since the beast in his skull was still whispering to him.

It wasn't howling to be let loose anymore, but it whispered.

You failed Verci.

Verci was curled up in the compartment, his elbow jammed into Asti's ribs, while Asti also had Win's knees in his back. Neither one of these things made quelling the beast any easier, especially with Asti's head pressed against the wall of the compartment.

You could have saved him.

Asti hadn't gotten much of a chance to look at Verci's leg, but it looked horrible as they loaded him into the carriage. Asti was pleasantly surprised at how well Verci was bearing the pain he must be in, especially crammed in this tiny space. Even if he wasn't making any noise, Asti could feel the cold, clammy sweat on his brother's brow.

This is your fault.

Pilsen gave a series of knocks indicating they were in the clear. Asti undid the latches and the secret compartment sprang open. He, Verci, and Win all tumbled out into the back of the carriage.

"Well, this has been thrilling," Pilsen said. "You're all lucky that Kennith and Mila have sharp eyes."

"Ow," Verci said loudly. "Ow, sweet saints, ow."

Pilsen looked down. "Great saints, son. You aren't supposed to bend your foot in that direction."

"How bad is it?" Verci asked. His face was horribly pale. Poasian pale. And his curly mop of dark hair was soaked in sweat. Asti looked down at his brother's leg.

There was no doubt it was broken. The foot was twisted at an unnatural angle. Now he truly was amazed Verci wasn't screaming. He certainly would have been.

"Win, help me get him up on the seat."

"I can barely move my—"

"Now, Win!"

Win scrambled up and helped lift Verci up onto the

carriage seat. Once Verci was in position, Asti half climbed out the window to see Kennith. "What's our time to the safehouse?"

"Just a few minutes," Kennith said. "We're already in Seleth, and the streets are clear."

"Don't spare the whip, hmm?"

"Should I go to Kimber's? Find Doc Gelson?"

Asti considered that for a moment. Verci probably would need the old drunk, that was certain, but they also needed to get whatever Verci found back to the safehouse, back to Miss Josie.

He couldn't let that get in the way of what Verci needed.

"Yes, get there," he said, pulling back in. He stripped off his coat from the job and grabbed a spare shirt from the secret compartment. Changes of clothes were always kept in there. "Pilsen, Win, get Verci's shirt changed. Pants will have to stay. Take his bags, whatever he got, back to the safehouse. Have Miss Josie start to look at it."

"I did get something, but I'm not sure—"

"Later, Verci," Asti said. He saw Verci was starting to have tremors. This was not good. "In a moment Kennith is going to pull up in front of Kimber's. I'll haul Verci out and get him to Doc Gelson."

"But—" Win started.

"Safehouse, boys," Asti said. "We'll meet up with you later."

The carriage came to a halt. Asti looked out the window—Kimber's Pub, Asti's occasional second home. And almost the first home for Doc Gelson, who spent most nights pickling his head in Kimber's cider. Asti kicked the door open and pulled Verci out.

"I can put weight on the good one, brother," Verci said.

"All right," Asti said, signaling to Kennith to drive on. Kennith wasted no time, and neither did Asti bringing his brother into the pub.

"Some help here!" he shouted. "Doc?"

Kimber—sweet, warm-faced Kimber—was the first one to react. She raced out from behind the bar, knocking over two glasses in the process.

"Asti, what happened?"

"He fell, hard," Asti said, deciding the best course was to give an honest account, if lacking in detail.

Kimber got on Verci's other side and held him up. "Let's bring him to the cot in the back. Then I'll drag Gelson out of his stupor."

They laid him out on the cot, and Kimber went off to get Gelson.

"She didn't press you further," Verci said weakly.

"She knows better," Asti said. "Blazes, she's—"

She'd seen the beast, seen Asti in his full red-eyed, pure murderous insanity. Seen exactly who he was and what he was capable of. She saw that, and hadn't chased Asti away. That was pretty incredible.

"Did you see who else was out there?" Verci asked.

"I wasn't really looking."

"Ren Poller. With a couple Scratch Cats."

"Blazes," Asti said. Ren was Nange Lesk's right-hand man, and the Cats were the gang Lesk and his crew had been using to try to get a grip on North Seleth. Lesk was in Quarrygate, thanks to Asti—or Asti's beast, more correctly—but it was clear that the rest of the crew hadn't broken up at all. Ren would definitely want to poke his poxy nose in their business, especially if he saw that Verci had broken his leg. He would make it his mission to know the hows and whys and wheres, and he'd put every Scratch Cat out to sniff around. Asti was going to have to warn Mila and Helene. They'd probably get it worst.

Kimber came back in, almost dragging Doc Gelson by the scruff of his neck.

"I have an office during the day for this sort of thing, you know," he said gruffly.

"Not exactly a wait-until-morning sort of thing," Verci said.

"Hmmph," Gelson said, squatting down next to Verci. "There is also Culver Ward."

"That's lacking in the personal service, Doc," Asti said.

"I am not your all-hours stitch, boys," Gelson said sharply.

"Then perhaps you shouldn't be so easy to find late at night," Kimber said.

"As long as you all don't expect me to be working for free."

"You'll be paid," Asti said. "Put his cider bill onto my account."

Kimber narrowed her eyes at Asti. "And you, Asti Rynax. Are you living at my inn again?"

"I've paid for the room, haven't I?"

"You've paid for you and Win Greenfield for the past two months, and the next four. But I haven't seen much of you, now, have I?"

"I've had business," Asti said.

"Business, hmm," she said archly. "I know I don't even want to know."

"You really don't."

"Keep that business out of my place, hmm?" She leaned in. "If the Constabulary come searching, I can't protect you, you know."

"I would never do anything to endanger you or your business, Kimber," Asti said. Gelson was now examining Verci's leg in earnest, and Asti went to sit at the small table Kimber kept in this room, her makeshift desk where she handled the business of the pub and inn. The desk was a mess of papers and ledgers. "Do you need help with the books here, or something?"

"I manage," she said. "However, I could stand to not be receiving so much post that is addressed to you." She lifted up a pile of papers and pulled out a bundle of letters tied together. "I haven't had a chance to give that to you because you haven't—"

"I've not been around, yes. You could have put them in my room."

"Then I wouldn't have gotten a chance for a word. Doctor, do you need anything?"

"The strongest spirits you have, Miss Kimber," he said.

"You aren't getting any of that."

"It's for the Rynax boy, you dilly," Gelson said. "I'm going to have to set this leg and he'll want to be out of his skull."

"Fine," Kimber said. She pointed a finger at Asti. "This will be from your tab, you know."

"Of course," Asti said to her back as she went off.

"What's with all the letters?" Verci asked.

Asti flipped through the mail, confirming his suspicions. "Another path to finding out about the fire, who was behind it. I've been trying to get the various newsprints engaged in the story, maybe they can dig places we can't. They've had the courtesy to write back." He opened a few, all of them saying variations on the same thing.

"So what'd they find out?" Verci prodded.

"They found out that they don't give a barrel of sewage," Asti said. He threw the letters on the floor. "I shouldn't be that surprised, but—"

"But what?"

"I thought there might be some, I don't know . . . crusading truth seekers."

"Rarely do people care about anything beyond their nose, brother," Verci said. "We're hardly exceptions to that."

Asti had to take that rebuke. It's not like he gave a damned blazes about the scandals and murders he read about in the newsprints.

Kimber came back with a bottle of Fuergan whiskey. "This is only for Verci." She poured a glass and handed it to him, hovering over them all. Verci threw the drink down his throat.

"That was—oh, saints," he said, coughing.

"Three more of those, at least," Gelson said. "I wouldn't hate one, myself."

"Not a chance," Kimber said.

"Four whiskeys?" Verci said, taking the second glass from Kimber. "Raych will not be pleased." He sent it down his throat.

"Yes," Kimber said drily, filling the glass again. "I'm sure the thing she'll be upset about is that you're drunk, not the foot."

Asti perked up at that. "I suppose I should go tell her what happened, hmm?"

"Yes, yes, you should," Verci said as he took the third drink. "That way she focuses the anger part on you—"

"Which she would anyway," Asti said. Verci's wife, at best, tolerated him. One reason why he was now officially living and receiving mail at Kimber's inn.

"And then all I get is the sympathy." He took a few deep breaths. "I recognize this is quality whiskey, Kimber, but four this fast is a challenge."

"I'll get a bucket," Kimber said, pouring his fourth.

"Good idea," Gelson said. "Even drunk, when I set this leg, it's going to be horrible, wrenching pain. You will probably pass out or vomit. Possibly both."

"Joy," Verci said, taking his fourth.

"Asti, come here and hold him down," Gelson said.

"Got it," Asti said. He knelt down by Verci's head, holding his brother's chest and arm down. Verci gripped onto Asti's arms.

"You ever have anything like this in your spy days?" Verci asked. He must be drunk. Verci never prodded about what had happened to Asti when he was in Intelligence.

"Arm, once," Asti said. "Out in the Napolic jungle, and Li—" Bile rose to his throat suddenly, just from thinking of Liora Rand. The partner who had betrayed him, got him captured and psychically tortured in a Poasian prison. Thanks to her, he now had this broken brain, this angry beast on a chain in his head. He swallowed it down. "My partner had to set it, splint it with a couple sticks and a torn shirt. That wasn't as bad as this."

"It's clean, though," Gelson said. "That's something. On three."

"Count it," Verci said.

"One, two, three." Gelson pulled on Verci's leg, and at once Verci screamed and vomited. Much of it got on Asti, but he wasn't going to complain.

"Is he out?" Gelson asked.

"Looks that way," Asti said. Verci's eyes were closed now, but he was breathing fine. "Went like you said."

"He didn't mention the screaming," Kimber said. She handed a rag to Asti. "I'm going to check on the rest of my patrons. They're probably spooked."

"I'll get this set and wrapped now," Gelson said. "Have him come see me in a couple days—at my office in the day, mind you—and we'll change out the wrapping."

"How long for it to fully heal?"

"Break like that might never fully heal," Gelson said. "I

mean, I'm pretty sure he'll walk again, we won't have to cut it off or anything."

"Good," Asti said.

"But he'll probably always have pain. Possibly will need a cane for the rest of his life."

That hit like a hammer.

"You're sure?"

"I'm not sure, no," Gelson said. "People all heal different. He might be running by Soran. The foot might turn black and we amputate. We'll have to see. But I know you boys are all running around and such, so best you know what's likely."

"Thanks, Doc," Asti said. He fished through his pockets for some bills.

Gelson held up a hand. "Just take care of the tab here, and pay me proper at my office. And get that mess off yourself, son."

Asti cleaned himself and Verci off while Gelson finished wrapping the leg. Verci stayed out the whole time, seemingly sleeping peacefully. Or at least the sleep of four whiskeys. But he didn't seem in distress, and Gelson wasn't concerned. When he finished cleaning up, Kimber returned.

"How is he?"

"He'll get through," Asti said, half to convince himself. "Now I've got to go tell his wife."

Chapter 4

RAYCHELLE RYNAX WASN'T ASLEEP, despite the late hour. Verci was out—"on a job," as he liked to say. Even though what he was doing was the furthest thing from a proper job as she could think of, and she could never sleep when he was out there.

At some point she was going to get word that he was dead or in Constabulary irons, and she honestly couldn't decide which one she thought was worse. And all because of his loyalty to his brother.

Stupid blasted Asti Rynax, she thought, quickly adding a prayer for forgiveness to Saint Bridget. Sometimes she cursed the day she had fallen for Verci Rynax and his disarming smile—she hadn't known he would come with a trunkful of trouble in the form of his mad brother. She had half a mind to shut Asti out of their lives completely.

But she couldn't do that to Verci.

She got up from the bed, checking on Corsi, asleep in his crib. Little boy had no idea where his father was right now, and with luck he would never know the things Verci had done. Was doing right now. She wondered sometimes why Verci and Asti spoke of their father with such fondness. The man had done nothing but put them on a path to an illegal and immoral life. A life both of them had almost freed themselves from.

They should be free of it now. There was no reason, save Asti's continued, burning anger.

The door opened downstairs—the back door from the alley. It caused the jangle bell in their apartment to go off. Raych tensed up, waiting to hear the next sound. If it was Verci coming in, he'd pull the hidden switch in the kitchen that made a different bell ring, and she'd know it was safe. If she didn't hear it soon, then she knew what she'd have to do—scoop Corsi up and hide in the lockroom behind the secret door.

Verci had already hidden her away there twice. She hoped she'd never have to go in there again. She still didn't understand why he was courting the risks that might force her to hide away.

The second bell rang. It was safe. Grabbing her housecoat and a candle, she went down the back stairs to the kitchen.

Asti was there, pulling Verci's inert form through the door.

"Saints and sinners, what happened?" She found herself shouting despite herself.

"Quiet!" Asti snapped. "You have neighbors."

"I'm aware," Raych said. "What did you do to my husband?"

Asti lifted Verci up and put him on the work counter. Verci's leg was bandaged up, which didn't explain why he was completely insensate. So many different feelings welled up inside of her. She wanted to scoop up her husband and care for him, she wanted to slap him and scream at him for being an idiot, she wanted to not be worried out of her mind every time he went off on one of these foolish "gigs" that his brother insisted on.

Asti spoke up. "He had an accident, and Doc Gelson set the leg—"

"Did he get hit on the head?" She went to check Verci's head for injuries, and then the smell hit her.

"No, he's out cold because of the four whiskeys he had."

"The four what?"

"Just so the leg could be set."

Raych couldn't hold it in. "This is your fault."

Asti had the decency to look down at the floor, abashed. "I know. I'm not sure how he fell, but I should have been there to—"

"No, Asti," she snarled. "You should not have been there. Neither of you should have been."

He glared hard at her. "And, what? Not find out who burned us out? Not bring them to justice?"

"Let it go," she shot back. "You already won—"

"Won?" he almost shouted, then pulled his voice back down. He stalked over to the back door and shut it with the latch, and turned back to her. "What in the name of all the saints makes you think we won?"

"You had your revenge on Tyne, robbed his place. Why wasn't that enough?"

"He was hired by—"

"And where is that money, Asti? If you went through all that, why don't we have that money?"

"I've told you—"

He had told her about keeping it hidden, about putting up a pretense of everything being normal, about acting like they were struggling, and they would slowly introduce the money into their finances. Make it look legitimate. But she thought it was just more excuses for Asti to do what he wanted.

And drag Verci along with him.

"I'm not interested in that. I want my husband safe." She wanted more than that. She wanted some sanity, some normalcy in her life.

"You think I don't?"

"Then leave him be, Asti! Let him just be a husband, a father. Let him get the Gadgeterium started again, let him run the bakery with me. Just be normal."

"That's what we're doing."

She shook her head. "I don't mean your game of looking normal. I mean actually doing it. Let it go. If you can't, at least let him go."

Asti's hands were shaking. "I need . . . I need to go check on the others. Make sure they all made it back. Let them know Verci's all right."

"Is he?"

"Doc Gelson said it'll heal. He should stay off it for at least two weeks."

"Gelson, saints." That man was more menace than medicine. Everyone around her was. "Fine, get out of here."

Asti went for the door.

"Wait," she said. "Help me get him upstairs and in the bed. Then go."

Asti came back and picked Verci up by himself. Raych was always surprised how strong Asti was for being such a small man.

"Do you have him?" she asked.

"He's my brother, Raych," Asti said. "I'll always have him."

It was nearly eleven bells at night when Mila made it back to North Seleth with Helene. They were stuck walking most of the way from East Maradaine, as neither of them had planned on not being able to ride back in the carriage. They managed to catch a tickwagon over to Trinital Highway in Gelmoor, but from there they were on their own, hiking through Shaleton and Seleth.

Helene had griped the whole way, mostly about her feet and how Asti must have screwed something up. She liked blaming Asti whenever anything went wrong on a job. She had preemptively griped this job for the week beforehand.

"Still don't quite get why we didn't just bribe the guards," Helene groused. "It's not like we don't have the money."

Asti had explained exactly why, and while Mila wasn't good at articulating it, she understood. Asti pointed out that a bribed guard isn't a trusted friend, and bribing eight or more guards means a high likelihood that one of them will take the money and turn on you.

The bigger reason was that while the money they had from robbing and burning down Tyne's Pleasure Emporium was an immense fortune, it wasn't safe for them to spend too much in one place, or for any of them to suddenly have so much money. If anyone realized that a crew of North Seleth dregs now had thousands of crowns on them, it wouldn't take much to figure out why.

There were deeper matters, politics-of-the-underworld stuff that Mila didn't really understand. Elements of Tyne's network, as well as other criminal enterprises throughout the city, who were searching for whoever had taken out Tyne. Miss Josie had referred to a "Mister Gemmen" who was rather put out. Mila didn't know who that was, but anyone who made Miss Josie speak in hushed tones was someone to worry about. But Miss Josie made it clear that Gemmen was someone who needed to be handled before the money was safely theirs.

Asti agreed with her, and was adamant about it with the rest of the crew. Laying low kept them safe. They had to put on the long show, like nothing had changed. That meant no extravagant spending, like taking a cab back to North Seleth. No bribing guards. No anything that would send whispers back their way.

Mila was reasonably sure that Helene understood, she just hated it. That was Helene's real issue. Especially since Helene had to keep pretending being a poor girl who never quite recovered from the Holver Alley Fire. She hadn't accepted that.

Mila didn't mind. She rather liked being the richest street beggar in Maradaine. But that was her: her cover was still being a street urchin, one who commanded a small gang of boys who called her "Miss Bessie." No one in the neighborhood really knew her beyond that.

Helene was known, especially by folks like the Scratch Cats and the crew running them. She had to put on more of a front, and that meant working in a shop so people wouldn't wonder how she was getting by.

Working in the shop was killing Helene.

"Eight bells tomorrow," Helene griped as they made it back to the neighborhood. She handed over her crossbow kit to Mila. "I do not have time to 'check in' with anyone at the safehouse. Tell them I went home to sleep. Tell Julie to come home."

"Don't you want—"

"No, Mila, I really don't," Helene said. She shook her head. "I screwed up, and Verci paid the price. I can't—I don't want to see him, not right now."

"I doubt he—"

Mila found Helene's finger in her face. "Don't even try that with me. I do not want to hear your mewling, little girl."

Mila let that wash over her. Helene was upset, and she tended to snap—especially at Mila—when she was.

"Fine," Mila said. "Go home. I'll let everyone know you made it back fine."

Helene trudged off, and Mila made her way to the safehouse alone.

From the outside, the crew's safehouse looked like just another warehouse by the bank of the Maradaine River. There was a whole row of warehouses, most of them owned by companies whose offices were in Inemar or East Maradaine. Rent was cheap and few questions were asked. Carriages coming in and out didn't look strange, nor did beggar girls looking for a place to sleep. It was a good place for the crew to work out of.

Inside the safehouse, it was a different story. Once one got through the complicated locks that Verci and Win had installed, it was almost—not quite, but almost—like a cozy home. There was a stove and icebox, large table, cots, an office that Miss Josie would sometimes work out of when she was around, and a warehouse floor that held Kennith's carriage and horse stables, Almer's chemical lab, and Verci's workbench.

When Mila arrived, Asti was at the table with a bunch of papers, talking with Miss Josie. Win was curled up on a cot, and Almer, Kennith, Mister Gin, and Julien were all at the other end of the table, eating bread, cheese, and stew.

"Where's Helene?" Julien asked when he saw her carrying the crossbow kit.

"She went straight home," Mila said. "She said you ought to do the same."

"Right," he said with a nod, getting up from the table. "Have to work tomorrow."

"Night, Jules," everyone said as the big guy left.

"And Verci?" Mila asked.

"Leg broken," Asti said. "It's set, and I brought him home to Raych."

Mila raised an eyebrow as she sat down with Asti and

Miss Josie. Miss Josie gave Mila a slight nod, which was typically the limit of direct interaction Mila ever had with the woman. She knew—blazes, she had always heard the stories—that Josie Holt had once ruled the criminal underground in all of Seleth. Now all she had left, apparently, was this crew and a few remnants of her empire. Even still, she had such a strength of presence that Mila couldn't help but be a little cowed by it, even though she was a small woman with graying hair and a walking cane. Miss Josie couldn't claim credit for taking down Mendel Tyne, but getting rid of him had helped her from losing further ground in the neighborhood.

"What did we get?" Mila asked Asti.

"Verci grabbed a few papers, most of which involve the purchase of properties in North Seleth," Asti said, thumbing through the sheets. "There aren't specifics about who the purchases are for. It may be that the details we need are not here."

Mila picked up a file and looked at the pages. "So we didn't get anything?"

"I wouldn't say that." Asti put some sheets to the side. "While most of these don't name names, or even companies, they all are marked on the bottom with Andrendon Project."

"Like this one," Mila said, holding her file.

"No, that's nothing. So far there's no sense of who or what the Andrendon Project is—"

"It's right here," Mila said. She wasn't the best reader, but she could make out her letters and words well enough.

"What do you have there?"

Mila did her best to read it, sounding out the words. "It's a purchase order of material for the Andrendon Project."

Asti snatched the file out of her hands. "How did I not see this?"

"You're not exactly at your sharpest," Josie said softly.

"True," Asti said. "All right, this might be something, then. It doesn't say much, but it does have an account listed for billing. The Creston Group."

"Is that a company?" Josie asked. "So what are they buying the land for?"

"Far too soon to think about that," Asti said. "For all we know, it's just another layer between Chell and the buyers, or one member of the Creston Group is using it to protect their identity, or . . . there's a lot of things this might mean."

"But it's a lead," Mila said.

"It's a lead, the first real one we've had," Asti said.

"We've got something?" Kennith asked from the other end of the table. Those boys all approached.

"We've got something to look into," Asti said. "Creston Group."

"What is that?" Almer asked.

"Sounds like a formal association," Mister Gin said.

"What does that mean?" Kennith asked.

"Whatever the group is, it's making a purchase, right?" Mister Gin said. "You want to be able to do business under the name of something—like, say, a theatrical troupe, that's how I know that—you have to declare who you are so the city knows how to classify what you are, how to tax you, and so forth."

"You think this Creston Group is one of those?" Asti asked.

"Likely," Mister Gin said. "And if it is, then the right city offices have paperwork on it."

"I'll look into it," Asti said. "We should probably all rest, and tomorrow start investigating the Creston Group." The rest all nodded and went off, Josie limping her way over to her office.

"Tomorrow, I presume that's going to be you and me, right?" Mila asked Asti.

"Yeah, I got a plan cooking," Asti said. "And it's one that's just you and me. Saints know Verci won't be up for it."

Mila nodded. Saints knew that Raych wouldn't let Verci out her sight.

Chapter 5

VERCI WOKE SUDDENLY, his body infused with pain. There was the dull, throbbing pain in his leg, and the pounding, splitting pain in his skull. He also, for a moment, didn't know where he was.

His own bed, in the apartment over the Junk Avenue Bakery. No idea how he got there. Also, sunlight was streaming through the closed shutters, so it was clearly morning.

He didn't remember much, save four Fuergan whiskeys.

That was what caused the headache, certainly. Verci only had vague memories once they went into Kimber's, but he remembered the whiskeys. He could still feel them in his throat. Somewhere after the whiskeys Asti must have gotten him home.

"Bah!" Corsi was on the bed with him, curled up in the crook of Verci's arm.

"Hello," Verci said to his baby son. "Good morning to you as well."

"Bu-bah!"

"I agree," Verci said. "We should seek out your mother."

Verci pulled off the covers and saw his foot. It was wrapped up in a mess of bandages, and it didn't hurt like it had last night, but he still was in pain. That was the best he could hope for, really. He stretched forward and gently probed the bandage with his fingers.

Shooting pain.

There was no need to try to walk on it, then.

"Geh bah?" Corsi crawled over to Verci's foot.

"Yeah, your pop really messed up," Verci said.

"That's for certain."

Raych stood in the doorframe, a cup of tea in her hand. Somehow she managed to look gorgeous, even with flour on her face.

"I don't suppose that tea is for me, is it?" Verci asked.

"It is," she said. "It shouldn't be, but it is." She came over and handed him the tea, then scooped up baby Corsi. Verci sipped the tea and slid backward so he could sit up against the wall.

"So, my memory of last night is foggy," he said. "But I presume you have a series of choice words for me."

"Oh, I did," Raych said. "I used them on your brother, who took them like a kicked dog. It did take some of the steam out of me."

"Still, if you want to tell me how stupid I am—"

"You are very stupid." She sighed. "You're broken right now, thanks to your brother . . ."

"Not his—"

She quickly interjected. "But you're also not in jail, and that's also thanks to your brother. Even though . . ."

She sat silently for a moment.

"Even though?" Verci prompted.

She sighed. "I know *why* Asti is bent to blazes on going after these mysterious people behind the fire. He . . . he needs a project, he needs someone to focus his anger on."

"Right," Verci said. This was a conversation they had been dancing around for the past month or so.

"But we—Verci, we've now got this bakery, this apartment, and supposedly there's money to keep paying the debt on the burned-down shop. I even understand why you insist on that . . ."

"It's because—"

"I know why," she said, a bit of snap in her voice. "I understand why you think that matters. But . . ."

"But?"

"Isn't that enough?" she asked. "We're all right. We'll be all right."

"For now," Verci said.

"Isn't that all anyone gets?" she asked. "But you—you could have died. You could have been arrested. And for what? Asti's mad quest?"

"It isn't mad," Verci said. "Asti isn't . . ."

He almost said that Asti isn't mad, but that wasn't true. Asti hadn't had one of his spells—or, at least, hadn't told Verci about one—since the night at Tyne's. But Asti was hardly a model of sanity. And Raych was right about one thing: focusing on this job, going after whoever was ultimately behind the fire, it kept Asti's head together.

"I can't just abandon him," Verci ultimately said.

"Well, you aren't running around, breaking into buildings on that foot," Raych said.

"See, I'll be staying out of trouble now."

She glowered at him. "Doc Gelson popped into the bakery already this morning. He says no weight on that foot for at least two weeks, and to go see him in his office in a couple days."

"Right," Verci said. "Which means I need to get around without putting weight on my foot." A challenge for him to solve.

"It means you should stay in bed—"

"Nonsense," Verci said, drinking the rest of his tea. "For one, I have to use the water closet, and I hardly think you want to play nursemaid to me for the next two weeks and beyond."

She scowled. "No, but—"

"Because you have a bakery to run, a baby to care for . . ."

"I've brought Lian in to help in the bakery." Raych's sister.

"Did you tell her what happened?"

"That you fell down the stairs while carrying a bag of flour?" Raych said with fake sweetness. "Yes, of course I did."

"Good," Verci said. He handed her the now empty

teacup. "In the meantime, I'll need to make some crutches. But first—" He rolled off the bed and landed on his hands, feet high in the air. Walking on his hands, he made his way across the room.

"Verci!" Raych squealed.

"I told you, love," he said as he flashed an upside-down smile. "I really need to use the water closet."

Asti barely slept. Too many things swirling in his head. Too much blame, too much anger. Sleep was worse. When he was asleep, nothing held the beast on its chain.

Well before dawn broke, he was on task for the next step in what they needed to do. They had a name for an organization, now to put a few faces on it. Gin had the right idea— if the Creston Group was a formal association, then there would have to be paperwork filed with the right city offices. And over the night, a plan for how to get what they needed.

Most everyone else had left, even the Old Lady, wherever she slipped off to when she left here. Except Mila, curled up on one of the cots. Like him, she spent more nights in the safehouse than not. He felt guilty about that, but mostly because he was breaking the rules, and he was letting Mila do it as well. They were supposed to maintain their cover, pretend like they were still living a normal, legit West Maradaine life. He should be spending every night in his room at Kimber's, and Mila should . . .

Mila should be sleeping in alleys and under bridges, to maintain her cover. That's why he never made a thing about her sleeping here.

The sun would be up soon. Time to put the plan in motion. He grabbed some paper and ink from the office, and wrote out a few things. Then he selected some clothes from the wardrobe of costumes Gin had pulled together and laid them out by Mila.

"Wake up, get dressed."

Bleary eyed, Mila squinted at him. "What time is it?"

"Bit past six bells, but I've got a plan."

"A six bells in the morning plan?" she asked, sitting up. "That's not your usual plan."

"Just hurry up."

"Is there tea? Breakfast? Is that part of your plan?"

"Get dressed," he said. "I'll get you some bread and preserves, deal?"

"Deal," she said.

He went off to the kitchen and got the kettle going. In a few minutes she joined him, dressed in the clothes he laid out for her. A smart skirt and waistcoat, the kind that Uni girls would wear when not in uniform, especially the ones who went to work in offices or courts. For his part, Asti had dressed in the same sort of style, so he looked like any other clerk or bookman in the city.

"Fancier than you usually have me wear."

"You've been working with Pilsen on accents, yes?"

"Some," Mila said.

"Give me your best college girl."

She smirked. "You want a Mary or a Royal?"

"I honestly don't believe you can make the distinction."

"Not really," she said, doing a passable job of an educated girl. "Mister Gin insists there is a difference, but I'm not hearing it."

"That'll do. Worst case, you'll come off like a Westie who went to U of M." He thought about it as he passed over her tea and bread. "That might even work."

"So what's the plan, and why is it so absurdly early?"

"It's early because we've got to get to Inemar before eight bells, and the streets are going to be packed by seven."

"What's in Inemar?"

"The city archives," Asti said. "Eat up, everyone's got to work this morning."

"Right," Mila said. "Poor Helene."

"Poooooooooooooooooooooooork and cheese! Get it hot! Get your hot goxies! Get your poooooooooooooooork and cheese!"

This was the center of the sinners' blazes, where Helene was forced to work her trade each morning. Slinging Monic-style pork sandwiches—goxies—from the shop underneath the apartment she shared with her cousin.

This was the deal she had worked out—the cover of still

being a broke North Seleth girl who lost everything in the fire. So she and Julie had an apartment, "rented" from Mister Inderick in exchange for them working the goxie stand each morning and lunch. Julie made the goxies—and he did a damn fine job of that, Helene had to admit—and she was in the window, selling to the morning crowd.

And there had to be a crowd. Mister Inderick made it very clear that they had to sell at least a certain amount, or they'd be out on their ears.

Helene had to laugh at that. She had her share of tens of thousands of crowns, just waiting for the Old Lady to call it safe and dole it out. That was Baroness money. She could move to Monim and hire muscle-bound boys to feed her goxies.

But the money wasn't safe, and they had to maintain appearances. The only money they had access to was the bit Josie and Asti had put with some creditor account for "job expenses." Whatever that meant. Helene didn't quite understand what the difference between goldsmith notes and creditor accounts were, but both were things a person used when they had a lot of money. Helene would far rather deal with real coins. Helene understood one thing: this business with creditor accounts meant no coin in her pocket right now, save what she earned slinging goxies with Julie.

"Watcha got for me, Kesser?"

Ren Poller was at her window with Ia, that blonde mountain of a Bardinic woman. Ia had taken up wearing a fur cap, probably to replace the green newsboy cap Helene had taken from her.

"I've got goxies for five ticks, and nothing else," Helene said. "You want?"

"Yeah, give us four," Poller said, flipping a crown at her. "Ia's a hungry girl."

"Why are you working with meat, girl?" Ia said, her Bardinic accent thicker than the pork fat in the air. "You cannot fight anymore?"

"You wanna spar?" Helene asked. "I could use another hat."

"Helene!" Julie yelled from the stoves. "Order up!"

Helene grabbed the goxies, wrapped in yesterday's newsprint. "Four more," she told Julie.

"Four more, aye," Julie said.

"Hey, Dusky!" Helene yelled at the customer who was waiting near the window. "Got yours."

"Took long enough," he muttered, grabbing the sandwiches and stalking away.

"Real charmer, Hel," Ren said.

"Your order's in," Helene said. "Step to the left. Next!"

The next order up started to step to the window, but off of a glare from Ren, he stayed back.

"I saw something funny last night, Hel," Ren said.

"Well, I'm glad you bought a mirror. Step to the left."

"Verci Rynax came into Kimber's last night. Or, rather, he was carried by his brother."

"I've got goxies to sell, I don't care about gossip."

"Ain't the Rynaxes your boys?"

Helene scowled at Ren. "Known them since I was a kid. Same as you."

"But they are your friends, *sjat*?" Ia asked, leaning into the counter. "You are around them much, *sjat*?"

Helene wasn't sure what "*sjat*" meant in Bardinic, but she felt vaguely insulted. Though maybe it just meant "yes." "Sometimes," she said, while trying to get the next in line to give his order. "But I'm not mother or wife to either of them."

"So you don't know what they were up to last night?"

"I try not to have late nights, Poller," she said, taking the order and money from the next customer.

"Right, because you have to work here," Ren said.

"That is why she is not dusting knuckles," Ia added.

"You wanna dust, ivory?"

"Order up!" Julien yelled. She turned to grab the order, and saw Julien scowling at her.

"What?" she asked as she grabbed the next set of goxies.

"You don't fight," Julien said coldly. "You make sure I don't fight, I do the same to you."

"I'm just mad," she said. "I just—"

"Order's up," Julien said, pointing to the wrapped sandwiches. "Talk later."

"Right," she said. She grabbed the goxies and brought them out. "Take your food, Poller. Stop bothering me."

"Or what?" Poller snarled.

Julien turned to the window. "Or me."

"Fine," Poller said. He handed the sandwiches to Ia, who started eating the first one as menacingly as anyone can eat a sandwich. They strolled off.

"Next order!" Helene called out. "Pork and cheese, hot goxies!"

The orders kept coming, and Helene kept working. But she knew that Poller wasn't going to let it go. That was going to be a problem for the crew. And the only thing she could do at the moment was put up the front that nothing was going on.

That, or knock Ia's teeth out. That would be satisfying.

Chapter 6

"THE FAR HEART HAS hard wars to harden its home for hurricanes," Mila repeated as they walked down Promenade Street in the heart of Inemar. One of Mister Gin's exercises to work her accent, knock the Westie out her speech patterns.

"You can stop that now," Asti said. "You'll be fine."

"First time I've really tried this," Mila said.

"You've got to do the real thing sooner or later," Asti said. "This is a good field assignment for that."

"Because the stakes are low?" Mila asked. She knew that if this didn't go right, Asti probably had six other plans to get the information he wanted.

"They aren't low, but . . . the risk is. You're not going to have to pull a knife or bolt if this doesn't work. Worst case is you'll get insulted and told to leave."

They reached the steps of the City Archives building, a bright giant of white stone steps and pillars. It looked like what she imagined the royal palace on the other side of the river must. Several young men, well dressed, were standing at the bottom of the steps, waving pamphlets and shouting out to whoever came close.

"Put the path of God in the Parliament! Vote for Acarrick!"

"Government that works! Hentin Parinal is the Functionalist for you! Learn about the whole Frike ticket!"

"You sir, you sir," one of them said to Asti as they approached. "You look like the sort of fellow who supports the average man of business."

"I suppose," Asti said. Mila noticed he had shifted his accent a bit, just like she was supposed to be working on.

"Thus I'm certain that Turncock and Winfell have your support to be returned to the Parliament. They've been working hard for the merchants and artisans of this archduchy and country, and they need your help as well."

"Sure, sure," Asti said, taking the pamphlet. "They're Minties, right?"

"Yes, of course," the young man said. "Now as I'm sure you're aware, there's a special election for a third chair from Sauriya. I'm sure you heard—"

"Yes, of course," Asti said. "Tragic, tragic. And therefore Good Misters Turncock and Winfell are supporting who?"

"Pentin Oswin! He's a key member of the business community in Kyst, a man of enterprise, who's also served in that city's Council of Aldermen . . . ."

"Oswin, all right," Asti said. Mila couldn't tell if he was playing a role or was really interested. "Give me just a moment, and I'd like to talk to you about our own aldermen here in Maradaine."

"Of course."

Asti pulled Mila to the side. "You better get in there."

"You think this will work?"

Asti handed her the papers. "Confidence, but mixed with nervous desperation. You know what you're saying?"

"I've got some words in my head," she said.

"Say that again without your Westie accent."

"I've got some words in my head," she said again, making sure to round her vowels and articulate her w's and h's.

"Good, go for it."

"You're not coming?"

"No, of course not."

"Why did you even dress for this?"

"So you wouldn't look strange walking with me."

Mila rolled her eyes. "Are you really interested in this election stuff, or is this part of the role?"

"Just go."

Inside the main lobby, there were two guards, whose uniforms looked more official than the ones in the Pomoraine, but weren't quite Constabulary either. King's Marshals? Sheriffs of the Archduchy? She had no idea, and she felt she should know.

"Pardon me," she said, going up to one of them. Confident. She's supposed to be here. "I need to get to the office for City Registrar Archives?"

"Second floor, to the right," he said, pointing up the stairs.

"Thank you, kindly," she said. "Have a good morning."

He just grunted. She might have oversold it.

She made her way up the stairs, putting on the best "harried" expression she could as she went. "Be in character well before you approach the mark," Mister Gin had said. She allowed herself one more "The far heart fought hard wars to harden its home for hurricanes" before she went into the Archives office.

"Oh, thank every saint you're already here," she said to the clerk as she went up to the desk. "I was worried no one would be here before nine bells."

"No, no," the clerk said. An older man, thick spectacles over his mousy nose. He wasn't unlike Almer, actually. "Here at eight, closed at twelve, open again at two, and closed at six. Every day."

So that's who this guy was. The by-the-rules official. That would be challenging.

"Glad to have it." She slapped the papers Asti had written out on the counter. "I'm in a bit of a bind, sir."

"Well, I don't know what that has to do with me, young lady."

"My boss is an attaché for one of the aldermen, who is expecting a report on several formal associations that are involved in a project on the west side."

"Right, that's pretty standard. Requests for those

records should be put in five days in advance of receipt, so we can have that on the twenty-third."

"Ah, no," Mila said. "You see, I need this so he can present it at nine bells."

"Well, young lady, that sounds like you didn't plan properly."

"But I did," Mila said. She had to get him on her side, give him a story he'd respect. She lowered her voice. "One of the other secretarial girls is trying to sabotage me—she wants my job."

"Again, I don't know how this concerns me."

"So she hid one of the associations they want a report on. Gave it to me last night after you closed. I have all the rest, I just need information on this one."

"That isn't how things work, young lady. You put in the request, then I pull the file, and then I check it for security concerns—"

"Security concerns?"

"Not every file can be released to any secretary or functionary, young lady . . ."

"I have an alderman's attaché—"

"I'm talking potentially. I don't know about yours. Still, then I send it to the scribe on the third floor, who makes a copy, returns the copy and the file to me. I'll send a page to your office to let you know to come get it . . . there is procedure."

"We did that. But there's this one."

"Even if I could help you, the scribes are very busy. They can't possibly . . ."

"I don't need a copy," Mila said.

"Well, I can't very well give you the original . . ."

"No, I mean . . ." She was getting flustered, and almost letting her accent slip. "I can copy what I need. If you can just put it in front of me for a few moments."

He nodded sagely for a moment. "This girl, the one who has it in for you. What's her name?"

"Helene," Mila answered without blinking.

He chuckled. "What's the file?"

"Creston Group."

"Let me check," he said, going into the back.

Mila let out a deep breath. Surprisingly, he didn't even

look at the papers Asti had forged. Who knows what those even said.

After a few minutes he came out carrying a handful of papers. "You might have a real problem, young lady."

"What's that?"

"Well, the Creston Group has been filed with quite a few security precautions. I can only release the file—or let it be copied—by one of the aldermen themselves. Not his attaché and certainly not you."

"But I—" She stopped. This guy was going to play by the rules. "Is there anything you can tell me from the file? An address or . . ." She struggled to think of what the official term might be. "Or a responsible party?"

"Responsible party?"

She leaned in close. "This report is about . . ." What was the word? Verci would use it sometimes. "Liability. If someone is injured . . ."

"Who the aldermen can pass the lawsuit onto," the clerk said. "I understand." He thumbed through the papers, humming tunelessly. "All right, there is a name listed as the primary signatory, and that's not in the protected portion. It is literally just a name, now . . ."

"That will help," Mila said.

"Lord Nathaniel Henterman, the Earl of Hinton Hollow." He clicked his tongue. "Privacy of the Peerage is quite a thing, still."

Mila put on a smile. "That helps, quite a bit. Thank you so much."

He smiled back, his teeth a bit crooked and blackened. Leaning closer he added, "I know some of us have to work a bit harder to stay ahead of the Helenes in this world. Mine was Mitchell."

Mila laughed. "I appreciate it. Now I have to run."

"Good luck."

She scurried out of the office, down the stairs and through the lobby, to find Asti waiting outside, thumbing through the pamphlet the campaigner had given him.

"Any luck?"

"I have a name."

"That's something."

"Lord Nathaniel Henterman, the Earl of Hinton Hollow. Now we just have to find out who he is."

"I have an idea," Asti said.

Asti had a name now, the man behind the fire. He sent Mila off to check on her boys—he had a feeling he was going to need them—and went back to the safehouse to do more research. But even after going back through the paperwork, he had nothing else to go on. Presuming Lord Henterman was a client of Mister Chell's, none of what Verci had stolen indicated that. He needed more information. Surely Druth Intelligence had a whole file on Henterman—they had files on everyone in the peerage—but he could hardly go into the Office and pull it himself.

So he had to do the next best thing.

By midmorning he had camped outside the spice shop that was the residence of Khejhaz Nafath, the Poasian spy turned double agent for Druth Intelligence. Nafath was really the only asset Asti had left from those days, and he wasn't really Asti's asset. Nafath had other handlers, both Poasian and Druth, and he had signals for contacting any of them. Nafath might know something about Henterman, but it wasn't likely. Nafath didn't have any reason to follow nobility. So Asti needed an active agent.

Asti was the one who had initially turned Nafath, made sure his spice shop was placed here in western Maradaine. So he knew all the signals, and odds were Druth Intelligence hadn't bothered to change theirs.

So Asti turned the marked stone in the outer wall of the spice shop, and waited to see who would respond.

It was nearly eleven bells when someone made a note of the signal and slipped away. It was subtle, and Asti wouldn't have noticed if he hadn't been looking for it.

A half an hour later, someone else came to Nafath's shop. This was a face Asti recognized: Tranner. Not a friend by any means, but a decent enough agent. Asti didn't even wait a beat before following him in, which was good, because once he was inside, Tranner and Nafath were already confused.

"Hey, you called for me," Tranner was saying. "So you tell me—"

"Hello, Tranner," Asti said. "Sorry to bother you."

"Rynax?" Tranner asked. "What the blazes are you doing here?"

"He lives in this neighborhood," Nafath said coldly. "This explains why you got the signal from me."

"I sent it," Asti said.

Tranner scowled. "We need a new signal, then. And I'm going to report this, Rynax."

"Wait," Asti said, holding up his hands peacefully. "I know I'm not well liked back in the Office."

"We don't think about you at all, you crazy bastard. But maybe that will change now."

"I need some information."

"I don't care what you need."

Asti steeled himself. This wasn't going to be easy.

"Mister Tranner," Nafath said. "I strongly suggest you listen to his request."

"Why should I, ghost?"

"Because I have seen that look on Mister Rynax's face before. And it is not one many people see twice."

"You going to fight me, Rynax?"

Asti was tempted to go for bluster, or even threats, but that wouldn't give him what he needed. "No, Tranner, I'm not. But given what I've sacrificed for Intelligence, for the Office . . . this isn't too much to ask. It could have been you on Levtha."

Tranner gave a conciliatory shrug. "Rand tricked us all. You're just the one who took the arrow. What do you want to know?"

"Lord Nathaniel Henterman. Earl of Hinton Hollow, I believe."

"What do you need to know about him?"

"Anything you have," Asti said.

Tranner mulled for a moment. "Is he a threat to Druth security?" Tranner glanced at Nafath. "You think he's been turned or something?"

"I don't know much of anything yet," Asti said. "I don't

have anything concrete, but . . . I think it might need to be looked into."

"We can't just casually look into a member of the peerage, Rynax."

"All the more reason for me to look a bit deeper. Deniability."

"That's the dumbest thing I've ever heard." He shook his head. "Off the top of my head, he's got a manor house in East Maradaine, in that part where the south side nobles have their houses. He spends most of his time in Maradaine, letting the affairs of Hinton Hollow be handled by his staff."

"All right," Asti said.

"His father served on the Council of Lords under Maradaine the XVII, as High Lord of Finance. His grandfather was a Noble Officer in the war. He was one of the commanding adjuncts in the Khol Taia occupation."

Nafath made a strange noise at the mention of Khol Taia.

"Wait, Captain Willman Henterman? That one?" Asti had been forced to read about the various heroes of the war in his training, and most of it was just lists of places in the islands and names of officers that he didn't bother to keep straight. But Khol Taia was different.

Khol Taia was the one place where the war had been brought to Poasian shores. Druth forces occupied the city in 1158 and held it for three years. Supposedly, once the Poasians forced them off, they burned the city to the ground, considering it now "sullied." Captain Willman Henterman was a minor name in all that, but he had the distinction of being the only officer who was both part of the initial invasion and one of the last people to leave in the retreat.

"That's the one. As for the current one, he's recently married, just a few months ago or so, but I don't recall the details. But it was a large event. He's got close ties to a few members of Parliament, as well as some of the lords on the King's Table. He's big on creating events, being seen. He throws some kind of gala at any opportunity."

"Gregarious?" Asti asked.

"Possibly to a fault." He thought for a moment. "Though that might be masking deep debts, leaving him vulnerable—"Tranner stopped. "That's just my speculation right now, not any official opinion."

"Can you bring me something official?" Asti asked.

"Why would I?" Tranner said.

"Fine, then," Asti said. "Do you know anything about the Creston Group? Or something called Andrendon?"

"Not a clue," Tranner said, going to the door. "I'll let my superiors know you're asking, how about that? Then we'll find out what they think of you."

"Fair enough," Asti said.

"And I better not see the two of you at the same time again," he said, and left the store.

Asti went for the door. "Asti, dear friend," Nafath said. "You use me like that, and don't even make the courtesy of a purchase?"

"I'm not really in the market for Poasian spices," Asti said.

"But you are always in the market for information, as we can plainly see. I may not know about noble lords, but I do know this neighborhood." Nafath pulled a jar out and put it on the counter. "I do hear things, you know. You might find what I know to be of use to you." He tapped on the jar.

Nafath's true job, as far as his Poasian masters were concerned, was to seek out dissidents in the poor neighborhoods of Maradaine. Druth people who could be turned into Poasian agents. Even though he had been turned to work for Druth Intelligence, he still went through the motions of his job for the Poasians.

"And what do you know?"

"I know you have not been as subtle or as clever as you think, Asti Rynax. I know you have been, and continue to be, up to something. Likely involving the true reasons behind the fire months ago. And others have noticed."

"Really?"

Nafath raised up his hands in a Poasian gesture that roughly meant "Do not kill the truthteller." "I do not know exactly what you are doing, nor do the other eyes on you, I think. But there are other eyes on you. And I imagine this business with the Lord Henterman is part of that."

Asti dropped a half-crown on the counter. "I'll be going."

Nafath pushed the jar forward. "Your purchase."

"I don't need it. Consider it a down payment for future truthtelling."

"Then I await you. I may even send you a warning if you deserve it."

"Why would I deserve it?" Asti found himself asking.

Nafath chuckled and tapped his skull. "Because my people are responsible for you. Therefore there is a certain . . . obligation placed upon me."

Asti left, knowing that he would never understand Poasians.

Mila stood on the street corner next to Nafath's shop, now dressed in her Miss Bessie street rat clothes.

"What are you doing?" he asked her.

"Waiting for you."

"How did you—"

"I followed you," she said. "So do we know where we're going now?"

"Yeah," Asti said. "Back out to East Maradaine."

Verci couldn't just stay up in bed. In a few minutes, he had rigged together some crutches, and with a little practice got adept enough at hobbling around with them. He did notice that his foot started to swell after being upright too long. At least for the time being, it was best to stay seated with it raised. So he'd have to figure out a way to do that and still get around.

He placed himself in a chair on the Junk Street walkway outside the bakery, where he could prop his foot up, and started sketching out a plan. Shouldn't take much to make a chair he could roll around in, even if it wasn't going to work well on stairs. Or cobblestones.

But it would be something, and it would let him be more available for whatever Asti needed next. Shortly after midday he had already received a coded note from Asti—sent by one of Mila's Bessie's Boys—saying that the new target was a noble with a manor house in East Maradaine, and he was heading out there with Mila to investigate. He should call on Helene with the bread delivery excuse if any trouble reared its head.

"Oy, no beggars here." A Constabulary handstick prodded Verci in the arm. Verci looked up to see a stick with lieutenant's stripes on his arm. This could be that trouble.

"Not a beggar, sir," Verci said. "Just injured. This bakery is my wife and mine's."

"Why are you sitting out on the street?"

"Sun and fresh air?" Verci offered. "I can't exactly be carrying the flour bags right now, you see."

"Fine," the lieutenant said. "Just . . . try not to look like a vagrant."

"My lifelong goal, sir," Verci said. There was something off about this lieutenant that he couldn't quite place. "You're not quite on your beat, are you, Left?"

"Does it show?" the lieutenant asked with a strangely sheepish smile.

"Most of the sticks in these parts are lifers, even the officers. Few get assigned Seleth from somewhere else, unless they screw up."

"Nah, I'm not on Seleth beat. Or North Seleth," the lieutenant said. Verci took a closer look at his badge. Jarret Covrane. "Funny thing, though. North Seleth."

"Funny place," Verci said.

"Born and raised here?" Covrane asked.

"More or less, though I've seen my share of the city and the outskirts."

"Good," Covrane said. "What's funny about North Seleth, it isn't really a place. You know, on the map. Sort of Seleth, sort of Keller Cove. Sort of Benson Court."

"I never was a map man, sir," Verci said. This lieutenant was very odd, and it set the hairs on the back of Verci's neck on end.

"I would say the folks in the Constabulary Houses aren't either."

"I don't follow." Verci wracked his brain. Covrane. Was that a name he should know? Was there a reason this fellow was talking to him?

"You ever notice there aren't many constables who really walk these streets? 'North Seleth'?"

"I never gave it much thought until this moment, sir," Verci said. A few folk were walking by, giving Verci and the constable an odd regard. Including Kel Essin. Essin was a window-man, like Verci had been back in the day, but not as good. And three times the drunk as Doc Gelson.

And he was one of Lesk's crew.

Essin stood on the other side of Junk Avenue, staring at Verci talking to a constable like it was a nightmare horror he couldn't look away from.

"This is the funny thing I found out. See, I'm stationed in Keller Cove."

"All right," Verci said. "So, you're off your beat."

"By the map in my stationhouse, you're right. Our beat ends at Ecsen Creek. Then it's Seleth's beat."

"Sounds right."

"But the Seleth stationhouse? Their map says their beat ends at West Birch, and this here stretch is Benson Court."

"Well, that's just absurd," Verci said. "We're definitely not in Benson Court." Anyone living in North Seleth would argue that contentiously.

"You're confused, aren't you?" Covrane said.

"Rather, about a number of things."

"It gets better, sir," Covrane said. "You, as a business owner here on Junk Avenue, should be concerned and aware of what I'm telling you."

"I'm quite intrigued." Verci wasn't lying about that, even if he didn't understand why the lieutenant was telling him this.

"Because I went to the Benson Court stationhouse, and guess what their map says?"

"That their beat ends at Junk Avenue, and this is Keller Cove?"

"Very good, sir."

"So we're in no house's beat, really?" Verci had suspected such a thing—sticks were always in short supply in this neighborhood—but he had never complained about that. He remembered he was supposed to be an honest businessman, though. "That's quite troubling."

"Well, don't be as troubled, sir," Covrane said. "I'm making North Seleth my own special project."

"That's . . . very kind of you, sir."

"So I'm getting to know the locals, Mister—?" He let it hang.

"Rynax," Verci said. "Verci Rynax. Proprietor of the Junk Avenue Bakery, with my wife. Raychelle. She's the baker. I'll be opening the Rynax Gadgeterium in the near future."

"Gadgeterium?"

"Indeed!" Verci said. "A fine selection of unique gadgets, tools, and toys for the discerning customer who embraces our modern world." He showed his sketchbook to the lieutenant. "Working on something to help with my current predicament."

"Interesting. I've got some sketches as well." The lieutenant reached into his coat, pulling out a notebook. He thumbed through the pages. "So you are, as you said, a long-time local."

"That's true."

"And you heard of the big fire and robbery over in Keller Cove a few weeks ago."

"It made the newssheets."

"Reports are they escaped west. Are you familiar with any of these people?" He handed the notebook over. Inside were sketches of faces, seven total. Far from perfect representations, but there was a certain likeness to Asti and Mila, and to a lesser degree himself, Helene, Julien, and Pilsen. None of those were too incriminating or damning. He could recognize them all only because he knew exactly who he was supposed to be looking at. The one of him was poor enough that even sitting right here with it, the stick didn't seem to suspect. For six out of the seven, it was nothing to worry about.

But the seventh was Kennith. It was definitely close enough to be a problem; there were only so many Ch'omik-skinned folk in North Seleth.

"Not overly, Left," Verci said.

"What about this one?" Covrane said, pointing to the sketch of Kennith. "You know a chomie carriage driver?"

Verci put on his best incredulous smile. "I did hear about this one. What did they call it? 'A driver black as night on a horseless carriage.' Sounded like drunken ramblings."

"Quite a few people made the same ramblings, Mister Rynax. It has some credibility."

"If you say so, Lieutenant. I heard some say it was Sinner Sethisar himself tearing through our wicked streets."

Covrane nodded calmly, putting the journal back in his coat. He took out a calling card and gave it to Verci. "Well, if you should think of something, pay me a call. I would be most grateful, Mister Rynax."

"I'll do that," Verci said.

Lieutenant Covrane nodded and went off down Junk Avenue. Across the street, Essin was still standing wide-eyed. When Verci looked at him, he squealed and went off down the road.

Verci looked down the road. Covrane was out of sight. He got up on his crutches and went into the bakery.

"Raych," he said as soon as he saw his wife. She was rolling dough with her sister. "I need to deliver some rolls over to the goxie stand."

"You'll do nothing of the sort," Raych said.

Verci sighed. "Then . . . then you'll need to go over there and tell Helene to come here to *pick up her order*."

"She doesn't—what are you?" She looked at him, then at Lian, and back to him. "Oh, her order. For making more goxies. At her stand."

"Yes," Verci said. "And it's a rush. It might be too big for her to carry, so she should bring Julien with her."

"This is a bakery, we don't do rush orders," Lian said snidely. "Or did you already prep it?"

"It's all right," Raych said, dusting the flour off her hands while she removed her apron. "Keep working on the sweet rolls. And Verci?"

"Yes, my love."

"Work the counter while I'm gone. You can manage that, yes?"

"Absolutely," Verci said, hobbling behind the counter and putting on an apron. "I'm a pillar of the community. And I have to stress: rush job."

Raych rolled her eyes and went off.

"Well," Lian said as she portioned out her dough. "I'm glad an honest trade has done you well. If only the same could be said of your brother."

Chapter 7

MILA WAS GETTING ANNOYED by Asti's precautions, which he was going overboard with. First he wanted to get word to Verci and the rest, but he felt he needed to be extra careful. So he wrote coded notes—even though Mila reminded him that only Verci knew the code, so sending that to everyone else was absurd—and then had Mila send those notes to everyone else through her Bessie's Boys. Mila had to go back over to the boys, even though she'd just checked on them. She had a feeling that Asti was going to want them on message duty for a while, so she told them to be on point. No hiding out today.

Asti told her to meet him at a safe drop spot by half past one bell. That spot was under the creek bridge, where Asti had a set of new clothes for both of them to change into. Once they changed under the bridge, he brought her over to the apartment in East Maradaine—the one they had just used for the Pomoraine Building job—and had them change clothes again.

"Is this all really necessary?" she asked as she switched into the prim dress that had far too many buttons and clasps to be useful. And layers. Far too many layers for this summer heat.

"I think we've been a little too careless of late," he said as he changed on the other side of the sheet he had hung up in the middle of the apartment. "Verci's out of commission right now, with his leg, and a couple of Lesk's crew saw that. Nafath said—"

"That's the Poasian spice guy."

"Yes."

"Who is a spy *for* the Poasians."

"Yes, but—"

"And sells spices in North Seleth."

"Mila!" Asti snapped at her.

"Look, I just wonder why you even talk to such a person."

"Be—because he pays attention to what's going on. And he knew we were up to something, and people were watching us."

"Like Lesk's crew. Even though Lesk is in Quarrygate."

"We're going to have to do something about them. Well, maybe not us. Maybe your boys?"

"Asti," Mila said calmly. "I'll remind you that Lesk's crews are a bunch of thieves and thugs."

"Like us," Asti said with a shrug.

"But we have morals."

Asti gave another shrug to that.

"And they run the Scratch Cats, who earn their name by *cutting other people*."

"Yes, they're bad people, which is why—"

She pulled the sheet open and glared at him. "And my boys are literally *children*. You can have them run messages and use their eyes all over town, but that's all you'll use them for."

He nodded quickly. "You're right, you're right. Sorry. I—" He paused, sitting down on the bed. "A bunch of things with Nafath, and Tranner, and what happened to Verci—it's got me spooked. And that part of my head . . ." He tapped at his skull. "It's a growling dog right now. So I'm—"

"Being more careful right now," Mila said. "I'm for it. But before we go back out there, actually tell me our plan. Deal?"

"All right," Asti said. "So we're heading deep into East Maradaine now, to find Lord Henterman's estate house. There are quite a few noble estate houses out there, so . . ."

"I thought all of those were on the north side," Mila said.

"Some of the Sauriyan lords prefer having their city homes south of the river so they're in their proper archduchy."

"Wait, are we in Sauriya?"

"Depends on who you ask and to what end. As far as voting for Parliament goes—"

"Like that matters to me." Though in her rounds of panhandling, she had seen women starting a movement for the right to vote.

"We're Sauriya. But in other ways the Duchy of Maradaine—which is the city—is its own thing, separate from the archduchies on either side."

"Let me tell you something," Mila said, her blood suddenly coming up. "We are governed by way too many people, you know? I mean, there's a king, the Parliament, the Duke, the Council of Aldermen, and what else? Is there a Baron of Seleth?"

"No, of course not," Asti said, though it didn't sound like he was sure. "You're dragging my point away from our mission, here."

"Sorry."

"So we're changing into these outfits so we fit in for that part of town."

"We're not dressed like noble swells, Asti." In fact, the dress he gave her was rather plain. Plain and reserved, despite all its buttons and clasps. It was very different from the suit she wore this morning. His suit was different as well, with a coarse wool jacket despite the summer heat.

"No, but there is a certain look to the service class, and we've got to hit that."

"Service class? How were we not already dressed for that? How are we not always dressed for that?"

"We're working class, which is different. And these people take note of that, trust me. I'm talking about the people who work for the nobles, in their homes. It's a very certain type. There's a sort of modesty, a willing submission to their roles."

"They believe they're supposed to serve the nobility?" Mila asked.

"And they believe that they're above folk like us for it," Asti said. "Blazes, you complained about the Parliament? Some of those folk came from the service class. Literally working for their nobles in the Parliament."

"The world is a terrible place," Mila said, rubbing her eyes. She understood gangsters burning them out for land far more than stuff like this. Blatant criminality at least made sense to her. These people, she couldn't even imagine. "So that's what we're pretending to be? And why this outfit has three layers of skirting but still looks like a washergirl dress?"

"That's how we need to look, so we won't look out of place walking through the neighborhood. Though if we have to speak—has Pilsen worked on the service accent with you?"

"I didn't even know there was a service accent."

Asti shook his head. "Then you'll have to just be a West Maradaine girl . . . all right, if you have to speak and someone asks—"

Mila was already on it. She had learned enough from Mister Gin about making up stories. "I spent too many years with my drunken father in westtown before my aunt got me out of there and on a proper path in a decent home."

Asti looked impressed. "Not bad. Though it shouldn't come up."

"Because that's our cover, but we aren't actually going to interview for any work."

"Spot on," Asti said. "Once we're there, we'll see what we can scout out."

The morning rush had long passed, and midday hadn't heated up, so there was a chance for Helene to get off her feet and sit in the chair by the stove while Julien pulled more supplies out of the stores. As much as she hated working this job as a cover, she admired how much her cousin seemed to really love it. Of course, it was honest work, and it involved four of his favorite things: cheese, bread, pork, and pickles. Their deal meant that they could eat as much as they wanted, as long as sales stayed steady.

Julien could happily eat goxies all day long. Which was probably why he cooked them with such love.

One of Mila's annoying brats had delivered a note, supposedly from Asti, but Helene couldn't be bothered to figure out what it said. It was in his stupid code that only Verci could crack. Though she would have to go and face Verci sooner or later. She wasn't sure what she could say to him when she did.

"Helene?" A woman was calling her.

Helene looked up to see someone leaning through the window, and it wasn't Mila or Josie.

It was Raych Rynax.

"What do you want?" Helene asked.

"I . . . I don't rightly know," Raych said. "Verci was—"

"I know, he got hurt. I saw it."

Raych scowled hard at her. "My husband is at the bakery now, and something has spooked him. He said you needed to come get your order of rolls. And you'd need Julien to help you carry them."

"We do need more rolls," Julien said.

"Jules, we get rolls every third day. That's tomorrow."

"I know that," Raych said. "So obviously Verci meant something else."

"Something's wrong and he wants us both," Helene said. "But he didn't tell you, hmm?" She might have been a bit too coarse with that, giving Raych a look that would normally start a fight. Helene couldn't quite help herself from trying to raise this woman's dander up. Raych Rynax always got hers up just by existing. The woman was too pretty—just enough Acserian in her face to make her exotic—to the point where she didn't fit in North Seleth.

"He couldn't speak freely. My sister is at the store right now. Helping out because of his foot." Raych leaned farther in the window. "I don't know what it is, but he was sitting outside, and then hobbled in as fast as he could on those crutches, just to tell me to come get you. So whatever trouble you're all mixed up in—"

"We're all mixed up in, Raychelle," Helene said. "Don't act like you aren't part of it, and that you don't benefit."

"I don't—"

"Why do you have a bakery right now?"

Raych fumed, thin-lipped. "Even still," she said with hard punctuation. "There seemed to be some urgency."

"We'll be right out," Helene said, closing the window.

"We're not supposed to close the shop," Julien said.

"I know that," Helene said. "And so does Verci. There must be a reason he's asked for us to come right now."

Julien shook his head. "It isn't right."

"Then you stay. He asked for us both, but you stay."

Julien bit his lip. She rarely saw him so burdened with a decision.

Finally Julien said, "We need to help Verci and maintain our appearance. I will stay."

"All right," Helene said. She handed him the keys to the lockbox. "Remember, five ticks per goxie. And a crown is?"

"Twenty ticks, I know," he said. He quietly added, "Haven't made that mistake in a long time."

"I'll be back as soon as I can," she said, taking off her apron and putting on her green cap. "Don't stay open past three bells."

"But—"

"No exceptions." She went to the alley door. "Lock—"

"Lock it behind you, I know."

Helene went out to find Raych waiting at the mouth of the alley.

"Where's Julien?"

"He's staying. Someone needs to keep the shop."

Raych didn't give her any push on that, and they started walking at a heavy stride toward Junk Avenue. That suited Helene just fine; no need for idle chatter with Raych.

"Now this is interesting."

Poller stood in the walkway, with his whole crew shoulder to shoulder. That skinny drowned rat Kel Essin, the bald bruiser Sender Bell, and of course Ia. Rutting Ia.

Helene took Raych by the arm and pulled her across the street.

"Where you going, Kesser?" Poller asked, walking into the street with the rest.

"Going to none of your business."

"She thinks this isn't our business," Poller said.

"She's with Rynax's wife, walking to the bakery," Essin said. "They've got something working."

"It's called bread," Raych spat at them. "She works a sandwich shop, they need bread."

"Don't talk to them," Helene said. "Don't even look."

Poller jumped in front of them, and in a breath all four boxed them in.

"What's the story?"

"Story is get out of the rutting way, Poller," Helene said.

"Or you'll call a stick?" Essin asked.

"Your cousin isn't here," Sender added.

"I don't need my cousin," Helene said. "Back off."

"What are the Rynaxes up to, Kesser?" Poller asked. "What's the Old Lady up to?"

"Back off."

"Ain't no one seen the Old Lady in weeks. She's off the table. Or is she?" He leaned in close, so she could smell his rotten teeth.

"You think you're scaring me, Poller?" Helene said, though Raych had wrapped her sweaty palm around Helene's wrist. She was probably terrified. "You're a two-pence nothing. A lapdog for Nange, cooling his heels in Quarry-gate."

"He ain't going to be in the 'gate forever," Poller said.

"Nope." Sender put his hand on her shoulder. Helene pushed it off.

"And we've been making more friends," Poller said. "We can't have plans screwed up by your boys."

"Roll your rutting hand, Ren," Helene said. "Step off or we scream."

"Scream," he said. "You think I don't have this block locked down?"

"You don't have anything."

"I'll ask again. What are the Rynaxes up to?"

Ia grabbed Raych. "Maybe the wife will tell us, *sjat*?"

"Get your hands off her," Helene said. "Now."

"Or?"

Helene shot a quick punch into Ia's nose, and another one into the center of her chest. That was enough for her to lose her grip on Raych, who scrambled away. While Ia staggered back, a hard punch came at Helene's back, knocking her to her knees. Sender laughed, straddling her.

Helene flipped over and pounded him in the tenders. It was his own fault for presenting them so prominently to her. He bent over double, and she didn't let up. She grabbed him and squeezed his tenders as hard as she could until she felt something pop.

Sender fell over with a sickening gasp.

Helene turned to Poller, who stood agape in the middle of the road. "I'll ask again. Do you think you're scaring me?"

"No wonder you've thrown in with the Rynaxes," he whispered. "You're just as crazy."

"Let's move, Helene," Raych said. "Before the Constabulary comes."

"They ain't gonna come," Essin said, his hand shaking as he pointed accusingly at Helene. "But Treggin is going to hear about this!"

Helene had no blazing idea who Treggin was, but it was clearly a name Essin wasn't supposed to say. Poller smacked him across the head and told him to shut it. She didn't waste any time hearing more—these bastards had already eaten up enough of her day. She grabbed Raych's hand and bolted to Junk Avenue.

They were out of breath when they reached the bakery, not stopping until they were inside.

"The blazes?" Verci said when they came in. The man was sitting behind the counter, his bandaged leg propped up. He looked adorably pathetic like that, wearing a baker's apron over his shirtsleeves.

"Verci—" Raych gasped. "Those terrible—and she—"

"What happened? Are you all right?"

"Fine—but—"

Helene caught her breath. "Lesk's crew gave us some hassle. I gave them some back."

"What's this ruffianary?" A woman who looked like a pudgy version of Raych came over, her eyebrows judging Helene. This must be the sister. "Is this the woman with the rush order?"

"Yes, but it's all right. Raych explained some things to

me on the way," Helene said. "As long as I get my rolls for tomorrow, I'll be fine. But we should go over my accounts?"

"Yes," Verci said, pulling his leg off the counter. "Raych, you'll be all right? I should go over the accounts with her in the office in the back."

Raych looked hesitantly between him and Helene for a moment. "Yes, I suppose it's important that you do that. Just don't be too long about it."

"Never, love."

She leaned in and kissed him. "And be careful," she added in a low whisper. Presumably so her sister wouldn't hear.

"Always."

Verci led Helene through the back, his usual calm reserve melting as soon as they were through the doors. "Where's Julie?"

"He stayed to work our shop. Thought it was important to maintain the cover. And Lesk's crew, they've got a fly in their nose about us—"

"Can't worry about that just yet. We've got a bigger problem."

"Is it Asti? Because I don't know why you'd call me—"

"Asti is scouting something out east with Mila. Didn't you get a note?"

"You know I can't read that code you two use."

"Fine," Verci said, leading her to the back alley doors. "We need to find Kennith and get him locked down in the safehouse, and quick."

"Ken? Why?"

"Because there's a Keller Cove stick who's got some sketches. Witness reports from the night of the Tyne fire."

"Sketches of who?"

"You, me, Asti—but vague enough not to matter. But Kennith—"

The chomie stood out in a crowd. "I'm with you. Let's go."

Chapter 8

AFTER WALKING THROUGH EAST Maradaine, Asti and Mila found their way to Tully Road, a ring wrapping around Flynn Lake. The largest and most opulent of the East Maradaine manor houses all were on Tully Road, backed up to the lake.

Every one of them also had fifteen-foot walls around the property with steel gates and multiple guards at each one.

"There's no sneaking in, hmm?" Mila asked once they had done two laps on Tully. Asti still wasn't sure which house was Henterman's, though he had eliminated a few of the options.

"At least not in the front," Asti said. "Especially not you or I. Verci, if he were in form—"

"Not for a couple months."

"I'm aware of that," Asti said.

"And the houses all protect each other, in a way. Can't sneak through the back without coming from the lake, can't get into the lake without starting on another house's grounds. Rather clever."

Asti nodded. "There are two points of access to the lake itself—the creek in and creek out. Those cut through these properties, and could be weak points that can be exploited."

"But we have no idea if the lake shore is watched inside—"

"Right now, it's all just information," Asti said. They walked past the house with the inbound creek, approaching its gate. This was now the third time they passed it, and any guard worth the crowns he was paid would have taken note of them. Time to do something or move on. A loaded cart of goods was pulling up to the gate, and an empty cart was being let out. "Fair amount of activity here."

"Loaded carts entering each time we passed," Mila said. "None of the others have anything like that."

"All right, keep walking, make toward the main road."

"We're leaving? But—"

"For the moment. I have a theory, and I want to test it. Follow along."

They neared the main road; the empty cart came clopping up toward them. Asti waved to the driver.

"Good day to you, sir," Asti said, using his best north country accent. "Business is treating you well?"

"Well enough," the driver said.

"I hate to trouble you, but we're walking back to Inemar. My cousin's feet are killing her, and we would appreciate a ride."

"We've been walking all day," Mila added.

"I'd appreciate an extra half-crown in my pocket," the driver said.

Asti knew that a man like he was pretending to be wouldn't give up a half-crown very easily. "Would you settle for six ticks?"

"Fine," the driver said, waving them up. "You looking for work?" he asked once they were settled in the cart and paid up.

"Does it show?" Asti asked.

"You wouldn't be out here unless you were working for these swells, or were hoping to. And if you've been walking long enough for her feet—"

"Clever man you are."

"What sort of work are you looking for?"

"I'm a handyman by trade," Asti said. "And Bessie here is a cook's girl. Sadly, no place that we've talked to is looking for either role."

"Did you try Henterman Hall there?"

Perfect.

"Is that where you came from?"

"Just delivered as much flour, honey, and salt as I sell to the University. Seems like they're having something of a grand ball in a few days."

"Oh, they are?" Asti said. What was it Tranner had said? Henterman uses any excuse for revels. "Is it for Saint Jontlen Day?"

"I suppose," the driver said. "I mean, who else but the swells bothers to celebrate Saint Jontlen Day?"

"How do you celebrate Saint Jontlen Day?" Mila asked.

"I thought you were a cook's girl," the driver said.

"The places I worked never did Jontlen," Mila said.

The driver shrugged. "Well, since you say that, sir, it makes sense. Because they're clearly going to be making cakes, and when I arrived another cart was unloading pigs. Like thirty. So I guess they are doing the Bloody Feast."

Mila looked like she was going to ask about that, but Asti waved her down. No need to make the driver more suspicious. He'd explain it later.

"So they're making preparations," Asti said.

"That's how it seems to me, but I don't think much on it," the driver said. "I hear they do that from time to time. Good for business, though."

"Absolutely," Asti said. "Very helpful, don't you think, Bessie?"

She glared at him. Clearly his shushing waves had not been appreciated. "Quite."

Now they knew where, and there might be a way to just be let straight in the front door.

Verci was in the safehouse, and the last thing he wanted to do was go back to the bakery. The idea of puttering around on his crutches while other things were happening almost made him ill. Raych would be unhappy with him if she knew that. She thought Asti was pushing him, forcing him to be a part of this plan.

It wasn't completely untrue. He wouldn't be doing this if

Asti wasn't involved, but he wanted these bastards to pay for what they did to Holver Alley just as much as Asti did. Once that was done, he would be more than happy to live a simple life of baking and gadgets.

Right now, at least, he could work on his new chair with Kennith. That was fun. Kennith hadn't been happy when Verci and Helene had pulled him out of the inn's stable and brought him back to the safehouse. Verci wasn't sure if it had really sunk into Kennith's skull how much danger he was in.

"How long will I have to hide out in here?" Kennith asked as they were attaching the wheels.

"I don't know. Might be a while," Verci said.

"Ha!" Josie came down from the office. "I got pegged by the sticks in '03. Why do you think I never show my face in public?"

"Damn and blazes," Kennith growled. "I ain't staying in hiding that long. I've got my own job. I've got my garden. Peppers and okra."

"What's okra?" Helene asked. She was mostly hovering over Verci, but not contributing. Verci suspected she was in as much of a hurry to get back to the goxie shop as he was to the bakery.

"Ch'omik vegetable. I grow it every year, starting with seed stock from my father, just like my peppers."

"I remember that sewage you made with your peppers," Helene said. "You can keep the okra."

"Here's the thing about okra, Verci," Kennith said, ignoring Helene. "Harvesting it is like a gig. You got to do it just in the right moment, or it gets hard and tough. And then it's no damn good."

"I understand," Verci said. "Let's just wait a few days, maybe the lieutenant will get bored."

"Still, go check on my garden."

Verci pointed at his foot.

"Fine," Kennith said. For a moment, he looked over at Helene, and then at Josie. Sighing, he said, "I'll get Almer to do it."

"Probably wise," Helene said.

"Hel," Josie said, coming over closer. "Tell me about

your little run-in with Poller and his folk." She limped her way to the table and sat down. Verci never knew exactly how she had hurt her leg. It was possible he was looking at his future.

"Ain't much to tell," Helene said. "He tried to give some hassle to me and Verci's piece of butter—"

"Can we not call my wife that?"

"And after things went too far, I smacked that Bardinic slan in the face, knocked Sender in the tenders—ha—and got Raych the blazes out of there."

Helene sounded collected about the whole thing now, far from the half-panicked mess she was when she got to the bakery.

"You shouldn't be risking your hands in a street brawl, girl," Josie said.

"I should get in a high window and keep an eye for Poller, that's what I should do."

"He's not worth that," Josie said, drumming her fingers idly on the table. "He's not a leader. He's just wanting to keep the boots warm for when Lesk gets out of Quarry."

"You think Lesk is going to make a real play at us?" Verci asked. Josie had already lost so much of the empire she had built—mostly because she couldn't trust any of her old lieutenants anymore. She barely trusted Asti and Verci, and that was because she knew neither of them were interested in taking anything from her.

"I think Lesk wants North Seleth, has decided he's supposed to be the new boss in this neighborhood." She chuckled to herself. "They all know who'll stand in their way of that."

"I do not intend to be a neighborhood boss, Josie," Verci said.

"I know that," Josie said. "But any idiot with his ear on the street can see you and your brother aren't the types to lie down and let Lesk do it either."

"Seems we're alone in that," Helene said pointedly. "They've got places like the Shack, and quite a few folk under their thumbs."

"They've got a few holes and corners is all," Josie said. "But that's not something we're going to let them hold onto."

Verci held his tongue. Every time Josie talked like this,

like they were her lieutenants to reclaim the neighborhood with, Verci wasn't sure how to respond. He didn't like it, but at the same time, he couldn't pretend that he didn't owe Josie for so much. If she needed help, he couldn't ignore her.

But the idea of actually being part of some street war with Lesk's crew or some other boss made his palms sweat.

"Essin said a name, and it made Poller mad," Helene said. "Treggin? I ain't never heard it before."

Josie shook her head. "That ain't a player I've heard of."

"And you've heard of everyone?" Kennith said with a bit more spite than he probably intended.

"Apparently not," Josie said. She looked like she was about to say something else when Asti and Mila came into the place.

"We've got a target, and I've started to cook up a plan," he said boldly. Then he noticed Verci. "Glad to see you aren't moping around."

"I tried it for the morning," Verci said. "It didn't suit me."

"Target?" Josie asked. "Plan?"

"Lord Nathaniel Henterman, the Baron of Hinton Hollow, whose manor house in town is in East Maradaine. Number 7 Tully Road, to be precise."

Verci didn't know the specifics of East Maradaine or Tully Road, but he knew the kind of houses nobility lived in out there. "I hope your plan doesn't involve me scaling my way into an East Maradaine manor house."

"Nothing doing," Asti said. "I know you're going to want to lounge about for this one."

"So what is the plan?" Kennith asked.

"Didn't expect to see you here, Ken," Asti said. He glanced about at the bunch of them. "Why are you here, actually? I—what's wrong?"

"There's a lieutenant with a picture of my face," Kennith said. "So I have to stay hidden."

"This about the Tyne job?" Asti asked Verci.

Verci nodded. "He's got more faces, but his sketch of Kennith is the one to worry over."

"Also Lesk's buddies are getting frisky," Helene said. "I might have beat some calm into them, but—"

"It's more likely you've got their attention, girl," Josie said.

"Then all this sounds like my plan will make even more sense," Asti said. "We're going to need a base of operation in East Maradaine, or near enough. Josie?"

"Why are you looking at me?"

"Because this is what you usually do," Asti said.

"I ain't got any fingers out east, boys. I barely have any here, anymore. Didn't you already rent a flop in Inemar? Use that!"

"That's tiny, and doesn't have sights on our target."

"Oh, you have to have a special place for each job," she snapped. "Everything perfect for Asti's plan, which will likely roll up anyway."

"Is there a problem, Josie?" Asti shot back. "We're working a plan, and we need a safehouse for it. This isn't some wild hare I'm running. This is the man who had our neighborhood burned down."

She scowled. "I know that. It's just a lot of things faster than I thought."

"But you can make it work, right? It's not like money is a big problem here."

She sighed. "I'll see what I can find. It won't be much. Definitely won't be East Maradaine. Probably Colton."

Asti nodded. "That's fine. A place we can stage and scout from. And also a better place for Kennith to lay low."

"A Ch'omik, laying low in Colton?" Helene scoffed. "If he wants to hide, he should bury himself in the Hodge in the Little East."

"Roll yourself," Kennith told her. "I'd rather spend the rest of the year in here than live in the Hodge."

Verci waved the two of them down. "Presuming the base of operations, what's the plan?"

"Slow down, both of you," Josie said. "Start with what you know."

Asti went over to the icebox and pulled out a couple of ciders, handing one to Verci as he came back to the table. "So, Mila and I did some groundwork. We've got a sizable city manor house, probably the largest on Tully Road. Gates, high walls, all the houses in a circle. No way in from the back. Possible soft point through the creek and the lake, but I'm not sure. There's a lot I'm not sure of. We need a hard scout without it being a jangle."

"We can't repeat last night's debacle, that's for sure," Kennith said. Asti glared at him, but he just shrugged. "Am I wrong?"

"No," Asti said. "So, this is what we know. Henterman, he's throwing a party in a few days. More deliveries, more food, and so forth. That might give us some scout entry. But that party is our moment."

"What sort of party?" Helene asked.

"Apparently, Lord Henterman is throwing a gala party for Saint Jontlen Day, and—"

"Who celebrates Saint Jontlen Day?" Verci asked.

"Lord Henterman," Asti said. "But that's our moment to strike. That's what we have to be ready for."

"Hold up," Josie said. "I like your enthusiasm, but can we be clear on what 'strike' means? Especially if we're talking in three or four days."

Asti stared at her dumbly for a moment. "I mean, that's when we do it."

"Do what?" Josie asked pointedly. "I mean, with Tyne, we robbed him. Took from him like he took from us. So, are we robbing the manor house? Are we killing Lord Henterman?"

"If he's the one—"

"Are we talking about murdering a member of the peerage? Because if you think there's heat over Tyne, that's nothing compared to a dead earl. Or even a robbed manor house. No amount of coin spread to the right corners will quiet that rattle."

Helene piped up on that. "You're spreading coin to where? Ain't that all our money?"

"Hush it, Helene," Josie said. "I'm keeping the noise off our backs. All of us. So what is it, Asti? What's the goal?"

"I'm not sure," Asti said quietly.

"You're what?" she pressed.

"Not sure," Asti said.

"And yet, in just a few days, you want us to make our move?"

"This is the moment!"

"Asti," Verci said quietly. "She's got a point, the moment for what?"

"To find out what we need to do," Asti said. "I mean, you're right, we don't know. We don't know who Henterman is, what he's trying to do out here, whether he's the real brains of this or just another pawn. We need to find out."

"So when you say strike, you mean the party is an opportunity to figure out who he is and what we need to do about it." Verci looked over at Josie.

"Right," Asti said. "Though that might burn our entry. But we don't know how to do an entry unless we get in there for a proper scout."

"Sounds like a job for a spy," Verci said. "Since you don't have a window-man right now."

"You're going to be fine," Asti said, almost like he was trying to force it into truth with pure power of will. "I'd want you at the base while we're running, but I imagine Raych would object."

"You think?"

"She did tear my face off last night," Asti said. "You were out cold for that part."

"Probably for the best."

"So, the plan?" Helene prodded.

"Sorry," Asti said. "Henterman Hall. Gala party. We need to use that—"

"They're hiring," Mila said idly.

"What?" Asti's eyes bugged out at her. "How—Why didn't you—"

She pulled some papers out of her shirt. "You remember when the wagon driver told us to try the Henterman House? He wasn't being idle, they are looking to hire folk. He had sheets for a paper job, and it's in the adverts for the *Gazette*." She took out a copy of the newssheet.

"When did you grab those?"

"Didn't see me, did you, Mister Rynax?"

Verci stretched to grab the newssheets from Mila, but he couldn't reach far enough from his chair. Helene snatched them and handed them over.

"They're looking for a few things. Kitchen staff, handyman ..."

"Stableman?" Kennith asked.

"No, sorry. But that gives us an in," Verci said. "With some forged credentials—"

"That is something I can handle," Josie said.

"So who will try to be hired? I can't be the handyman like this."

"I'll go for that," Asti said.

"You? Handyman?"

"I do have some skills," Asti said.

Verci tried not to laugh.

"Fine, who else?" Josie asked.

"I'd want to keep Gin out of this part," Asti said.

"Isn't that what he's best at?" Helene asked.

"We want to be able to infiltrate the party," Verci said, picking up what Asti was probably thinking. "Most of us can fake service class, but not the sort of person who would get invited."

"Right, that's Pilsen," Asti said. "Some distant fake lord who can get into Henterman's good graces, perhaps. But the rest of us should try."

"Even me?" Mila asked.

"No, we're going to need Bessie and her boys," Asti said. "Wherever the base house is ..."

"Runners for messages, right," Mila said. "Got it."

"Yes, but also for this Lesk crew business," Verci said, giving Asti a look. "We're going to need eyes and ears."

"Eyes and ears," Mila said. She also gave Asti a pointed look. "But that's all, right?"

"Right," Asti said.

"Don't Julie and I have to run the goxie shop, keep the cover?" Helene said. "I mean—"

Asti waved her off. "I'm not sure how useful that is anymore. Like you said, Poller is already sniffing around. You shutter the shop, he'll go nutty trying to find out why. Might slip up."

"We don't make sales, we get booted," Helene said.

Asti nodded. "Josie, in addition to the place to use as our

base, some money to cover Helene and Julien at the goxie shop."

Josie groaned a little and nodded.

"That a problem, Old Lady?" Asti asked, a little harsher than Verci would have.

"Of course it is," she said. "I wasn't anticipating this many expenses so quick after the last one. The money isn't easily—"

"Just get it done," Asti said. "We'll work on getting us hired."

"So, Mister—"

"Crile, sir," Asti said, using a north shore accent from the Yeisha region of Patyma. "Pander Crile."

"Crile." Mister Canderell, the butler for the Henterman household, glanced over Asti's forged letters of reference. Canderell was a jowly, ponderous man who clearly thought very highly of himself. He sat behind the desk in his small office, meticulously kept neat, with a half-filled decanter of wine the only sign of the man's vice. "That is an interesting name, given that you are clearly of Kieran stock."

"My mother's side," Asti said. "Always did favor her in looks, but my father in skill."

"So you worked in the household of Baron Grentin," Canderell said. "Your skills as a handyman are given commendation. I do not know the head butler of that household personally, or the Baron Grentin, but these papers are in good order."

"Thank you kindly, sir," Asti said. "I'm grateful for the opportunity."

"What brings a man like you to the city, Mister Crile? You've clearly come quite a way."

"I'd hate to speak out of turn, Mister Canderell," Asti said, lowering his voice, as if he was taking the man into his confidence. "I quite enjoyed the household of the Baron, but . . . they reached the point where regular repairs were not their priority."

Canderell nodded. "I understand."

"So I have a cousin who lives here who let me stay with

him while I started looking for work. The city seems like it has quite a bit of opportunity."

"Under normal circumstances, we would not be able to help you," Canderell said. "However, the Lord Earl has intentions for an event in just a few days, and his previous event ... did considerable damage to elements of the household. More than our man, Mister Ottick, can handle on his own. So a man of your talents—temporarily—would be useful."

"Mister Canderell, I would appreciate it," Asti said. "The opportunity to prove myself."

"If your work is acceptable, of course, we would provide you with references. Local references would help you in seeking a permanent arrangement. Which, perhaps, might even be available here."

"If Lord Henterman and his wife are pleased with my work, obviously. And I'll do my best to make sure they are."

"I'm sure you will, Mister Crile." Canderell sighed. "Are you able to start immediately? There is quite a fair amount of work to be done over the next few days."

"I believe I would," Asti said. "I've got my tools with me, of course—"

"Of course."

"I would like to send a note to my cousin, just to let him know that I've found work and not to expect me."

"It is the polite thing to do," Canderell said. He gathered a few items from his desk. "I can lend you stationery and ink, and you can give it to the third underbutler." He handed the paper and other goods to Asti.

"The third underbutler?"

"This way," Canderell said, leading Asti out of the office. "Is there a problem?"

"No, of course not, Mister Canderell, sir," Asti said, digging thick into the role. "Just that the Baron only had the one. And then none."

"There is no need to further detail the Baron's troubles, Mister Crile. We believe in decorum in this household."

"Of course, Mister Canderell," Asti said.

"As we believe in decorum, you should respect the proper order of discipline. You, of course, will answer to

Mister Ottick, and if there is a household matter to be discussed, bring it to one of the underbutlers. I should not be troubled unless there is a serious matter of immediate attention and none of those people are available."

"Understood, sir," Asti said as he was being led through the maze of servants' hallways in the lower levels of the household. It would take him some time to learn his way about.

"And the Earl and Her Ladyship—"

"I should not disturb in the slightest, sir," Asti said. "I understand my place."

"Lovely, Mister Crile. Ah, Mister Ungar." Canderell brought Asti over to a livery-clad man who was coming down the hallway, who was a familiar face. "Are you finding your way about well enough?"

"Well enough," Mister "Ungar" said.

"This is Mister Crile, who will be joining Mister Ottick as an assistant handyman," Canderell said. "He'll be writing a *short* note to his cousin and beginning work straight away. Would you watch over that, and then have one of the pageboys deliver his message?"

"Of course, sir."

"And then bring Mister Crile out to Mister Ottick so he can be assigned his first duties. Mister Crile, I look forward to seeing your good work."

"As you say, sir. Mister Crile?" Ungar—actually Win Greenfield—led Asti to a small nook as Canderell went off. He turned to Asti and smiled. "Looks like you got in."

"Not yet," Asti whispered to Win. "Close the door."

Win did so. "You think people are listening to us?"

"I think we need to make sure not to break character. How the blazes did you get hired as the third underbutler? I thought you were going for a footman position."

"Well, I was, but I am a bit old to be a footman, you know."

"I didn't know that."

"It's a young man's position." Win smiled. "Write your note. Like you said, in character."

Asti started writing a coded message to Verci. "Right, but ..."

"I grew up in a house not unlike this one. My father was the first underbutler for the Baron of Jontlen Cove, and in my youth I served as a footman. But then the household lost fortune . . ."

"That's the story for a lot of noble houses."

"So we came to the city to look for work, and I fell into an apprenticeship with a locksmith. But I know this work, as well as I know locks."

"And Canderell spotted that?"

"*Mister* Canderell. Always use that with him and any man above you in station."

"Right."

"He realized I was seeking a position beneath me, and well, I told him more or less the truth. Save the name. Thus he gave me this underbutler position."

"Well, that's useful. It puts you and me well placed to check out the whole house, and it gives us excuse to talk. I'm supposed to come to the underbutlers for any issue."

"Good, yes," Win said. "So what do we do?"

"Learn the house. Every room, door, and window. Find the weak points. Learn the patterns of the staff. Do you know if anyone else was hired?"

Win raised an eyebrow. "I know who wasn't."

Chapter 9

VERCI WAS JUST GETTING settled into the new safe-house in Colton when the door slammed open and shut again. Helene stalked into the kitchen where Verci was set up in his chair.

"I am not housemaid material."

"I think we knew that already," Verci said.

She pulled the pins out of her hair—done up in a prim bun that was common for the service class—slamming each one on the table as the curls of her dark hair cascaded down. "It shouldn't bother me," she said, "but that lady was so blasted snooty. Let me tell you something. Servants of fancy folk are far more stuck up than the actual fancy folk. Tell me there are ciders in the icebox."

"There are," Verci said.

"Who all is here?" she asked as she went to the icebox. She took out two bottles of cider, popped them open, and handed one to Verci.

Verci was surprised by the cider in his hand, but took a sip. "Almer is upstairs with Kennith, getting him settled in. Almer didn't get hired either. And Pilsen is . . . around? He's been in and out."

Helene looked about the kitchen. "This is a decent place. How did Josie swing this?"

"I'm not sure, but I think Pilsen did—and is still doing—the legwork for it."

Verci agreed with Helene—it was a good get for a safehouse, especially in Colton. It was a three-story townhouse—the sort of place that was incredibly narrow, wedged within a block of houses that were all identical. Each floor was only one room: root cellar, ground floor kitchen, first floor sitting room, and top floor bedroom. Verci had set himself up in the kitchen, so as not to navigate the stairs.

There was a knock at the door. Helene shifted her grip on the bottle, ready to throw it if she needed.

"Hold up," Verci said, though his own instincts made him want to go for a weapon as well. "It's just a knock."

Almer came down the stairs and went to the door, and then came to the kitchen.

"Boy at the door with a note." Almer Cort came over and handed it to Verci. "Addressed to Vernon Crile."

"That's the cousin in Asti's cover," Verci said, taking the note from Almer.

"So he probably got hired," Almer said, a little bitterly.

"He did," Verci said, looking over the note. "They want him to start working right away. And if I'm understanding his message, so did Win."

"Good for Win," Almer said. "How's your foot? You want anything for the pain?"

The pain in Verci's foot was just a hair below unbearable. "If you can."

"I can," Almer said. "But it's gonna taste horrible."

"Why, Almer? Why does it always taste bad?"

"It helps you to not like it too much. And this stuff . . . it's real easy to like it too much." He went into his bag. "But I'll leave you some for the next day or two, and send more later. Best not to have a lot on hand."

"Where are you going?" Verci asked. "I figured you'd be helping here."

"I'm going back home, I've got a shop to run."

Helene laughed. "I thought Asti said not to bother with our covers now."

Almer sneered at her. "It's not a cover, it's my shop. It's important to me. If you all need something, I'm there for you. But I'm not going to cool my heels here just in case."

"I understand," Verci said, though he didn't like it. "Just keep your ears open. And be there for Mila if she needs anything."

"What is she doing?" Almer asked. "I barely understand what you're doing here."

"So I'm not the only one?" Kennith called from the room upstairs. He came down. "I mean, I guess I'm just plain hiding. What about the rest of you?"

Helene shrugged. "Extra eyes, research. Backup if needed. Plus Asti has established a cover, including having a cousin—that's Verci, for all intents."

Verci nodded. "So I need to be seen living here, just in case someone else from the household comes by."

"And I need to not be seen at all," Kennith said. "Look, I'm just useless on this. I can't go anywhere. There's no place for a carriage or horses. I might as well—"

"Ken," Verci said. "I need you here because I need a pair of hands I trust with tools. And we need you safe. It's not fun, I know."

"I once spent a whole winter hiding in an attic, son." Pilsen came up from the root cellar.

"Weren't you outside?" Verci asked. "You didn't come back in, and you certainly didn't go down there."

"This house was used by wine-runners back in the ration days of the war," Pilsen said. "Oh, you're all too young. Point is, there's a hidden latch down there to a tunnel that comes out about a block away. I went to check on that. It's all good and safe."

"You could have mentioned that before," Verci said.

"Where's the fun in that?"

"I don't want to spend the summer hiding," Kennith said.

"I'm sure," Pilsen said, putting a hand on Ken's shoulder. He glanced out the window for a moment. "I do want to help you bear this, though."

Kennith raised an eyebrow. "How?"

"Here we are," Pilsen said, going to the main door. He opened it just as a man carrying a large bundle was about to knock.

"Is this package for Kendall Rell?" the man asked.

"You got his name wrong, dear," Pilsen said. "Probably for the best."

"I was supposed to do the whole thing with playing the delivery man."

"Get inside, you foolish boy," Pilsen said, pulling the young man inside. Verci recognized him as Pilsen's friend, the one he called his "puppy". As long as Verci had known Pilsen, he had kept a young man around as an "apprentice", and this one was just the latest.

"What's this?" Verci asked.

"You're off your foot, Ken can't be seen, I figured we needed some extra help," Pilsen said. He grabbed the man's face and squeezed it. "And look at him. He's so eager and adorable."

"Pilsen!" he said. "You're making me look silly."

"God and the saints did that, puppy," Pilsen said, kissing him on the cheek.

"I never caught your name," Verci said cautiously.

"Vellun," the young man said, extending a hand out to Verci while still clutching the bundle to his chest. "Vellun Colsh."

"All right, Vellun. If Pilsen vouches for you—"

"Of course I do."

"Then we can use you, I'm sure."

"How does this help me?" Kennith asked.

"Oh, yes!" Vellun said, shoving the bundle into Kennith's hands. "This is for you!"

Kennith took it and opened it up on the table. "My peppers! And okra!" He smiled at Pilsen and Vellun. "You harvested this for me?"

"Seemed the least that could be done, son," Pilsen said.

"It does mean a lot," Kennith said. He squinted at Vellun for a moment. "I'm going to send you to the market for me."

"Whatever I can do, Mister Rell."

"Rill," Kennith said. "Let's make a list."

Kennith and Vellun went over to the table.

"Nice thinking, Pilsen," Verci said.

"I have my moments. Now, I must be off."

"Again?"

Pilsen crouched down next to Verci's chair. "I'm not sure if you realize how bad of a hit Josie has taken in the past few months."

"I imagine," Verci said. "I knew she dropped most of her lieutenants."

"More like they vanished."

"She doesn't trust us enough to tell us straight?" Verci asked.

"I do know we're about the only ones who even see her anymore," Pilsen said. "Mersh is long gone, and he'd been with her for years. Blazes, boy, I'm pretty sure I'm the only one who does her legwork now. I've been running around half the city, playing her lieutenants."

Verci wondered when the blazes this had happened. Had he been so wrapped up in the plan on Colevar and Associates? Or was Josie being good about hiding it? "To what end, Pilsen?"

"Mostly to the end of protecting our nest, maintaining what power and contacts that she still has."

"Why'd she go to you?"

"Josie and I do go back a piece, son. We were already seasoned salts when your father got into the game. She trusts that I'm too old and tired to bother betraying her."

"You're being careful, right?"

"Do you even know me, Verci?" Pilsen shook his head. "I've played five different people in her 'organization,' and none of them are Pilsen Gin. I'm safe. She's safe. You and Asti are safe."

"I didn't mean to imply—"

"I know, son," Pilsen said, rubbing Verci's head. "I should get going."

"Stay sharp," Verci said.

He went to the door. "I'll keep you up to date on Josie, don't you worry."

"I'll head back with you," Almer said, putting a couple vials on the table. "Drink only half of that every twelve hours. No more. Less if you can manage, honestly."

"Fine."

"Are you staying here?" he asked Helene.

"I suppose I still can," Helene said, glancing at Verci. "I presume you need someone here to help you get around and such."

"I'm still working that out, but thanks," Verci said.

Almer nodded. "Make sure he doesn't take more than what I told him. Hide it from him if you have to." He pointed to Kennith and Vellun. "You two as well."

"Fine," Kennith said, waving him off. "See you later."

Almer and Pilsen left. Verci sighed and rolled himself over to the door to make sure it was latched. He was surprised to find Helene right with him, guiding his chair.

"You all right?" she asked.

"I'm wondering how much good I'll be to Asti and the plan from here."

She smirked and took a sip of her cider. "So Julie made it in at the fancy house."

"He did?" That was somewhat of a surprise. "What job did he get?"

"Get this," Helene said, pulling a chair over to him and sitting down. "Cook's helper."

"Really?"

"I only saw him from a distance, but he looked so rutting happy, you have no idea. And it's good, because I think it broke his heart to abandon the goxie shop."

"You two can go back to it once this is done."

Helene scowled. "I don't like it. I only worked it because you and your mad brother said we needed to keep a 'cover.' I could do with not smelling like pork and cheese every day."

"Then we'll come up with a better cover for you," Verci said. "You shouldn't be miserable."

"You've got it easy," Helene said. "Your wife runs a bakery, and you're still putting up the pretext that you're opening the Gadgeterium."

"We will still do it," Verci said. "Trust me, this business . . ."

Helene leaned in closer. "I know," she said in a soft whisper. "I'm in, because I want to make sure that the folks who

hurt us get what's coming. And I'm certainly not going anywhere while he's in there. But . . . I don't want thirty years
to pass and find myself like Josie or Pilsen, you know?"

"I know. I've got to do right by Raych and Corsi."

"Right," Helene said, leaning back. "And you should."

Verci mused quietly. Raych was not happy about him
coming out here, being gone for days. She didn't understand, even still. Helene, she got it. Why couldn't Raych?

Helene was still staring at him, had been for a bit. Finally
she broke away and took a long sip of cider. "We can get to
the roof of this place, huh?" she asked loudly.

"Laundry line up there," Kennith said from the table.

"Good," she said. "It's a bit of an incline walk from East
Maradaine to here. It's eight blocks, but maybe I can get a
clear view of Henterman Hall from up there."

"Maybe," Verci said. She stood up and went to the stairs.
"You gonna need a new scope that could see that far?"

"No need, Rynax," she said. "I can see everything just
fine right now."

Mister Ottick was an old man with stringy, thinning hair on
his head, and thick, bushy hair on his face and hands. The
constant look on his face was that of a man who had just
swallowed a fly. He seemed to take to Asti's presence as well
as Asti could expect. "Well, you don't seem to be completely
stupid. We've got a lot of work to do in the next three days."

"Three days?" Asti asked. "Is that when the party is?"

"No, you blighter," Ottick said. "It's in four days, but the
work's got to be done by then."

"Right," Asti said.

"So, first things first. Most important repairs are in the
ballroom. We've got to tighten up the candle sconces and
lamp fixtures. Damn fools were all hanging from them at
the last party."

"Is that how it goes at these parties, then?" Asti asked.

"I don't want to know what his Lordship and his friends
get into. And neither should you."

"Fair enough," Asti said, letting Ottick lead him up
through the back stairways through the household. He

spotted Julie hard at work in the kitchen. Good. Three of them in the household was solid. If one of them got caught or fired, the other two were still in there.

Not that he could count on Win or Julie to do what he could. He was already mapping the whole house out in his head, noting the various members of the staff, where they worked, where they went. Kitchens, services rooms, and staff offices on the lowest level. Back stairways leading to the main halls on the ground level. Foyer, dining room, breakfast room, ballroom, library.

Second floor had servant quarters on the east side, with more back stairways leading to the lower levels. Open stairways to the west side, where there were guest bedrooms and the Lord's private study. Two separate third-floor sections, with grand stairways leading up to them, for each of the Lord and Lady's sleeping and dressing chambers.

Strange habit of nobility, being married and sleeping in completely separate parts of the house. One couldn't easily sneak from one bedroom to the other without walking in full view of the hallway. You'd even be seen from the foyer. It'd be easier to sneak to—or sneak someone from—any of the guest bedrooms.

Perhaps that was the point.

"Ballroom," Ottick said as they entered the grand room. "Let's get to work on the floor paneling first."

Asti had worked with his brother on enough build projects to look competent at the job. Nothing extraordinary— certainly nothing to impress Ottick—but enough to keep working. He got his tools out, he asked questions, and worked with his head down.

All the while, he figured out the ballroom. For the event, this was the key room to focus on. Five exits on this floor. One to the foyer, one to the dining room, two service entrances, and one he didn't know. Two curving staircases that led to an upper balcony, and hallways that vanished, though there were smaller gallery boxes that overlooked the room. Those hallways probably led to the rest of the upstairs.

"What about the staircases?" Asti asked.

"Ayuh, the banisters are all out of heevy," Ottick said. "I think some drunk fool tried to slide down them."

"Is this how it goes?" Asti asked.

"You gonna keep asking that question?"

"I mean, the party wrecks half the house, we fix it in time for the next?"

"You haven't met his Lordship yet."

"No, sir," Asti said. "I got the impression from Mister Canderell that I shouldn't bother with that."

"I shouldn't talk out of turn," Ottick said, glancing around. "Let's just say I'm surprised he married her Ladyship."

"So that's a new thing, there being a lady in the house?" Asti asked. Not that he really cared about things like that, but any information might be useful. "And that hasn't changed the parties?"

"Changed the nature of the parties a bit," Ottick said. "At least from what I hear. I stay in my shed those nights. And—where are you sleeping?"

"I have a cousin in Colton. I come in from there."

"Probably wise."

"Mister Ottick." Win had come in through the main doors in his Ungar persona. He walked across the ballroom toward Ottick. "There is a situation with the main doors that Mister Canderell feels you should attend to personally."

"Rutting blazes," Ottick said, and Win put on an act of looking shocked. "All right, I'm coming. Crile, keep on these floorboards."

"Very good," Win said, nodding to him as Ottick went off. While Ottick was gathering up his tools, Win dropped a note in Asti's toolkit. Asti had to commend Win for his skill there. It was a good quiet drop.

"I'll keep on it, sir," Asti said as they went out the doors.

"Drop that 'sir' sewage," Ottick yelled back, and they were already gone before Asti could respond.

Not that Asti needed to. He moved to work floorboards in a far corner, and unfolded Win's note.

Second floor, Lord's study. Extra locks—very complicated. Special valet assigned. No regular staff admitted.

Asti ate the note. He knew all that he needed to from that. The study was now a key target. They just needed to find out why Lord Henterman put so much protection on it, and how to get around it. But whatever was in there, Asti was very interested in finding out.

"You're the best one to keep an eye on everything in the neighborhood," Asti had told Mila. "You've got your Bessie's Boys, and Lesk's crew don't really have you in their sights."

All of that was true, but that didn't mean that Mila had to like it at all. She most certainly didn't care for stomping down Frost in rags when Verci and Kennith were sleeping in the new safehouse in Colton. Didn't seem fair. She shouldn't have to keep pretending to be a street urchin while Helene and Julie had abandoned the sandwich stand.

Of course she, as Miss Bessie, could safely spend the night in the sandwich stand, or even Helene and Julie's flop above it. She could sleep in Helene's bed. That would annoy her deliciously.

"I'm worried about how this stuff will affect Josie," Asti had added. "If she's really lost her place, we won't have the clout or connections to pull off what we need."

So she was stuck in the neighborhood, while everyone else was working the gig. And everyone else seemed so blasted calm about things. They all acted like they could walk away at any point. All of them but Asti. Frankly, Asti was the only one she really understood in all of this, even with his crazy, dangerous ways. He was angry, and wasn't going to stop fighting until he had gotten them all. He made sense, at least to Mila. Choking the life out of Mendel Tyne hadn't quelled her anger one bit.

"Girl!" Mila turned instinctively. Too many people used that as a way to get her attention, but rarely was it a woman calling her. It was the stout woman who ran the pub Asti stayed in. Kimber? Nice enough woman. She was standing in front of her pub, wringing her hands and fiddling with a piece of paper.

"You calling me?" Mila asked, coming close.

"Yeah, you," Kimber said, pulling Mila the rest of the way in. "You . . . you're wrapped up with whatever business Asti is doing, right?"

"I'm, uh—" Should she trust Kimber? Did Asti? Mila didn't know.

"I don't want to know what he's doing. I know it's—I know I don't want to know. But he told me he'd be scarce for a while."

"If that's what he told you," Mila said as guardedly as she could.

"Can you get word to him? I went looking for Verci, but he's gone from the bakery, and his wife snapped at me."

"I can imagine," Mila said. She was going to have to go over to the bakery, to deliver a note from Verci. She would probably get some sort of earful from Raych as well. Verci's wife had always been relatively kind to her, but she definitely had opinions about Mila being involved in the things Asti and Verci did. "What sort of word?"

"Someone came here looking for him. Said they were from a newsprint, but I never heard of it. They left a note and a calling card for him."

"I can take it," Mila said. "I may not be able to—"

"It's fine," Kimber said, giving the note over. "I don't want to know what he's doing. I trust that it . . . he's got the right intentions behind it."

"I got it," Mila said. She was about to step away, when she turned back. "Has anyone been giving you trouble? I, uh . . . I'm told I should be looking around for it."

"Nothing out of the ordinary," Kimber said. "But if I know of something . . ."

Mila just nodded and walked off. No need to linger, especially with people watching on the street. It was true that the folks who were causing trouble didn't really know her, but the other side was she didn't know them, either. Verci had given her names: Poller, Essen, Sender, Ia. Helene had emphasized Ia. "Tall Bardinic slan in a stupid hat. You cannot miss her."

And Treggin. That was a name Verci told her to keep her ears open for.

Mila headed to the bakery, keeping an eye out. No sign of this Ia. Or anyone else that fit the descriptions she'd been given.

"No beggars, no," she was told as soon as she entered the bakery.

"I'm not—"

"I said no!" Raych yelled at her. No, not Raych. Same face, a bit thicker in the cheeks and hips.

"I'm looking for Missus Rynax," Mila said.

"Well, you got Missus Elman instead, and she doesn't cotton to beggar girls looking for day-old bread."

"Good for you I ain't one of them," Mila shot back. "What I am is someone who needs Missus Rynax, so why don't you run and fetch her before I get punchy?"

"You insufferable brat!" Missus Elman said, grabbing a broom. She raised it over her head, "I'm gonna—"

"I'll make you eat that broom, miss."

"What the blazes are you doing, Lian?" Missus Rynax came in from the back, baby on her hip.

"Chasing out this beggar girl."

"Saints, leave her be," Raych said. "You, girl. You buying something?"

"I might, if she puts the blasted broom down," Mila said.

"Lian!"

Missus Elman put it down, grumbled something, and went in the back.

"You're one of them, aren't you?" Missus Rynax said. "Forgive me if I've forgotten your name."

"Mila." Mila thought about it for a moment. "But for the time being, call me Bessie."

She sighed and shook her head. "That sounds like an Asti thing."

Mila pulled Verci's note out of her pocket. "I've got this for you."

Raych opened it up. "I shouldn't be surprised."

"He—" Mila stopped herself for a second. "He said he would gladly be going back and forth, but right now—"

"It's—" She smiled ruefully at Mila. "I was about to tell you that it's fine, but it isn't, and you probably know that. But it isn't your fault."

"Missus Rynax, starting tonight there'll always be a young boy in a newsboy cap outside your bakery. Not right on the stoop, but where you can see him."

"And why is that?"

"Because if you need to get word to me or to Verci, you know, fast, you tell that boy. And he'll run."

"You're Bessie to them?"

"That's right."

"And what's Verci called?"

"He's the Baker."

Raych chuckled. "Is Asti the Butcher?"

"No, he isn't," Mila said. "But that's good. I'll use that."

"You should be doing better things, girl."

"I ain't ever had better things, Missus Rynax," Mila said. "Not until Asti and Verci took me in."

"Be careful," Raych said.

"Any message for Verci?"

"Yes. Tell him to stop being an idiot."

"Would you like me to also stop the moons in the sky?"

Raych grabbed a roll and tossed it over to Mila. "Take that. You're skinnier than a twig."

Mila winked at her and went out.

That done, the last step was checking in on her boys. They mostly holed up in an abandoned assembly house down near the creek—a real rotten cesspool that one couldn't properly get to without crossing two bridges, one of which was falling apart. The building itself was crumbling, half fallen into the creek bank.

Mila wondered why no one burned it down to get the land.

"Hello, boys," she said as she came in. She always entered making it completely clear she was in charge. "I'm going to need one of you to go hang out on Junk—oh, saints."

Eight of the boys were there—Peeky, Nikey, Telly, Conor, Enick, Astin, Jede, and Tarvis—and all of them were laid up on the ground. Black eyes, bleeding lips, broken noses, and worse.

"What the rutting blazes happened?" Mila asked.

"Miss Bessie—" Peeky wheezed out. He was the oldest, only twelve, and he looked like he had gotten the worst of it from any of them. His left arm was twisted in a horrible configuration. "They just swarmed in here."

"Who did?" Mila asked. "Scratch Cats?"

"Some of them were Cats," Enick said. His right eye was

a swollen mass of blood and flesh. Mila wondered if he would ever see out of it. "A few others, too."

"Why?" Mila went to each one, looking them over. "What did they want?"

"Didn't want nothing," Conor said. He looked the least bad off, standing up and looking ready to dive into something, despite the caked blood on his nose. Mila wondered how anyone could be that ready for a scrap at the age of nine.

"They must have said something." Mila went to Jede and Tarvis—the babies, the twins, just six years old but looking like they were four. Half of Jede's teeth had been knocked out, and Tarvis had a shoe print on the side of his head. "How bad?"

"Bad," Tarvis said coldly and quietly. "I'm very mad."

"I am too."

"I'm going to cut them all."

"Not right now, hmm?" Mila said. She checked the rest. Everyone would live, everyone would have scars.

"They didn't say much," Peeky said. "Didn't ask anything. Didn't want anything besides giving us a beating."

"Where's everyone else?"

"Out and about," Conor said. "Can't rightly keep track."

"Can everyone walk?" she asked.

Most of them nodded, save Astin. Peeky scooped Astin up in his good arm.

Mila went to a crate she kept hidden behind some shelving. The Scratch Cats, whoever else was here, they didn't go digging through their stuff. They didn't do anything besides stomp her boys. She took out her rope, a couple knives.

"Conor, clean your face and plant yourself on Junk by the bakery. The rest of you all, scatter about, tell the rest of the boys that this place is dead. You all know the goxie shop on Colt?"

Some of them nodded.

"Gather up in there. Crack the back door quiet as you can. Rest up there."

"There? That rutting giant runs that place with his crazy wife!"

Mila kept herself from laughing at that description of

Julien and Helene. She would not tell Helene how the local boys saw her.

"They're not there right now. It's safe."

"How do you—"

"Because I'm Miss Bessie, and it's my business to know." She belted the rope and knives. "And those Scratch Cats hurt my boys, so I'm going to show them what else is my business."

Chapter 10

MILA WAS HALFWAY TO the Shack before she realized she had no idea what she was going to do when
she got there. She could hardly fight the whole lot of the
Lesk Gang or the Scratch Cats, even if she knew who they
were. Her head was full of steam and anger, especially over
her boys getting stomped. That was on her. It might have
even happened because of her.

Maybe she was fooling herself that Poller and the others
in Lesk's crew didn't know who she was, didn't know she
was with Asti and Verci. It wasn't like she had been particularly careful before they did the Emporium. It wasn't like
Kimber hadn't known she worked with them. Probably
Poller did as well.

But she didn't know them yet.

As much as she wanted to pay someone—anyone—back
for what happened to her boys, she knew she couldn't just
crash in there and crack skulls. She could scrap, but she
wasn't a fighter, not the way Asti was.

She needed to do this like Asti. Watch. Listen. Learn.

She hid her knives under her coat. She wrapped the rope
around her waist like a belt. She shouldn't need those things,

not tonight. Not if things went right. She went into an alley, found some refuse and dirt, and smudged up her face.

Mila went the rest of the way to the Shack, placing herself on the corner with her hat out once she was in sight.

Three hours later, she had made a fair number of crowns. If she had needed money, it would have been a good night. But she had learned little. The Shack was definitely a Scratch Cats hole—they were coming and going throughout the night. But if they were working something or planning anything unusual for the night, she hadn't heard anything.

"You need to stop being so scared, *sjat?*" Heavy accent. Mila glanced up. Tall woman, blonde hair, cropped short. Stupid hat. This had to be Ia.

"I'm not scared, I'm cautious," her companion said. Skinny rat of a man. "We shouldn't do anything unless we know what Rynax is doing."

"Rynax is a nothing," Ia said. "He was a washed out nothing before the fire, and he still is. Whatever he's doing doesn't matter."

"Don't be so sure," he said. "The Old Lady always liked him and his brother. He's got roots."

"I don't know roots. I don't know the Old Lady."

"Just because—"

"I do not care. The Old Lady, she does not matter. The snow is on the wind, and we can smell it."

"I don't know what that means."

"Bardinic saying. It means a storm is coming and we must be ready," she said, leading her friend down the street. "Treggin doesn't care what Rynax does, and neither should we."

There was that name again. Mila wanted to follow them, hear more of what Ia and the other one were saying. But there was no way she could do that without being noticed. Too conspicuous on empty streets.

"Hey, girl," someone came out of the alley right by her. "What you got for me?" Boy about her age. Scratch Cat mark on his face. His hand grabbed her upper arm quick and hard.

"You want something from me?" Mila gave her best soft coo, which probably still sounded ridiculous.

"Why you hanging around here?"

"Oh," she said in a breathy whisper. "I was looking for a Scratch Cat to play with."

"Were you now?" He pulled her close to him. "Well, you found one."

"Good," she said. With her free hand, she pulled one of the knives out of her belt and sunk it into his belly. He struggled to grab his own weapon, but she pushed him deeper into the alley, twisting the blade. He was twitching and struggling with her, but that meant he stopped holding her arm, so she managed to pull his knife from his belt and throw it away.

"So, Scratch Cat, were you on the stomp today on Bessie's Boys?"

"The what?"

"A bunch of Scratch Cats hit some boys, in the old assembly house. Kids. You part of that?"

"Just clearing out the trash," he said, coughing and flailing with his arm. He was trying to give a fight, but he was already too weak.

"Who ordered it?"

"Came from . . . from . . . Poller. Why do you care?"

"Those are Bessie's Boys. Can you guess who I am?"

The Cat could barely speak. "B—Bessie?"

"Tell that to the sinner that claims you," Mila said.

She pulled out her knife and let him drop. She wiped the blood off on his pants and skirted off down the alley. There was little point to staying. No need to hang around and have that body stuck to her. It was enough of a message for now. She even dropped half the money she made tonight onto his body, so they wouldn't think he was killed for coin.

She wasn't any less angry. This didn't change anything.

She needed to clear her head, come up with a plan, know what was going on. But clearly, whatever was going on involved this "Treggin." Not some random name that Helene had heard. So now, go to the goxie shop and sleep. She'd go see the Old Lady in the morning.

Not that she and Miss Josie had ever exchanged more than a few words, but it was time for that to change.

Verci stood over the kitchen table, admiring his sketch of the interiors of the Henterman household. For a sketch based on Asti's descriptions, he felt pretty good about it.

He didn't feel good about any sort of straight burgle. Walls were high, too much open ground between the walls and the household. Lower windows were iron barred, doors had double latches. And Asti had counted at least six house guards, armed with crossbows and swords. Probably all ex-army, based on Asti's assessment of them.

"You've got it solid," Asti said, leaning over him while chewing on some concoction Kennith had made.

"Don't eat that over my sketches," Verci said. "Saints, it'll stain if it drips."

"Sorry," Asti said, stepping back. "Kennith, I don't know what the blazes this is, and it's burning the ever-loving sewage out of my mouth, but *saints* is it good."

"Ain't it?" Kennith said, grinning to himself. "If I got to be stuck in this place, at least I can make it smell and taste good."

The three of them were the only ones still awake in the safehouse. Helene was passed out on the couch, Julie on the floor next to her. Vellun had taken off around eight bells, presumably to meet up with Pilsen for something or another. Win had been given quarters in the Henterman household. That was good for access, but it made getting word to and from him challenging. Asti and Julie could come back here each night, but they had to take pains to not be seen together.

"How else is it going?" Verci asked.

"It's work. You'd probably like it, but I'm rutting exhausted. And Helene's taken the couch."

"And the bed is Ken's."

"The bed is Ken's," Asti said. "He's earned that. So where are you sleeping?"

"Oh, it's easy," Verci said. He wheeled his chair away from the table, and then locked the wheels. Then he pulled a lever, and the chair leaned back. "Saints be damned, it's like I'm in bed."

"Saints and sinners, brother," Asti whispered. "This is rutting genius, you know this? We could make a pile of notes—straight, square goldsmith notes—selling this."

"I know that," Verci said, pulling the chair back upright. "That's why we're going to get the Gadgeterium open."

"I'm with you," Asti said. "And I wouldn't have been able to pull off faking this job without the work we did fixing up the old place."

"All right, before you go to sleep, what's the plan tomorrow?"

Asti took the last bite of Ken's concoction, whistling from pain and delight as he finished. Then he came back over to the table as he wiped his mouth with the back of his hand.

"So, it's clear that the Lord's private study, here on the second floor—that's something important. Extra security measures like you wouldn't believe. Win's absolutely right about those study doors. Five separate locks. And one of the house guards is always on that hallway."

"Just one?"

"That I've noticed."

"So who goes in there?"

"I imagine just Lord Henterman, but he hasn't come back from . . . whatever it is. Hunting trip, I think I heard. There's a special secretary—like his aide-de-camp, totally separate from the house staff. At least, that's what I hear, I haven't seen that guy either. Maybe Win or Julie has, but . . ."

"You don't get to talk to them much there."

"Not much. I took lunch with Ottick and a few other trade staff, and Julie and some of the other kitchen folk were there. But we steer clear." They must be working Julie hard, because he barely said a word—even when he ate Kennith's Ch'omik stew—and then fell asleep on the floor.

"Hel is worried about how he was doing." Really, she had spent half the day pacing and fretting, when she wasn't doing everything she could to make sure Verci was comfortable. Which only made Verci more uncomfortable. He had been of half a mind to send her back to Seleth to help Mila, but he needed someone here he could count on in case of trouble. Vellun didn't qualify, not yet, and Kennith . . . he didn't want to have to count on Kennith if it involved going out in the streets. If there really was a crisis, he'd need Helene.

"Near as I can tell, he's doing fine," Asti said. "Looked happy, others talking well with him, that sort of thing."

"Right," Verci said. "So, the study?"

"I got a look along the outside, and there's a window. Trying to get up to it from the ground will prove challenging. There's a clear view of it from all over the grounds, the walls beneath have some ivy creeps that look like bileworth."

Verci groaned. Bileworth was nasty stuff, a rich household's dream. Looked like beautiful ivy with small orange flowers, very tasteful. But grab hold of it, or even brush it too hard, and it oozed out a vile, noxious sap. One whiff would usually force violent retching, and once the sap was on your skin, it was nearly impossible to get off. Many a burglar ended up quivering on the ground in a pool of their own vomit and filth, a disgusting package for Constabulary to pick up, thanks to bileworth.

"Bileworth usually doesn't grow naturally," Verci said. "You think there's a house mage?"

Asti shook his head. "Not that I've been able to tell, and that's a big expense. Even for a lord like Henterman. More likely it was a one-time hire."

"Still, that's something we need to know about."

"Eyes open. If there is one, it couldn't be too secret. The kitchen staff would know for sure. I'll check with Win and Julie."

"All right, other ways in. Above?"

"That's what I'm going to look into tomorrow," Asti said. "Above it is the Lady's chambers. Her bedroom, salon, sitting room, water closet, baths, and wardrobe."

"That's a lot of chambers."

Asti just shrugged. "Nobility. What can you do tomorrow?"

"I'm not sure, honestly. I'm supposed to go see Doc Gelson to recheck the foot. But there's no way I—"

"No, do it. That's important. Can Helene help you get out there?"

"Oh, I'm sure she will," Verci said. Hel was being far too helpful, downright hovering. He knew she felt responsible for his accident, and if he didn't actually need her help through this, he'd have told her to shove off.

"While I rot in here," Kennith said.

"This is what I need from you tomorrow, Kennith. Take a scope and get on the roof. Start to learn these streets, between here and the manor house. When it's busy, where the clogs are, where the constables are running the crossways, all of it. Can you do that?"

"So we can make escape plans?" Kennith asked. "If I can get a carriage out here, that might be useful."

Asti pointed to the both of them. "Talk with, what's his name? Vellun? Have him help you with that."

"Right," Kennith said.

Verci was starting to feel a twinge in his foot. Almer's concoction was starting to wear off. "Hand me that vial over there," Verci said. "Time for another belt of that stuff."

"How is it?" Asti asked.

"This? It's pretty horrible going down. But then you don't feel anything and it's bliss," Verci said. He measured out just a capful of the stuff and swallowed it. "Almer said not to take too much, it's dangerous."

"Well, don't," Asti said.

"I won't," Verci said. "We never got mixed up in *effitte* or other nonsense, not going to let this take me."

"All right," Asti said. "I'm claiming some floor space in the sitting room, and Hel will have to cope with that. I need to sleep, or I'll be a wreck at work tomorrow."

"Saints, Asti. You almost sound like a respectable, honest man."

"Don't worry," Asti said, winking as he went up the stairs. "That won't last long."

Mila was woken by someone pounding on the back door of the goxie shop. She glanced around. The rest of her boys were all sleeping.

"Who is it?" she called out.

"It's Conor, Miss Bess. Open up, but quick."

She opened the door. "What's wrong? If the baker woman has a message . . ."

"Naw, but something's happening on Junk, and it's coming to the bakery. Youse gotta come quick." Conor looked spooked, which wasn't common for him. If whatever was happening hit him in the gut, it was probably a big problem.

First she had to get her boys safe.

"Peeky, Enick, eyes on the rest. Get them moving and out of here."

"Where to, though?" Enick asked. "Where we got now?"

Mila thought for a bit. "Head to the warehouses on Junk. Don't break into any, but stay low."

"There's no scraps or begging in that spot!"

"And no one looking for anyone, either," she hit back. "It's just for a bit. Raid the larder here before you go."

"You don't have to tell us that, Miss Bessie." The place was devoid of bread, cheese, and pickles in moments.

Mila would pay Helene back. Probably.

"Show me, Conor," she said, and let him lead the way.

Over on Junk, a passel of toughs were standing in front of the shop two doors down from the bakery. Might have been Scratch Cats, but Mila thought they were something else. Three were at the door, and through the window, Mila could see two more talking to the shopkeep.

"They've been working their way down," Conor said. "Thought you should know before the bakery."

"Those the boys that hit you all last night?"

"Not all of them, but you see that one with the strange eye?" Mila noted one of them had an eye that looked the wrong way.

"He was there?"

"Definitely him. Maybe one or two others." The boys inside the shop came out, one of them counting coins and dropping them in a sack.

"Good enough," Mila said. The boys were moving on

from that shop to the grocer next door. "You run to that house I told you about. Tell them I said someone's working a shake on Junk Avenue." She remembered Kimber's note, and dug it out of her slacks. "Give them this as well. You got that?"

"Got it," he said, and tore off.

Mila unhooked the rope from her belt and went over to the bakery door. Missus Rynax and her sister were hard at work, putting out loaves and rolls. Mila stuck her head in.

"Missus Rynax, ma'am," she said calmly. "Lock the door for a few minutes."

"What, why?" she asked, coming over. She looked down the street. "What's going on?"

"Nothing you have to worry about," Mila said. "I've sent word, and I'll deal with this."

"But—"

Mila shook her head. "Lock the door."

"You're just a little girl. Get Asti, get Helene. Or Julie . . ."

"They're nowhere close right now. I can handle this."

"Just—"

"Door, Missus Rynax."

Mila stepped away, and Raych shut the door, latching it.

The gang of boys came out of the grocer and started to move on the bakery. Mila brought her shoulders up, holding the rope with as much menace as she could muster.

"Move along, gentlemen," Mila said. "This place isn't for you."

The boy taking the center of the group looked her up and down. He had a good seven inches and two years on Mila, and a deep, ugly scar across his cheek. "Who the blazes are you?"

"I'm the one telling you to move along."

"You gonna make us, sweetling?"

"I ain't seen you boys in these streets before," Mila said, avoiding the question. She couldn't fight all five. She wasn't Asti. "Do you know who owns this bakery?"

"Someone who's gonna pay us," Cheek Scar said.

"Yeah, so open up!" Lazy Eye shouted.

"This your boy?" she asked Cheek Scar.

"We're all together," Cheek Scar said. "We're all here."

"This one smacked around my boys," Mila said. "And now you're going to try to muscle a bakery that's owned by the Old Lady?"

"What do I care about that?" Cheek Scar said. "Who cares about some old lady?"

"Oh, saints and sinners," Mila said. "You did a shake-down of Junk Avenue—right in North Seleth—without clearing it with the Old Lady? What kind of idiot are you?"

"What's she talking about?" the Waishen-haired one asked.

"You all ain't from North Seleth, are you?"

"I don't care who she is, I'm breaking the window with her head," Lazy Eye said. He took two steps toward her, and Mila whipped out with her rope. She got it around his neck and pulled tight, kicking him in the knee. He dropped down and she yanked him back.

"Don't," she said to the other four as they made to move on her. "Not unless you want him dead."

Lazy Eye clawed at the rope, but he couldn't get a grip on it.

"You ain't that hard, slan," Cheek Scar. "You wouldn't kill him in the street."

"You know nothing about me, or this street." She leaned in closer to Lazy Eye. "You worked with some Scratch Cats yesterday, didn't you? Smacking my boys about?"

"Yeah?" Lazy Eye didn't seem sure if he should be proud or afraid.

"Idiots. You muscle in here—" She yanked hard, forcing Lazy Eye to make horrifying noises. "You thought no one would notice? No one already owned this street?"

"That ain't what we were told."

"Oh, who told you that?" she asked. Now she had something. "Same folks who put you on my boys?"

"Your boys? Those kids?"

"My boys, gents," she said. "Eight of them you doled out pain to. Should I give him eight times over, make us even? What do you think, Lazy Eye?"

"Guhh—"

"That's what I thought." She looked at Cheek Scar. "So

I think you boys need to learn some manners. You got some coin out of your shake game?"

"What's that to you?"

"That coin, that's your walkaway money. You all can go back to your flop with it in your pockets right now. Or you can have a problem, and have no money."

"You think you—"

"Five clicks, and Lazy Eye won't be spending any money."

"And then the four of us drop you, little girl."

The shop door opened behind Mila. Damn and blazes. Raych must have caved.

"All of you do what she says, or you'll be having bolts for breakfast!" Raych roared.

Mila turned to see Raych carrying a monstrosity of a crossbow, which seemed to hold ten bolts at once. It was the most beautiful thing she could hope to see.

"Calm down, lady," Cheek Scar said.

Mila released Lazy Eye and kicked him over to his friends. "You heard the baker. Take your walkaway money and clear off this block."

The other boys helped Lazy Eye to his feet and moved away, while Cheek Scar stayed, staring for a few moments.

"I'm gonna remember you, little girl."

"Do that," Mila said. She had an idea, and this was the best place to try it out. "And tell Treggin that Miss Bessie wants a word."

"He don't talk to street slan like you," Cheek Scar said.

That clinched it.

"Then tell him I'm coming," Mila said.

Cheek Scar spat on the ground and went off with the rest of his boys.

Once they were around the corner, Raych lowered the crossbow. The hard expression melted into fear. "The baby isn't the only one who needs his skivs changed now."

Mila laughed despite herself. "That was rather brilliant, Missus Rynax."

"Mad, it was," Raych said. She pulled the crossbow trigger, to no effect. "Verci could never get this thing to work."

"Well, it worked well enough," Mila said. "For now, at least."

"What is going on?" Raych asked.

"I can't rightly say," Mila said. "I'm going to find out. I'm going to keep my boys on your block."

"That's just a patch on a bleeding wound, my father would say."

"It's all I have for now," Mila said. She coiled the rope at her belt. "I've sent word, but Verci is crosstown, working—well, working things out with Asti. But I'm sure once he knows what's happening here—"

"He'll do what his brother tells him to do."

Verci's wife knew him pretty well.

"This is all about protecting the neighborhood."

Raych's jaw tightened. "I'm sure they've gotten you to believe that. Blazes, I bet they even believe it."

Mila wasn't sure how to respond to that. "Verci said—he said this shop has hiding places. If something goes wrong . . ."

"My sister, the baby, and I will lock down, don't worry," Raych said. "Don't fret about me, just get my husband back home."

Mila nodded. There was nothing else she could do or say. It wasn't like Verci listened to her. And it certainly wasn't like he could pop back over to North Seleth any time he wanted. Not in his condition.

"You didn't need to do this," Verci said. Helene was pushing his chair over to the tickwagon stop. The wheels rumbled over the cobblestone, making his body and leg tremble to an unpleasant degree.

"What, like Vellun was going to get you over to Gelson's office?" Helene asked.

"I didn't need the help," Verci said, but that wasn't true at all. He would have barely gotten out of the safehouse, let alone on the tickwagon, across to Seleth to see the doctor, and now back to the tickwagon. He was pleased with the chair, and he and Kennith had done an excellent job building it—it was great for getting about the safehouse. But the wheels didn't agree with these roads, and there were too many little steps to navigate along the way. It couldn't be done alone. And Helene was right, Vellun would not have been as good of an assistant. He was an eager pup, but Verci found him a bit dim.

"We're only a few blocks from the bakery. We came out this way, sure you don't want to stop in?"

Verci did want to, he wanted to see his wife and child, but he didn't think it would be a good idea. Raych already didn't approve of this whole venture, so for him to pop in for a few minutes would be too painful for her. And for him.

"No, we need to get back. We need to—"

"It's fine," Helene said, pushing him a little harder toward the tickwagon stop. She brushed off the couple of swells who tried to shove campaign pamphlets into Verci's hands, though they ignored her. The wagon was coming up as they approached; she must have spotted it. "I know what you mean."

Waiting and watching while Julie was in the household had been hard on her. She had grilled Asti on a hundred things before he begged off and sent them away. Today he was going to slip into the Lady's chambers. That was what he had tried to make clear to Helene—he was taking the risks, and Julie and Win were just there for support if needed.

Helene waved down the wagon, which pulled to a stop. Helene helped Verci out of the chair to get up in the wagon. Gelson had changed the bandages for a proper brace, and had listened earnestly while Verci discussed the idea of building a device that could hold his foot in place while it healed. It was the first time Verci had spoken to the man while he was something resembling sober, and found him engaging, even charming. The new brace meant Verci could put a little bit of weight on his foot, enough to climb up in the wagon with Helene's help.

"Come on, come on," the driver said.

"Getting there, blazes," Helene said, picking up the chair.

"Let me help you with that," a well-dressed stranger said, coming up to Helene.

"He knows who he's voting for," she snapped.

"Not a campaigner, just want to be helpful," the man

said. He lifted up the chair and helped Helene load it in. As she climbed into the tickwagon, the stranger looked at Verci. "You're the younger Rynax, yes?"

"Yes," Verci said cautiously.

The man clapped his arm in a friendly way, but Verci noted that hint of aggression. "Tell your brother that Major Grieson wants a word."

"I'm afraid—" Verci started.

"He'll know," the man said. With a wink, he signaled to the driver, and the wagon started rolling down the street.

"What was that?" Helene asked.

"Probably nothing that we're going to like," Verci said.

Chapter 11

ASTI WAS JUST ABOUT out the door when one of the Bessie's Boys came running up to the safehouse at an impressive clip. "Where's the Baker?" the kid asked, gasping for breath.

"He's out," Asti said. "But you know me, hmm?"

"The Butcher?" the kid wheezed out.

Asti sighed. That must be Mila's idea of a joke. "You got something to tell me?"

The kid took another moment to catch his breath.

"I got to move, kid. Time is precious."

"I ran a long way, man."

Asti waved the kid off, walking down the street. The kid kept up with him.

"This is a thing, man."

"Tell me."

"So, Miss Bessie wants you to know there's a shake going down on Junk Avenue."

That stopped Asti. "What kind of shake?"

"Five guys. They were going from shop to shop, hassling them for coin, breaking stuff when they didn't get paid."

"You saw them?"

"Well, I see the quint of toughs coming up the street,

going in each shop. And one of them was the one what gave me this nose, and busted Jede's teeth . . . so I knew they were the trouble, you grig?" Asti just noticed the kid's nose was pretty banged up.

"You already had a tangle with them?"

"A batch of these new guys. And Scratch Cats. Working together. They came to our hole and cracked our skulls. Miss Bessie was mad about that, and about the shake coming up Junk."

"And the bakery?"

"I brought Miss Bessie to see before they got there. She said she would stop it."

Mila would stop five guys? Asti had a hard time believing that. "All right, kid, this is crucial. Did she say to get us, or just to tell us?"

The kid bit his lip, thinking for a moment. "I think she just said to tell you."

"You think?"

"No, she did."

Made sense. In the time it took this kid to run out here, at least a quarter hour had passed. Even if Asti ran full out, it would be far too late for him to do anything for her. He had to trust her. He had her stay in North Seleth because he believed she could handle whatever was going on there. If she needed help, she would have asked.

"All right." He had to think about what this meant, but he also needed to get to Henterman Hall, get to work. "Is that all?"

"Oh, no!" The kid startled. He pulled a note out of his pocket. "She said to give you this as well. But she already had this on her."

Asti took the letter. Another piece of mail for him delivered to Kimber's. He shoved it in his pocket. "All right, head back to the neighborhood. Find Mila, make sure she's fine. If she's not, head back out here. Hear?"

"Heard." The kid dashed off.

Asti did the same toward Henterman Hall. He needed to get there quick. Last thing he needed was to get sacked today for being late.

He made it to Tully, through the gates with a wave, and down the carriageway of the house just as distant church bells rang out the hour. There was a carriage parked in front of the main doors, with several of the house staff standing at attention, including Win in his disguise as Ungar. Asti noticed Mister Ottick was not present for this.

A well-dressed man was shaking Win's hand as Asti approached, hoping to make his way around to the work shed before he was really noticed.

"Ah, Mister Crile," Canderell said sharply. Asti turned and headed toward the large group.

"Yes, Mister Canderell, sir?" he asked.

"His Lordship has returned to the household. It would be ill-mannered to not present you, as you are here."

"If you think that's best, sir," Asti said. "It isn't necessary."

The well-dressed man came over, a broad grin on his face. Lord Henterman, presumably. He was every inch modern nobility. Smart waistcoat and topcoat, with matching ascot. Probably Turjin silk, by the look of it. The look was completed by a narrow-brimmed hat with a feather in the brim. "What's this one, now? You have been busy, Canderell."

"As the household needs, my Lord," Canderell said. "This is Mister Crile. He is helping Mister Ottick with the repairs."

"Oh, good show, Crile," Henterman said. He kept up the large smile, but barely looked at Asti. "I'm afraid we've given you plenty of work for the next few days. Good show, indeed. Back to it, then. Daylight will burn without us." Henterman strolled into the house with another smartly dressed man right at his heels. Asti had barely noticed that one.

Asti wasn't sure what to make of Henterman, but he hardly seemed the sort who would order the burning of a neighborhood. He seemed far too . . . disengaged. But at the same time, he might be the type to not care what happened, as long as it brought the money in.

"You heard his Lordship, no standing about," Canderell

said. He clapped his hands for further effect, but Asti was already on the move. He had plans to make the most of today.

Mila didn't find any of her boys in the warehouse blocks. That was upsetting, since she had told them to be there. They weren't at the goxie shop either, though the larders had been cleared out. Hopefully Helene wouldn't be too upset about that.

She made her way back to the warehouses, taking another pass to look for her boys. No luck. Finally, she decided she had wasted enough of the day, and went to the safehouse. Time to let Missus Holt know what was going on.

The safehouse doors were locked up, as they should have been, so she was surprised to hear voices when she came in. No one other than Missus Holt was supposed to be around. Perhaps Mister Gin was here—Verci had said something about him helping Missus Holt out with her problems.

Of course, Mila's problems were mostly the same problems now.

"Hello?" she called out.

"Is that you, dear?" That was Missus Holt, but she never heard Missus Holt sound like that before.

Mila came out into the main floor of the safehouse, to find Missus Holt holding court at the table with Mila's boys. Almost all of them—save Conor—were sitting around eating cookies.

The first thing that came to Mila's mind was to wonder where the blazes the cookies came from.

"There you are, Bessie," Missus Holt said. She was disturbingly sweet. She even got up from the table to meet Mila halfway, kissing her on the cheek like she was a grandmother. "I was wondering when you would get here."

"What is happening?" Mila asked.

"Well, these boys were all around, and once I realized that they were your little crickets, I had to invite them in. And they've been very charming." She led Mila over to the table and sat her at the head with her.

"You boys all right?" Mila asked.

"Miss Bessie, you didn't tell us you knew the score here in town," Jede said. He smiled big, despite the teeth knocked out. That didn't seem to stop him from eating another cookie.

"I'm the one who's supposed to know things, pip," she said. She might as well play along. What had Asti told her about running these boys? "Always be in charge." That was the first rule. She grabbed a cookie and took a bite. It was pretty damn good. "So she's been good to you all?"

"She's got a lot of knives," Tarvis said quietly.

Missus Holt took a bite of her own cookie and pointed to the twins. "I like these two. They remind me of our brothers, when they were that age."

Mila couldn't imagine Asti as a little kid, but now that she was thinking of it, he probably was a lot like Tarvis.

"Where are these cookies from?" Mila asked.

"Junk Avenue," Missus Holt said. Mila must have given her a look, because she added, "Dearest, I can always get into the Junk Avenue Bakery."

Mila was about to ask where else Missus Holt could get into when she turned to the boys. "So, now that Miss Bessie is here, let's talk something serious, all right, boys?"

"We got trouble in these streets, Miss Bess," Pikey said.

"Yeah, I'm aware," Mila said. "I just chased off five shakers on Junk Avenue, who shook out some coins from several shops."

"You did that alone?" Missus Holt asked.

"Pretty much, though Raych Rynax is nothing to scoff at."

"Saints, Asti was right about you."

"I suppose he was," Mila said.

"All right, boys, this is what Miss Bessie and I need you to do. Any of you know the egg game?"

The boys all shook their heads.

"You never taught them the egg game?" She gave Mila a very disapproving look, like she was personally offended by this failure.

"No one ever taught me the egg game."

Missus Holt sighed. "Children today, what will we do?

All right, what we're going to do is play the egg game, but the eggs are all of North Seleth. I see that confused look on your face, Nikey, and I'm gonna explain."

"We need to keep one parked outside the bakery," Mila said.

"Well, pick one whose face is intact."

"Best one was Conor, he ain't here."

"Is he already running to the boys out East?"

"Probably already back."

"Then, fine. The rest of you, since you all look broken and pathetic, you're all going to make lovely broken eggs."

"Thought you said the neighborhood was the eggs." Peeky was asking.

"It is. Each of you go out, find a corner. Different corner, each of you. But stick around Bridget, Frost, and Ullen. No farther south for now. When you get there, slump down and make with the tears. Tarvis, you can cry on command, can't you?"

Tarvis suddenly burst out a wail of tears that made Mila cover her ears. Then he stopped just as suddenly.

"That's real good, Tarvis. Have another cookie." Tarvis snatched the cookie faster than anything. Missus Holt smiled. "You cry your eyes out until you get a stick pay attention to you. Or anyone who looks fancy."

Jede objected. "A stick? We'll be thrown in Gorminhut!" Mila had heard horror stories about the west side orphanages. As bad as her uncle's home was, it was better than any of those places.

"Or Quarrygate!" Enick added.

"Or the church!" Nikey said this one like it was the worst of all options.

"You can handle slipping out of those, can't you, boys? And if anyone gets nicked, we'll take care, don't you worry. But when you get asked why you're crying, you show those bruises and cuts and busted teeth, and you say—" Missus Holt looked to Mila, obviously wanting her to fill in the answer.

"Treggin's boys," Mila said. "Say the name Treggin."

"He the one who did this to us?" Peeky asked.

"Yeah, and he's gonna get stomped," Mila said.

"We're going to stomp him?"

"No, dears," Missus Holt said. "It's a long game, and today you're setting up the board." They all nodded like they understood. Josie gave them one more warm smile. "So all of you, run along."

They scampered off, most of them grabbing more cookies before they left.

"Well," Missus Holt said once they were alone, her tone dropping like a hammer. "Looks like we've got a right proper mess brewing."

"That's why Verci and Asti had me stay back here," Mila said.

Missus Holt grumbled. "We shouldn't be rushing into this Henterman business. I don't like splitting our attention, especially since we've got trouble like this on our stoop. Here is what matters. But if it's you and me, that's what it'll be."

"And Pilsen is around, yes?"

"Pilsen is busy right now," Missus Holt said, with a tone that indicated there would be no further conversation down that path.

"And Almer is still around at his shop."

"Well, that might prove useful," Missus Holt said. Mila got the impression she meant anything but that. "As I said, it's you and me."

"I won't let you down, Missus Holt."

"Don't try to live in my bottom, girl. It's unseemly. You're clever and capable, I've seen it, and Asti certainly knows it. Now we really will put it to the test. So, Treggin?"

"That's a name that keeps popping up. The boys doing the shake responded to it."

"Never heard of this Treggin. Which is odd, if he's actually a player. Possibly someone from out of town or something, thinks this is a spot he can make his own little kingdom."

Mila wondered if that sort of thing was common. She imagined there was a whole secret history of the neighborhood buried in Missus Holt's head.

"So what do we do next?"

Missus Holt hobbled over to a cabinet near the kitchen.

"Next, you and I switch from milk to wine, and you tell me what you know . . ."

"Where are you going?" A stern feminine voice echoed up the stairwell. Asti turned back around. A matronly woman in a severe dress—likely a lady's maid, but not necessarily her Ladyship's primary maid—stood at the bottom of the stairs.

"Sorry, sorry," Asti said, laying his accent on a bit thicker. "I'm Mister Crile, perhaps you've seen me about? I'm working with Mister Ottick, getting everything in order before the big shindig, as it were."

"The new handyman," the woman said coldly. "I was aware there was one."

"Right, so, I was told to give everything in her Ladyship's quarters, you know, a onceover. Taps in the water closet, hinges in the wardrobe, that sort of thing."

"I don't think there's anything wrong with any of those."

"Begging your illustrious pardon, miss, but it's more mine than yours to assess that."

"How is that, Mister Crile?"

"Well, I'm sure you would recognize a bad water closet tap, but you might not know when it's, you know, about to go bad." Asti knew he was laying the character on a little thickly, but it was the best way to get where he needed to.

"And that's your business."

"That's my business, indeed. Very much so."

"Very well," the matron said. "Be about your work, Mister Crile. But do not be disruptive. Her Ladyship will be returning from a luncheon shortly, and she is partial to taking a nap at that time. She would not relish having it disrupted by your. . . . tinkering and such."

"Saints forbid, miss—" Asti said expectantly.

"Missus Heachum."

"I will be as the proverbial mouse in the tale of Saint Ilmer, Missus Heachum."

"Very good, Mister Crile," she said.

Asti went back up the steps.

That was a useful encounter, because he now had permission to be up here, even if he had made it up himself. Were he caught by someone else, he could cite that Missus Heachum was aware of his presence and he was doing his job. And now he knew Missus Heachum. At some point he needed to chart out the entire staff, but there was already too much in his head with just the physical layout of the house, and keeping track of being Mister Crile. It had been a long time since he had done any sort of long-term scout while staying in character.

The three months in New Acoria, with Liora—before Paktphon, before Levtha. That had been a good three months. They pretended being a married couple, creating a perfect cover, and she was an expert at the details. And the forging.

And the betrayal. That whole time she must have been laying the groundwork for giving him over to the Poasians.

Asti shoved that to the back of his skull. Not the time.

The top of the stairs opened up to a grand sitting room. The perfect setting for a lady of status and nobility to have a private tea with her peers—chairs and tables and everything just so. There was a grand window here, but this was not over the study. That would need to be farther to the right.

Asti went that way, counting his steps, which brought him to the bedroom. A wide sprawling room, with the bed against the far wall, near two sets of fireplaces. The bed faced another grand window, giving a spectacular view of the gardens, the lake, and likely the sunset if the time was right. It was absurdly perfect.

He went to check the fireplaces. Likely there were sets of flues that connected. Asti closed his eyes and pictured the layout of the floor below. They were above one of the guest rooms.

He needed another forty steps to the north to be over the study. Counting that out took him to the dressing room. Another bay window, surely to give her Ladyship plenty of natural light to see herself in the mirrors. Vanity was covered in face paints and rouges and perfumes, meticulously arranged. That window would be the one above the study window. It might just be that simple.

A quick glance told Asti otherwise. This window wasn't designed to be opened.

He moved back, away from the window, past the shelves of wigs, and into the wardrobe. Dozens upon dozens of dresses of every color hung along the walls—from elaborately fancy to elegantly simple. Every dress for every possible occasion a noble lady might find herself in. Asti was surprised that he had retained a fair amount of that information from Intelligence training—he knew all the dresses and the occasions and what one might wear for what.

Of course, he had been trained to blend with nobility, observe them, and know what he was observing. He was just amazed that all that noble swell stuff took root in his skull.

Helene would tease him relentlessly if she knew.

A board squeaked as he walked around. Not just squeaked, but gave slightly. There was a rug—a finely woven piece from a northern province of Lyrana, another thing he knew better than he wanted—which Asti quickly rolled up.

Asti couldn't believe his luck.

It was hard to see—one had to be looking for it to spot it—but it was clear as anything once he realized. Slight seams, designed to look like a natural part of the floor. Hinging was similarly hidden cleverly. But it was a trapdoor.

A trapdoor, right above the study, if his step counting was right.

Asti heard commotion from the stairs. He rolled the rug back out, making sure it was properly in place. Everything looked like he found it.

"It's just been terrible, with only a few days left," a highborn voice was saying. Her Ladyship had returned to her chambers.

Asti moved as quickly as he could to the door leading to the dressing chamber, pulling one of his tools out of his pocket.

"But nonetheless, we must persevere. Nathaniel would be disa—oh!" Lady Henterman had come into her bedroom, seeing him as plain as day. It couldn't be helped.

"Don't mind me, milady," Asti said, having knelt in front

of the lower hinge, making a show of tightening the screws. "Just keeping this door from causing you any trouble."

"I wasn't aware there was trouble." Something in her voice raised the hairs on the back of his neck. Instinct told him to get out. A noble lady would be incensed to find a worker in her chambers without explicit permission. He finished the facade of fixing and pocketed the tool.

"Aye," Asti said, getting to his feet. "And it's my job to keep it that way." He turned away, keeping his head down. He was playing at the lowest rank of service, the real Mister Crile would never look a noble lady in the eye.

"Then I commend you on your job, Mister—"

She gasped, only the slightest amount. Enough for Asti to notice. He looked up. Every nerve in his body shot on fire.

He knew that voice. He knew that face.

Lady Henterman was no noblewoman.

Instinct—and the beast clawing at the inside of his skull—pulled the tool out of his pocket. With a savage cry he leaped at her, all reason leaving his mind. Nothing mattered anymore.

Nothing except burying that tool into the heart of Liora Rand.

Chapter 12

ASTI HELD ONTO THE leash of the howling beast in his mind, even though it wanted the same thing he did. He couldn't lose control, not here, not now. Liora Rand was here, right in front of him, playing at being a noble lady for some reason. It was more than he could understand, but he didn't need to understand it. He just needed to pay her back in blood and anguish.

Liora gave him the barest of knowing smirks, and dodged his attack adroitly. She then turned to her lady's maid, standing agape in the sitting room. "Guards! We need guards!"

Asti didn't care. He dove in at her, releasing a flurry of punches and slashes. She scrambled out of his way, screaming in a performance of panic and fear.

The maid went running off, and as soon as she was down the stairs, Liora dropped her facade. Her face, her body language—all shifted in an instant as she dove in at Asti. A flurry of punches and kicks came at him. He blocked some of them, letting the rest hit him in unimportant ways. Judge her strength, test her resolve.

Plus he couldn't possibly block all of them.

She was hitting hard, nothing held back. Asti returned the favor. There was nothing he wanted more in the world than to bleed her out on the Tyzanian carpet.

Words to that effect must have left his lips.

"Oh, you mad about something, dear?" She chuckled. She drew a knife out of some mysterious location and swiped at his belly.

"You have no idea," Asti said. He drove his tool at her hand, hoping to force her to drop the knife. He got in a good slice, opening up her flesh, but she held onto her blade.

She opened her mouth, as if to banter further, but Asti was having none of that. Hard punch to her face. Blood from her teeth.

"Not bad, but not your best," she said.

"You want to see my best?" Asti asked. The beast was screaming to be let loose, to let him become a monster of rage and death, but he held it back. Not even to kill Liora would he let it have control of him.

"Wanna see mine?" She hit back with a wink. In a flash, she threw another hard swipe with her knife, opening up his arm. He dropped his tool despite himself. Then her manner shifted again, as she held her hands in front of her face, her expression cringing with fear. "Help, oh help!"

Six hands grabbed Asti from behind, and before he realized it, he was dragged to the floor. He struggled to pull free, but whoever had him had weight and surprise on their side. He was pinned down before he knew what was happening.

"Oh, thank goodness and every saint," Liora was saying, in full effect of her noblewoman character. "Thank goodness you gentlemen came so quickly."

"Yes, ma'am," one of the people holding Asti down said. "Ropes! Or irons!" he yelled out.

"This ruffian would surely have killed me. You saw, Issie, he came at me like a madman!"

"He did, indeed, milady."

"And I'm not done, traitor," Asti snarled at her, despite his face being buried in the floor. He tried to wrench his arms free, but they were being held strongly enough that they would break before he got loose. Saying this earned another hand smashing his face down. He couldn't see anything but carpet.

"Traitor!" she said haughtily. "Fine words for a man who attacks his employer. Who even is he?"

"This is Mister Crile, the new handyman," a voice said from behind him.

"He said he was coming to fix things in your chambers."

"Hmm, yes. Seems he had a fix in mind for my person," she said.

"I have irons." The voice of someone running up the stairs. Win. Win as Mister Ungar. His voice was like a bucket of cold water on Asti's rage. The rest of the job still needed doing, even though he wanted nothing more than to choke every ounce of life out of Liora. Win had to maintain his cover. Same with Julie, wherever he was. Asti was skunked, no helping that, but they could keep in place.

So he struggled, but now only for show, as the irons were put on him.

"Are you all right, my Lady?" Asti heard Win asking.

"Your hand, my Lady! We must fetch a surgeon!" someone else said.

"It's a scratch," she said. "My girl can wrap it for me."

"My Lady, are you well, or should we call for a doctor?" This was Win.

"I believe I will be, but I simply must lie down. Yes, cancel everything I have this afternoon so I may recover."

"As you say, my Lady." Her handmaiden.

Asti was hauled onto his feet, irons secure on him. Irons secure, but a key secreted into his hand. Bless that Win. He would have found his own way out of the irons before too long, but that did make it faster and easier.

"Should we call the constables?" Win asked.

"Of course you should. Have him hauled off." Liora gave him the slightest twitch of her eye, just a hair short of a wink. "That should teach him not to assault his betters."

"Very good, my Lady," Win responded. "You're certain about the—"

"No doctor is required," she snapped. She probably

wanted to be alone as soon as possible. She had a ploy at the ready, so Asti needed to be ready as well.

The three mooks who held him brought Asti down the stairs. Asti put up a good fight as they brought him down—enough to be believed, not enough to hurt them.

No, the pain was to be saved for Liora.

When they reached the lower levels, Win got in Asti's face. "Mister Crile, I have to believe you've gone quite mad. We will have to turn you over to the authorities."

Asti held his composure, but kept character, leaning in. "Do what you have to do, I couldn't care less."

Win grabbed Asti by the chin and said, "It's quite a disappointment." He leaned in further to speak to the guards. "Take him down to the storage closet off the laundry rooms. Lock him in there while I summon the constables."

That put Win's ear right next to Asti's lips. "Gentle Shepherd, seven bells. I'll explain," Asti whispered.

Win pushed himself away from Asti. "It shouldn't be more than half an hour before they come." Asti was impressed that he didn't show a sliver of a crack in his facade. Asti almost believed Win wanted him arrested.

Almost.

But a half hour was plenty of time to get out of the irons and escape the closet.

And then Liora Rand would get what she was due.

The roof of the safehouse was quiet, and with the scope of her crossbow, Helene could almost see Henterman Hall. She could see a snip of the wall, at least, which was impressive even at this distance. She might be able to make such a shot, if the crossbow could handle the overcrank. Four wouldn't be enough. Maybe five. But Helene didn't think she had the strength in her arm to get that fifth overcrank. Maybe if Julie did it for her.

She wished she could check in with Julie, make sure he was doing all right. This was the first time he'd ever worked any sort of job without her there. She knew she was probably worrying too much, that he'd be fine, but—he needed her.

No, that wasn't true.

She wanted to believe he needed her. Saints knew no one else did.

Well, right now Verci did, and she was more than happy to be there for him. If he was stuck in the house in that wheelie chair and just Kennith for company, he might go a bit nutty.

Kennith had slipped out, despite Verci's warnings. "I ain't nothing for us if I don't have a carriage and horses, and Vellun has a plan to get mine and keep them nearby." So he left.

Which meant that it was now just her and Verci in the house, and that was even stranger. Not that she hadn't entertained several idle thoughts about what she might do if she had time alone in a house with Verci, nor could she deny those thoughts kept percolating into her head despite herself right now.

All the more reason she fled to the roof to look at the city through her scopes, and check out her crossbows.

She now had three different Verci Rynax crossbows, and all were beauties. There was the distance one—the Rainmaker—with the powerful lensescope and that could handle overcranking. There was Orton, the hip-hanger, named after Poppa. Small and easy to hide under a coat, but it didn't have much range. Good in a pinch, solid craftsmanship, trigger lock to keep it from dry-firing under the coat.

And then the one she called The Action. That one was something spectacular. Powerful, but not a sniper crossbow. This was a street brawl weapon, designed to be shot and reloaded something fast. That was the one she wanted in her hands when things turned left.

Verci should be making these and selling them to the Constabulary; he'd make a killing.

Instead he kept making crossbows for her.

Helene wondered how Raych must feel about that.

She took another look through the scope, up the roads leading to Henterman Hall.

Asti was in the streets—she could spot him out because he was making a spectacle of himself. Running full tilt for them like the sinners were after him.

Whatever just happened, it couldn't be good.

She grabbed The Action and went down.

✹

Verci was surprised by the front door flying in. Asti stormed into the house; he must have kicked it open.

Asti looked a hair away from completely losing it. He wasn't in the feral, horrible state he had slipped into a few times, but he looked like he was barely holding it off.

"What's wrong?" Verci asked as his brother pounded up the stairs.

"New plan!" Asti shouted.

"What new plan? Where are Win and Julie?"

Asti crashed and rummaged upstairs.

"Blazes is going on?" Asti carrying on had made enough noise that Helene had come down from the roof, yelling out. "Verci, you all right?"

"I don't even know," Verci said. "Asti? Asti?"

Asti came down the stairs like a mad bull, carrying his belt of knives and Verci's bandolier of darts, as well as a set of dark clothes and a short sword as well. Asti almost never used a sword. Verci didn't even know he had one here. Verci did know those clothes. Those were Asti's "work clothes" from his Intelligence days. Those were assassination clothes.

Helene was right behind him, crossbow in hand, though she looked like she might have to use it on him.

"All right, Asti, I'm a bit scared," Verci said. "Blazes is happening?"

Asti didn't acknowledge, instead he looked at Helene. "What's that you got?"

"My crossbow."

"Right, the brawler," Asti said, stripping out of his Mister Crile outfit. "Good. Get loaded up."

"Asti!" Verci shouted. "Talk!"

"Nothing to say. New plan. The others are fine, no worries, but for me ..." He stopped for a moment, his hand trembling. He clutched his wrist with his other hand. "I have something else to do."

"Oh, no," Verci said, wheeling his chair closer. "No, you do not get to do this."

"You don't get to tell me—"

"Yes, I do, Asti. Yes, I do." Asti abandoning the plan, abandoning everything they were working for to do something crazy—and whatever this was, it was pure madness— that was too much. Verci would walk through blazes with every sinner at his heels for his brother, but he would be damned if he let Asti sabotage things now.

"Not about this!" Asti snapped.

Anger burst forth like a dam. "You were broken and I was there. You wanted to live clean and I gave you a place. When we lost it I was with you. When you wanted to chase whoever was behind the fire, I backed you. I'm here in this chair right now and you 'have something else do to'? How dare you, Asti?"

Verci had been so riled in his anger, he hadn't even noticed his brother had dropped to the floor, weeping. Knife in one hand, Asti jabbed it into the floor over and over.

"Hey, hey," Verci said. "Hold it down, brother. You are stronger than this."

"Should I go or—" Helene muttered.

"I'm not," Asti said. "I am—I am this shattered thing and she—she—"

"She who?"

"She's somehow the rutting lady of the house? How the blazes does she—"

Verci didn't know what was going on. "All right, Asti, just stop, breathe. Tell me what happened. Who is she?"

"She's—" Asti stopped and looked up. Verci was about to speak when Asti put his finger to Verci's lip.

"Who else is here?" he whispered. "Ken? Anyone?"

"No, it's just us," Verci said.

"No, it isn't," Asti said, grabbing the shirt and bandolier and putting them on. "She's here."

"Who?"

Asti drew out darts in one hand and a knife in the other. "Liora Rand."

That name hit Verci in the center of his spine. It had taken him weeks to get Asti to talk about anything that had happened to him in Intelligence, and even then he had gotten very little. But he knew the name Liora Rand: Asti's partner, lover, and betrayer. Verci didn't know the hows or the whys, he only knew the who.

Liora Rand, the woman who broke his brother.

Asti crept over to the stairs, primed to throw a dart as soon as he saw anyone come down.

Verci's attention was so focused, he barely noticed when someone burst through the kitchen window.

In a flash, there she was—Liora Rand with no disguise or pretense. No wig or face paint or bodice-dress. She was dressed almost the same as he was. She crashed through the window like a hawk, heading right for her prey. Asti threw the three darts he had in his hand, one hitting its mark in her leg. It didn't slow her down. A hard punch felled Helene before she even touched the floor. She had a knife, but the way she dropped Helene reminded Asti how effective and brutal an unarmed fighter she was. Liora Rand's bare hands were as lethal as a fully armed Spathian knight. Asti drew his blade and closed in, but she was already in motion. Her knife touched Verci's throat just as Asti's reached hers.

"Stop," she commanded.

Asti was pressing his blade against the flesh of her neck—just an ounce more pressure would slice it open. Her blade was in the same place on Verci's neck, and she held a clump of his hair in her other hand. One foot kept Helene on the floor.

"I should—"

"This is your brother, isn't it?" she asked. "I remember how fond you were of him. Oh, you'd be thrilled to know how he prattled on about you. 'Verci this' and 'Verci that'—"

"Liora—"

"So I know he's not going to do anything to risk your precious throat. Are you, Asti?"

"You will not—"

"Are you, Asti?"

"I'm not taking this blade off your neck."

"Of course you aren't, you aren't an idiot. You need the assurance. I'd be disappointed if you did."

Her calm, cold manner—always such a sight when he had worked with her—was infuriating. It took every ounce of will Asti had not to slit her throat right away. But she was right—he couldn't do that and stop her from killing Verci. And he . . . he couldn't survive without Verci. It was the only thing he truly had in this world.

"I'm not going to let you walk out of here," Asti said.

"I came in here, Asti," she said. "And I'll walk out when I'm ready." She tensed for a moment. "Skirt, ease it down."

Asti let his gaze lower slightly, to see Helene bringing up her crossbow.

"You know what this would do if I—" Helene croaked out before Liora pushed down on her chest with her heel.

"I know you're not. Slide the crossbow away. Gentle."

Helen stared defiantly.

"Do it, Hel," Asti said.

Helene pushed the crossbow away, so it was only a few feet from her.

"We have more people coming here," Asti said.

"And they won't do anything as long as I got Verci primed for his closest shave."

"Most of them don't like me," Verci said.

"Doubt that. He's the ideas, you're the charm. I know how it works."

"You know nothing, Liora," Asti said. He could feel the anger creeping up his arm, but he wouldn't let it make his hand tremor. Not right now. Verci's life depended on his nerves holding still. On the beast staying on the leash.

"You should realize I'm not here to kill you," Liora said. "Use your damn brain."

"I wouldn't trust you to—"

"I let you live at the house. I let you get away."

"So you could follow me here."

"You think that was easy?" she snarled.

"Because you're playing at being Lady Henterman?" Verci asked.

"Worst assignment ever," she said. "Worse than Gerrindack Bay."

That job involved swimming through the septic system of a Kieran facility in Napoli, in the sweltering heat of the broiling tropical sun.

"That was just a month before you betrayed me," Asti said.

Her eyes met his—cold, hard, and determined. "I was following orders."

That was not the response he expected. "Sewage. When I got back—"

"They told you that I was, what, disavowed? In the wind?"

"You gave me up to the Poasians for a piece of rutting paper!"

"A list. A list of names that Central Office wanted, no matter the cost. They said to—"

"Trade me for it? I don't believe it!"

"That's why they asked me instead of you. Because you were always a little too . . . idealistic."

"I've never heard anyone describe him that way," Verci said.

"Shush, Verci," Asti said.

"Yes," she said, adding a hint of pressure on Verci's throat. "Mommy and Daddy are talking now."

Asti's memory danced. He had played out the moments of her betrayal in waking dreams for months, even though it was a jumble. He and Liora had penetrated the Poasian facility—looking for some mystical weapon they were developing. The *Adzafhat*. And then she touched him with something, and he dropped down. Drugged. The rest was a blur. But he remembered her standing over him. Talking to the Poasian officers. Then she bent over and kissed him on the forehead.

"The—'mumble'—thanks you for the sacrifice."

He could never remember—never make his brain fill in—that missing word. Was it "The Service"? It might have been.

"Do you know what they did to me?" he snarled at her.

He wanted to slash her neck open more than anything. No—he wanted to tear it open with his teeth.

A tear welled up in her eye. "I didn't want to think about it. I didn't want to believe that . . . it was the mission."

Asti couldn't believe it. "Who ordered it? What protocol did they use to contact you? Verification numbers? Authorization method?"

She didn't even blink. "Major Chellick. Dead drop in Linsilla Square, written in Tenori Cypher Three. Six-five-six-nine-one-two-nine. Authorization by Standing Order Nineteen."

That all sounded fine, but it could be nonsense. He could recite the same legitimate-sounding terms off the top of his head as well, and make it sound believable. And Major Chellick was dead, so that could be an easy scapegoat. He told her as much.

"I don't care if you believe me or not. The point is I'm glad you escaped. I'm glad you got back to Maradaine safe and sound—"

"I am not sound!" Asti shouted. "I am barely keeping myself—every day—from tipping over the edge of madness."

She was silent for a moment, and her grip on Verci's hair relaxed by just a breath. "I am sorry about that."

Asti looked at Verci again, to make sure he was all right. He seemed calm, but his right eye was twitching.

Not twitching. Quiet code. Twitching a message to Asti.

Find out what she wants.

That pulled Asti back down to the ground. He still wanted her dead, but Verci was right. She wanted something else. That was the only reason she hadn't killed the three of them, or at least tried.

She had said the words of an apology, so that gave him the opportunity to shift the conversation.

"So why did you come here?"

"Verci," she said calmly. "With just your left hand, I want you to reach around my hips to the pocket on my other side. Very slowly pull out what's in there."

"Do it," Asti said.

Verci did as instructed. "He really does have the hands," Liora said. "I didn't even feel that."

Verci's hand came back holding a card.

"What is that?" Asti asked.

"Show him," Liora ordered.

Verci held it up, and Asti read the fine calligraphy. *You are cordially invited to Lord and Lady Henterman's Annual Saint Jontlen's Day Gala and Feast.*

"It's very simple, Asti. I came to invite you to the party."

Chapter 13

"I DIDN'T SEE THAT COMING," Asti said. "You've intrigued me enough to not kill you right now."

"So you'll take the knife away?"

"You want me to trust you with this?" Asti said, looking her in the eye. "You move first. Let go of Verci, step off Helene, move over to the well spigot."

Liora raised an eyebrow. "Why the spigot?"

"Because you're bleeding pretty badly from that leg and you're going to want to clean it properly."

She glanced down. "I've been trying not to think about that." Asti noticed that her hand was wrapped from where he had sliced it earlier. His own arm was bleeding, and while it wasn't critical, he was going to need to take care of it in short order.

"I've been thinking about it," Helene said. The blood had dripped onto her chest and face.

Asti carefully took the invitation from Verci. "If you want me to take this seriously, then step away."

Liora eased her blade from Verci's neck, and then in a singular fluid motion, sprang away from them all to the spigot.

Asti held his knife out, ready to throw it to bury it in her heart if he had to. He still wanted to. But this idea of hers—even though it was clearly a trick or trap or some other derangement—it had his curiosity. She had no idea—probably had no idea—why he was infiltrating the Henterman household, so he could use that to his advantage.

"You two all right?" he asked, eyes mostly on Verci.

"This is disgusting, and I'm going to go and clean myself properly," Helene said. She gave Asti a look, and Asti wondered if it was some sort of cue for her to do something crazy with her crossbow to take out Liora. Asti gave a small shake of his head.

"Don't you go anywhere, skirt," Liora said. "No one leaves my sight until I leave."

"You don't make the rules here, Miss Rand," Verci said, rubbing at his neck. Her blade had left a mark, a red indentation. That would pass in a few hours, long before Raych would ever see it. Asti didn't need another thing for her to yell at him about.

"We're negotiating at this point," she said. Wincing, she pulled the dart out of her leg. "Not too deep, I don't think."

"I'm better with knives than with darts," Asti said, still holding his blade, ready to throw. She knew what he could do.

"Yes, and you want to kill me dead," she said in almost a mocking tone. "That can wait. We've got a more pressing problem."

"The Saint Jontlen Gala," Asti said. "You want me there as a guest."

"Well, obviously not you as *you*. Or as this Mister Crile persona. I trust you can come up with something."

"Why?" Asti asked.

"Because I need a partner on this mission, and I don't have anyone else to trust."

Asti laughed, an explosive, enormous laugh that flew out of his lungs. "You trust me?"

"I—no, obviously. Except . . ." She sighed while unfastening her pants. "Let me explain."

"Why does explaining involve taking off your pants?" Helene asked.

"Explaining doesn't," she said. "Treating this wound does." She grabbed a rag and wet it under the well spigot, tossing it over to Helene. "Wipe yourself off."

"What is your mission?" Verci asked. "Why are you playing at being Lady Henterman?"

She hesitated for a moment, and then proceeded to strip off her trousers. Asti had to stop himself from admiring her fine, muscular legs. She was a horrible human being, but she was an incredibly attractive woman all the same, damn near perfection in skill and movement. She glanced back up at the three of them. "I really shouldn't—"

"Because it's classified?" Asti asked.

"It's a Black Rat mission."

Asti let out a low whistle. He knew that would be what it would have to be, but it was still a surprise to hear her say it.

"What's that mean?" Helene asked.

Liora took another rag and wet it down. "You wanna tell them, Asti?"

Asti sighed. "A Black Rat mission means Druth Intelligence investigates someone in the nobility, Parliament, or other prominent position, for suspected foreign influence."

Liora went rifling through the drawers. "So I had to get in close. Established credentials as a minor noblewoman, seduce him enough to get a bracelet, and then—find out what's going on. Three months later, I have no idea."

"So why is this my problem?" Asti asked.

"Because I need to get into Nathaniel's private study. If there is evidence of him being influenced, it's there, I'm sure."

Asti hid any reaction from his face. She wanted to use him to break into exactly where he wanted to go. It was almost delicious. Also too easy, so he didn't trust it in the slightest. He had to assume she was setting him up, but for what? How much could she know about his intentions?

"Why come to me?"

"You fell into my lap, Rynax."

"Not good enough."

She found a cloth in one of the drawers and started to wrap the leg. "Because I don't trust anyone in headquarters.

Information is filtering in a strange way. I think there are Black Rats throughout Intelligence."

"I'm not still in Druth Intelligence. They drummed me out because of how the Poasians rutted up my skull."

"Exactly," she said. "So I can trust a few things about you. First, I know that you want me dead—"

"That's the truth."

"And that you aren't a rat in the walls."

"Convenient," Asti said. "Your story is perfect. I can't go to anyone to confirm it, because they might be compromised."

"True. But if Henterman is compromised, doesn't that need to come out? If I bring in someone from Headquarters to help me—it could scuttle the whole mission."

"And I wouldn't?"

"We know how we work, Asti," she said. "Whatever else happened, we've got a silent understanding that we used in the field, a shorthand of signals and gestures." She pointed between him and Verci. "Just like the two of you. I know you've been talking in code to each other all this time. I've got no one else who has that."

"Except me," Asti said, letting his bitterness drip from his voice. "Presuming I say yes, what's my advantage?"

"I imagine I'll be helping you get whatever you were casing Henterman Hall for," she said. "I know you hadn't tracked me there."

"Really?"

"Please, Asti." She finished dressing the wound and pulled her trousers back on. "You're not the most guarded of men. You saw my face and nine different emotions played over yours. You had no idea you would find me. Else you would have had a better thing to kill me with than a hingelocker."

Verci glanced back at Asti. "That is my tool, you know."

"It's fine."

"It's a delicate tool and I lent those things to you—" Verci went on with his rant, while also sending another bit of Quiet Code with the eye that Liora couldn't see. *Play along. Keep her on the line.*

Asti agreed with that.

"Fine, sorry," he said to cut off Verci's distraction over the tool. He looked to Liora. "We're going to have to discuss this. Come back here tomorrow, and we'll have an answer."

"Or you might kill me," she said with a smile.

"That's the calculated risk you take."

"Fine," she said, securing her trousers and belting her knife. "It's been lovely catching up with you, Asti. Verci, it's been marvelous. You're everything he said you were and more."

"Forgive me if I don't get up to see you to the door, Miss Rand," Verci said coldly.

"I understand," she said. "Skirt, until later."

"Ma'am," Helene said, making the word sound like a threat.

She walked past them all to the door, now every bit the noble Lady Henterman in her demeanor, despite her current outfit. "I'll see you tomorrow, Asti. And if you do decide to kill me, please do me the courtesy of a proper fight. These last two skirmishes were quite wanting."

And she walked out the door.

Verci let out a deep breath. "Well, that was . . ." He froze, for once apparently at a loss for words. Finally he said, "I presume that was what the trouble was? Or is there something else?"

"Horrible," Helene said. "Can I go to the roof and shoot her?"

"Not right now," Asti said. "Now we really do need a new plan, and it's going to involve going to that party."

"Miss Bessie needs to be a presence now," Missus Holt said. "She needs to be a force in North Seleth."

Mila frowned, partly at the things Missus Holt was saying, but mostly at the outfit she was being dressed in. Missus Holt had given her a skirt and blouse that looked like it was sixty years old, with brass hooks instead of buttons, closing up all the way to her chin. If Mila had felt strangled in the service dress Asti had given her yesterday, this thing was going to choke the life out of her.

"This is absurd," Mila said. "Are you dressing me in your clothes from when you were my age?"

Missus Holt smirked. "Slightly. But Miss Bessie is going public now—"

"Yeah, that wasn't supposed to be a thing. Asti said—"

"I don't care what Asti said right now."

"My cover, both as me and as Miss Bessie, is to lay low. Not get noticed."

"How did not getting noticed help your boys, hmm?" Missus Holt asked. "They came for them."

"Even still, if Asti needs—"

"Asti can worry about Asti. What we need to do—what matters most—is keeping this neighborhood out of the hands of scum like Lesk and that other one."

"You need to explain this egg game thing you sent the boys on," Mila said.

"In time." Missus Holt had a tone that made it sound like that conversation was over.

Mila bit her tongue. "This collar is choking me, you know."

"That was the fashion. High, tight collars and no corsets. Which was a lot smarter than what the ladies wear today."

"No one I know wears a corset, Missus Holt."

"Not in these parts, no."

"I still don't get—"

"A style that defines the persona, Mila," Missus Holt said, bringing a bright red hat over. "You dress like a standard street rat, you won't be noticed. You dress like this, you'll own the room you're in."

"And the hat?" Mila said, looking in the mirror. The hat was just as much of a throwback, but something about the bright color and sharp brim worked for her. Mila lowered one side so it went over her eye.

"That was mine, back in the day," Missus Holt said. "I doubt anyone you'll be dealing with will really know or remember, but ... it sets a tone."

"Of who still runs North Seleth?" Mila asked. She had to admit, between the red hat and the blue waistcoat, it was probably the brightest, cleanest thing she had ever worn. Also hot. When she got out in the sun, she'd be a swamp. "What else?"

Missus Holt put a wide leather belt on her, with a knife prominently at the hip. The other side of the belt had a hook, and Missus Holt handed her a coiled rope. "You prefer using that rope, don't you?"

"I know how to use one, that's for sure," Mila said. One of the few decent remnants of her mother, of her horrible uncle she spent too much time with. Mila couldn't remember what trade their family was, but they knew ropes, and Mila held onto that and used it in her years squatting the streets with her sister. A good rope could keep her alive. She hung it on the belt hook. "I'm not usually one to be so conspicuously armed."

"Well, you are now," Missus Holt said. "And if a stick gives you guff?"

"Quote the Rights of Man at them," Mila said. "Though I don't know how much . . ."

"It usually makes them shove off." Missus Holt gave her some red gloves to match the hat. "That should complete the look."

"Fine, I've got a look," Mila said, putting on the gloves. "But I don't know what I'm supposed to do with it."

"Next part of the game," Missus Holt said. "So, the egg game. That only works when you're young . . ."

"So you have me do it."

Missus Holt chuckled. "In this case. With a real egg game, you need a little kid, like your boys. Normally, you have a bag of eggs, and you drop them on the ground, so they're a broken mess. And you cry your eyes out."

Mila got a whiff of what Missus Holt was selling. "Right, I seen this. You put on a show like your pop is going to beat the sewage out of you for dropping the eggs, wasting his money. And some kind stranger will give you a crown to buy new ones."

"And you do that for a few hours, you get a few strangers," Missus Holt says. "It's a good, old bit."

Mila thought about it for a moment, and was more confused. "But my boys don't have any eggs out there. They're just crying."

"Right, they don't have eggs. They *are* the eggs."

Mila didn't know what to make of that. "Yeah, but how does that help?"

"Saints, your little boys picked up on this a bit better, girl. Didn't think you were this dim."

"I ain't, but they knew they'd end up in Gorminhut." Her short time in that orphanage was enough not to wish it on anyone.

"That's better for them, but not by much," Missus Holt said. "But if a passel of beaten boys all get swept up by the sticks, sent to Gorminhut, and they all say Treggin's men did it."

Mila got a whiff of what Missus Holt was selling. "Sticks will push a bit harder in North Seleth."

"Especially since at least one lieutenant has decided to make our little neighborhood his priority." Missus Holt went over to her desk and sat down, putting up her cane. "Now, you're going to head out there, and I'll eat crowns and glass if you won't find the streets with a few more sticks walking the beat, and nobody working a shake."

"I suppose," Mila said. "But that's probably just going to last—"

"A day, maybe two. Which is all we want. We want those Scratch Cats, Lesk's crew, anyone else all going to ground for the night. They'll hole up in their pubs and other dens. And here's your job."

"My job," Mila said, taking a deep breath. The fact that Missus Holt was more than willing to have her boys swept up to Gorminhut made her nervous. What else would she sacrifice? Where did this game end for her?

"You go out there, and you walk the street like it's yours, girl. Chin high, hear? Powerful woman who isn't going to be cowed."

"All right," Mila said, looking back in the mirror.

"You start at the Birdie Basement, and then Kimber's, see if any of those rats are trying to take up space there. You see anyone you think is in league with Lesk or Treggin, step up. Tell them to hit the stones and walk."

"And that I want a parlay with Treggin?"

Missus Holt scowled for a bit. "I think that's a waste of time, but sure."

"You don't want to meet with him?"

"I wouldn't want him to have any sense that he matters that much, but that's me," Missus Holt said. "Miss Bessie needs to be a presence, but that means you've got to get a size of things." She went into her desk and pulled out a few ten-crown notes. "Use those liberally as well."

"And if I get into trouble?"

"Use that knife and rope, girl," Missus Holt said. "But try to draw blood and leave someone who can tell a story." She scoffed. "I'm sure that dead body in the alley felt good, but it didn't make much of a point for you."

Mila held her tongue again. But Missus Holt was probably right there. She didn't need a trail of bodies.

And she didn't want to get too much blood on this outfit.

Chapter 14

HELENE WANTED TO PUT a crossbow bolt in that Islan. She was of half a mind to put one in Asti for good measure.

"Tell me what the blazes happened there," she said. "Who the rutting blazes was that again?"

Asti had explained, while he bandaged his arm, what had happened in the manor house, how the lady of the house was really his old spy partner. Helene swore she'd make her pay for it.

"What happens to J—"

Before she said Julien's name, Asti was on her, putting his hand over her mouth. She bit him in response, which Asti took surprisingly well. He didn't even flinch when she tasted blood.

He came in too close and whispered in her ear. "Don't say their names here. Someone may be listening."

He took his hand off her mouth and shook it for a moment. "Who would be?" she whispered.

"Maybe no one, but we should presume she has someone." He took a moment and then added, even quieter, "Julien and Win are fine, though."

"How do you know?" she whispered back.

"There's no reason for them not to be."

That didn't make her feel any better.

"What's our plan?" she asked louder.

Asti grabbed some paper and started writing things down. "We have to presume this place is skunked. But we don't have anything else we can use, so we're stuck with it. But we've got to seriously consider the offer. But I need to think this over."

He passed the note to her: *Can you carry Verci?*

She nodded. "How much time do you need to think?"

Get him out through the basement exit. Find Kennith and Vellun. Then get Julien in the street before he comes here. Asti talked some things about finding the right clothes to wear if he decided to do what she wanted.

"You sure it'll be safe?" she asked.

Julien can't be seen in here. Or any of the rest. All of you meet at the apartment we used for the Pomoraine.

Helene nodded again. She'd be able to check on Julien. Whatever else was happening, the most important thing was making sure he was safe. If something happened, if he got caught in the household, with that woman . . . she wouldn't forgive Asti for that.

"I'm going to clean this place up," Asti said. "Why don't you two get some rest?" He showed the notes to Verci briefly, then set them to a taper and left them in a bowl to turn to ash.

"Rest, right," Verci said, wheeling over to the root cellar door. "We'll get on that."

Helene got behind him and tipped the chair backward to bring him down to the cellar.

"You get all that?" Verci asked when they reached the bottom.

"Got what I needed to," Helene said. "Are we supposed to disguise ourselves?"

Verci shrugged. "I would want to, but I kind of stand out in this chair."

Helene shook her head. "We're not taking the chair. Where are Ken and Vellun?"

"They were checking out a carriage club a few blocks away."

"What's a carriage club?"

"The kind of thing you find in a neighborhood like this," Verci said. "People can afford a carriage, but the houses don't have space for it or horses. So it's a place they can store them, share horses, that sort of thing. For regular fees."

Helene didn't bother with any more questions, not right now. There was enough going on. "Hold on," she said, scooping him out of his chair. He wrapped his arms around her neck—and for a moment her heart fluttered. She tamped it down—this was not the moment to even think about that, even with his hot breath right on her neck.

She took him down the passage to its exit point—a forgotten basement stairway in an alley where the backhouses had long been abandoned. "I need to leave you here while I go find Ken," she said, putting him down on the stairs. "You'll be all right."

He laughed. "I probably won't be arrested for vagrancy. And I have my darts if I need them."

"I won't be long," she said.

"Hurry," Verci said. "I'll stay out of sight."

She found her way over to the carriage club, two blocks away. It was the exact sort of place she pictured—a popinjay bother filled with swells and aspiring swells. When she arrived, Vellun was in full regalia as some sort of fancy businessman, with brass-button waistcoat and matching cravat and suspenders—talking to some other men who looked exactly the same—and Kennith was underneath one of the carriages.

And she was dressed like a West Maradaine meat slinger, complete with blood still on her face. She couldn't have looked more out of place. Someone who looked like her would never come to this place unless she was collecting coin for someone like Missus Holt.

She could use that.

"Oy, you," she said, as thick and Westie as she could, marching up to Vellun. Poking him in the arm, she continued, "You've been skiving out. You think you could hide here? You owe me money."

The other businessmen that Vellun was chatting with all

raised their eyebrows. "You let her talk to you that way?" one of them asked.

Vellun let the back of his hand fly at Helene. She was shocked at first, but realized as soon as it made contact with her, he wasn't putting any force into it. She played into the hit, rolling away from it.

"How dare you?" he said. "You have an issue, you talk to my man." He pointed over to Kennith.

"You've got debt to settle," she said, pointing her finger in his face. "Don't think it'll be just me next time."

Helene gave him a good glare, and then stalked over to Kennith. Let him explain that to his swell friends.

"He's enjoying that role a bit much," she said as she got to the carriage.

"Why are you here?" Kennith asked, pulling himself out from under it. "Whose blood is that?"

"An obnoxious lady. Something went wrong—"

"What?"

"Asti got skunked, and hard," she said. "Apparently we can't talk about it in the house, because it isn't a safehouse anymore. Oh, and Asti says you and Vellun can't go back there."

"What?"

"Or anyone else. It's compromised."

"What?"

"Is that all you're going to say?"

"I'm just deeply confused about. . . . everything."

"You and me both, Ken," Helene said. "All I know is this slan burst in, slapped us around, and she and Asti had a whole . . . thing. Asti says he has a new plan, but . . ."

"You don't trust it?"

She shrugged. "I think he's just trying to keep his head up."

Kennith gave a big sigh, like he was disappointed in everything in the world. "All right," he said, getting to his feet. "So what do we need to do?"

"First we need to pick up Verci—I left him at the exit to the passage. Then get Julie before he gets to the safehouse, and meet at the flop we used for the last gig." She sighed. "I think Asti intends to keep Win and Julie in the household.

Even though he got skunked, he thinks keeping them there is fine."

"But it's not fine?" Kennith asked.

"I don't even know. I think this is one of those 'Rynax brothers' moments where something has gone wrong, and they react extremely to stop anything else from going wrong, while at the same time they're convinced this new plan is going to go without a hitch."

Kennith nodded. "What do you usually do in those moments?"

She had to give the honest answer. "Go along. They're usually right."

He moved a bit closer to her, lowering his voice. "So, you've been doing this for a lot longer than me. Is this typical?"

"Things going wrong? Constantly." On his worried look, she added, "But this is different, you know. This isn't us being desperate for a score. We're flush, we're just working this to get things square."

"Square," he said wistfully. "Yeah, right." His dark face scowled as he went over to his toolkit.

"What?" she asked.

"Nothing, just . . . I know this stuff with the fire and all, it's a bit more personal for you . . ."

"We all were in back when Asti told us it went deeper."

"I know," Kennith said. "Just that was three bells in the morning, a bit of wine in my stomach, and riding fast from the whole gig . . ." He bit at his lip, struggling for something to say.

"I get it," she said. It made her angry that he was talking like this, but she also needed his help if she was going to see Julien and make sure he was all right. She kept it tamped down for now, but Verci would need to know Kennith was thinking things like this. "Why not walk away?"

She must have let a little too much of her anger slip into her words, because he glowered at her. "Can't now, especially with a stick looking for me. It's different for you, in a lot of ways."

"True," she said, trying to sound calm. "Look, I know I

mostly only have skin in this because of Julie. He—he's all I got, you know? And I need to get to him, make sure he's safe. Can you help me do that?"

"Yeah, I think I can," Kennith said. "But then what? He goes back in, and we keep charging through with whatever Asti says the new plan is?"

"For now. There's more . . ." Anger was bubbling up in her gut. She looked around at the swells, still chatting up Vellun, but giving the two of them a strange eye. "We probably shouldn't talk here too much."

"I get it. Sometimes what Asti wants is sewage." Kennith shook his head. "I mean, I ain't going to just hide up in here, or play manservant to Vellun, or . . . I'm gonna have my life."

"So what does that mean?"

Kennith furrowed his brow. "I'm thinking maybe *we* need our own backup plan to Asti's backup plan. A contingency to get us—and Julie and Win—safe if things go truly skunked. You with me, Hel?"

Helene nodded. She almost never saw eye to eye with Kennith, but he was right—they couldn't just be Asti's pawns now. Not with Julie's life at risk. Blazes, she never should have let him go in that house by himself. And Ken was at risk, just for standing out in the crowd, being a chomie and all.

"You got a plan?" she asked.

"I think I'm starting one. And, blazes, we been watching the Rynax boys and Mister Gin play all these plans and tricks. Like we can't pull our own? Course we can."

Of course they could.

"So what do we do?" Helene asked.

"Right now, we follow along and meet up with Asti in the flop. We got to find out what he's planning."

"So play Asti's game."

"Hey, one thing I've learned with these boys?" Kennith smiled. "You got to do the scouting work before doing the gig. We need to know more about what happened with Asti so we don't make that worse. And maybe make things worse for Win and Julie."

"All right," she said. "Now drag Vellun out of there. Damn fool is enjoying himself far too much. No more fancy boy jobs for him."

Kennith laughed, and clapped her on the shoulder as he walked over to Vellun. For the first time since starting up with this crew, Helene actually liked the chomie.

Asti made a lot of noise once Helene and Verci were gone, setting up a few obvious traps and getting rid of anything that could lead someone back to North Seleth and the rest of the crew. Some of it was show, just in case he was being watched. But most of it was necessary. The safehouse was burnt, and even though he planned to use that as best he could to get advantage over Liora, he had to do a certain amount of scrub to be safe. To keep the rest of the crew safe. Some bottles Almer had left behind had his shop name on them, and a few bits and pieces that could trace back to Kennith or the North Seleth Inn. Asti wasn't going to leave that to chance.

He had to make it look like a rushed, sloppy scrub while really locking down anything he needed in case Liora had any allies who might check the place.

Did Liora have allies? Her story didn't scan, not really. She had to be on the outs from Intelligence. But if she was, what the blazes was she doing with Lord Henterman? What possible agenda could she have had there on her own? He could understand if she just wanted to hide in a cushy life, pretending to be a noblewoman. He might have tried such a thing himself, if he could have trusted his own brain to hold together.

And if there wasn't Verci.

His hands trembled again at the thought of her pressing her knife into Verci's neck. She wasn't ever going to get that close again. She wouldn't ever be in a room with Verci again, if Asti could help it.

He should check with Central Office, see what they said about her. Not that they'd tell him. But that might skunk her gig, and therefore skunk his own. He'd already raised enough of a flag about Henterman. Saints, Tranner surely reported he was asking. That wouldn't have mattered much, but with Liora in the house, on a mission . . .

He shoved it down. What mattered was finding out why Henterman was messing with North Seleth, who else was in on it, what further intentions they had. They want to buy up the land, of course, but to what end? Surely not merely to own it. There were deeper things in motion, he was sure of it.

You're going to get everyone killed or arrested.

"Shut it," he said out loud.

Drop the rest, kill Liora. That's all that matters.

He pushed that voice down to the back of his skull. He wasn't going to let it control him.

Asti took one last look around the house, satisfied with what he had done. Then he switched back to his normal street clothes. No hunting, no prepping for a fight. Except for taking his belt with the knives, and the bandolier with the darts. He wasn't about to leave Dad's weapons behind. Despite the warmth of the day, he put on his checkered coat to cover up the weapons. He didn't need anyone giving him too much hassle for walking about Colton armed.

He walked to The Gentle Shepherd with purpose, but taking a roundabout route, ducking through alleys. If he had a tail, he didn't spot it, but he had to have lost it if there was one.

Hopefully Win would be there. He honestly wouldn't blame Win for not wanting to hear what he had to say.

He made it there by half past six bells, and waited on a barstool with a cider to cool his nerves. Seven bells came and went, and for a bit, he thought Win wasn't coming. Twenty minutes after the bell, Win came in, still in full aspect as Ungar. He even wore a gentleman's cap, taking it off as he entered. He took a seat next to Asti, but first gave far more regard to the barman. Once he had his own beer, he gave Asti a bit of his attention.

"You seem cooled off."

"Somewhat," Asti said. "What happened—"

"Does it matter?"

"It does, Win," Asti pressed. "Look, that woman. Lady Henterman? She and I have history."

"You have history with a noblewoman?"

"No, Win, she—" He lowered his voice a bit more. "She's not really a noblewoman. She's—she's an agent in Intelligence."

Win raised an eyebrow. "So why were you trying to kill her?"

"Because she . . ." Asti's hand shook. "You know I'm not quite . . . right, you know?"

"I remember," Win said. "Raychelle talked to us at length about it when you first moved in."

Asti wasn't aware of that. Win had never let on back in the days of renting the apartment over his shop.

"Right. Not to go into details, but that's because of—"

"We've all had trauma, Asti," Win said icily. "We don't all attack people for it."

"It's her fault, though. She did it to me, and when I saw her—"

"Fine," Win said, taking a sip at his beer. "Look, Asti, I know you're under a lot of pressure, and you want . . . you want some measure of justice. I feel the same."

"So we're in the same cart, still."

"Are we?"

"The plan has changed, but we still have things working. We still need to—"

"You need Julie and me to stay in the house?"

"Yes."

Win nodded. "I will. In fact . . ." He paused, pursing his lips. "Look, I know that you and Verci . . . the two of you pulled me out of that fire, you've been there for me all this time."

"Of course, Win."

"But my life has had a hole in it, and, frankly . . . I need to change it. Maybe being Mister Ungar can let me find some . . . solace."

"What are you saying?"

"I like the work. It's honest." Win quickly put his hands up. "I mean, I'm not like the rest of you. I'm not made for this kind of . . . gig. We both know that."

"Of course, Win. I . . ." Asti took another drink. "I understand completely. We all want to get clean. If this is a path for you, I want you to be happy."

Win smiled. "Good. But that means—"

"However we do this plan, we make sure it doesn't burn you with it." Asti said that with pure conviction, but he wasn't entirely sure how he could pull it off. He still wasn't sure what the plan was going to be. Maybe it shouldn't involve Win at all. Maybe he couldn't be trusted in a pinch. "Go up to the flop we used for the Pomoraine. Everyone else should be there. I'll be right up behind, and we'll work out the rest."

Win drank up his beer and dropped a coin on the bar.

Asti waited a bit longer, finishing up his cider.

You're going to get everyone killed or arrested. They're all trusting you.

"Shut it," he muttered into his mug. He wasn't going to let that beast whisper him to death. He was going to beat it. Beat Liora, beat Henterman, beat them all.

There had been a couple Scratch Cats in the Birdie Basement, mostly drinking wormwood swill and hooting at the girls on the stage. Mila had taken quite a bit of pleasure in kicking them out. She was surprised that the goons of the Basement were right with her when she did it. There was no chance Josie had had the chance to alert them that Mila should have authority. She just acted like an authority, and they listened.

The manager of the basement—a short woman of undeterminable foreign birth—came over to Mila after the Scratch Cats were kicked out.

"She send you?"

Mila raised an eyebrow. "You already know the answer."

"Those boys we need to keep out?"

"For the time being," Mila said.

"You tell her, right. That we're good with her?"

"I'll make sure she knows," Mila said. Looking around for a bit, she decided to add, "And mop the floors, it's vile."

Mila went back out into the hot afternoon, walking like

Josie had told her. Chin high, almost a strut. She made her way over to Kimber's, keeping an eye out for her boys or any of Lesk's folks.

The outfit and Josie's advice did have an effect. People were giving her way as she walked, like she had never seen before. A couple even tipped their hats to her.

Her hat. Josie had mentioned it had been hers. Maybe people recognized the look, and were respecting it? Anything was possible. But it felt good.

That feeling evaporated when she went into Kimber's. Kimber raised an eyebrow at her. "Are you in a play?"

"Just here on business," Mila said, doing her best to keep her facade up. "Can I get a cider and some supper?"

"Soft cider," Kimber said. Glancing about, she leaned in and added, "Is this one of those Asti things I don't want to know about?"

"It not unconnected," Mila answered. There was someone she noted in one of the corner tables, alone, head deep in his bowl of stew. "I'll be over there."

She didn't wait for Kimber's response, and sat down with the man she was pretty sure was Kel Essin. Skinny waste of a man, looked like he was coming down from a bad dose of *effitte*.

"Mister Essin," she said calmly.

"I know you, girl?" he asked. His eye was already twitching.

"We've never met, but you did something to my boys yesterday. So I have some concerns."

"Your boys? I don't know what you—" He started to get up.

Mila's mind raced. What would Josie do? What would Asti?

She grabbed his wrist and pulled him back into his chair. If he had weighed more than a gust of wind, she'd never have been able to do it.

"Who do you think you—"

"I'm Miss Bessie," Mila said. "And your boys went and stomped on *my* boys, so we've got a ruckus to settle here."

"I ain't got a—"

What was it Mister Gin had told her? Establish contact

and dominance. Eye to eye. Mila still had her hand around his wrist, so she drummed her fingers on it, all while staring hard into his eyes. "You've got a ruckus, with me and with the Old Lady."

"I ain't a guy you talk to about this," he said, pulling his arm free. "I ain't what you think."

"I think you're a lieutenant with Lesk's guys, trying to prime this place for him to come home to." That was a load of sewage she just said, but she made it sound strong. "I think you've got the ear of people."

"I ain't got—"

"I'm getting real tired of hearing what you ain't, Essin," she snapped. He startled a bit at that. "Let me make something clear. Your folks have pushed on my boys, on Junk Avenue, here on Frost, and the Old Lady noticed. You're going to pull yourself and yours south. Pull everything back to Elk Road."

"Why would I—"

"Because if you and your crew are lucky, the Old Lady *might* let you all keep Elk Road. For the right price."

"She can't—"

"You're going to say what the Old Lady can't do?" Mila spoke in a low growl. "Is that you? Or is that Treggin?"

Essin went pale. "It's Treggin. He's gonna—"

"No, he ain't. Whatever you are about to say, he ain't." Mila was enjoying this far too much. Essin was almost quivering. "So here's what else you're going to do. Tonight, nine bells at the Elk Road Shack. I'm going to come there with some of mine, and we're going to have a little parlay. Treggin better be there."

"But—"

"Now scat."

Essin sat dumbly for a moment, than bolted to his feet and went out the door.

Kimber came over with stew, bread, and cider. "What in the name of the saints was that, girl?"

"The things you don't want to know about," Mila said.

"Things I don't want in here, understand?" Somehow Kimber made Mila feel like a child with just the tone of her voice.

"Yes, ma'am."

"Eat up," Kimber said. "I'm sure you need it."

Mila dug into the stew, her mind now twirling on how she was going to meet the bluff she just pulled on Essin. She had set a parlay, and now she had to show up with the juice to match it.

Chapter 15

BEING STUCK WITHOUT THE chair had been a challenge. Verci ended up crouching in the stoop, looking like a vagrant for the better part of an hour. Colton was not a neighborhood to look like a vagrant in. One person came over tentatively, not sure if he should call a constable or a Yellowshield. Verci had managed to convince him that he was indeed fine, and that his friend had gone for a carriage and he would be on his way shortly. The clean shirt and the faked South Maradaine accent helped sell it.

Helene arrived with the carriage—and Kennith and Vellun along with them. With their help, he got into the carriage, where Helene spent a bit too much time fussing to make sure he was comfortable.

"I shouldn't have left you there alone, you've had a . . . are you thirsty, or . . ."

"I'm fine, really," Verci said. Though he did like being able to sit with his leg up again. And he hadn't eaten much today. Something probably should be done about food, but that wasn't a priority right now. "We need to position ourselves to intercept Julien."

"Go on Flynn," Helene said. "That's the route he'll take."

"You're sure?" Kennith asked.

"Julien doesn't like learning too many new routes anywhere," Helene said. "He takes the one he knows."

"All right," Kennith said, moving up to the driver's seat.

"Hey, Vellun," Verci said. "You know how to drive this, if you have to?"

The young man smiled a little emptily. "'Fraid not really, sir."

"Then get up there with Kennith and learn."

Vellun frowned and went up top, closing the carriage door on Verci and Helene.

"Am I punishing Kennith?" Verci asked.

"Nah, they're cream and honey," Helene said. "You thinking we need to have Vellun drive?"

"I'm thinking a Ch'omik man stands out in the streets. A Ch'omik driver, triply so. We shouldn't be putting Kennith at risk."

Helene nodded. "All right, I kept my trap shut back in the house because I saw you two eye twitching at each other, and I figured you had a plan," she said. "But what the blazes are we doing?"

"We're playing along with this idea," Verci said. "We wanted to run the party, and now we can, so . . . still a plan."

"And this lady that Asti has history with?" She shook her head. "Look, I know there's stuff about Asti's past he don't talk about. But I can see a tinder show that's about to burn down."

"Yeah," Verci said. "You know how Asti isn't, you know, quite in his skull?"

"You mean those episodes where he went barking mad?" Helene asked. Verci must have made a look, because she added, "You think no one talked about that? Kimber was there when he tore into the Lesk gang, and Almer couldn't shut up about it."

"Yeah." Verci sighed. "Well, short version is, that lady is why."

Helene let out a low whistle. "Well, I'll gladly shoot her, given the chance."

"Asti might resent that."

She shrugged. "If I get my shot before him, he can cry in his cider."

The carriage came to a stop, and they could hear some voices. Then the door opened, and Julien got in. Helene grabbed him in an embrace. "Are you all right? Everything good?"

"I know something went wrong," he said. "Asti did . . . you know what he did?" He seemed shook.

"Asti got burned, that's all that matters," Verci said. "But part of why you're in there is so we have a backup in case of something like this."

"Yes," Julien said. "They like me. They say I do good work."

Helene jumped on that. "They're nice to you in that kitchen, yes? No one treating you badly?"

"No, it's very kind," Julien said. He started talking about the kitchen, and Helene was completely engaged in his stories. Verci sat back and shut his eyes.

As soon as his eyes were closed, he saw Liora Rand with her knife at his throat. He sat up and shook that off. He had to admit, that woman was everything Asti had said she was. Capable, charming, and extremely dangerous. He knew exactly who she was and what she was up to, but yet he felt some sympathy for her.

She was going to be one step ahead of them, whatever they did. She knew Asti and thought like him. However they played this, they ha   keep that in mind.

They trundled through the neighborhood to Low Bridge, eventually reaching the apartment they used in the Colevar gig. Getting up to the apartment was a blazes of a problem, as there was no real way to do it without calling much attention. Julien ended up carrying Verci up the stairs while Vellun and Kennith brought the carriage around back.

The place was cramped with the three of them up there, and even more so once Vellun and Kennith arrived. They did have the sense to come with beers and strikers for everyone when they came up. Verci took that happily. Food in his stomach and washing something down his throat made a world of difference.

Win came up, dressed like an underbutler, and said polite hellos. A few minutes later, Asti arrived. He pressed his ear against the door. "I doubt we're being watched or followed, but on the off chance of that, it's not likely that whoever Liora has is good enough to listen in here with no notice. So we have a bit of time to talk."

"You mind telling us the full truth about what's going on?" Win asked.

"I will," Asti said. "Short version, everyone—it turns out that the lady of the house is an old partner of mine. She's pretending to be—"

"We all figured that part out, idiot," Helene said. "What are we going to do?"

"We're going to work with her," Asti said. "Use that to our advantage as best we can, but we have to keep the rest of the crew isolated. As far as Liora knows, our crew is me, Verci, and Helene."

Kennith nodded. "Makes sense. And is your plan to act like we were just planning to rob Lord Henterman?"

"Believable," Verci said. This was probably the best plan to go forward, as long as Asti could hold it together with regard to Liora Rand. Asti's temper—or whatever was in his skull beyond that—was the real dice roll in this plan. "The main thing is, we don't trust her, obviously. And she won't trust us."

"So we have to expect a double cross from her, and she's sure to do the same. All we have to protect ourselves is hiding who we all are and what we're really after."

Win nodded. "So Julien and I need to stay in the household, working our jobs and our covers. Are you sure we're safe with her?"

"As long as we don't let her suspect you two, you'll be fine. Julien, you can't go back to the other safehouse. So this apartment is where you'll stay now."

Julien frowned. "Helene, are you staying here?"

"Sure," she said.

"Hel, I need—" Asti started.

"Sure," she said firmly.

He fumed a bit and then said, "Fine, but I'm going to need you to come back to North Seleth in the morning, Hel. We're going to need to work with the Old Lady and Pilsen a bit."

"Why?" she asked.

"Here's the one thing we have right now." He pulled out the invitation from his coat. "We have an invite to the party. That was exactly what we wanted. We're in. So at the party, it's you and me going in."

"What, like I'm your escort?"

"Exactly," Asti said.

"How do I always end up with that job, Rynax?"

"We still need to hash the details," he said. "But the rest of us will go back to Seleth tonight to lay the groundwork with Josie."

"And I should stay there," Verci said. "I'm too much liability on this whole thing, Asti."

"Maybe," Asti said, squatting next to him. "Which puts you on par with me." He tapped on the side of his head.

"You can hold it." Verci was certain of that. He had held it together enough to talk it through with Liora, even as she held a knife to Verci's throat. Asti had to be able to keep his troubles in their cage, or they might as well scrub the whole thing.

"For the moment. But I'm also fighting every urge to just go to the Henterman estate with knives and fire, leave nothing but ashes and dust."

"And blood," Verci said.

"That hardly serves the rest of us," Win said coldly. "Or the good people who work there."

"Why I'm not doing it," Asti said, looking up at Win. He turned back to Verci. "But I need you to help me keep my skull on straight."

Verci was afraid Asti would say something like that. The original plan was skunked, and Verci had already been useless enough on that. He'd far rather just go back home and rethink everything. Let his leg heal while they crafted a new, proper plan to find the true reason behind the Holver Alley Fire.

Verci remembered the man from this morning.

"Something happened," Verci said. "In all the everything . . . I forgot to tell you. A man came up to Hel and me in Seleth, told us that . . . who was it?" The name had left his memory.

"Major Grieson," Helene said.

Asti groaned. "That bastard."

"Who is he?"

"Someone I know from Druth Intelligence."

"In the what?" Vellun asked. Asti turned to him, as if he'd just realized the man was there.

"It doesn't matter," Asti said. "Though it does confirm one thing, I think. He's probably worried we're going to stomp on Liora's mission."

"So, maybe that should mean something," Verci said.

"What are you saying?"

"I'm saying, maybe we let this one go, call it skunked."

"Push through, just like Pop said," Asti said.

"That's probably what got Pop killed," Verci shot back. "We're racing from one plan to the next, one gig to the next, without even taking a breath to—"

"Probably," Asti said, cutting Verci off. He pointed to the invitation. "But what we have here is an opportunity, one we can't waste. We can figure out what Henterman is up to and deal with Liora in one blow, if we roll our dice right."

"Deal with Liora isn't what we signed up for," Helene said. Then she shrugged and added, "Though, personally, there is some appeal to that. But I doubt anyone else sees it that way."

The rest just looked confused, save Win, who definitely seemed angry with Asti.

"Look," Verci said. "If we do this, we've got to be razor edge with everything. No mistakes, no foul-ups. That's hard to do with you and me both handicapped here."

"And Liora is that for me," Asti said. "I won't deny it."

Verci nodded. "So what do you all say?" he asked the rest.

"I think it sounds exciting!" Vellun said.

That wasn't quite what Verci was expecting, but no one else said anything against it.

"Push through," Kennith said. "What else are we going to do?" He looked over to Helene.

"Push through," she said.

"Fine," Win said, putting his cap on. "One thing is certain, our system of communication between the two of us and the rest of you will have to improve."

"I agree," Asti said. "We had to scramble today to intercept Julien, and that's my fault."

"Glad he admits it," Kennith grumbled.

"So how do we get messages to you without compromising you?" Verci asked, trying to steer things back to useful subjects.

Win thought for a moment. "There's an oil lamp sconce at the western gate of the house. The housing is a bit loose, so you can leave me a message behind that, and you can check if I've left you anything. And I can freely pass word to Julien, yes?"

"Right," Julien said, sitting on the bed.

"I'll see you in the morning, then," Win said, going to the door. Helene almost pounced on him, saying a few things too quietly for Verci to hear.

"Yes, of course," Win told her, adding, "Best to you all," before he left.

"All right," Asti said. "Then we'll go back to the safehouse to plan the next step. Unless you want to be dropped off at the bakery, Verci?"

The bakery. It was a shame Verci knew Asti didn't intend for him to stay there. Right now all Verci wanted was to lie in bed with his wife, child, and the scent of fresh bread.

But that wasn't where Asti was going to lead him.

Mila had waited on the corner for Mister Gin for ten minutes before she realized he had been there the whole time. He was leaning against the wall, his hair blackened and slicked back, skin bronzed, thick mustache and cropped goatee. He looked twenty years younger, and with the thin rapier at his belt, he looked formidable.

"Pleasure to see you, Mister—" She knew if he was in character, he'd only use that name.

"Entrimáriz, scourge of the Acserian coast," he said in a subdued accent.

She gave him a raised eyebrow at that. "You're a pirate?"

"Former pirate," he said. "Walk with me."

"So, are you supposed to be my muscle," she said as they

headed toward the Shack. "Or are you also doing the talking?"

"I'll talk as needed," he said. "As far as muscle goes, I'm more to imply the idea of muscle at our disposal. The two of us need to give the sense that we represent a larger organization."

"I've got that," Mila said. "But they know that I'm supposed to be Bessie, and they've already stomped Bessie's Boys."

"And you've given them some pushback. We'll see what that makes them do."

"And what might they—" Mila didn't finish the thought, as she noticed a boy hanging back in the alley they were approaching. Not just hanging back. Skulking, with a knife. But she wasn't worried, he was one of hers.

"Tarvis," she said as she came up. "What's going on?"

"Why you look all fancy?" he asked her. "I don't like it."

"Part of a scheme."

"This the scheme that got the boys thrown to Gorminhut, or a new one?"

"A new one," Mila said cautiously. Tarvis never showed much emotion beyond a low simmering rage, so while he was clearly angry, she wasn't sure if he was angry at her. Or if it was anything beyond his usual state of vaguely angry.

"This geezer part of the scheme, or do I stab him?"

"Don't stab him," Mila said.

"Already did a few today," he said. She noticed the cuff of his ragged shirt had blood splattered on it. "They grabbed me and took me to Gorminhut. So I had to stab a couple to get out."

"Good on you, chap," Mister Gin said. "That place was awful when I was your age, and I'm sure it still is."

"Jede is still there, I think. So I'll have to hurt some people to save him."

Mila had to remind herself that this tiny monster was only six years old.

"We're gonna get your brother and the rest out, in a bit. Right now we got to help the Old Lady and the neighborhood."

Tarvis made a face that was somehow both a smile and an angry sneer. "I don't like her. I don't want to help her."

"Well, help me," she said. She turned up his sleeve to hide the blood. "I see you've got your knife."

"Always," he said.

"Hide it good. Now give me a sad face. Best sad, scared little boy face you can do."

"Do I need to cry?"

"No, just the face."

His expression changed instantly, and the angry little monster was gone. All of a sudden, he turned into a poor urchin who any decent person would want to sweep into their arms and take care of.

"Boy has a gift," Mister Gin whispered.

"Now what?" he asked.

Mister Gin knelt down near him. "Stick with us, stay close to Miss Bessie's skirts. Anyone comes too close to her, you stab him in the leg. Got it?"

"Even you?" he asked.

"Not him," Mila said. "Let's get moving."

They made their way to the Elk Road Shack, where there was now a Julien-sized bruiser at the door. "You can't carry that belly sticker in here," he told Mister Gin about the sword.

"Then where should I put it?" Gin asked, now fully in character as Entrimáriz. "Because you aren't going to take it from me."

"Keep it and walk away, or hand it over and come in," the bruiser said calmly. "I don't care either way, except to tell you that you don't come in here with it."

"Do it, 'Máriz," Mila told him. "We're here to parlay, not fight."

"Because you asked, Miss Bessie," he said. "Else I'd—" He made a gesture like he'd skewer an invisible opponent.

The bruiser took the sword and let them in. Mila was surprised he didn't take the knife on her belt or check Tarvis. Then she saw that most of the slakes and steves in this place had knives on them.

"It's fine," Mister Gin whispered. "It's a prop anyway."

"I'm not really worried about that," Mila said as they

approached the table in the back corner. "One more sword wouldn't make a difference in here."

"Remember Verci's first rule," Gin added.

Verci's first rule. Know all your exits. Main doors. Twenty feet, seven tables, and at least fifteen people in between. Dirty windows, several just above eye level. All small, too small for anyone but Tarvis. Two sets of doors by the bar. One probably to the basement, the other to a back room. Narrow hallway, just five clear paces from the table they were coming up to. Probably to the water closet or outside to backhouses, depending on this place.

"Well, someone wanted a parlay," the man at the table said. Weasely man, sitting with Poller and Ia. Essin.

"You're not Treggin," Mila said, sitting opposite them. Gin took a chair, spun it around and sat on it, leaning on its back. Tarvis stood, leaning on Mila like she was his mama.

"Of course I'm not," Essin said. "And you two are not the Old Lady."

"I wanted—"

Essin spat on the floor. "Neither I nor Mister Treggin are particularly desirous to succumb to your wants." He said this with a certain air of uncertainty, though. Like he had memorized the phrase and wasn't sure if he had gotten all the words right.

"Mighty cocky, Mister—" Gin said. "I'm afraid I don't know all the little people here."

"It's Essin. Kal Essin. You two are Miss Bessie and Entrimáriz. Don't think I don't know what goes on in this neighborhood."

"And who is the little boy?" Ia mocked. "Do we need to get him milk?"

"He's one of mine," Mila said. "Don't come near him."

"Yes, the Bessie's Boys," Essin said. "This is what the Old Lady has now. A posturing girl and her cadre of toddlers. Did we not crush your Boys and send them scurrying?"

Mister Gin tapped Mila's foot with his.

"Like rats," Poller said nervously.

"The thing about rats," Gin said. "Is you never actually get rid of them."

"That's all the Old Lady is going to be, though. A common pest." Essin again. Gin gave Mila another tap.

"You think she's going to hand North Seleth over to you?" Mila asked. "She's willing to let you stay up on your toes, for the right price. But that's the best you get."

"She has nothing left, Miss Bessie," Essin said. "I know you think you're saddling a winning mare here, but it's a tired nag that has no races left in her."

Another tap, but Mila didn't need it. Essin was speaking oddly.

"She's still got a network, favors," Gin said. "Your man Treggin can't compete with that."

"You don't have an inkling about Treggin," Essin said.

"I think I do," Gin said. "I think he's a nothing, and you all are petty ants who follow the nothing."

Essin nodded, and then said, "You'll see what an army of ants can do, then."

"We're done," Gin said, getting to his feet. "Come along, Miss Bessie."

Mila got up, not sure at all what just occurred.

"Hope your boys all sleep well tonight, Bess," Essin called after her. Gin was already going to the door, and Mila followed his lead, not letting herself rise to the bait.

Once they were a block away, Mila finally spoke up. "You want to tell me what was going on?"

"We weren't talking to Essin, that's what," Gin said.

"He was a bit strange, yeah," Mila said.

"No, girl, listen. I know words, I know character, I know people. Essin is a half-pence half-wit who thinks he's clever, but has nothing approaching charm or learning."

That clicked in her head. "But he talked like he was educated."

"Words and phrases that I doubt Essin even knows," Gin said. His entire character of Entrimáriz was gone now. "I threw him a line from an obscure play—"

"The thing about the ants?"

"And he gave me the next line back." Gin grabbed her by the arm and pulled her along. Tarvis, who had been quiet all this time, pulled his knife.

"We said not him, Tarvis," Mila said quickly.

"Sorry," Tarvis said. He put his knife away again.

"Come on, double time," Gin said. "We need to get to Josie. We need to tell her what Treggin really is."

"And what is that?"

"Saints and sinners preserve me," Gin said. "Use your skull, girl. He's someone who could listen to our conversation with Essin and immediately feed him things to say. Or he's someone who can make himself look like Essin. Either way, the answer's the same. We're dealing with a mage."

Chapter 16

"**WHY DO YOU STILL** have that horrible thing there?"

Raych looked up from the kneading counter at her sister, who was pointing at the crossbow sitting nearby. This one was a functional one—light and easy to use. Verci had made it for her, but until today she had left it in a closet upstairs. The events of this morning were frightening enough, and the idea that she might actually have to use the crossbow petrified her. But she still felt safer with it near.

"Just in case," Raych said, continuing to knead the batch of dough she was working on.

"I'm sure this morning was nothing," Lian said, bringing her tray over. "Though we should make sure all the doors are locked. I swear we had more cookies here . . ."

Raych wiped off her hands. "Can you portion this into proofing bowls? I'm going to make sure everything is shut down up front." She picked up the crossbow and headed to the windows.

Verci had told her once that this shop was probably one of the safest places in the neighborhood, and she knew the lockdown rooms would be very hard to get into, if she had to go in there. But that didn't change the fact that it was still a shop, with windows and a door that needed to stay open to do business.

The streets were quieter than usual in the twilight. She was used to a certain degree of foot traffic and carousing at this hour, but the walkways were sedate. She went over to the door and stuck her head outside.

At least three Constabulary footpatrolmen were strolling on Junk Avenue. She had never seen that many constables in one place in this neighborhood. Even when she and Lian both had lived in Birdtown in the Little East, there were more sticks in the streets than North Seleth.

Maybe they were actually doing something about the business from this morning.

"What is it?" Lian asked from the back.

"Constables," Raych said, closing and latching the door.

"What do they want?"

"I don't think they want anything, Lian. They're just patrolling."

"Well, put that monstrosity away before they give you a rattle for it."

"We're latched up, Lian. It's fine."

"Fine for you, perhaps."

"Are tomorrow's breads proofing?"

Lian sighed. "Almost done."

"Thank you for your help, by the way," Raych said. "It's meant a lot."

"That thank you better include a 'here's three crowns.'"

"Three crowns?" Raych asked. "Now I know who the real shakedown thug of this street is."

"For the week," Lian said. "I'm not a monster."

Raych laughed. "I would like to have you here more often."

"You mean once Verci's on his feet. And where is he again?"

"He's . . . I told you." For the life of her, Raych couldn't remember the lie she had told Lian about where Verci was all day.

"Right, the special commission in easttown," Lian said. "I'm glad he's getting work, but . . ."

"Lian."

"I know, I know," Lian said. Putting the last of the dough in a bowl and covering it with a cloth, she added, "And I'm sure he's not the most helpful in the bakery, even when he is on his feet."

"Bread is not his passion."

"Hmmm," Lian said. "Saints know we could use the extra crowns, and until they bless me with a child . . ."

"You want to stay?"

"What would Pop say about us now?" Lian asked. "By Acser's eye, we must have fought him with every inch about learning bread. And you! 'I will never be a baker!'"

"That was once and I was nine."

"Still, we—"

Someone pounded on the door, and Lian screamed and threw flour in the air.

Raych hushed her and pulled up the crossbow, cautiously training it on the window, until she saw who it was.

"It's Asti," she said wearily.

"Why is he here?" Lian was almost in tears.

"No good reason, I'm sure," Raych muttered. Even still, she opened the door.

"Hey," Asti said, looking around like a mad squirrel. "Just you here?"

"Me and Lian."

"Hmm," he said. Even for Asti, he looked out of sorts. "All right, we need to move quickly."

"I'm not going anywhere."

"No, just hold the door open." He went back out.

Raych did as he said, now seeing that there was a carriage in the street, stopping just in front of the bakery. Before it came to a halt, Asti jumped on the runner and opened the door. The Ch'omik man—Kennith?—came dashing out of there and into the bakery, which caused Lian to scream again. Then Verci and Asti came in, Verci half carried by Asti. The carriage was moving again before they even got all the way inside.

"Shut the door," Asti said as they got in.

"Are you being chased?" Raych asked.

"Raychelle," Lian called, her hand on her chest. "Who is this . . . gentleman?"

"Kennith is an associate of mine, Lian," Verci said pointedly. "You'll be respectful of him."

"I . . . I'm sorry, I just found having this . . . strange man charge into the bakery to be a shock."

"Verci," Asti said sharply. "We need to keep moving."

"What are you talking about?" Raych asked. "What is going on?"

"Raych, it's all right," Verci said, though he hardly said it with any conviction.

"It is not all right," she said. "You come in like the sinners are after you, after being gone for two days, and—"

"I'm sorry," Verci said, in that irritatingly calm way he had that always worked. "But things are happening."

"What things?" Lian shrieked.

"Verci," Asti said sharply, going over by the oven. "We should keep moving."

"You aren't staying here?" Raych asked.

"I'll be back," Verci said, hobbling over to her, putting a hand on her cheek. "I'll be back tonight." He said this, giving a pointed look at Asti. Making it clear to his brother not to gainsay it.

"Right," Asti said. "He will be." With that, he reached behind the stove and moved something, and a panel of the wall opened up to a staircase. "Ken, can you help Verci?"

"Got it," Kennith said.

"Two hours," Verci said, giving her a kiss. "That's a promise."

"I'll hold you to that."

"Come on," Asti said. Kennith let Verci drape an arm over his shoulder, and they went down the stairs. Asti followed behind, and the panel slammed shut.

"What—what the blazes just happened?" Lian asked. "And *why* is there a secret door in the back of the shop? Did you know about this?"

Upstairs, Corsi started crying.

"Just go home, Lian," Raych said, as she went to her child. "Lock up when you go, and don't mention any of this to anyone. Especially Hal."

After a horrible day, Asti found it oddly gratifying to see Josie shriek when he came out of her secret door that went from the bakery to the safehouse. She was puttering around her office, making herself a pot of tea. She knocked it off the counter in her confusion, and Asti scrambled to catch it before it shattered on the floor.

"How did you come through—" she started once she regained her composure.

"Please," Asti said, putting her teapot back on the counter. It had been hot, but he didn't let the fact that it hurt show on his face. It was a good exercise for maintaining control, keeping the beast in its cage. "You think I didn't know you had that passage?"

She shrugged. "I figured you knew I had it. I just didn't think you'd actually find it."

Verci came limping in, supported by Ken. "Some respect, Josie. You gave me the bakery to live in. You think I didn't scour it top to bottom."

"I can guarantee you didn't find all my secrets."

Kennith put Verci in a chair. "I don't understand how you had tunnels and such built without anyone else knowing about them. I mean, it would have taken hundreds of men—"

"I didn't," Josie said.

"But how—"

"Boys," Josie said, going to her desk with her tea. "This part of the city is old, over a thousand years. And like any old lady, it is full of secrets you'll never discover."

"She's saying that there are hundreds of forgotten tunnels and catacombs in the city," Asti said. He had heard some stories back in his Intelligence days. He had even heard rumors that there were ones deep enough to go under the river. "The westtown ones are probably the most forgotten."

"You're here for a reason, and clearly not a good one," Josie said. "So spill."

Asti waved her out. "Let's go out to the main floor. Where is Mila? We sent word for Almer to come out."

"Mila is on our local problem," Josie said, getting her cane. "How's the foot, Verci?"

"Hurts like blazes," he said.

"Yeah, yeah," she said, coming over to him. "I know for that. Hope you do better than I did."

"I'll be running rooftops soon enough."

"Hmmph." She looked down at the brace. "Grab my tea, Asti, bring it out. I can tell you, a clean break like that, treated well, you got a shot. I never did."

"How did you hurt your leg?" Kennith asked, helping Verci out to the main floor. Asti grudgingly grabbed the tea and took it out.

"Cudgy Ottin and his people decided they wanted to end my career as a window-girl," she said. "So they took a hammer to my knee."

Asti bit his tongue. He had been a part of the crew that Josie had used for her revenge on Cudgy and his gang. Way back in the day, when she was grooming him to be one of her enforcers.

As they sat down at the table, Vellun and Almer came in.

"Who the blazes are you?" Josie asked Vellun.

"Vellun Colsh," he said. "I'm with Pilsen. Where is he? I haven't seen him for a bit."

"He's working. So you're his young sweetmeat. I can see why he fancies you."

"He's been useful," Verci said. "And Pilsen trusts him."

"He fancies him, there's a difference," Josie said. "Sorry, boy. You're very pretty."

"As you say, miss." Vellun took a seat at the table. Kennith tapped him on the shoulder.

"Help me in the kitchen. I think we all could use something in our stomachs."

"That's a good idea, Kennith," Josie said. "There's bread and cheese and mustard—"

"I've got it, Missus Holt," Kennith said, pulling Vellun with him to the kitchen.

"He's really quite gifted in the kitchen," Verci said.

"I'm sure," Josie snarled. "He knew to get that pretty boy out of here, as well."

"You don't trust Vellun?"

"I don't know him. Trust isn't even an option."

She was looking at Asti expectantly, but he didn't want to say much more until Mila and Pilsen came in. "How's business, Almer?" Asti asked.

"Terrible," Almer said. "Half the folks in this neighborhood are thugs, the other half are scared out of their gourd."

"We're trying to do something about that," Asti said.

"Are we?" Almer asked. "I wonder. You've got that girl peacocking around—"

"Mila?" Asti asked. "What does he mean?"

"Her Miss Bessie act needed some work," Josie said. "So we're establishing some bona fides for her."

"Peacocking," Almer said again.

"All right, it doesn't matter," Asti said. "This has to do with Lesk's crew?"

"Amongst other things," Josie said. "You're stalling."

"Fine." Dragging this out wouldn't help. "We've got some good intel on the house, the employment scam worked. I was able to case the whole household. Win and Julien have jobs there."

"And you, too, yes?"

"Not anymore. I was skunked."

That got Josie's interest. "How the blazes did you get skunked but not them?"

"Because the lady of the house is a ringer as well. Old . . . acquaintance from my days in Intelligence."

"Your days in what?" Almer asked.

"Not now, Almer," Verci said.

"The kind of old acquaintance that leads to you clawing each other's eyes out?" Josie asked. "I didn't ask about why you're all banged up."

Asti hadn't realized it was that obvious.

"But we've reached an accord, which puts us forward to a new plan—though needless to say, this woman is not someone we trust."

"Not someone we trust are words I live by, Asti," Josie said. "Here they are."

Mila and Pilsen had come in with a little boy in tow. She was dressed in some strange outfit that looked thirty years out of date, bright blue and red. Pilsen was done up like an actor's idea of how a pirate on the Napolic Straits dressed.

"I should never let anyone dress themselves," Asti muttered. "Who's the boy?" The kid had tottered over to Josie and got in her lap.

Josie smiled, stroking the boy's hair. "This? This is Tarvis. If we ever lose you, Tarvis is ready to take your job."

"What does he do?" Tarvis asked. "Does he stab people?"

"Very well," Josie said in the sweetest voice Asti had ever heard from her. "And he comes up with plans."

"Yeah, I can do that. I need to come up with a clever plan."

"Oh?"

"My brother is in Gorminhut. I need to get him out."

Asti chuckled. This kid was him.

Mila sighed and sat down. "We just parlayed with Essin and his crew."

"Not his crew," Verci said. "They're all Lesk's folks."

"Now they're Treggin's," Pilsen said. "And Treggin is something to worry about."

"You meet him?" Josie asked.

"Not directly. Asti, you know this Essin fellow. Smart man? Erudite?"

"I would not use those words for him."

"Right," Pilsen said.

"The Essin we met talked pretty fancy," Mila said.

"And not in that, 'I'm using words I think are fancy but I don't know what I'm saying,' way," Pilsen added.

"So what do you think?" Asti asked, though he guessed the answer.

"That this Treggin fellow could hear us, and feed to Essin what to say. Which means he's a mage of some sort. And we need to worry about that."

"What's a mage?" This came from Tarvis.

"Trouble," Asti said. "We're sure about that?"

"If it isn't magic or something like that, it's a damn good trick," Pilsen said.

"Did he ask about us?" Verci asked, indicating himself and Asti.

"You two?" Mila looked to Pilsen for confirmation. "I don't recall. No, he didn't."

"That's definitely odd," Verci said. "Helene said Essin was obsessed with what we're up to."

"Right," Asti said. More signs that Treggin—or someone else—was now pulling his strings. But Asti couldn't worry about that, not right now. "Speaking of, we've got a new development at the Henterman house. Short version, my cover is blown, but we have an in for the big party." He pulled the invite out of his coat. "We need to forge a copy of this, combined with a reasonable cover for the nobleman you'll be playing, Pilsen."

"Ah, good," Pilsen said. "Playing a nobleman at a feast will be something enjoyable."

Kennith and Vellun came out from the kitchen with trays of hot cheese sandwiches. "Not much in stores, but I did what I could," Kennith said. "I'm famished."

"Darling, sit with me," Pilsen said to Vellun, who dutifully took a chair by him. "We're going to a party."

"You're going," Asti said. "As am I. Helene will be my escort, and Mila will be yours."

"Is that going to work?" Mila asked.

"Or as his niece or something," Asti said. "Work it out and make it play. But that means you'll have to work like mad for the next two days on being a noblewoman."

"Same with Helene?" Pilsen asked. "She's going to be a challenge."

"She'll be here in the morning," Asti said. "So that's the plan. The four of us as party guests. Win and Julien are still our inside men. Verci, you'll run the observation from a carriage with Kennith, Vellun, and Almer as support."

"What support?" Almer asked.

"And what about Lesk's crew, the Scratch Cats, Treggin?"

Josie answered that. "Between calling out the sticks and the parlay you had, that should keep them busy for a couple days." She looked pointedly at Asti. "But this isn't something we can sit on, hear? I want us to move on them soon."

"Calling out sticks?" Verci asked.

Asti had noticed more than usual in the neighborhood when they came to the bakery. "You did that?"

"Doesn't hurt me none," Josie said.

"Hurt me," Tarvis said.

"And you should go to sleep," Josie told him.

"Can't make me."

"You'd be surprised what I can make happen."

That was a flash of the Old Lady that Asti had known when he wasn't much older than Tarvis. Somehow sweet and terrifying at the same time.

Asti grabbed a sandwich and tucked into it. "The point is, tomorrow, Pilsen will work with Mila and Helene. Josie, get a forgery of that invite made."

"Pardon me?" Josie said.

Asti sighed. "Could you please get forgeries of that invitation?"

"Yes," she said calmly. "Since you asked so kindly."

Asti continued. "Verci and Kennith lie low in here and get the carriage ready for whatever we might need. I'll head out east to meet with . . . Liora." He almost choked saying her name.

Mila perked up. "Who—"

"It doesn't matter."

Mila still had her attention on him. "Did you get that letter?"

Asti stared at her confused for a moment, then he remembered. "I did, but I never got the chance to look at it." He dug into his coat pockets and got it out.

"Who's it from?" Verci asked as Asti started reading it.

"Huh. It seems there is a newssheet that is interested in finding out more about the fire. *The Veracity Press.*"

"Never heard of them," Almer said.

"I have." This was Vellun. "North side paper, mostly distributed in the neighborhoods around RCM. One of those former-student, radical-idea papers."

Vellun clearly wasn't quite as vapid as he sometimes played at. Worth noting.

"Good to know," Asti said. "Then I'll check in with them tomorrow as well."

"Is that wise, in all of this?" Josie asked.

"We need information, first and foremost," Asti said. "*The Veracity Press* might know something that will open up what we know about Henterman."

"Or render running on him pointless," Verci said. "If that's it, Asti, let's go."

"Go?" Asti asked.

"Yes, go," Verci said. "I promised my wife I'd come home, and by saints and blazes, you'll get me there."

Verci was glad that Asti didn't give him any push about helping him back through the tunnels to the bakery. It was a long walk hobbling with the crutches he assembled from spare wood at the safehouse. He wished they hadn't left the chair behind. But the challenge of the walk put his mind to work on some ideas for a new foot brace, maybe a special cane or crutch. Necessity brought ideas, after all.

It was rather late, nearly the midnight bells, by the time they got inside. Asti got Verci up the stairs—ringing the right bells so Raych would know it was him—and then said goodnight.

"I'll sleep in the basement," he said. "Josie left enough furniture in her bunker down there that it's pretty comfortable."

"Asti," Verci said gently. "You know you can just move in down there. You don't have to—"

"I'm not good to have around your family too much."

"You've been—"

"I've been holding on pretty well of late, but today . . . Liora. It's gnawing at me. For them, for you, I need to keep some distance."

"Basement is some distance, Asti," Verci said. "Think about it."

"I think on everything," Asti said, and went back down.

Verci pushed himself up the steps—the pain in his leg was nowhere near what it had been two days ago, and Doc Gelson's brace helped—but it was hard and slow going to make it to the apartment. Raych had opened the door, waiting for him when he reached the top.

"So you did come back."

"I said I would," he said, coming in and getting himself to the comfortable chair.

"I don't know what happened tonight . . ."

"I'll tell you if you want to know. I can tell you everything."

She narrowed her eyes at him. "I don't think I want to hear it."

"If you don't, you don't," Verci said. "But I said from the beginning, I'm not going to keep secrets from you."

"Things went wrong today, didn't they?"

"And how." Verci wasn't sure how to say this, exactly. "We're casing a lord's manor house in East Maradaine right now."

"Because this lord was behind the fire." She somehow managed a tone that made it sound completely reasonable and utterly insane at the same time. Which it was.

"We think. Or he's connected somehow. The point of this is to find out exactly what his role was."

She had gone over to the kitchen and come back with a cup of tea. "So how are you casing it? Obviously not you, with your leg like that."

"Asti was doing the legwork inside with Win and Julien."

"Oh, Verci," she said. "That's just not right. Poor Win isn't made like Asti is. Or Julien, sweet man."

"They're doing fine. Blazes, Win is thriving, strangely. But Asti was discovered today."

She sat in the opposite chair. "Sounds like you're covering for him. He made a mistake, yes?"

"In a way, but . . . the woman, the lady of the household. Somehow, it's her."

"Her who?"

"*Her*."

Understanding dawned on Raych's face. While they never truly discussed the particulars of what had happened to Asti that broke his brain so badly, they had talked about how he had been betrayed by his partner. The "infamous woman" Raych had called her.

"That woman? From the Islands? But how . . . she's a lady married to the lord?"

"I don't fully know," Verci said. "I know she's skilled, she's dangerous—she's everything that Asti is, but as a woman. And not broken."

"And you know this for certain?"

"She came for us," Verci said. This was a moment in which Verci thought it best to minimize the full truth to his wife. She didn't need to know about the knife to his throat. "I don't trust her, but she seems to want to hire us, or use us . . ."

"For?"

"She says to spy on the Lord Henterman, that's her mission, but . . ."

"You don't believe it."

"There's no reason to believe her, but I think we have to use her."

"And you have to stop her." For a moment Verci wasn't sure if Raych was confirming his feelings, or giving him an order.

"You mean—"

"That woman wrecked your brother. If that translates to even half of what I would do to someone who hurt Lian—"

"I have an idea. I saw the crossbow in your hand."

"Right," she said. "I get where your head is at."

"I'm not sure what I'm going to do," Verci said. "I'm not sure what I can do." He pointed to his foot.

She got up from her chair and came over, grabbing his face. "You are going to use that brilliant rutting head of yours, and you're going to take care of it. Because you have to. Saints know Asti will not be able to."

"He's awfully riled—"

She kissed him once, stopping him from speaking. She did it again, getting Verci awfully riled himself.

"Listen to me," she said quietly. "You've got a blind spot when it comes to your brother. I know he's the one who comes up with the plans and drives things forward and all that stuff you always say. You need—I need you—to be the calm head. You need to see all the pieces moving."

"Like the gears in a machine," Verci said.

"Right," she said with a softer kiss. "And her gear is going to grind deep into his. You've got to be the one ready for it. Do you know what you need to do?"

Verci thought for a moment. He had a few ideas, but they all involved doing a lot of building in the next few hours.

He looked up at her eyes, seeing the love and fear deep in them. "Does this mean you approve?"

"Never," she said. "But I *accept*." And then she kissed him again.

Chapter 17

HELENE SLEPT BETTER THAN she imagined she would, given the circumstances. Maybe it was just having Julien nearby, knowing he was safe and happy. He really seemed to be loving this kitchen job. She half wondered if, in another set of circumstances, he could have gotten a job like that ages ago, straight and clean, and none of this business would have happened.

None of that mattered. Everything had happened, and she had to live with it.

"Let me make one thing clear to you," she told Julien while they ate breakfast. "No matter what else happens, if you have to choose between being safe, and keeping the rutting plan afloat for Asti Rynax, you choose yourself."

"But if I don't have to—" Julien started.

"Just listen to me. Choose yourself."

"We said we would be with him in this," Julien said. "We gotta get these people. We said we would. They killed Gram and destroyed our home."

"Ain't nothing we do will change those things," Helene said. "But in the end, we take care of each other. So I'm telling you—"

"I ain't that addled, Hel," he snapped. "I get what you're saying. Just don't like it."

"If Asti gets dragged down under—"

"Then we reach down and pull him up," Julien said sharply. "He did that for us after the fire, and he didn't have to. Ain't no one wanted us, and I know that's my fault."

"It's as much mine," Helene said. Julien probably could have gotten plenty of jobs cracking skulls if Helene had let him. But she knew that couldn't be his life. Not anymore. Bruiser work had already busted his head, made him a portion of the man he might have been. She wouldn't lose another drop. Not for any crowns, and not for Asti Rynax.

"We got each other in this," he said slowly. "But Asti, Verci, the rest. Still family. I remember that."

"Fine, fine," she said. "You need to be getting over there."

"I do," he said with a grin. "Today we need to do the tomatoes, and the summer jelly. All these foods for the Feast of Saint Jontlen."

"Who came up with that?" she asked him. "These are things only rich people could possibly do."

"It looks really tasty, though," he said. "Maybe we should try to do our own, smaller version or something. With the family."

"Julie," she said gently. "That night we're going to be working the gig. At the house. Remember?"

"Right," he said, giving that little nod he always did when he had forgotten about something. "You're going to be there, right? But disguised, like at the Emporium?"

"Probably not the same disguise," she said. She let out a groan. "I need to get over to the safehouse, so I can be taught how to be a proper lady."

"Be safe," Julien said, giving her a grand embrace.

"Always am," she shot back.

They left the flop together and parted ways in the street, him heading out east, her to the west.

It was an absurdly hot, muggy morning, and she surely looked out of place wearing the coat she had on. But she also had both the hip-hanger and The Action under her coat, as well as two quivers' worth of quarrels at her back.

To these East Maradaine and Inemar dandies, she probably looked like a right scary piece, trouble in the making. That felt good, and people gave her a wide berth all the way to North Seleth.

"Where are you strolling to, Moonlight?"

This was called out to her as she came into Saint Bridget's Square. Even though it came from behind her, a good pace away, she knew whoever said it was talking to her. She turned on her heel, walking backward to keep her pace, expecting to see someone like Ren Poller ready to give her sewage.

She was not expecting a Constabulary lieutenant.

"You got a question, left?" she shot back.

He headed over to her. "I think I asked. Where you strolling to?"

She stopped walking. "Why you asking?"

He came right up to her. "Because you stand out, Moonlight."

Normally this would be the sort of thing that she'd give someone a thumping for, but even she wouldn't dare that on a constable. Especially this constable. There was something about his eyes, his demeanor, the jaunty way he walked over that made his approach charming.

"How is that?" she sent back at him.

"Long coat, hot weather," he said. "You armed?"

"Ain't I got the right?"

"And I got the right to ask," he said. "Especially since you aren't a knife or club kind of girl, I gather."

"No," she said. "Far from."

"What are you carrying?" he asked.

She pulled back her coat and showed him the hip-hanger.

"You're not walking with it loaded," he said.

"Because I'm not stupid," she gave him back. "I see the way your boys carry their gear. Miracle half of them don't shoot themselves in the foot."

He nodded and flashed a grin at her. "I've seen a few of those among the cadets."

"So can I go?" she asked.

"Depends where you're going."

"My flop is a block or so that way. But I might stop at Kimber's for a cider."

"Bit early for that."

"Not with my throat this dry."

He gave her a bit of a nod to walk, but kept with her as she went. "So this neighborhood is your patch, hmm?"

"Born and raised, for the most part. Though I've been out and about in the wide world for a time."

"Hmm," he said. "So which is it?"

"Which is what?"

"See, I can only think of a couple reasons for a lady like you to be carrying quality crossbows—yeah, I saw the other one—on her person. So are you the type who's gonna start trouble, or the type who stops it?"

"I like to think I'm the one who stops it," she said, but not entirely sure why she was saying it. She wasn't sure why she wasn't charging away from this stick, beyond the fact that it would look even more suspicious. And this stick was clearly thinking of her suspiciously.

Or maybe he was thinking of her elsewise. Elsewise thoughts were certainly creeping into her brain, despite herself. And he was giving her that sense. She had enough experience with men in these streets giving her that sense.

"Let me see that other one," he said.

She moved over to the side of the walkway, leaning against the wall, and pulled The Action out from under her coat. "Careful with her."

"It's a her to you?" he asked, taking it from her. He held it with some reverence, checking its weight, holding it up to his eyeline.

"She's a good girl to me."

"Where'd you get this one?" he asked. "Never seen one like that."

No need to lie. It wasn't worth it. "Rynax. He was opening the Gadgeterium, but it burned down a few months back. He does some work on his own."

"Bakery man," the stick said. "I met him. Good bloke."

She took a look at his badge. "Covrane," she said in a bit of a purr. "So, Lieutenant Covrane, you in the market for a new crossbow?"

He pointed to his on his belt. "City issued. But they might be looking to place an order, you never know." He gave it back to her. "That's a serious weapon, miss . . ."

"Kesser," she said. "Miss Kesser. And I'm a serious girl with it."

He raised an eyebrow at her. "Bounty hunter?"

"I'd need papers for that, wouldn't I?"

"To do it proper," he said.

She chuckled to herself. It would be a far more interesting cover than slinging goxies.

"I might have to look into that," she said. "Legit papers and everything."

"Legit would be good," he said. "Now, you came from east of here. Where were you coming from?"

"Inemar," she said. She almost bit her tongue as soon as she said that. This was still a stick, even a cute one. He was working her. "I got a muscled bloke over there who I like spending the occasional night with."

"He got a name?"

"He does. And a wife. So I ain't gonna wreck that for him."

"You usually carry your weapons when you go see him?"

"Like I said, he's got a wife," Helene said, giving Covrane a wink. She put the crossbow back under her coat. "Can't be too careful. Now I'm gonna go get that cider. You wanna join me, that's your business."

"Another time, Miss Kesser," he said, tipping his cap.

She nodded back, and started walking again at a measured pace. She probably should get to the safehouse, but now she should take a roundabout route. Make sure this stick wasn't on her tail.

As she came into Kimber's, it hit her. He had recognized Rynax from the bakery. This was the one who had the sketchbook, the picture of Kennith. This was the trouble.

And she had half walked into it, like an addled schoolgirl.

"What are you doing here?" Asti was at one of the tables, nursing his own cider and looking through some papers.

"Same as you, getting a cider," she said, signaling Kimber and sitting down.

"You need to get to the safehouse. You've got two days to learn how to fake being a lady for the gala."

"It's got to be me?" she asked.

"Who else am I going to take to this?" he asked, just as Kimber came over with her cider.

"Take to what?" she asked pointedly.

"One of those things you don't want to know about," he said. On another look from her, he added, "It's not like that."

"Definitely not," Helene said.

"I just didn't know you were the take-people-to-things sort of fellow, Asti," Kimber said. "It's nearly nine bells. You wanted to know." She left before Asti could say thanks.

"You know she's—"

"Yes, I know, Helene," Asti said. "Saints even know why. She even has me go to Saint Bridget's with her every once in a while."

"So you are the take-people-to-things sort of fellow."

"I'm the wrong-in-the-head and she-could-do-better sort of fellow," Asti said. He picked up the papers he was looking at, his hand trembling.

"You all right?" she asked.

"Not even remotely," he said. Grinding his teeth, he said, "I have to go meet with her, figure out the full plan. I don't know if I can handle it."

"You want me to come with you?"

"No, no, I need you—I need you to be ready for the party. I'm going to need you . . ." He hesitated for a moment. "Hel, listen, right now, Verci's off the board. Mila's a great kid, but she's learning and still fresh as all get out. And lately something about the Old Lady—"

"You never really trust the Old Lady."

"Yeah, but in the past week or so she's . . ." He shook it off. "Maybe it's just my busted skull."

"Even busted, your skull is usually on the game," Helene said. "She has been arguing your plays a bit more lately."

"And maybe they're bad plays. Saints know, I've been rutting it up."

Helene couldn't argue with that. "But you're seeing that. Eyes open."

"Yeah . . . I need a clear head, and good open eyes." He tapped on the table. "That's why I need you, Helene, to keep this all on course. Feet on the ground, head in it. Because I'm not sure I can be at the reins. And if it ain't me or Verci . . ."

"Then it's me," Helene said, not sure what else to say.

He gathered up the papers. "Get to Pilsen."

"Sure," Helene said. She had to do this, and do this blasted well. For herself, for the neighborhood, for Julie and Grandma. For Asti and Verci Rynax. "Once I finished wetting my throat, hmm?"

"Yeah." He looked over to Kimber, and then back to Helene. "And tell her . . . tell her to pray for me." He drank down the rest of his cider and went off.

Kimber came back over. "He's getting worse, isn't he?"

"He's Asti Rynax," was all Helene could respond. "Worse is where he thrives."

"I wear the gown to go to town and never frown while looking down."

Mila repeated the phrase—again—not hearing any difference in how she said it from how Mister Gin said it.

She could definitely hear a difference between how she said it and how Helene did. Helene's was especially bad.

"Hel, you aren't even trying," Mister Gin said.

"Can't we just do the same thing we did at the Emporium? Where I don't bother?"

"No, you have to pull this off."

"We're not even sure what we're each supposed to be doing," Helene said. "Go to this feast, play at being nobility. We can't even do our accents, let alone behavior."

"We have to learn about manners and bowing and all that, don't we?" Mila asked.

"Yes, most likely," Mister Gin said with a sigh. They had been at it all morning, and while Mila felt she was getting it, this process still seemed somewhat hopeless. "I have to basically give you a year's worth of finishing school—and a lifetime of indoctrination—in two days."

"Finishing school?" Helene asked. "I don't even want to know about that."

"Let me think," he said. He got up from the planning table and went to the stove for more tea. "I don't suppose there's anything stronger than cider in here?"

"You'd have to ask Josie," Helene said. She paced about, heading by the door to the stables. "What are those two up to in there?" Mila had been around when Verci arrived in the morning on his crutches, with Almer in tow, and then sent Almer off. Ever since then he had been holed up with Kennith, sending Vellun out to shop for supplies.

"Verci said he had to do a lot of building," Mila said. "He's got a plan."

"Everybody has a plan," Helene said.

Mister Gin came back over. "All right, table accents for now. Mila, you at least have the fundamentals for it. Helene, I . . . we'll figure it out."

"So what do we do now?"

"Small talk. Election is today—"

"Did you vote?" Helene asked.

"Saints, no," Mister Gin said. "No one cares what I think. But people will expect you to be versed on it."

"Us?" Mila asked. "Can noble ladies vote? Because we can't."

"Go vote, Pilsen!" Verci yelled from the stable.

Mister Gin ignored Verci. "No, but the lords and other men there will probably want to hear you say things that they'll approve of."

"Which would be?" Helene said.

"Probably some variant of 'I know it's poor taste to politicize the tragedy, but if it means more Traditionalists in the Parliament, then at least some good will come from it.'"

"Tragedy?" Mila asked. She had heard Asti mention something like that earlier. "What tragedy?"

Helene answered. "Some swells in the Parliament were murdered, or something." She shrugged. "I just wrap sandwiches in the newsprints, I don't read them."

"It doesn't matter what the tragedy is, honestly," Gin said. "There's always *some* tragedy."

"Fine," Mila said. "Is there anything else, Mister Gin?"

"I've been trying to remember what a Feast of Saint Jontlen even is. I don't think I've ever seen one or . . ."

"I don't even know who Saint Jontlen is," Mila said.

"The bloody saint," Helene said. "That's what I remember."

"The bloody feast," Mister Gin said, snapping his fingers. Then he stopped. "No, I don't remember. Damnation and sins. It'll come to me." He sat down for several moments, a blank look on his face.

"Mister Gin?" Mila prompted. "What should we—"

He looked up at her. "We should get to the Elk Road Shack. We need to—but I was supposed to meet you on the street, and . . ." He stopped and shook his head. "That was yesterday. Today is lessons of ladyship. Sorry."

Helene moved a bit closer. "Things we need to know for this party? Table manners? Dancing?"

"Dancing!" Mister Gin said enthusiastically. "There's no possible time. If you're asked to dance, politely decline. Saints and damnation, we need to know where we're supposed to be from. That would help. Where is Asti?"

"He's meeting with the lady," Helene said. "He should be here in the afternoon."

"Then we'll know more," Gin said. "All right, girls, on your feet."

Mila stood up from her chair. "I thought we weren't going to do dancing."

"No, something far more important," Gin said. "Walking."

"I know how to walk," Mila said.

"Yes, like a common urchin, the two of you," Gin said. He stood up himself, spine straight and chin high. "Now to walk like a proper lady. Which reminds me, at five bells we're going to see a friend of mine to get you proper gowns and shoes."

Mila sighed and got on her feet. "This will be worth it, yes?"

Helene shrugged. "I suppose we at least get to go to a fancy party. That's something."

Once he had arrived, Asti spent the morning pacing in the ruined safehouse, his hands continually going to the knives at his belt. She would be here, and he could just slice her open the second he saw her. That would be good.

Except that wasn't the plan.

But she would get what she deserved.

He found himself drumming his fingers on the handle of the knife.

Maybe she did deserve it. Maybe she had been ordered. She could have defied the orders, told him. Or maybe that line was just sewage, keep him guessing.

He hadn't slept well the whole night, eventually wandering over to Kimber's so he could get a good look at the rest of the mail she was holding for him. It was all rubbish. Even *The Veracity Press* one was probably rubbish, but he wrote back to them to come meet him at Kimber's at five bells.

That should keep him from trying to kill Liora. He had an appointment later, he didn't have time to kill her and ruin the rest of the plan.

Killing her would ruin the plan.

He kept telling himself that.

The door opened and he drew his knives before he even knew what he was doing.

"Hey, hey, none of that." It was Almer.

"What are you doing here?"

Almer hauled a small crate into the kitchen, putting it on the table. "Verci sent me with this baby and my own stuff."

"But why?"

Almer rummaged through the crate, taking out a strange contraption of Verci's. Asti didn't recognize it. "Because he felt you needed someone with you for this, and thought I was the best choice."

"Why you? No, Liora's going to be here, she doesn't know about you and—"

"Verci said you'd say that, and he said to tell you 'we should bump to hide the pull.' I don't know what that means."

Asti knew, and he even understood what Verci meant. "He means letting Liora see you is a way to get leverage on her. Tells her we have a crew and she doesn't know the half of it."

"Fine, whatever," Almer said. He took out two vials and handed them to Asti. "Drink those down."

"What are they?" He had had far too much of Almer's nasty-tasting sludge for one purpose or another.

"First one's my own special distillation of the oils from *phatchamsdal* and *hassper*. Calm your nerves, because you're a wreck."

"No, I need to stay sharp—"

"You're already razor sharp, and you're going to cut yourself, now drink it." Asti did, and found it oddly pleasant to the tongue. Not like most of Almer's concoctions.

"How long will it—"

"Shouldn't be too long, nor will it last long either," Almer said. "That's the mild one. Just enough so you aren't getting stabby at the slightest twitch." He poured a liquid into the top of Verci's device.

"I'm not—"

"I saw you when I came in."

"Fine," Asti said, looking at the second vial. "And what's this one?"

Almer pulled out a vial of powder. "That's the antidote to the poison I'm about to make." He poured the powder in the hole and then slammed the lid shut.

Asti drank down the second liquid. It tasted not entirely unlike what a dead horse smelled like.

"That was horrible."

"Yeah," Almer said. "I just took it myself a few minutes ago."

"And why?"

Someone was opening the door. Almer took note and grabbed a handle on the device, squeezing it.

"Because we need some protection right now, I gather."

Liora walked in, this time fully in her aspect as Lady Henterman. Regal dress, dazzling jewelry, long clothes, and a ridiculous hat with a veil. "Well now," she said, maintaining the accent. "I'll have you know my driver is down there with a whistle, and he will call for Constabulary if anything untoward occurs."

"Stop it, Liora," Asti said. Almer's concoction was working, because while he did still want to slice her throat open, it was more of an abstract idea rather than a pressing urge. And the beast, for once, was quiet.

"I have to maintain some illusion," she said, now normally. "Who's the rat boy?"

"Insurance," Almer said with a sneer. "See this handle I'm holding shut? I let go, the vents on this open and fill this room with *nilari* smoke. Are you familiar with that?"

Liora looked slightly fazed. "I am."

"Good," he said. "So talk to Asti and don't give me a reason to let go."

"Like stabbing him," Asti added.

"Yes, like that," Almer said.

"I see you haven't changed in the important ways," Liora said. "Did you vote?"

"Always," Asti said. Not that his opinion on the Sauriyan Chairs of the Parliament and the city's 15th District Alderman really made a difference, but he stopped in Saint Bridget's and did it. Dad always said, "Voting don't matter, but it lets you gripe with authority."

"You, rat boy?"

"Minties down the line," Almer said.

"I would have pegged you both for Salties or Frikes . . ."

"This isn't why you're here," Asti said.

"No, of course not." She cautiously reached toward a chair and pulled it over to sit down. "I'm guessing your brother is not here right now. Or the lady with the crossbow."

"They're elsewhere, preparing for the party."

"So you've agreed to my proposal."

"I really need to know what the proposal is," Asti said. "Obviously, you want to use me at the party to get further intelligence on your . . . husband." The absurdity of it was almost amusing. Almer's potion really was working. "How did you manage that?"

"The usual way. He was looking for a wife, and I was available."

"Presenting yourself as of noble birth, minor enough and from somewhere far enough away to not be questioned."

"Third daughter of the fourth daughter of the Earl of Greckinvale."

"Where is Greckinvale?"

"Utterly fictional, but supposedly in northern Patyma. That's the trick, you know, the fictionality."

Asti shook his head. "Don't tell me my own tradecraft. I need to know because we're going to need to use it. Helene and I will play your cousins who have come down from Greckinvale."

"You want to be related to me? And her as well?" Liora looked a bit put off.

"Minimizing our fictional earldoms is probably for the best," Asti said. "Plus I imagine you want to minimize the potential scandal of you inviting a strange man to your husband's party."

She sighed. "You're right. That would look better. Though I did relish the idea of a good scandal."

"Why would you?" Almer asked.

"Because, rat boy, this particular assignment is deadly dull." She gave Asti a sly grin. "Frankly, your attempt to murder me was the most fun I've had in ages. I have missed you dearly, Asti."

"Stow that," Asti said. He didn't need to hear her sewage, and through the calming haze of Almer's drug, he could see it for the clear, naked attempt at manipulating him that it was. He wasn't going to rise to it. "Tell me what we need to know about the party itself, and what our objectives are."

"The party is the Feast of Saint Jontlen. That's going to give us our chance."

"How can that give us a chance?" Asti asked.

"Do you know how the feast goes? What it entails?"

"Never had the pleasure," Asti said. "Though I know the story of Saint Jontlen." After that old soldier had compared Asti himself to the saint—"red-eyed and anointed in blood"—he had done further reading. Kimber had been quite pleased to go over that particular Tale of the Saints with him.

Jontlen had been an old soldier who had become a priest, taking charge of an orphanage in the outskirts of a small town. The orphanage had been sacked by slavers, all the children abducted, and Jontlen left for dead. But Jontlen tracked the slavers down, and singlehandedly killed them all, calling out "Free! Free! All free!" to the children before he succumbed to his wounds.

Asti wasn't sure how a one-man killing spree qualified someone for sainthood. Kimber had said it wasn't about the killing, it was how he had been driven by godliness beyond his mortal endurance so he could save the innocent. Several stories of the saints involved rescuing children from bad men.

He had no idea how that translated to a feast, though.

"The meal is laid out—all sorts of dishes made to suggest bloodiness," Liora said.

"What?" Almer asked.

"Things like roasted lamb, sausages, beets, and berry pies. As much bright red as you can get. All placed out on a table in the center of the ballroom."

"I'm not seeing. . . ."

"Then most of the guests—really, it's supposed to be children, but this party will be adults playing the game—"

"This doesn't shock me," Asti said. "Most nobles act like children."

"True." She sighed ruefully. "Especially Lord Henterman. But the guests all go hide, all over the house. Then the host—that's Nathaniel."

"Of course."

"The host plays Saint Jontlen. He goes around and collects the 'guards'—some of the guests play the slavers—"

"Of course they do," Asti said. This whole thing was a strange and morbid way to celebrate slavery and slaughter. "Go on."

"He'll bring them back to the table, and feed each of them a bit of the food with his bare hands, making a point of smearing it on their faces and his hands."

"Symbolizing Jontlen's bloody rampage," Asti said.

"And once he's done that, he calls out 'Free! Free!' to the household."

"And all the people hiding come running out, right?" Asti said. "Like the children ran to Jontlen as he died."

"You've shot the bunny," she said, with an infuriating wink.

"So our opportunity is when we're supposed to hide,"

Asti said. "Henterman will be focused on his game, and we can go through the trapdoor in your wardrobe to get into his study."

"So you did find that," she said wryly.

"Why did you think I was in there?" Asti asked. He then realized he might be giving too much away, at least in terms of what his real agenda was. Before she could ask why he wanted into the study, he gave her a fake answer. "Trying to find the best way to Henterman's safes."

"You think he has safes in there?"

"We're not in this for the challenge of it," Asti said.

"Our crew needs a good score, lady," Almer added.

"Well," she said curtly. "Once we're in there, you can get whatever you want for your . . . score. And then we'll part amicably."

"As in we don't try to kill each other once the gig is done?"

"I'll point out, dear Asti, that I've not actually tried to kill you."

"Don't worry," Asti said. "I haven't really tried, either."

She stood up. "Then we are arranged. I'll see you at the feast."

"Cansling," Asti said. "As your cousin, my name will be Cansling. And Helene will be Jennidine."

"You always loved making up your character," she said. "You should know that I'm Anaphide in that household. Lady Anaphide Henterman."

Asti gave her a mock bow. "Lady Henterman. What's your old family name?"

"Onterren."

Asti nodded. Cansling and Jennidine Onterren. He locked that in.

"Get to work on your aspect," she said. "No one can see a hint of Mister Crile in you."

"Please," Asti said. "I'm a professional."

She rolled her eyes, and then with a slight shift of her shoulders, fully became Lady Henterman again, gliding out the door.

"Well, that was horrible," Almer said. "I was of half a mind to let go of the handle just to kill her."

"Do we need to disarm this thing?" Asti asked.

"Yeah," Almer said. "Probably for the best. There's three pins on the bottom there."

Asti noticed the pins, familiar with Verci's typical designs. He slid them into place, and Almer let go of the handle.

"So this stuff that you had me take," Asti said. "That . . . that was a big help."

"Glad I could help," Almer said. "I'm going to warn you, though—"

"Of course there's a downside."

"When you come down, it'll probably hit you hard. So be ready for it."

"And I suppose I can't just take more."

Almer touched Asti on the chest, feeling around for a moment. "Yeah, I don't recommend it. While you're calm, your heart is pounding like a hummingbird. It can only take so much of that."

Asti scowled. "Fine. I just thought—"

"I know, Asti," Almer said. "I know what you need. Right now, this is the best I have, and you shouldn't abuse it."

"I understand," Asti said. He wasn't sure if he truly did, or if it was the drug talking. "What about the antidote? Any side effects I should know about?"

Almer nodded, rubbing his stomach a bit, and then let out a noxious belch. "We're both going to be doing that for the next hour or so. Sorry."

"You've done worse to me," Asti said. "Come on, let's get back to the neighborhood. Plenty to do."

Chapter 18

VERCI HAD DRAFTED OUT sketches of a new brace for his foot, one that would let him walk without hurting himself. But he needed parts to get building, and that meant waiting for Vellun to get back. So, in the meantime, he worked with Kennith on trying to improve the spring-engine carriage. It had been an ongoing project of theirs, and if they got something working in time for this gig, all the better. It wasn't like escaping at high speeds wouldn't come in useful.

The improvements to the spring engine weren't working. Verci had tried several different tweaks and changes, and Ken had come up with quite a few good ideas, but nothing they tried gave them the results they wanted. It didn't help that, without Julie, they had a blazes of a time cranking it up to its maximum torsion. So they couldn't do a proper test. Nor could they really test it in the stable of the safehouse.

The problem was, the engine always only had one charge. Let it loose, and it unwound like mad, sending the carriage off like a sinner. That had limited use. Without a flattened street, without a straight path, like they had after the Emporium, it was pointless. Turning it at full speed would be a nightmare. Verci had tried to make a device that could clamp the torsion release, so they could accelerate in controlled bursts, but it kept getting torn apart.

Nothing worked.

"What about a series of smaller springs, working in concert?" Kennith asked.

Verci tried to visualize it. "I see what you're saying. Like how eight horses could pull a carriage faster than just two. But I wonder if they can generate enough push."

"Working together, they should," Kennith said. "And not have so much torque that it shatters the clamp."

"I can't see how we can build that in two days, though," Verci said.

Kennith nodded and went over to one of his horses. Edlan, his favorite. "You're not out of a job yet, boy."

"What about pure muscle power?" Verci asked. "Like a pedalcart?"

"You would need several people pedaling."

"Or some serious gear work," Verci said. Then an idea hit him. "Or—this might be it. We've been struggling about controlling or containing the spring power once it's released."

"Right, because you only get one shot."

"Yes, but what if—" Gears and pulleys and machinery were already swirling and assembling in his head, making it hard to actually form words with the ideas he was having. "What if instead we focus on recharging the spring quickly within the carriage. With the pedal work!"

"Leg power, torqued with the gear work," Kennith said. "I think I can see it working."

Verci grabbed his notebook and started sketching. "And if you had two or three springs, then you could be charging one with the pedal while discharging the power of the next. It'd be complicated."

"Too complicated to build in two days?"

"Likely, but until I can make a new boot, what else are we going to do?" Verci said. "We need some old pedalcarts. Where is Vellun?"

"You sent him to the market an hour ago."

Verci noticed little Tarvis sitting in the corner, cutting

away at a block of wood with his knife. "How long have you been there?"

"Long enough to see you guys being stupid. Why mess with this? Build a clever trap, that's what I'd do."

"Clever traps won't help us here," Verci said. "Those are what you have to keep someplace safe, like our defenses here."

"I didn't see any traps," Tarvis said.

"You're not supposed to," Verci said. "Point is, we're running a job out east, and they're the ones who'll have traps for us."

Suddenly an idea hit him. A crazy idea, but an idea nonetheless.

"Kennith, you've got gardening tools, right?"

"Yeah," Kennith said. "Over at the inn. Why?"

"Oh, we need to get them, and get to work. The kid has given me a huge idea."

Asti helped Almer with carrying his crate of chemicals and Verci's contraption back to his shop at the corner of Holver Alley and Rabbit. "This thing is actually pretty interesting," Almer said of the device once they got in the store. "I should talk to Verci about making some modifications to it."

"What sort of modifications?"

"Well, there are causes for, say, aerated or steamed medication. Something like this could come in handy. It's not just for poison on a deadhand trigger."

"Speaking of medication," Asti said. "Should I be feeling like ants are walking on the inside of my skin right now?" That was an understatement to the sensations he was having.

"How bad is it?" Almer asked.

"I mean, I don't want to claw my flesh off in a fit of madness, if that's what you're asking. Especially if you tell me it will pass in, say, an hour or so."

Almer went behind the counter of his shop and took out a notebook. "I can tell you that, but I'd just be saying things to placate you. I honestly don't know for certain."

"You don't know?" Now Asti felt his temper clawing up

from inside his gut. "You gave me something and you don't know what it'll do to me?"

"Hey, Rynax, chemistry is more complicated than that. Every person's body and mind is different. What that drug does to you won't be what it does to Verci, and it certainly wouldn't do the same to Helene or Josie. I got kicked out of the Apothecary Guild for even bringing this up."

"That was why?"

Almer looked around sheepishly, and wrote more things in his notebook. "It was related to that."

Asti had long known that Almer wasn't a proper member of the Apothecary Guild—a fact that Almer tried to keep quiet, but Asti had figured it was the reason a man as gifted at chemicals as Almer would have a run-down west side shop.

"So what can I do?" Asti asked. "I imagine that I can't keep taking doses of that stuff."

"No," Almer said. He tapped his charcoal stylus on the desk. "But did you feel it was helpful at first?"

"I didn't slice Liora open, so I suppose," Asti said.

"Right. Look, ever since the night of the fire, when you, you know . . ."

"Went feral and killed two boys right here?"

"Yeah, that . . . I knew that you had some real problems. And since we've been working on all this together, helping you out has been on my mind."

"And so you gave me that drug. It's not a cure."

"Nothing is going to be a cure," Almer said hotly. "Saints, the body is a bizarre balance of organs and fluids and we don't know how much of it even works. Do you know what your pancreas does?"

Asti was a bit dumbfounded. "I don't even know what it is."

"An organ you have right here," Almer said, pointing to Asti's side. "I know what it is, but I don't know what it does in your body, or why you need it. Nobody does."

"What does—"

"My point is this, Asti. If I don't know what your pancreas does, then I don't know what this stuff does to your pancreas." He held up the vial. "Good, bad, I don't know. Is that making your skin crawl? I don't know."

"So what good are you—"

Almer tapped Asti in the center of his forehead. Asti fought down the urge to grab Almer's finger and break it. "Now think about how anyone's brain is so much more complicated and unknown. A lot more than your pancreas or heart. I know this stuff does something to your brain, but I'm not sure what. I'm definitely not sure why. But I'm doing what I can because I want to help you."

Asti tamped down his anger. "I get that, Almer. I appreciate it, I do. But . . ."

"Don't just give you things to drink without discussing it?"

"Yeah."

"Fine. What I gave you was what I considered a quarter dose. A test. We need to test these things, that's how the science needs to work."

Asti sighed. Almer deserved some truth if he was doing this. As much as he didn't want to say it, he made himself push the words out. "Even if my brain wasn't broken by science?"

"Magic or something like it?"

Asti nodded. It would be too hard to explain otherwise, how Poasian telepaths barraged his mind with psychic attacks until he shattered, creating the feral, animal beast in his head. It was nearly impossible to articulate it.

Almer gave a sly smile. "Let me tell you something I know, Asti. I've seen some things in my time, and magic— and things like it—can do some crazy things that defy the order of nature and science. But in the long run? *Science wins.*" He held his hand up in the air. "A mage can make something soar up high, but as soon as he runs out of juice . . ." He slammed his hand onto the counter. "Gravity. Science."

"I don't know if this makes me feel better or not."

"It won't. Look, the dose I gave you, it helped you out for a couple hours. The aftereffects should be about the same. I won't give you anything to help with that, because— then you have one chemical hitting another and . . . who knows what it's doing to you. If you're still feeling the same by around sunset, come back and we'll talk."

"Fine," Asti said. Knowing that it should pass, that helped. "Thanks for today, though. I mean it."

"Go on," Almer said. "You've got things to attend to, and I might get some business today. Saints know none of this that I do for you all is cheap."

"Well, make sure Josie gets you covered for your costs," Asti said. "I'll have a word with her if she's being difficult."

Almer frowned. "Do you trust her?"

"I trust that Josie will be Josie. She's in this not out of some moral duty, but because this whole business has challenged her power and her stake."

"Yeah, but you've got your sharp eye on her?"

"Sure, yeah," Asti said. "If this is about money, I'll—"

"No, it's—" Almer shook his head. "I'm following your lead here. If you've got it, that's good. I'll see you later."

Asti made his way up Holver Alley—the first time he had been in weeks. The husk of the Rynax Gadgeterium, across the way from Almer's shop, had become marked up with paintjobs from a few different local boys. Asti noticed a Scratch Cat symbol, as well as a couple he didn't know. They'd have to do something about that.

The rest of the Alley was much the same way: vandalized, burned-out husks or torn down, empty lots with exposed brickface of the Kenner Street buildings behind it. Plenty of shops, homes long gone. Plenty of dead friends and neighbors.

Until he reached the other end of Holver Alley, where it hit Ullen. There, just a bit away from the corner—right where Win Greenfield's locksmith shop was, where Asti and Verci had lived in the Greenfields' spare apartment, was a brand-new house. Bright and vibrant, surrounded by cinders and ash.

"How the bloody blazes did I not see this before?" Asti said out loud. Was this part of the plan behind the burnout? Was this house the first step in whatever the Andrendon Project was?

There were a couple of guys—masonry workers—laying out a walkway up to the front door. "Hey, oy," Asti said as he came up. "When did this get built, and who owns it?"

One of the mason guys shrugged. "We're not from here, pal."

"Yeah, but who hired you?"

Another shrug. "Our boss tells us to come out here, do a job, we do the job. Ain't your business."

Asti felt the beast growling and stirring in his skull. "Who's your boss?"

"Keep walking, pirie," the guy said.

The beast woke up completely, and Asti had to bite his lip to keep it on the chain. It hit him a bit harder than he had expected, and he realized he had been standing, staring and fuming at the masonry workers for a minute, while they glared back.

"Something troubles you, Asti Rynax?"

Asti turned around to see Nafath, looking especially out of place in the middle of the street. Asti had never seen the man out of his shop, and with his milky-pale complexion and pitch-black coat and trousers, Nafath was especially singular in appearance. Asti almost wanted to laugh at the idea that this man was a fellow spy, since he was anything but inconspicuous.

"Are you following me, Nafath?" Asti asked.

"Hardly," Nafath said. "I have my own business, you know. There is always hunger in these streets for the things I sell."

"Spices or information?" Asti asked, brushing past him.

"Both, of course," Nafath said. "Though I still have some of the former waiting for you."

"I don't need spices," Asti said.

"You might be surprised what you need, Mister Rynax," Nafath said. "But for now, I'll leave you to that little thing seeking your attention." He went off.

There was a tug on his sleeve. "Hey, you. You're the Butcher, hmm?"

Asti looked down to the little boy who was pulling on his shirt. "The what?" The boy was familiar, now that he got a look at him. "What is it, Tarvis?"

"I'm Jede. Tarvis is my brother. You seen him?"

Asti nodded. The beast still howled, his skin still crawled with spiders, but he pushed that all down. It had taken the telepaths of Levtha Prison many days to beat him; he could hold up through this. "He said he got out of Gorminhut."

"Me too. Just took me a bit."

Asti pulled the kid away from the house, back out onto Ullen. "So you looking for him?"

"Or Miss Bessie. You know where they are?"

"I do, but it's a secret, kind of."

"Oh, the warehouse place with the Old Lady," Jede said. So much for secret safehouses.

"Yeah, you know it?"

Jede nodded. "I was gonna go looking for him there next."

"Last I knew, your brother was there. But I need you to do me a favor."

"What's that?" Jede didn't look like he enjoyed doing favors.

"When you go there, tell *my* brother . . ."

"That's the Baker?"

The Butcher and the Baker. Asti would have been amused if he wasn't beating down the urge to stab everyone he could see and then peel off his own flesh.

"Yeah. Tell him to meet me at Kimber's at five bells, so we can see the newssheet guys together. You got that?"

"Kimber's, five bells, newssheet guys. Fine."

"And make sure they feed you," Asti called out, as Jede was already scampering away. His own stomach was empty. Maybe eating something would improve his situation. It probably wouldn't hurt. He headed over to Kimber's to do a bit of scientific research of his own.

"How much are these dresses going to cost?" Helene asked as they made their way down into Seleth proper. Gin was leading the way to his "friend", while she and Mila trudged behind him.

"That's not your worry," Gin said. He had been annoyed with them most of the damned day, probably because neither of them were getting those blasted fancy accents or noble postures right. Blasted waste of time. But the day had been too much work, not enough food, and now they had to get their stupid dresses for the blazing party. But, according to Gin, they first had to get money from their creditor. Josie had gone off somewhere, but Gin knew where the creditor was and how to get the money. At least, that's what he said.

"I worry," Helene said. "Maybe we're spending way too much of our shares on chasing this sewage. It's not like this will be sure to have a payout at the end."

"I thought some things were more important than a pay-out."

"Principles are fine, but I also need to live."

"Hel." Mila nudged her as they walked, her head bowed down. "You're armed, right?"

"Yeah," Helene said. She was still walking with the hip-hanger and The Action under her coat. "Why are you acting strange?"

"I spotted a couple Scratch Cats walking the same way as us. And a couple others from that other gang."

Helene glanced behind her, but didn't see anything unusual. "You sure?"

"Pretty sure."

"I don't know what we can do about that," Helene said. "It's a crowded street, they aren't going to try anything."

"That other gang was shaking Junk Avenue on a crowded street."

That didn't sound good. "And are you armed?"

"Two knives and a rope."

"A rope is not a proper weapon."

"Says you," Mila said. "Killed Tyne with one."

Helene rolled her eyes. "Gin, are we almost there?"

"Right here," Gin said, coming up onto a block of narrow, cramped buildings. "I should go up by myself," he said, getting a letter out of his pocket.

"I ain't waiting here on the street," Helene said. She glanced back down the street. Now she spotted the Scratch Cats. Four of them, cooling their boots on the front stoop just across the street.

"Me either," Mila said.

"Fine. But let me speak."

He led them through one door up a stairwell that was

barely wide enough for one person to go up it. Julien probably wouldn't be able to fit.

"How is a letter of credit different from a goldsmith note?" Mila asked.

Helene had no idea. This whole credit holder thing never made a blasted bit of sense to her. Apparently you paid some guy to hold your money so that you could tell him to pay someone else, or give you a bit of your own money.

Because holding onto your own money was just too sensible.

"Mister Kannic," Gin called out as they entered the fetid-smelling office. All the window shades were pulled shut, so only the barest creeps of sunlight found their way in, not that Helene wanted to be able to see anything in better detail. She already saw that the desk in the corner had more than one half-eaten meal rotting away. Helene couldn't believe that anyone who had access to large sums of cash would submit themselves to being in a room like this, unless Kannic was the type who liked this atmosphere.

A man with pocked skin and patchy hair came shuffling out from behind a curtain. "Yeah, what, what?" he asked, his accent indecipherable to Helene.

"I have a letter of credit . . ."

"Course you do, that's why anyone comes up here." He came closer, sucking on his own lip. "You need some coin to pay for this fine bit of business." He nodded at Helene and Mila.

"No, I—"

"Hey, yeah, I get it, what. She's a ripe plum, for definite." He leered at Helene, and then looked at Mila. "Plum and peach, plum and peach. Well, indeed."

"Please let me shoot him," Helene said, reaching under her coat to put her hand on The Action.

"Hey, what, what," he said, holding up his hands. "Ain't my peach and plum. All for him, all for him." He went back over to Gin. "Oh, yeah, now I got a look at you. I know you. Why are you out strolling with this plum and peach when we know you are more of a sausage man?"

Gin shook the letter at him. "We need two hundred fifty crowns, Mister Kannic."

Kannic took the letter. "I'm just saying, does a heart good, seeing an old parcel like you, walking around with some finery like these birds. Gives a man hope."

"You must live on a lot of hope," Helene said.

"I ain't too proud," he said. He went over to the desk and pulled out a ledger. "Give me a tick."

Helene went over to Gin, grabbing his arm. "Our money is entrusted with this crumb of sewage?"

"We had to have someone who wouldn't ask trouble-some questions," Gin said. "That minimized our options."

"Oy, oy, parcel," Kannic said, looking at his ledger. "You got a big dyno here."

"What is he saying?" Mila asked.

"That isn't possible," Gin said. "Our line of credit—"

"Is dyno. Denied. No."

"What does that mean?" Helene asked.

"It means no money," Kannic said.

"You don't give it or we don't have it?" Mila asked.

"Either, both. It's the same, really."

"No, no," Gin said. "I'm certain, I'm certain. . . ."

"Our money is here," Helene said, opening up her coat to show The Action, resting her hand on its stock. "I expect you to deliver it."

"Hey, oh, what what?" he said. "It ain't how it works. No hinth, you hear?"

"Where's our money?" Helene asked.

Gin shook his head. "I distinctly recall going over the numbers—"

"And I said dyno!" Kannic spat on the floor. "Absie!"

Absie—at least who Helene presumed was Absie—lumbered out from the back room. He was easily Julien's size, with hands as big as Helene's head. He rubbed those giant hands together. "There a problem, boss?"

"These folks are dyno and they seem to think a crossbow would change that, what?"

Absie came over to Helene, towering over her. "Are you engaging in threats against my employer?"

"I don't make any threats," Helene said, hovering her right hand over the hip-hanger. This guy wasn't about to chase her off right now. Gin was staring at the letter, muttering about how he was certain that it should be right.

"We just want to know what is going on with our account," Mila said. "We're confident that we have good credit. Perhaps there was a clerical error?"

"Are you challenging my acumen?" Absie asked. "My record-keeping is exemplary."

"He's the bookman?" Helene asked.

"And a damn good one," Absie said. "Which account?"

Kannic chuckled. "The, um . . ." He then just made a little whistling sound.

"That one?" Absie said. "Closed down."

"But—" Mila said.

"Closed down. Talk to your matron if you have issues." He flexed his fingers for a moment. "Now, please move along, before I am forced to be violent."

"He'll do it, what you know," Kannic said.

"Fine," Helene said. "But don't think I don't have my eye on you."

"Oh, your eye, what? I ain't afraid."

"You have our money and my eye," Helene said. "That should make you nervous." She stormed out, and Mila was right on her heels with Gin stumbling out behind them. Since they went in, the sun had dropped down behind the buildings, and the lamplighters, as usual, hadn't gotten around to illuminating this part of town. The whole street was in dusky shadow.

"That ain't right," Helene said to Mila. "You're with me on this?"

"I agree," Mila said. "We should tell Asti."

Gin shook his head. "Now, now, it wasn't too bad. Perhaps we have new options. And for the dresses—"

"He said to talk to our matron," Mila said. "Does he mean Missus Holt?"

"Saint Hesprin, he must have," Helene said. She couldn't imagine that Missus Holt, as protective of her privacy and identity as possible, would risk herself to deal with these petty knee-breakers. Was there someone else who would take their money? "You're sure this was right?"

"Of course I am," Gin said.

"You did seem awfully confused, Mister Gin," Mila said.

"Ladies, I'm sure it's just some sort of misunderstanding, and—"

Gin was cut off by a blow to his head, sending him to the ground. One of the Scratch Cats stood behind him, knuckle-stuffers on both hands, looking thrilled with himself for knocking down an old man.

"You shut your mouth!" he shouted. "You all better get ready, because it's time."

"Oh, it's time," another boy said behind Helene. She spun on her heel, sending an elbow back into him. He jumped out of the way before she connected. There were at least four Scratch Cats, by their scars, and four of the other boys. One of those was the one up on Helene. "Time for you all to get yours."

"Didn't I teach you boys something the other day?" Mila snarled back at them. "You need another lesson?"

"Ain't nothing Miss Bessie needs to teach us! We're the Crease Knockers, and we've come to knock!"

"Knock you both around!" another Crease Knocker said. "This is our night, Treggin said!"

Their attention was on Helene and Mila, they didn't notice Gin scramble to his feet and run away like a sinner. For the best. Helene couldn't scrap with these fellows and protect the old man.

"We get ours!" a Scratch Cat said. "You gonna pay, girlies."

"You and that bakery bint!"

Terror had taken hold of Helene's heart, pounding up to her throat. She and Mila were surrounded on all sides, deeply outnumbered. Penned in like dogs. And no one else was on the street, as far as Helene could see. If anyone was around, they were keeping their heads down and ignoring it.

"Walk away, boys," Mila said. Blazes, that girl had some iron in her spine. Even still, Mila had backed up against Helene. Her body was quaking.

"Or?" the Crease Knocker moving in on Helene asked. The mouth-breathing tosser reached out to touch her face.

Helene pushed down her fear and let her anger rule. She whipped up the hip-hanger with her right hand while grabbing the tosser by the head with her left. She pulled his head down on her knee while snapping off a shot at the guy behind him. He was hit in the shoulder, crying out. She smashed the hip-hanger across the head of the tosser who pawed at her, dropping him to the cobblestone. With enough of a hole in the circle of street boys, she grabbed Mila's hand and ran with everything she had.

"Hel, Hel!" Mila was shouting.

"Run!"

She wasn't even sure which way they were going, and the other six boys were right on their heels, hooting and howling at them as they gave chase.

Helene turned into some alley, Mila still shouting in protest as she dragged her along.

"Mister Gin! He just left us!"

"No choice," Helene said, pulling Mila down with her as she dropped behind a refuse bin. It was dark as all depths and blazes back here.

"Why did he—"

"He's an old man, and he's no fighter," Helene said, pulling out the Rynax Action.

"How could he—"

"Ladies! We're going to find you!"

Helene started loading The Action, taking up extra bolts in her shooting hand. "It's good he got away. Now we gotta do the same." She had practiced this, shooting and quick-loading. It was what this crossbow was for. She could do this, if her fingers would stop shaking. If she could see.

"Hel!" Mila managed to shout and whisper at the same time.

"Just let me—"

"The bakery," Mila said. "They said they're doing the bakery."

Raych and her stupid sister. And Verci wasn't anywhere near the place to protect them.

"All right, on my count, I'm going to come up and—"

Hands grabbed Mila and dragged her out from the refuse bin. Mila screamed her head off, and Helene scrambled away from there before a second Scratch Cat pounced on her.

"We're gonna—"

The Scratch Cat didn't finish that thought before earning a bolt in his throat.

Mila twisted in her captor's arms, and before he got a good grip on her, she came up with her knife and sliced open his arm. He cried out, and Mila pushed off from him.

"Come on!" she shouted, running back down the alley. Helene raced with her, reloading her crossbow as they ran. At the mouth of the alley, one of the Crease Knockers was blocking their exit. Helene took a shot, hitting him in the leg. Somehow he didn't drop from that, and Helene put her shoulder down to charge into him.

She barreled into his chest, and Mila hit him in the waist. He hit the cobblestone like a bag of onions. Helene didn't stop, charging down the street as fast as her feet could take her. She was on Colt Road, and turned to run over to Junk Avenue, not stopping until she was at the bakery.

"Mila, you need to—"

She turned to look at the girl, but Mila wasn't there.

"Mila!"

No sign of her. The night had already gotten absurdly dark. They must have gotten separated, or Mila was grabbed.

Helene loaded another bolt. She had to get back over there, find Mila, find Pilsen, get them both out of the street. It's what Asti would do. Asti would kill them all and save his crew. He said he wanted her to hold them together. That's what it meant.

A scream pierced through the air behind her. Instinctively, Helene turned toward it. She didn't see where it came from, but she saw something else that chilled her bones.

The door of the bakery had been kicked open.

Chapter 19

VERCI HAD DECIDED THAT leaving his chair behind had been a mistake. With his crutches, he could
hobble around effectively enough, but being upright for
more than a few minutes would become excruciating. He
hadn't gotten any more pain reliever from Almer, either.
But hopefully once he built the new brace, all that would
change. Hopefully.

What really convinced him of the error of neither re-
trieving or rebuilding the chair was heading over to the
North Seleth Inn with Kenneth. It was only two blocks,
shouldn't have taken more than a few minutes to head over.
Instead it was a painful slog, even with him pushing himself
hard through his agony. He didn't want to leave Kennith by
himself, exposed on the street. Sticks were still out in heavy
numbers, and one of them even stopped them to give Kennith a bit of hassle. Fortunately, this guy was not looking for
a Ch'omik man based on Lieutenant Covrane's sketches.
He was just being difficult. But that kept them both standing on the corner for several more minutes.

By the time they arrived at the stables of the North Seleth Inn, Verci was in a cold, clammy sweat.

"Let me put it up," he told Kennith as they got inside. He found a bench and collapsed on it, putting his leg up high.

"No worries," Kennith said. "You and Hel hustled me out of here so quick, I didn't have time to settle myself. Let me get some things, check on the other horses, all that, and I'll hitch up the carriage."

"Fine," Verci said. "I definitely need the time."

"I won't be too long."

Verci was really tempted to undo Gelson's brace and let his foot breathe. He had the idea that it would feel really good, but Doc Gelson also told him not to do anything like that. He was probably pushing himself too hard to let the damn thing heal properly.

Because they were rushing. Everything they were doing was a rush. Even the new brace he'd come up with was a rush.

"Hey."

Verci looked up to see the kid. "What do you want, Tarvis? Why'd you follow us?"

"I'm Jede," he said.

"Tarvis's brother?"

"Yeah, he wasn't at the warehouse."

"You went there?"

"Yeah," Jede said. "Nobody there, and you all were hobbling away. So I followed you here. Thought he might be with you."

Verci didn't remember seeing Tarvis leaving. Was he supposed to watch him? No one told him he was supposed to watch kids. That definitely wasn't part of the deal. He'd have to talk to Mila about that. "I don't know, kid." Where had Mila and Helene gone? Or Josie? He was shocked that she had slipped out.

"Your brother had a message for you," Jede said. "Saw him on the street. Go to Kimber's to meet the newsprint guys."

"What?"

"What he said."

"He say when?"

"Five bells I think."

"Hey, Kennith," Verci called back. "You know the time?"

"Almost five bells, I reckon."

"Rutting saints," Verci said, taking his crutch. "All right, kid, you stay here, stick close to Kennith back there."

"The chomie?" the kid asked.

Verci leaned in, bracing himself a bit on the kid as he got to his feet. "You call him that, you'll get a taste of his riding crop."

"I ain't afraid."

Verci called back. "Kennith! I got to meet Asti. You've got an apprentice here."

Kennith came out, his sleeves rolled up. "Tarvis, what are—"

"I'm Jede."

"Oh. Well, come on. Horses need to be looked after."

"Ugh," Jede said, following Kennith.

Verci limped his way out of the stable and down to the street, slowly heading to Kimber's. He did wonder where Tarvis had gone off to. Possibly to make his one-man assault on Gorminhut Orphanage to rescue Jede, not knowing he had gotten out on his own.

A memory triggered, when he was no older than Jede. Pop had sent him out to practice lightening purses, and he'd been caught by some beet-faced shopkeep. The guy had dragged him into an alley and pulled off his belt to whup Verci within an inch of his life.

Then Asti had shown up. Only eight years old, Asti beaned the shopkeep with two rocks, then raced in and wrenched the belt out of his hand. Dropping him with a kick to the knee, little Asti proceeded to give the shopkeep the whupping he had planned to give to Verci.

"Get running," Asti said then. "I got this."

Verci had lost count of the number of times Asti had been looking out for him. Even when Asti had left to join Intelligence, and Verci was doing window jobs for Josie, Verci would feel invulnerable, unstoppable, because he believed that if he got into trouble, Asti might appear out of any shadow to rescue him.

Somehow he wondered where that faith had gone.

Verci stumbled into Kimber's, his foot throbbing with agony.

"Should you be up already?" Kimber asked as he came into the taproom.

"Probably not. Is he—"

"Right there," she said, pointing to Asti in the back corner. "You two are meeting someone?" She sounded concerned.

"Newsprint folk. Talking about the story of the fire."

"So something respectable," she said. "That's a pleasant surprise."

"Night's early."

Verci sat down with Asti, who pushed a half-eaten striker over to him.

"Not hungry?" Verci asked.

"Yes. But yet also nauseous," Asti said. "Almer."

"He said he was going to give you something. He swore it would be safe."

"Yeah. I think that's probably true, but it wasn't pleasant. Though I think it worked, for the short time."

Verci wasn't sure what to say to that. "So, who are we meeting with?"

"*Veracity Press*. Small thing, up in the north side. Intellectual idealists."

"What does that mean?"

"It means we value truth in the story over what is politic or expedient." A tall man with a wide smile stood over them, with a young woman at his side. "Hemmit Eyairin," he said, extending his hand boldly.

"Asti and Verci Rynax," Asti said, taking it.

"Lin Shartien," the woman cooed in a thick Linjari accent, offering her hand to Verci. "Whatever happened to your foot, Mister Rynax?" She sat down on the chair next to Verci, leaning on the table.

"Accident," Verci said.

"Do they have a decent wine here?" she asked. "Or is this one of those beer and cider holes?"

"I've never been much of a wine drinker," Verci said, feeling like Lin was a bit too close to him for his comfort.

"There is wine," Asti said, signaling Kimber to come over.

"Wine?" she asked as she approached, looking at Hemmit and Lin.

"Whatever red you have," Hemmit said. "Just bring the bottle. Lin?"

"That's fine," Lin said.

"Two bottles," Hemmit said.

Lin pointed to Asti's half-eaten sandwich. "Two of those as well."

Kimber gave a bit of a look to Verci and Asti. Verci presumed she was subtly asking if these two were good for the ten crowns' worth of food and drink they just ordered.

"It's fine," Verci said. "Soft cider, please."

"Soft?" Lin and Hemmit both asked at once.

"My apothecary is giving me something for the pain," Verci said, pointing to his foot. "He says not to mix it with hard drink."

Hemmit shrugged, as if to say that he thought passing up hard drink was a difficult sacrifice. "You wanted to talk about the fire that happened a couple months ago," Hemmit said.

"First, tell us a bit more about you two," Asti said. "Are you two the whole newsprint?"

"We have another partner, plus a small group for actual printing and distributing. We also put out that pamphlet telling the whole story of the Parliament murders." He said this with a lot of pride.

"I'm afraid that didn't really make it down this way," Verci said. The pamphlet certainly didn't. The only news of the murders he had heard was something about dissidents trying to kill members of Parliament who then got captured and arrested. Not anything that concerned or affected him.

"I get that," Hemmit said. "Down here across the river, it's all just northside swells fighting other swells, right?"

"Saints, Hemmit, don't pander to them. They're west-towners, not idiots."

Asti sighed. "And I'm sure part of our neighborhood burning down doesn't really measure up to members of Parliament or political radicals, hmm?"

"On the contrary, that's what really matters," Hemmit said passionately, tapping a finger on the table in emphasis. "These people—you people—you're the ones we need to help bring voice to."

Lin handed over a copy of their newssheet. "Getting your story, the story of this neighborhood, into the hands of people who could make a difference, that matters. That's what we're here for."

Verci looked over the newssheet for a moment. It was what he expected. Fiery rhetoric and idealistic politics. He wondered if either of these two ever had struggled or gone hungry.

Kimber came over with the cider and wine bottles and glasses. Hemmit uncorked it and poured out for himself and Lin. "This is what I know so far," he said. "Fire burns down your alley, where your home and shop are. Fire brigade doesn't come until it's pretty much burned out. Brigade chief spends some mad crowns for a few days around there and disappears."

Verci almost choked on his cider when Hemmit said that. Brigade Chief Yenner didn't so much disappear but was caught and tortured by Asti. Yenner led them to Tyne, which led them to Colevar and Associates, which led them to Andrendon and Lord Henterman. He wasn't sure how much of that should be told to Hemmit and Lin.

"All right?" Lin asked.

"Fine," Verci said.

"Next, most of those lots were bought out above market price. Someone was collecting the land, and that's the mystery."

Asti nodded. "We know this, and you know this. So what's next? What can you discover? What can you do?"

"We can get more people to know it," Hemmit said.

"How does that help us?" Asti snapped back.

"It's been my experience that the city is filled with bits of knowledge," Lin said calmly, pouring herself her own glass of wine. "Several people may know something else about the fire, or the land purchases, but not know what we know. Publication—"

"Puts the bits together, yes," Asti said. "I was hoping you might have some bits we don't have."

"Hard to say," Hemmit said. "We don't know all that you know."

Kimber came with two strikers and put them in front of Lin. "Anything else?"

"Fine for now," Lin said, picking one up and taking a bite, quickly devouring it. Verci was surprised, given how lithe she was.

Asti gave her an odd regard. "She's an eater, isn't she?"

"We all have our appetites," Hemmit said, pouring himself another glass of wine. "Let me tell you why we're interested in what's going on here, and in the two of you." He pulled a sheet of paper out of his satchel. "Did you two vote?"

"Of course," they both said in unison. Verci chuckled. Dad, despite being a thief and a scoundrel, always spoke of voting with a strange combination of disdain and reverence. Verci hadn't taken it seriously until recently. Opening a shop, going straight, being part of the community . . . voting seemed like it ought to be an important part of that.

"Who's your Alderman seat?" Hemmit asked.

"The 15th," Asti said. "It's been Lammart for a few years."

"You voted for Lammart?"

"He's a decent enough bloke for a Uni swell," Asti said.

"What if I told you Lammart isn't going to win the 15th?"

"How could you know that?" Verci asked.

Hemmit placed the paper on the table. It was a map of the city, roughly sketched out. Hemmit tapped on the part of the map that showed North Seleth. "Because they've redrawn the 15th."

Verci turned the map for a better look. The seat districts were drawn out on it, and it was not what Verci remembered. The 15th ought to be Seleth and North Seleth, Benson Court and Holmwood. Instead it was North Seleth and Benson Court, and a part of the neighborhoods on the other side of the river.

"What the rutting blazes is that?" Asti asked. "When did that happen?"

"Very quietly three months ago, when most of the newsprints were busy with that mistress scandal that ousted Strephen. It was a perfect time to get something like this drawn up and approved by the Duke."

"You know what this means?" Asti said, more to Verci than the others. "There's probably enough votes to drown us out, so our seat in the council will go to some north bank tosser who's never stepped foot in this part of town."

Verci looked more closely at the map. "And what was the 15th is now part of four different seat districts. Lammart probably won't get many votes in any of them."

Hemmit nodded. "Whoever takes the 15th won't argue against some sort of project in this part of town that would inconvenience his voters, because he won't need these voters."

Asti let out a low whistle, staring at the map.

"Now," Hemmit said, "you were going to tell us more things you know."

Asti drummed his fingers on the table. Coded message. *How much do we trust them?*

Verci tapped a quick response. *This much.*

"We've heard a bit on our end, something called the Andrendon Project," Verci said. "We really don't know much of what it's about, but it seems the land purchases are tied to that."

Asti nodded. "And something is being built already."

"What?" Verci asked in unison with Lin and Hemmit.

"I just saw it," Asti said. "Someone is building a house there."

"A house?" Lin asked. "Amid the burned-down wreckage?"

Verci was surprised by that. He would have thought, if anything, it would have been something like a factory. Anyone spending the kind of money that Colevar and Associates were offering must have been expecting a high degree of return, and that had to mean something industrial or commercial, like the stuff being built out in Shaleton.

He had presumed that was the whole point.

"Just a single house?" he asked.

"Well, so far," Asti said.

"Where?" Verci asked.

"Right at Win's place."

Verci's stomach turned. "That's horrible."

"A single house hardly sounds like something that would be called 'Andrendon Project,'" Hemmit said.

"Unless it hides something else," Lin said as she gazed off to the distance. "You're sure about that name?"

"It mean something to you, love?" Hemmit asked.

"And it might to you if you had stayed in school," Lin said. "Andrendon. It's an old Saranic myth, or more to say, a myth about Saranus."

"Saranus?" Verci asked. He didn't know what she was talking about.

"Ancient city that was the seat of power in what would become Druthal," Asti said. "It's half-myth in and of itself. Fell to the Kieran Empire a few thousand years ago."

"Why do you know that?"

"Because I know things. But I never heard of Andrendon."

"That's because it's rather obscure, taking a rather deep study into mysticism."

"Oh, was this that course you did with Professor Jilton?"

Lin shuddered. "Horrid. But if I remember correctly, the Andrendon was sort of a magical citywide transportation system. The word even comes from Old Kieran for 'wind riding.'"

Verci was thoroughly lost. "Why Old Kieran?"

Lin took another sip of wine. "Because the only things we really know about Saranus come from Kieran reports."

"What might it—" Asti started to ask, when something crashed through the front window. Glass flew into the taproom, and something hard knocked one of the patrons in the head. He went down like a sack.

Then another came hurtling through. Asti was getting to his feet, but before he was up, Lin was struck. Blood gushed out of her nose as she fell to the floor.

Verci noted the weapon. A brick.

"Graces, what—" Kimber shouted, interrupted by a few more bricks flying into the place. These were wrapped in burning paper. Asti was already launched at her, pulling her to the floor before she was clobbered.

"What is going on?" Hemmit asked.

Verci looked around. For once, Doc Gelson wasn't deep in his cups in the place.

"No idea," he said. "Get her out of here."

Asti was checking on Kimber, who was in something of a panic. "Stay down, stay down!" he shouted.

"Who—why—" Kimber sputtered.

"Verci, fires!" Asti said, pointing to where one of the flaming bricks landed.

"Got it!" Verci bounded over to it, before he remembered he shouldn't be bounding anywhere. He almost collapsed from the pain. Hemmit raced over, taking off his vest and beating down the nascent fire with it.

Hoots and hollers came from outside, and then the race of footsteps as they ran away.

"Is this typical?" Hemmit asked.

"No," Verci said. "I've never seen anything—"

Verci was cut off by a primal yell. Asti was on his feet, knives in hand, eyes red with rage. Before Verci could say anything else, Asti ran out into the night.

Asti was in a deep red haze of rage, but it was his own. The ants crawling under his skin were marching with him. The beast was right at his side, for once a partner. Right now, they all wanted the same things. They wanted to chase those boys, run them down and bleed them out.

They weren't even running, just hooting and howling as they went down Frost, toward Saint Bridget's. At a shop down the way, they threw two more bricks through windows.

Asti charged in, knives out. One of the gang boys wound back to throw another brick, and Asti was on him, stabbing him in the chest and back at once.

"Saint Hesprin!" one boy shouted. "Run, run!"

They dashed off, and Asti was on them. They gave him good chase, they could run fast—but he could run long. He'd run them down. The beast always did.

They turned off down an alley, and Asti was about to dive in there after them when a voice broke through the red haze.

"Mister Rynax! They got him! The sticks nabbed the chomie!"

Asti turned. The kid—Asti forgot his name, but he was

one of Mila's. The kid was running over, out of breath. "The sticks pinched him good."

Asti could barely find voice, forcing each syllable was work. It was almost as if his brain didn't know how to make words anymore. "They got . . . Ken?"

"Three of them, loaded him into a lockwagon!" The kid pointed down the street, where a Constabulary wagon was trundling down the road. Kennith was in there. Kennith had been arrested.

Kennith needed him. If that wagon made it to the stationhouse, that would be the end for him. He'd be in Quarrygate after that, probably for the rest of his life.

Kennith needed him. That was the anchor Asti needed to pull himself out of the red haze and back into his rightful skull.

"I've got it," Asti said, pushing the beast back in its cage. "Go into the pub, tell my brother . . ."

A brick flew out of the alley, cracking the kid across the skull. He hit the ground, blood pouring out of his head.

Asti saw the two hooligans standing halfway down the alley, both howling with laughter. The beast wanted them both, wanted out of its cage, but Asti held it fast.

These two boys, these bastards, were nothing. Not worth losing himself, what scraps of his soul he still had. Instead he scooped up the kid. The poor thing had half his head caved in.

Asti ran back into Kimber's with the boy.

"I've got a kid here! He needs help!"

Verci and Hemmit were up and at it, helping Kimber and the other folks. Verci came limping over, looking like each step was agony but he wasn't going to let it stop him.

"Oh, saints and sinners, is that Jede?" Verci asked.

"I thought his name was Tarvis."

"They're brothers," Verci said, looking meaningfully at Asti.

Asti nodded. "He said Ken's been pinched. I've got to—"

"The sticks have him?" Verci asked. Asti just nodded. "Asti, if they've grabbed him, that's an arrest, lawful. You can't—"

"It's Kennith," Asti said. He took a kerchief out of

Verci's pocket. "He's only in this because of us. I ain't going to let him pay for us, not a chance."

Asti didn't wait for a response, tying the kerchief around his face as he went back out into the street.

He was half a block away before he realized Verci wasn't right at his side.

Of course he wasn't, not with his foot messed up. But Asti couldn't shake the feeling that even if Verci was in top form, he still wouldn't have come.

Chapter 20

MILA WAS ONLY A couple of steps behind Helene
when she was grabbed and thrown against a brick
wall.

She gasped for breath, unable to cry out to Helene as a
fist drove into her chest, another cracking against her nose.
A third blow came, but she gathered her wits enough to
drop out of the way. Her attacker punched the bare brick
wall. He howled in pain, shaking his hand. That gave her a
chance to scramble out of the way, pulling her rope off her
hip. As he turned around to face her, she had it looped
around one hand, and then the other. In half a click she had
his arms bound behind his back.

"Who sent you?" she hissed in his ear.

"These blocks are ours, girl," he said. "None of you or
yours are going to have them."

She kicked his knee, and as he dropped down she yanked
up the rope, dangling him by his arms. A disquieting pop
came from both his shoulders, and he cried out.

"Me and mine?"

"You know what I mean. You and your boys. The Old
Lady. The Rynax crew."

She jumped onto the small of his back. "Who sent you?"

"These streets are Treggin's, and you know it."

"Where is he?"

"I ain't going to—"

His words were cut off by the knife in his throat. Little Tarvis had leaped out of the shadow, burying his blade in the kid. Tarvis looked up at Mila, his eyes full of rage. "He wasn't gonna talk."

"Tarvis!" she shouted, dropping to her knees. She grabbed hold of his shoulders. "Are you—why did you—"

"Because he was a waste of time," Tarvis said.

Mila looked around. She wasn't even sure where she was, the night was so dark, and her head was still spinning. She wasn't sure if there were any other Scratch Cats or Crease Knockers nearby, but she could hear the hollers and cat calls in every direction. They were everywhere.

"We need to get out of here," she said, coiling her rope back up. "We've got to get off the street."

"Street's where I belong," Tarvis said. "Can't find Jede. He's not in Gorminhut no more."

"He's probably looking for you," Mila said. "Let's get to the safehouse. We should—"

"I know what I need to do," Tarvis said.

Mila put on her best strong face, even though her gut was churning with fear and terror. "You and me need to get out of here. Come on."

She started back out of the alley, knife in one hand, rope in the other. Tarvis was right with her, his own knives at the ready.

On the other side, she heard the boys still hooting and hollering, but then another voice broke through, asking something, almost politely.

"You told me you had found Miss Bessie. Why did you waste my time?" He spoke like an educated man, hitting those same vowels and consonants that Mister Gin had been teaching Mila.

"She and that other skirt ran this way—"

"Yes, but you don't have them yet," he said.

"Sorry, Mister Treggin. We chased after—"

The gang boy earned a slap. Possibly for saying Treggin's name.

This was Treggin. He was right here, in the street. Mila signaled to Tarvis to stop.

"Don't be sorry, just keep up with the trouble. That's the main thing tonight. Show these streets who they need to fear."

He started to walk away.

"Tarvis," Mila said quietly. "I'm going after them. Treggin's there, I can't let him go."

Tarvis nodded. "Who do I stab?"

She sighed. She knew she shouldn't bring him into this. But he was here, in it, and she didn't have anyone else. "Anyone who gets in your way. But if things get hairy, run."

She took the rope off her belt and strolled out onto the street, playing at being Miss Bessie, Josie Holt, Asti Rynax—anyone other than Mila Kendish. She had to be someone who could win.

"Hey, fools," she called out. "You think this little brannigan means you own these streets?"

"Brannigan" was a word Mister Gin liked to use. She was pretty sure she used it correctly. Treggin stopped in the middle of the street and turned to her.

"Who in the name of the saints are you?" Treggin asked. The rest of them were dumbfounded for a moment, giving Mila a chance to get a good look at Treggin. He looked like a man out of place, a swell dressed in the costume of a street rat. Teeth too straight, face too clean.

"You know who I am," she said. "Don't act like you don't."

"The infamous Miss Bessie," he said. "The way these boys spoke, I didn't expect a child."

"You're the one they all follow," Mila said. She needed something more in here, something with drama. Keep their eyes on her while Tarvis slipped through the shadows. "But you're just a petty nothing, so I can't see why they mentioned you with such hushed voices."

"Kill her, boys. Leave her body in the middle of the street as a message."

"Yeah, let's—aah!" One of the gang boys cried out, because he had earned Tarvis's knife in his leg. Tarvis stabbed him a couple more times.

"How do you like that trick?" Tarvis yelled.

"Hey, he's—" the second gang boy started, but Mila

leaped on him, wrapping her rope around his neck. Third gang boy tried to stab Mila, but she twisted herself behind the second. The third one ended up stabbing the second by accident. Mila spun the second around so he landed on the first, still howling in pain. She got her hands tangled up in the process, and couldn't get her rope free of his neck before the third was on her.

Fortunately, he had lost his knife in the chest of the second one, and instead pummeled her with punches to the head and chest. Mila took a few hits before she was able to get her arms up, block and dodge.

He jumped at her, wrapping his arms around her body to crush her. "You're gonna die now, missy!"

"Not by you," she hissed. Her arms were held tight, but she had enough leverage to grab her knife off her hip and drive it into his. He squealed and let go.

Mila dropped him with a boot to his tenders.

Out of the corner of her eye, she saw that Tarvis had his boy down. Everyone but Treggin was taken care of. Just the sauce atop the pie remained.

She turned her gaze to Treggin, trying to make her eyes look like Asti's did when he was fully wild.

"You were saying something about a message?" Knife out, she stalked over to him.

He chuckled and twisted his hands. The air twisted with him, and he seemed to make a great blade out of what looked like a broken reflection of the world. "I was."

He swung the blade at her, which she blocked with the knife as best she could, sparks flying everywhere. Asti had never taught her anything for a fight like this. She backed up, away from Treggin and his sword of twisted air. He kept coming to her.

"You thought I would be easy?" he mocked. "Did you have any idea?"

She dove out of the way of another thrust of his magical blade, putting her far too close to the three gang boys on the ground, at least one of whom was dead. He had her rope around his neck. She feinted toward him, grabbing the rope and untwisting it so she could put it to use as quickly as possible.

Treggin was laughing at her. "I don't think that will help you, missy."

"You'd be surprised who I've killed with a rope," she said. She got it loose, but he managed to get a thrust in, hitting her in the shoulder with his strange broken-mirror blade. It only brushed her, but the pain was an explosion of ice throughout her body. Mila screamed and backed away.

"You think you can stand up to me?"

Mila tried to remember, what did Asti say about mages? They needed to concentrate, stay focused.

She had an idea.

She pushed through the pain—she had never experienced anything like what she was feeling in her arm—and whipped out the rope. With a perfect shot, she wrapped it around the bottom his legs.

"You think—" he started, before he realized he was tangled. Mila yanked with everything she was worth, despite her shoulder feeling like it was being eaten by a bear, pulling him off his feet.

He cracked his head on the cobblestone, and the blade vanished.

Hands grabbed her arm. That Crease Knocker that Tarvis had stabbed was trying to grope her, pull her down. He must still have had some fight in him, and Tarvis was running down the street. She responded with her fist in the Knocker's face, again and again, until he let go and dropped back down.

She turned back, but Treggin was gone.

But I've got your face now.

She coiled up her rope and stumbled her way down the street to catch up with Tarvis. Blood was dripping off her arm, her head. They must have gotten more of a piece of her than she realized. Maybe she should get herself looked at. She knew she must be a fright.

But that was all right. These streets were hers now.

Her world started to spin, and she couldn't keep to her feet. "Tarvis!"

She couldn't quite see if the boy heard her.

"Tarvis!" She wasn't even sure if the word escaped her lips as she dropped to the street.

Raych was out in the back alley, sweeping the last of the crumbs from the kitchen floor, when the bakery doors were kicked in.

"Hoo-oo!" a boy's voice called. "Where are you, baker lady?"

"She's here, she's here!"

"We're coming to settle up!"

Three voices. At least three of them. There might be more. They were still in the storefront, so they couldn't see back into the kitchens, to the back alley door.

She couldn't just run, as much as she wanted to. Saints, she had every urge to just run down the alley to the street and find a constable or a neighbor or by Acser himself, even Asti.

But she couldn't run. Lian and Corsi were upstairs. Lian wanted to take a nap with the boy, and if Lian still slept like she had as a girl, that racket didn't rouse her.

Verci had always joked that the bakery, which used to belong to the Old Lady, Missus Holt, was the safest building in all North Seleth. But that was only if someone knew its secrets, and in the past two months Raych had barely learned any of them. She only knew the crashdown room in the apartment upstairs. A very safe place she could hide with Lian and Corsi, if she just could get up there.

Lian had no idea about any of that. She had no chance if those boys went upstairs. She had to get to Lian and the baby first.

There was a hidden staircase from the apartment to the alley. She knew how to get to it from the apartment, but had no clue how to open the door from out here, hidden in the brickwork. Maybe there wasn't a way. Verci had never come up that way.

Raych found herself trembling, her breath quickening. Her heart was like a hummingbird.

She tried to quiet her breath. What would Verci do? She couldn't fight, not with just a broom, or even with the knife on the counter a few feet away.

The knife was just a few feet away. The staircase was a bit farther the other way. She could still move now, get to the stairs. Or get the knife, then the stairs. That's what Verci would want her to do. Get upstairs, get Lian and Corsi, and hide in the crashdown until morning.

The boys were knocking over shelves out in the front. Now was her moment, if she could get her feet to move.

She took two steps in, mouse quiet, like Verci liked to say. Even still, the floorboard creaked as she stepped. It was probably almost inaudible, but to her, it was like a clatter of pans.

"Come on, baker lady. Let's settle some accounts."

She stretched her hand to the counter, slowly wrapping her fingers around the handle of the knife.

"Come out, come out . . ."

One of the boys came through into the kitchen. He grinned wickedly as their eyes met.

"Got her!"

He lunged at her, and she scrambled back to the alley door. She lost grip on her knife, it clattered to the floor as the boy grabbed hold of the front of her apron. She was half out the doorway, so she flailed to grab hold of the door and slam it against him. That loosened his hold, and she was able to pull herself away from him, out to the alley. She started to run to the street.

They were chasing her outside, which meant they weren't going upstairs. That could save Corsi and Lian, if nothing else.

"Baker lady!" the boy taunted. "You can't get away!"

She was almost out of the alley when two other boys emerged in front of her. She tried to stop and turn away, but slipped and crashed into one of them.

He grabbed her by the hair, and yanked her up.

"She didn't want to pay. Didn't want to play."

The other boy slapped her across the face.

"Let's take her back inside," he said.

She kicked at the one who was holding her by the hair, but it did no damn good. He dragged her back down the alley.

"You nearly let her get away," the slapper said to the first boy, still in the alley doorway.

"Knew you boys were coming," he said.

"Help!" Raych screamed. "Help!"

"No good'll come of that," the slapper said. "Folks here are learning who owns Junk Street."

"Help!" she screamed again. Someone must be nearby, someone would help her.

The hair-dragger brought her over to the first boy, and they each grabbed an arm and held her up on her feet, so she could look at the slapper right in his ugly face.

"See, this whole neighborhood is going to change," the slapper said. "You belong to us and ours."

"Like blazes," she said. Every ounce of her body was filled with terror, but she had to fight, had to defy them.

"Well," he said, pulling a knife out of his belt. "You're going to learn."

They dragged her back inside, and despite her kicking and thrashing, hauled her up on the dough table. The leader—the one who slapped her clearly was—stood over her, caressing her face with the flat of her knife.

"You're going to say it," he said. "You're going to say these streets belong to us."

"To who?" Raych snarled.

"To the—"

The rest of his speech was impeded by the crossbow bolt buried in his throat. The other two boys gasped and turned, and one of them earned a shot in the chest. He and the leader fell on the floor, while the third let go of Raych and charged in at his attacker.

Raych heard a scuffle, flesh hitting flesh, and the third boy grunted. Then there was a twang, and he dropped to the ground.

A moment later, the face of Helene Kesser came into Raych's vision.

"Are you hurt?" Helene asked. "Can you walk?"

Raych wrapped her arms around Helene's neck, never before so happy to see this woman.

Carriage job, no prep or plan. Just Asti, all alone. One lock-wagon, slowly working its way toward Keller Cove, with one driver and two footpatrol sticks on the runners, keeping watch.

Three dead sticks would be easy right now, but would bring a hammer of Keller Cove Constabulary onto North Seleth, a manhunt for Kennith and anyone else working for him. But leaving the three of them alive would leave three witnesses, and the same result.

Brute force, as easy as it would be, would have too many consequences. For Ken, for the rest of the crew, for the whole neighborhood.

He needed to get Ken out without them knowing he did.

The lockwagon was heading toward Bridget Street Bridge over the creek. That was something he could use, if he could get ahead of it. A choke point—he just needed to stop the carriage, distract the sticks, and crack open the lockwagon and pull Ken out.

Alone, with just a kerchief around his face and two knives at his belt.

The rage from before had washed away the effects of Almer's medication, and purpose had focused him. Right now his head was in a cool, clear place, seeing the job in front of him and what he needed to do. Even the beast was quiet for once.

"If I had someone else to be a distraction, that would be something," he muttered.

Someone else.

Those rutting gang boys were heading toward Saint Bridget's.

He ran back toward the alley they were in, scooping up a stray brick from the ground as he went.

Those two boys were still hooting and hollering in the alley. They had grabbed someone else—Asti couldn't see who it was—and were busy taking turns kicking and pissing on him.

Asti pulled down the kerchief and hauled the brick at them, hitting one of them square in the back. Not bad enough to injure him—Asti needed these bastards alive and moving—but it should damn well hurt.

"Hey!" he shouted. "Forget someone?"

"Oh, pal, we gonna pike you!" They tore down the alley at him.

Asti was off like a crossbow bolt, toward the creek bridge. Let them have a sense of where he was going, just enough so when he lost them, they'd keep heading to the bridge.

Losing them was child's play. He dashed into an alley, scurried up the backstairs to the rooftop, then raced across it to shimmy down the drainpipe and drop in the creek bed.

Bastard street boys served as a distraction, but it wouldn't stop the lockwagon. For that, he would need brute force.

Asti crept his way over, hoping he wasn't too late. Thank the saints he wasn't, and that lockwagons were easy to spot in the night, with their green-and-red tinted lamps hanging on each side. It was just approaching the bridge. Creek bed was all but dry—it had been hot as blazes without a proper rain for weeks. He scooped up a sizable rock and hurled it at the lockwagon wheel spokes.

It hit with a decidedly satisfying crunch. Asti slipped under the bridge to hear the wheel collapse.

"Saints and blazes!" one of the sticks yelled.

"Blazes happened!"

"Wheel went out!"

Then the gang boys came running up, keeping up their hoot and holler the whole time. "Where is you? You're going to get a thumping!"

"Who's thumping?" one of the sticks called. "Oy, you boys trying something?"

"Rutting sticks!"

"Show you a thumping!"

Two sets of feet went running into the street. A third dropped down onto the planks of the bridge, walking over to the broken wheel on the right side.

Asti scrambled up the left side of the bridge to the lockwagon door, which was easy enough to open. Asti was surprised by that. Seemed "lockwagon" was just a name. Kennith was there, ironed at wrists and ankles.

"They pinched you good, hmm?"

Kennith's eyes went wide. "Are you crazy?"

"Quite," Asti said, grabbing Kennith by the front of his

shirt. He wasn't going to be able to run, but that was all right. Asti didn't need him to go very far. "Hold on."

"To?"

Asti pulled Kennith out of the carriage and threw him off the bridge into the creek bed. Then he slammed the wagon door shut and dropped down.

"Saints and sinners," Kennith moaned, lying on the dusty creek bed. "You could have killed me."

Asti pulled Kennith up to his feet, half-carrying him, which was awkward, since Ken had about half a foot of height on Asti. He dragged him into a sewer tunnel that emptied into the creek.

"What are we—"

"Shh," Asti said. "Can you walk?"

"I can shuffle."

"Go in the tunnel for a piece. I'll stick by here in case they follow us."

"How far? Why?"

"Go!"

Kennith went off into the darkness. Asti crouched down, knives drawn, ready to cut open anyone who dared come in there.

He could hear the lockwagon driver complaining about fixing or changing out the wheel. The two footpatrol had beat the stuffing out of the gang boys.

A bit more scuffle, and they brought the two boys over to the lockwagon.

"Where did he go?"

"I thought you—"

"We need to—"

"Rutting blazes. Let's just haul these boys in and deal with finding the chomie later. It's not like he's gonna fight."

"This wheel still—"

Asti had heard enough. Better to put distance between him and the legitimate law. He caught up to Kennith shortly. Kennith clearly couldn't move very well in the irons, and had fallen over, lying in the fetid waste of the sewer tunnel.

Asti sat down next to him, pulling him up to a sitting position.

"I don't know about you, Ken, but I've had a lousy past couple days."

Kennith burst out laughing, and then quickly bit his lip to stifle it when he heard it echo through the sewer tunnel. Finally he said, "Asti, that . . . that was stupid. What if—"

"I don't worry much about 'what if,' Ken." Asti checked out the irons on Ken's wrists. Unlike the lockwagon door, they were serious, beyond Asti's ability to crack open.

"But you can't risk yourself to—"

"You're on my crew, Kennith."

"But that doesn't—"

"Ken," Asti said sharply. "You're on my crew. Nobody does anything to my crew."

Kennith smiled. "Now how do I get out of these?" He held up his ironed hands. "And how do we get out of the sewer?"

"We'll get to that," Asti said, leading Kennith a bit deeper into the sewer tunnel. He quickly found what he was looking for. Pushing one of the loose masonry stones, he added, "Luckily, we have a way out of here." A part of the masonry opened up, revealing a passageway.

"Is this the Old Lady's?"

"It's one of her exits from her old office," Asti said. "Right below the bakery."

"And then?"

"And then, we figure out what went wrong tonight, and we set about making it right."

Chapter 21

HELENE PACED AROUND THE bakery kitchen, knowing full well that no amount of walking and wishing would get rid of the three dead bodies.

Raych came back downstairs, now wrapped in a housecoat. "They're fine up there. A little scared, but it's fine." She looked about the kitchen. "I thought you were going to—"

"Hide the bodies?" Helene knocked back to her. "Yeah, I'm not sure where to even begin with that, Raych."

"We can't just leave them here, we have to . . . you have to . . ."

"I have to?" Helene shot back.

"You are the one who . . ." Raych almost choked on the words. "Killed them," she finally eked out.

"It was them or you."

"I know," Raych said. "I very much . . . I'm not questioning it. But . . ." She paced about for a moment and then dropped into a chair. "This isn't something I . . . I don't know what to do. This isn't my world, Helene."

Helene didn't have time to deal with this sort of nonsense. "It is. It kicked through your door and forced itself on you. This is where we live, and this is our world. It burned us down, killed the people we love, and it came in here.

You're lucky you still have something. So spine up, because this is what we live in."

Helene hadn't realized how much that had been building inside of her until it flowed out onto Raych. And now Raych was crying.

"Oh, saints, don't do that."

"How . . . how can . . . how can you stand it?"

"What choice do we have?"

Raych was on her feet in a shot. "Didn't we have a rutting choice?" she snarled right in Helene's face, tears flowing. "Couldn't we have taken that blasted money you all stole and gotten out of this place? Couldn't we?"

Helene took a deep breath, not letting the anger in her belly rise up more. "You want to shout that a little louder? Maybe your sister didn't hear you."

"Maybe she should! Maybe she should know what kind of person I am, that I condone this sort of thing!"

Helene grabbed her by the shoulders, but resisted the urge to shake her. "Raychelle. I'm sorry you married into this blazes of a family. Believe me—"

Raych's eyes narrowed and sharpened on her. Darts of steel, despite the tear pools at the corners. "Oh, I believe it. I see how you look at my husband. And I know the two of you—you have all the little things, all the history. You get him in ways I never will."

"Maybe I do," Helene said. "And I know what it would do to him if something happened to you. That's why I came."

Raych was calm again. "So what do we do?"

"We do what any honest businessperson would do in a case like that," Helene said. "We call the Constabulary."

Helene went out into the street, which was now quieter—no sign of any other gang boys at the moment. She went to the whistlebox on the corner—the door had long since been torn off, and it had been covered in paperjobs and paintjobs so may times that the original wood was nowhere to be seen. But the whistle itself was still there. Helene gave a quick blast, which should call any footpatrol or horsepatrol that might be in the area. Though surely they had their hands full.

She strolled over to the bakery idly, waiting at the door. In a few moments, Raych came to join her, resting her head on Helene's shoulder.

After a few minutes, a pair of footpatrol came over, looking tired and drawn. "You make a call?" one asked. "You shouldn't do that if there isn't a situation."

"There is," Helene said. "Call for a bodywagon, and I want to talk to Lieutenant Covrane."

The first one shook his head. "Covrane don't work the dark."

"Why do you need a bodywagon?" the second asked.

Raych spoke up. "Three hooligans broke into my shop here, tried to assault me or ... worse. ..." Her voice broke just a bit there, and Helene was sure it was no performance. "Fortunately my friend Helene here showed up with her crossbow."

The first stick raised an eyebrow, signaling his partner to go in and check it out. "You just ... carry a crossbow around?"

"It's my right," Helene said, holding it up for them to see. "Why I wanted to talk to Covrane. He's familiar with it."

"Huh," the stick said, looking at the crossbow. "So you were just in the area, fully armed?"

"Yeah," Helene said. "Helene Kesser, I live over on Ullen, over the goxie shop. Work the goxie shop, so I do business with the Rynaxes and their bakery. I was walking home up Junk when I saw the door was kicked open, so I went in. Three animals had her pinned on her kitchen counter, ready for ..."

Helene found her own throat choking up.

"So I did what you do to wild animals."

The second stick came back. "The boys, look like Crease Knockers by their signs. They've been all over the neighborhood tonight."

"I noticed," Helene said.

"This seems pretty clean," the second said. "We can just call the bodyman in, take their statements, and be off."

The first nodded, took out his whistle and blew a few trills.

"Have a seat, ladies," the second said, directing them to

a couple chairs he had brought over from the kitchen. "We'll try and have this done as quick as we can."

Helene nearly collapsed into her chair, and Raych did the same. It took a bit before Helene realized Raych was squeezing her hand.

"Hey, Hel," she said quietly. "Thank you. I'm glad you were here."

"I got lucky, Mila said—" The words crashed into Helene's skull with realization.

Mila.

Jede was dead. Verci didn't need Doc Gelson to tell him that. The Doc really did try his best, saints bless him, but there was nothing to be done, especially on a pub table.

Verci couldn't do anything but sit in a chair and watch. He wanted to be out in the street, be at Asti's side. Or be at the bakery, with Raych. He had no idea what was going on out there. The streets seemed quiet right now, best as he could tell. He pushed himself to take a look out the door, despite his foot.

"Are we all right?" Kimber was behind him, peering out into the darkness.

"As much as we can be," Verci said. "You want me to fix that window?"

"You work with glass?" she asked.

He grinned. "No, but I can put some boards over it until you can get a glazier."

"I appreciate it," she said. "You don't need to."

"It's what we do here. And I need to do something."

Hemmit and Lin came over to the door, him supporting her. Her head had been bandaged up, and she seemed mostly all right. Hemmit still had a wineglass in his hand.

"Your brother is gone?" Lin asked.

"It's his way," Verci said. "Trouble in the streets, his people in danger . . . he'll fight every sinner in the blazes to there to keep them safe."

"And you too?"

"For me, he would tear this city apart, brick by brick."

"I believe that," Hemmit said.

"Mister Rynax," Lin said. "I was thinking about Andrendon, and this house that's been built. Tell me, are there any Circle chapterhouses in this part of town?"

"You're talking mages?" Verci asked. "No, none that I'm aware of."

She loosened the laces of her blouse, opening it up slightly to show a tattoo over her heart—a wolf head in red. "I know something of Mage Circles. Some are less scrupulous than others."

Verci remembered that Pilsen suspected Treggin of being a mage. "You think they—that the house and the fire— that some Circle is behind it?"

"I've heard some whispers that some Circles—the smaller, less influential ones—have been forced out of their chapterhouses in neighborhoods in the east and north of the city."

"So they'll come west," Verci said. "And might make some sort of a deal to get a new house on recently vacated land."

"Something to look into," she said, tightening her blouse up again.

"There's one other thing, Mister Rynax," Hemmit said. "Before all this madness, I told you there were two reasons I was interested in this story, and the two of you."

"Right," Verci said. "The change in districts on the map, so votes in North Seleth don't matter." And Verci imagined the fear and mischief in the streets also kept people from voting. That this happened tonight, maybe that wasn't a coincidence.

"Well, they won't, I would bet my ink," Hemmit said. "But to me, they very much matter. You see, I've been asking around this neighborhood for the past couple days about who they were going to vote for Alderman."

"Most probably said Lammart."

"Several, indeed. But a name that kept coming up?" He raised up his nearly empty wineglass, as if looking disappointedly at it would cause it to refill. "Asti Rynax."

If Verci had been drinking wine, he would have spit it out. "Asti? For Alderman? He's never . . . he has no interest . . ."

"Which is why I wanted to meet him. It's clear he's

looked at by some as an important part of this neighborhood's community . . . a leader . . ."

"You're off base," Verci said, even though he found the idea strangely fitting and compelling. "We're just a couple of folks who live here and—"

"And care about what's happening. A man like Asti, a man who would write letters to every newsprint in the city? Maybe that's a man who needs to be fighting for this neighborhood in a real way."

"Maybe. But he's not going to win, of course."

"No, of course not," Hemmit said, handing his empty glass to Verci. "But that's something to think about for next year."

Next year. That seemed so far away it felt pointless. Where would either of them be? Still chasing the Andrendon people? Working a bakery and the Gadgeterium? Locked up in Quarrygate? Verci had no idea.

He only just realized that. He couldn't see where his life was going right now, and that was far more terrifying than anything else.

"Give our best to your brother," Lin said. "And stay in touch."

They went out into the night.

Verci stayed in the doorframe for a bit, looking up at the stars in a vain attempt to find some solace. "Kimber," he said finally. "If you've got any tools—"

"Oy, help!" a tiny voice cried out. Out of the darkness, two figures stumbled toward the pub: tiny Tarvis, propping up Mila as best he could. Mila looked a fright, face bloody. Verci fought the urge to run out—he'd only hurt himself worse. Once they were in reach, he took up Mila. Once he had her, he could tell the injuries on her face were superficial. She'd get a good scar over her eyebrow, probably. But her blouse was torn and her shoulder was covered in black marks, like lightning.

"What happened?"

"Something of a scrap, Mister Rynax," she said. She almost sounded like Asti. "Don't worry, I gave pretty damn good as well."

"Tarvis, stay here," Verci said. "Just wait in the door."

"I ain't—"

"Just wait." Verci brought Mila inside. "Can you walk?"

"Course I can," Mila said. "But if the Doc is here, getting a look over wouldn't be a bad idea."

"Gelson," Verci said, putting Mila in a chair. "Doc, we need you."

Gelson turned his attention toward Mila, and then the room was filled with a soul-wrenching cry.

"Jede?" Tarvis was at the table, his tiny hands grabbing his brother's crushed face. "Jede! Stop playing a trick, Jede, it isn't funny!"

"Tarvis," Verci said, stumbling over. "Tarvis, I'm so sorry . . . he . . ."

Still clutching Jede's face, Tarvis looked up at Verci with flowing tears and white-hot fury in his eyes.

"Who?"

"I don't know, some gang boys—"

"The ones out tonight?" He was fuming with rage. He took Jede's blood-soaked cap and put it on his own head. "I'm going to show them."

Verci tried to grab the boy's arm. "Tarvis, wait, you should—"

"Don't touch me!" he screamed, kicking Verci's broken foot. Verci fell over in agony. "None of you touch me! None of you stop me! I'm going to make them all pay!"

He drew out his knife and ran out into the street.

Verci stumbled to the door, calling after Tarvis, to no avail.

Doc Gelson came over to Verci, hand on his shoulder. "I'll make some arrangements for the boy."

"Thanks, Doc," Verci said.

"And, saints, get off that foot, or it'll never heal right." He shoved Verci's crutches into his hand.

Verci hobbled over to Mila. "How are you?"

She sat up woozily. "Doc says I'm an idiot, but I'll be all right." She stretched her arm a bit. "Hurt like blazes in the moment, but he says he can't see anything wrong with it."

"What happened to it?"

She noticed Jede before she answered. "Oh, saints and sinners. Did—Tarvis?"

"He's gone."

She slammed a fist against the table. "They're . . . damn it!"

"Hey, I know—"

"No, Verci, they're . . . they're just little boys. They're my responsibility." She started crying. "Those blasted Scratch Cats and Crease Knockers, I'm going to—" She gasped and looked up. "We need to get to your wife."

"My wife?"

Mila pulled herself to her feet, grasping at Verci, "Yes! Those boys said they wanted to get 'that lady from the bakery' as well."

She started running, and Verci didn't waste any time heading out the door.

Chapter 22

THE BASEMENT BUNKER BENEATH the bakery was still well stocked and furnished, fortunately. Asti helped Kennith into a chair, poured him some wine, and went about finding some tools to remove the irons. While he worked on that, he could hear things happening up in the bakery. The earhorns that drew sound from upstairs were open, everything loud and clear.

Things happening in the bakery involved Constabulary, bodywagons, and Helene answering questions. Asti thought it best to stay below and keep his ear open.

"You're not going to help her?" Kennith asked.

"It sounds like she's got it," Asti said. "But if they take her off in the lockwagon, I'll be on that as well."

After nearly an hour, the sticks left.

"Stay here," Asti told Kennith. "I'm going up."

He came up through a trapdoor in the pantry, causing both Raych and Helene to scream when he came out.

"Saints above and below, Asti, tell me you haven't been in there all night!" Raych shouted.

"No, of course not," Asti said. "The way up from the bunker comes up in there."

"How long you been down there?" Helene asked.

"Long enough to hear what you two went through."

"Why were you downstairs?"

"Kennith got grabbed by the sticks. I got him clear, and he's hiding down there."

"Well, gear up," Helene said, picking her crossbow up off the counter. "Because Mila got caught in the middle of things, Pilsen's out there too, somewhere, and we need to find them. And maybe drag Ren Poller and his people through the streets by their ears."

"You gonna do that on my account?" Mila was in the alley doorway, her face a mess of blood and bruising, her shoulder a spiderweb of black lines. "Thank saints you're all safe."

"Oh, saints, Mila," Helene said, going over to her. "I should have held onto you, but when I realized I lost you, I was—"

"It's fine," Mila said. "I know this looks bad, but I gave better than I got. Doc Gelson said I'm fine."

"You saw the Doc? Did you see Verci?"

That question was answered when Verci raced in as fast as he could on a crutch. "Raych?" He went right to his wife and swept her up in his arms.

"Right behind me," Mila said weakly.

Verci looked up from his wife. "Why . . . why are you all here?"

"It's been a night," Asti said.

"Kennith?" Verci asked.

"Safe. Downstairs."

A few pounding knocks came from the floor.

"See?"

Mila nodded. "Jede's dead, and Tarvis is out there, doing . . . I don't know what. And Pilsen is in the wind. What should we do?"

"Sleep," Raych said. "It's late and we all should sleep."

Asti shook his head. "We need to take care of our people. Gather and figure out what's what."

"We do?" Verci asked. "Can't that wait until morning?"

"That might be best," Helene said.

"Mila?" Asti asked.

"I'm exhausted," she said. "But Tarvis—"

Asti looked at his people. All of them were in bad shape.

Even Helene, who wasn't obviously injured, looked like she had been shaken to the core. As much as he wanted to drive forward, figure out the next thing, he had to do right by them. They were his crew, he had to keep them straight and safe.

And they were here. Despite the madness of the night, and despite getting pinched or hurt, they were still here, still here with him. That gave him more peace than anything else he had tried in the past weeks.

"Right. Here's the plan. Verci, go upstairs with your wife, get some sleep."

"Lian is still up there," Raych said. "Hal must be in a state."

"All right. I can walk her home. Everyone else, go down to the bunker. It's cozy enough for you all to flop out there for tonight."

"And safe," Helene said.

"But Tarvis, Pilsen—" Mila said.

"I'm going to take Lian home," Asti said. "Then I'll see if I can find Pilsen, and look out for Tarvis as well."

"Follow the trail of bodies," Verci muttered.

"Verci!" Raych admonished.

"I'll see what I can do," Asti said.

"Thank you," Mila said.

Asti pulled her aside. "You tangled with a mage."

"How can you—"

"The shoulder. I've seen things like that before."

She nodded. "Looks worse than it is. He only grazed me."

"He being Treggin?"

"Yeah," she said. "I got a good look at him. We'll be ready next time."

He admired the attitude, but she had to be putting on a brave face. If that mark on her shoulder was a graze, she was lucky to get away alive.

"All right, get some rest." He turned out to the rest of the room. "Tomorrow morning, eight bells, we'll all go to the safehouse. We've got a big day tomorrow."

"What's tomorrow?" Raych asked.

"It's Saint Jontlen's day," Asti said.

Verci woke in his own bed, nestled between his wife and his son, and for a moment, everything was right with the world.

"Someone's downstairs," he said. He could hear someone thumping around down there.

"Many people are downstairs," Raych muttered. She opened her eyes and looked up at him. "It's Saint Jontlen's day, yes?"

"Right," Verci said, worried about what Asti still had in mind right now. Of course Asti wanted to drive forward.

"I'm not opening the bakery today, in observation. Plus there's such a mess to clean up downstairs."

"I'll help with that."

She propped herself up on her elbows on his chest. "Oh? I thought today was a big day, Asti has a whole plan for you."

"I'm sure he does, but I won't leave you in a lurch." Verci smiled. "Besides, if anything has been drilled into my head in the past few days, it's that I'm not much good to the rest of the crew with my foot like this."

"What are you talking about?" Raych asked.

"Last night. Asti was out there on his own to rescue Ken. Mila got beat hard, and you were only saved because Helene was nearby. Meanwhile all I did was sit in Kimber's and fret about things."

"Well, I would rather have you sitting and fretting in here, so you could have done something brilliant and clever when those boys showed up."

"Like get beat as well?" he asked.

"Bah," she said. "Verci Rynax with a broken foot is still worth twenty of those boys. Your strongest tools are right here." She tapped his forehead.

"Let's go see what's going on down there," Verci said.

Washed and dressed, Verci hobbled his way down the stairs with Raych right behind him, Corsi in her arms. "Who's up?" he called as he got to the bottom.

"Morning." Asti was by the front door, Verci's tools neatly arranged around him.

"Are you fixing the door?"

"I do have some skills along those lines," Asti said. "I know it's remarkable."

"Asti, did you sleep?" Raych called out from the kitchen.

Verci hadn't failed to notice that it was now pristine—absolutely no sign that the place had been vandalized and three people killed in there.

"Too much to do," Asti said, getting to his feet. He opened and closed the door, showing that it now was fixed. "We've got a busy day ahead, and I couldn't let this stuff tie you up when I could take care of it."

"You . . . you still want to do the ball and everything?" Verci asked.

"Blazes, yes," Asti said. "Golden chance, brother. Pop always said—"

"I know what he said. Didn't he get killed on one of those?"

Asti nodded. "And that won't happen to you."

Verci grabbed his brother's face, pulling him in close. "You think that's the only thing I think about?"

"I'm just saying, if the choice is ever between me and you, choose you."

Raych came over. "I'm impressed. You never would have guessed—"

"Three people were killed here?" Asti asked. Raych flinched a bit at that, and nodded. Asti shrugged. "I may not be much for the honest life we all want, but I know how to clean that up."

Raych looked down at the floor and stammered for a moment. "I have some pastries from yesterday, we should bring them down to everyone. With some tea and preserves?"

"That sounds capital," Asti said.

There was a knock on the door—Almer Cort.

"You all ready?" he asked as Verci opened it. "Asti told me to come by around eight bells."

"Last night you did that?" Verci asked.

"Like I said, we've got a busy day. I've been at it all night—checked in with Almer, brought a message to Win, came here and cleaned up."

"Pilsen? Tarvis?"

"Pilsen made it to his flop with Vellun. He seemed addled, nasty bruise on his face, but . . . he's safe. Tarvis . . . kid went into the air."

"What do you think he's gonna do?"

"Same thing I'd do," Asti said. "Kill every bastard he finds."

Verci nodded. "So now?"

"Now, we need to get everyone over to the safehouse and crash into readiness for tonight."

Raych sighed. "And what are you all doing tonight?"

"We're going to a fancy party in a manor house," Asti said, a little too flippantly for Verci's taste. "We're invited by the lady of the house, an old friend of mine." He was clearly being a bit too condescending to Raych.

"Oh, this thing, and her," Raych said.

"You told her?" Asti asked him.

"No secrets from her," Verci said. "That's the rule."

"Fine," Asti said. "Let's feed the crew and get moving."

Everyone else downstairs was in surprisingly good spirits, despite the bruising on Mila's face and black scarring on her shoulder. Even Ken was a bit more joyful than Verci had expected.

"You all right?" Verci asked him.

"I'm not thrilled that I'm a wanted man," he said in a hushed voice. "But . . . look, I've always respected you and your brother, but I figured when the number came, I'd be the one alone in the cart."

"Is this an Oblunic idiom?" Kennith had grown up in eastern Druthal.

"Probably," Kennith said. "I'm just saying, the last thing I expected when I was put in that lockwagon was for Asti to pull some crazy play to get me out. So . . . I don't know, I'm just sorry I had any doubts about you two." He grabbed Verci and embraced him.

"If it makes you feel any better, Ken, I frequently have doubts about us as well."

Once everyone was ready, Asti led them all through the door to the safehouse. "I'm going to remember that one," Raych said to Verci before they left. "You're going to teach me every secret this place has."

"Every one," he told her with a kiss.

Asti helped him walk down the tunnels as they made their way to the safehouse, where they found Josie alone in the kitchen.

"I was wondering when you all would show up," she said. "I heard there was quite a bit of excitement."

"Where did you hear from?" Asti asked as he brought Verci over to his chair at the planning table.

"I still have a few sources," she said. "I'm still Josefine Holt."

"That you are," Asti said. "All right, tonight is gig night, and we are deeply behind, so let's talk about what we need to do. Do we have the forged invites for Mila and Pilsen?"

"Yes," Josie said, joining them all at the table. "And are the girls ready?"

Asti shrugged. "Hel? How's your accent?"

"It hurts when I hold the ham in my hands over my head." She overemphasized her h's, but it sounded passable.

"Good enough," Asti said. "When Pilsen gets here, he can keep working with you."

"Of course, we don't have anything to wear," Mila said.

"How's that?" Verci asked. That sounded like a critical detail.

"We were out to get the dresses when everything went crazy last night," Mila said.

"There was also an issue with the money at the creditors," Helene said. "Pilsen tried to play it off, but something's wrong. What's going on there, Josie?"

"Why did you go to the creditor?" Josie asked. She sounded quite put off.

"To pay for the dresses we need to buy," Helene said. "It's a fancy party."

"How do you even know where he is?"

"Pilsen brought us," Mila said. "Where is he?"

Josie sputtered. "He shouldn't have—he knows he shouldn't—"

"We needed the dresses," Helene said. "And you weren't here."

"Fine, fine," Josie said. "Just next time let me know what you need."

"Speaking of," Asti said. "Almer was saying something about not getting covered for his supplies. Josie, I know we have to look clean, but we also need to have his expenses covered."

"My supplies aren't inexpensive," Almer said.

"I'll figure it out," Josie said curtly.

Verci saw Asti's eye twitch. Something didn't sit right with him, and Verci had the same bad feeling in his gut.

"Figure what out?" Verci asked. "Josie, just move the money to where it needs to be so we can pay these things."

"Yes, but it's a complicated—" She shook her head, looking very annoyed. "Stupid Pilsen. If I had known, I could have covered it."

"Josie," Asti said sharply. "Where is our money?"

She looked up at him, and that annoyed face melted into calm. A facade Verci had seen too many times to trust. "It's tied up, being cleaned, covering—"

Asti stood up. "No, Josie. I know your stories, I know your tells."

"It's fine, Asti, you just—"

"What did you do?"

Verci was up as well, as best he could be on one foot.

"Josie, tell me you didn't do anything stupid."

"Saints above, Rynaxes. I'm the only smart one here."

"Josie, what does that—" Asti reached out toward her, and she sprang up defensively.

Then her face betrayed everything. Verci saw it, and it was clear Asti did as well.

Asti leaped on her, but before he got close, she pulled something out of her pocket and threw it on the ground. The room was suddenly filled with choking, yellow smoke. Asti's eyes bulged out and he collapsed. Everyone else fell to the ground, coughing. Verci felt his body seize up, and he dropped down. He couldn't move a muscle, despite wanting to crawl across the floor to claw Josie's eyes out.

"You foolish boys," he heard Josie say as his world went dark. "You always want to do things your way."

Chapter 23

ASTI WOKE WITH THE contents of his stomach emptying out of his mouth and nose. Hands held his shoulders to the ground, despite his vain attempts to thrash and fight back. Those same hands turned him onto his side and cleared his mouth out.

"Breathe, Asti." Asti's vision was still a fog of blurs, but he recognized Almer's voice.

"Wha—how—" was all he managed to say. His head was full of questions. What the blazes just happened? What did Josie do? Why the blazes did she do it? And where was she now? That last part was crucial, as he wanted to know exactly where she was so he could slice her open.

"Come on, get it out," Almer said, pouring water on Asti's face.

Asti coughed and heaved some more, but there was nothing else in his system to get rid of.

"You with me?" Almer asked. A strong scent hit Asti's nose, bringing a wave of clarity to his head.

"Here," Asti said, his eyes focusing on Almer. "What—what happened?"

"Talk while you help me," Almer said, pulling Asti to his feet. Surrounding the table, everyone else was on the ground: Verci, Helene, Mila, and Kennith, all of them unconscious and a decidedly unnatural shade.

"What do I do?" Asti said, going straight to Verci, as Almer went to Mila. Almer tossed him a small vial.

"Get that down his throat first."

"What the blazes happened?"

"I should have known," Almer said, pulling open Mila's mouth. Asti only now noticed Almer had a bleeding gash across his forehead. "I saw it, and I thought you did as well."

Asti pried open Verci's mouth and poured the potion into it. "I didn't, not like this—did you sell Josie something?"

"She bought it from me—or said she was going to pay for it—a few weeks ago," Almer said. "The *callit* smoke and the immunity. Said she needed it for personal protection."

Verci shook violently, vomiting up everything he had eaten. Mila was doing the same.

"I thought it was sketchy," Almer said, holding Mila down as she shook. Asti grabbed hold of Verci. "Water on the table, get their mouths clear so they don't choke."

"You thought she might use it on us?"

"You said not to trust her, you had your eye on her. So I thought it would be a good idea to dose myself with the immunity, keep the counteragent on me. Just in case."

"You . . ." Asti wasn't sure what to make of this. "You thought she would do this?"

"I wanted to be prepared if she did."

Verci was coughing. "What . . . Asti?"

"Shh, you're all right. Next, Almer?"

"He's good. Move to someone else."

Asti went to work on Helene, while Almer went to Kennith. Verci tried to pull himself up to a sitting position.

"What was that?" Verci asked.

"You didn't notice, Asti, how cagey she always got when the money came up? I noticed, because she would dodge and change the subject when I asked her."

Mila crawled up onto her chair, wiping off her face. "I thought it was strange, about the account being empty."

"Do you think Pilsen knew?" Asti asked. If he was Josie's accomplice, then Asti wanted answers. If Pilsen had them, Asti would have to do something drastic. "Almer, what the blazes would have happened to us if you hadn't been prepared?"

"We'd have woken up in a few hours, with the worst headaches of our lives."

"I think I have that," Mila said.

Kennith and Helene were roused, hacking up terribly. Asti went to his cabinet to get some knives.

"Where are you going?" Mila asked.

"To find Pilsen. I want to talk to him."

"What the blazes?" Helene asked.

"That's what we're all asking," Verci said. "Almer, I'm guessing from your head that you confronted Josie?"

"She clobbered me with her cane. Sorry I'm not good with the physical stuff, boys. She sent me foggy for a minute while she went into the office."

Verci hobbled toward the office, pointing at Asti. "Don't go anywhere. I'll check it out."

"Oh my saints!"

All heads turned to the door, where Vellun and Pilsen had just walked in. They looked utterly appalled, which made sense, given the floor was covered with vomit.

"What happened here?" Pilsen looked shocked, but faking his way through things was what he did. He also had a great gash across his head, which had been inexpertly bandaged. Asti put the knife in his belt and came over.

"Hey," Asti said, as gently as he could manage. His gut told him Pilsen knew something, but it was possible Josie had also played him. Blazes, Asti hadn't suspected this from her. As much as he knew—*knew*—not to trust Josie within an inch of her life, he had been presuming she was fully together with him on this.

He had let her fleece his whole crew.

"Asti," Pilsen croaked. "What happened?"

"Josie had a trick up her sleeve," Asti said. "We were asking her about the money—"

"You're talking about the empty accounts?" Pilsen asked.

"You knew, then?"

"I knew things were wrong with the accounts, but—" He looked up at Asti, his eyes filled with honesty. Blazes, either he was legitimate or this was an excellent performance. But Asti had to remind himself that Pilsen was an excellent performer. "I—I had done a few things for her, delivered some messages, played some parts. Paid a few bribes. She was definitely concerned with reclaiming her hold over this neighborhood."

"Which Lesk and Treggin were taking."

"Treggin!" Mila said excitedly. She moved herself in between Asti and Pilsen, as if to prevent Asti from getting too violent. "I actually squared off with him last night. You were right about him."

"Is he a mage?" Pilsen asked.

"Blazes, yes," Mila said. "That was some scary sewage."

Helene stumbled around the room, still working off the effects of the smoke. It seemed to hit her harder than most. "Let me understand something. Rutting Josie Holt, the Old Lady of North Seleth, just poisoned us all and ran off, because she had stolen all our money?"

"We think she did," Asti said.

"So that whole, keeping it safe, keeping it clean thing? That was sewage?"

"No, I think that was a real thing," Pilsen said woozily. "But she used that as an excuse to keep hold of it. I think—I think—" He looked off in the distance. "What was I saying?"

"Josie taking our money, Pilsen."

"She did? Is that why the credit accounts were empty?"

"Yes, Pilsen!"

"I was afraid of something like that, but I—what did she do? Where is she? Do we have the dresses?"

Saints, maybe the years had addled his brain. Or that blow to the head. Or he was playing them. Any one was possible. And Pilsen was good enough that Asti couldn't tell.

Verci came out from the office. "She was ready, I'll tell you that. She had a ton of papers in her desk, spark loaded or something. They all burned up with the turn of a knob."

Asti was on his feet. "Which way did she go?"

"Brilliant," Verci said. "She left the door wide open, and the tunnel is collapsed ten feet in. There's no following her."

Asti put his fist through the wall. Then he did it again. And again.

"Asti," Verci said sharply. "Keep it together."

"I'm together," Asti said. For once, the beast was still on its chain. "This isn't me losing it, this is just me angry."

"What are we going to do now?" Vellun asked.

"What are you doing here?" Asti asked him.

"I thought I was supposed to come to help train the ladies for tonight. But clearly something bad has happened. Can we still do this?"

"Something indeed," Asti said. Things were clicking in his head. Tonight still had to happen. Drive forward, like Dad always said. "All right, the plan is shifting, and we all need to be on top of it. If you're not on top of it, I need to know right now."

Verci put his hand on Asti's shoulder and squeezed. A simple message that he was in.

"Tell me part of the plan involves blood from Josie," Helene said.

Asti nodded. "Not tonight—we've got to settle the business at Henterman Hall, and find out what's next with the enemies of North Seleth—."

"But—" Helene started.

"And Josie has earned a spot on that list," Asti said. "Have no doubt."

"Well, you're telling me we're all broke again. And Julien is still in that household. If nothing else, I need to pull him out. So I'm in."

"It's funny," Kennith said. "Yesterday I might have told you to piss up a rope. But . . . yeah. However you need me, I'm in."

"That's good, Kennith, because I've got a blazes of a plan for you."

"A carriage plan?" Verci asked.

"No, but—Almer, Pilsen, Vellun? In?" Not that he fully trusted either Pilsen or Vellun right now, but he needed bodies. He could put them in positions that minimized their risk to the plan.

"Saints, you got to ask?" Almer said.

Pilsen nodded. "Though I'm afraid . . . no amount of greasepaint will cover up this gash in my head."

"Yes, please," Vellun said. Asti immediately saw why

Pilsen kept calling him a "puppy". There was such an earnest eagerness to him.

Asti turned to Mila. He didn't need to say or ask anything. She held her head high and delivered in a perfect highborn accent, "I can't possibly imagine a better use of my time than making all of those rat-rutters suffer."

"Far be it for me to be the raincloud," Pilsen said. "But we are definitively lacking in resources. Money, certainly. Dresses and other appropriate outfits. How could we ever pull this off tonight?"

"Verci, Kennith, we have two carriages at our disposal, yes?"

"Yeah," Verci said. "We were working on a repeated spring engine for one, but—"

"Scrap that, doesn't matter. Speed won't help. I need those carriages looking appropriate for nobility, with as much secret space as you can muster."

"Both?" Kennith asked. "I can only drive one, you know."

"You won't be driving either," Asti said. "But also, go through this whole place, and find out every damn thing we've got on hand. Every spare crown, every loose screw. I want a list."

"Dresses," Mila said. "Do we still have the dress I stole for Tyne's Emporium? And the one Helene wore that night?"

"Probably," Helene said. "Though they would hardly be high fashion for the ball. And they are kind of filthy with ash and dirt after that night."

Almer perked up. "I can get them clean and sweet smelling."

Pilsen pointed to Vellun. "And this one is decent enough with a sewing needle to get the dresses to fit correctly."

Vellun smiled. "I also know of a theater company in town that would have appropriate outfits for the men to wear. I could call in a favor or two."

Asti had a list. "We'll need three outfits for lords and two for fancy drivers."

Pilsen raised a bloody-gashed eyebrow. "Three? What are you playing at?"

"We need something to draw those swells' attention," Asti said. "And I've got just the thing."

Pilsen shook his head. "Yes, but like I said, my face is a mess. Mila's as well, honestly, but we should be able to cover it decently enough. But if I try to pass for a lord, there will be questions."

"That's fine, you won't be playing one," Asti said. He had already figured out that part of his plan. In part due to Pilsen's face, but also to put the old con man at arm's length. No need to give him too crucial a job right now.

"Then who will be Mila's escort with the forged invitation?"

Asti looked over to Vellun. "Suit up, kid. You're going on."

Verci had spent much of the day in a blur—going through the crates and boxes in the safehouse, getting both carriages ready, preparing a satchel for his gadgets.

And finalizing two special gadgets—his new boot and his cane. The cane hid a spring-loaded blade. He wanted to build a dart-launcher and hide it in there, but that would take a few days. No time for that.

"How's it feel?" Mila asked when she saw him trying it on.

"Wrong," Verci said. "I mean, it still hurts to put weight on it, but I can do it. The framework in the brace takes most of my weight, so I'm not putting any stress on the ankle. But I can't run well or be too sneaky. Bit too much clang when stepping. But nothing to be done about that. Still need the cane."

"You can walk."

"I can walk." He looked over at Mila, and saw something sad and angry in her eyes. "What is it?"

"Tarvis, Jede, the rest of my boys," she said. "I mean, I was supposed to be responsible for them. And Josie just used them for . . . whatever her real plan was. Got them scooped up into Gorminhut. And now Jede . . ."

"Right," Verci said. "Look, we all got played by Josie this time. I should have . . . I know her well enough that I should have known better. But she still knitted our eyes. And Jede—you can't take blame for that. There were boys who did that to him, and we'll . . . we'll add them to the list."

"Those boys got the lockwagon," Asti said, coming over to them. "Hopefully, they'll stay in Quarrygate for a while."

"And Tarvis?" Mila asked. "We need to find him, help him—"

"If we can," Asti said. "He might not want our help."

"He knows where to find us."

"Part of what I wanted to say, Verci," Asti said. "This place—"

"It's not safe, yeah." Verci had had the same thought. Surely Josie had other secrets here, just like in the bakery. As much as he scoured the place, he doubted he could find them all. "You think we've got to burn it out?"

"I don't think we should come back here after tonight."

"There's the bakery, but that's just as suspect," Verci said.

Asti nodded. "It's no safer. You should get Raych out of there."

"Go where? To Hal and Lian?"

Asti sighed. "It would be safer. I haven't told Kennith yet, but his stable over at the North Seleth Inn has been nailed down by the constabs."

"So where are we going to go?"

"There's the empty factory, by the dead bridge," Mila said. "It's where my boys would hide down and flop out, when they could. Decent enough."

Asti frowned. "That place is boxed in, nowhere to run. But I'll take a look. In the meantime, we should get everything we have that we want to keep and hide it in Almer's shop."

"Why there?"

"It's a secure enough place, and it's controlled. It's all his."

"Fine," Verci said. "But only equipment and such. I think, for now, for tonight, we can consider the bakery and the bunker below as safe."

"Safe?" Mila asked.

"Look," Verci said, more for Asti's benefit. "I've known Josie a long time, and worked with her longer than anyone else here, save Pilsen. She can't be trusted—"

"Especially now—"

"But she has a style that we know," Verci said. "She's not

going to hit back at us, not right away. In a couple days, she's going to reach out and offer us some sort of settlement."

Asti frowned, but nodded. "Right. She's running from us. She'll lock away from the places we know too well, like the bakery."

"So we go back to the bunker tonight?" Mila asked.

"If we make it through this, it's as good a place as any," Asti said.

"Not as swank as this," Mila said.

"You'll get your share of swank tonight," Asti said. "How's your dress?"

"Vellun and Almer are working miracles. Explain to me what I'm doing tonight."

"Basically, we want to get all of us on the grounds. Once inside, it's a hot run with little plan, when we come down to it. I really don't like that, but there isn't much choice. I'm going to be making decisions as we go, and you need to be able to respond to that. Take initiative if something goes wrong."

She took that better than Verci expected. "What can I do when that happens? And what's our ideal situation?"

"All right," Asti said. "The ceremony of Saint Jontlen has to do with everyone going off to hide around the house. At that point, Liora and I will be going up to her quarters—"

"Saints above, Asti, I don't need to hear that."

"To use the trapdoor in her wardrobe to get into the study."

"Which she hasn't used herself, why?" Verci asked. Everything about Liora and why she was pulling Asti in set his hair on end.

"I'm sure that there's a reason that I'm not going to like. We're clear, she's using me for some reason, and until we know it, I got to play the part and hope I don't end up the tiger in a cage."

"So," Mila said. "What I should be doing is backing you up in a way that this Liora woman doesn't notice. Because we're expecting a double cross from her."

"The double cross is a given," Asti said.

"Which is what you and Vellun are there for," Verci said.

"We have no idea what we're going into with that study. We don't know what Liora wants, or what she's wanting to use us for."

"Or even what we hope to find there."

Mila nodded like she understood. "She knows about Helene and Almer, so you're putting them up front. He's your driver and she's your date."

"Actually, in the context of the characters, Helene is my sister."

"Who decided that?" Helene yelled across the room. She was wearing just corset, skivs, and stockings, and if she had any reservations about being underdressed in front of him and Asti, she didn't show it.

"I did," Asti said.

She came closer. "I appreciate that I don't have to play that we want to roll each other."

Mila coughed to get Asti's attention back. Asti took note and continued, "Right, so: she knows about Helene, Verci, and me. And Almer. A big part of Verci's job is to be the obvious trick we want her to think we're playing. He's the secret backup she'll presume I have. She won't know about the rest of you."

"Are we not playing a trick?" Helene asked.

Mila mused for a moment. "Jede and Tarvis and their tricks."

Verci tried to ignore that. "Of course we are. But we're giving an obvious trick—Almer and I placing ourselves to back up Asti—to hide the real one. With Vellun, Mila, and Kennith."

"Vellun and Kennith will capture everyone's attention, right," Mila said to Asti. "So when you sneak off with Liora, I have your tail, and pull you out when it goes bad."

"Why do you say 'when'?" Asti asked.

"Because I know you."

Asti rolled his eyes, and turned his attention to Helene. "Why aren't you dressed, anyway?"

"Because Vellun is putting together some dress hoop thing that looks frightful, and I'm waiting. I have to wear this stuff?"

"We all have our burdens."

"I'm going to be a lumbering cow, you know," Helene said. "But it's a place to hide some hip-hangers."

"See, thinking in solutions," Asti said. "That's much better."

"Verci," she said sharply. "Take The Action and the Rainmaker in the hidey-hole with you. If we're smuggling stuff in . . ."

"You want it handy," Verci said.

She winked and went back over to the table.

"Where's Kennith?" Asti asked.

"Introducing Almer and Pilsen to the horses. I think all three of them are out of their element today."

"Aren't we all?" Asti asked.

"Kennith made that char-duck again," Mila said.

"Chr'dach," Asti said. "Is that our gig night ritual?"

Verci shrugged. "It makes Kennith happy, and given what you're having him do, somewhat appropriate. I actually like it."

"All right, whatever else happens, we need to be in carriages, rolling by five bells. The party starts at six, and we've got to get across town."

"Paint's barely dry on those carriages," Verci said.

"Then blow on it or something," Asti said. "I've got to put on a stupid suit. Five bells."

"Five bells," Mila said. "I better figure out how to hide a rope in my dress."

"What is it with you and those ropes?" Verci asked.

"I'm good with them," Mila said. "Kept me alive this long."

As she went off to Vellun and Helene, Verci turned to Asti.

"So then what's next?"

"After tonight? Josie, whoever else is behind Andrendon, Treggin, and Lesk's crew. We'll figure it out."

"Not quite what I meant," Verci said. "What's . . . when do we try to be normal again? Decent folk of the neighborhood? The Rynax Gadgeterium?"

Asti took the sides of Verci's head and pulled him close, touching their foreheads together. "Soon. I promise you, that little boy of yours will not know this life of ours."

"Raych already knows it too much," Verci said. "It came for her."

"We'll keep them safe, keep them clean. You know—you know—" Asti's eyes started to well up.

"You haven't been holding it together," Verci said. "Last night . . ."

"I've got it under control," Asti said. "Finish up your gig night ritual."

"It's not—"

"Of course not," Asti said. "Just make sure you're ready for whatever tonight throws at us."

"I'm ready for that, brother," Verci said, kissing Asti on the forehead. "I'll be there with you. That's the only thing I need."

Raych had to admit, Asti had done a fabulous job of cleaning the bakery. That meant she could spend much of the day—whenever Corsi wasn't being fussy—going through the place to find all the hidden secrets Verci had mentioned.

The bunker in the basement was the most fascinating. The upstairs apartment was comfortable and well apportioned, but this could be more living space—a lovely office or reading room. Or it could be Verci's workshop. There was no reason why he couldn't use it that way. It was a perfectly livable room, but Verci was so set on it being this secret bunker and part of all the Old Lady's mystique, he couldn't bear it being anything else.

Sometimes she wondered if Verci and his brother were so stuck in their ways, being sneaky and secretive, that they just didn't see the obvious.

She came back up into the bakery to find a man standing in the middle of the shop, carrying a small case.

"We're closed," she said cautiously.

He turned to her—and she stifled the immediate instinct to scream or run. He was milky-white pale with stringy pitch-black hair. A Poasian. Raych always tried to have an open mind about people from all parts of the world, but a Poasian? That still filled her with dread, even if she felt ashamed for it. Her uncles who had served in the War in the

Islands talked about the "ghosts" in a way that made them sound inhuman. This was the first time she had been this close to one. Did any live in this neighborhood? Asti would know.

"My apologies," he said with the harsh accent. "The door was open."

That was troubling. Hadn't she latched it?

"I—it's a holiday. I decided to stay closed."

"Of course," he said. "A saint day, yes? You seem to have quite a lot of those, and observe them with irregularity."

"Me?" Blazes, her voice quivered there. She wished she could hold some composure here, show no fear.

"Again, apologies. I was referring to . . ." He paused for a moment, as if thinking of the best way to express himself. "In my native language, several ideas translate to 'you,' including addressing a national character as a whole. I know nothing about you, an individual person, as we have never met."

"No, we haven't."

"Which is a terrible shame, as I engaged in a robust business with the former owner of this shop."

"Oh?" Did he mean the baker, or Missus Holt?

"I am being obtuse and poor," he said. "I ask forgiveness, for I should be plain. My name is Khejhaz Nafath, and I am a spice merchant with a shop in this neighborhood."

"Spice shop!" Raych was almost too loud in her exclamation. She had heard of a Poasian spicery in the neighborhood, but she had never dared. Nor had anyone she had ever spoken to. She wondered how the place stayed in business.

Probably through shady dealings, like so many things in this part of the city.

"Yes, of course, Mister Nafath. I didn't realize there had been business with you before. Mister Mersh didn't leave me with complete records of his accounts. Is there an outstanding payment or such?"

"Not at all, Missus Rynax," he said. "Though I would welcome the opportunity to gain you as a customer."

She managed a weak smile. "We get our spices from Remeniux's."

He sighed. "Yes, indeed. I am . . . familiar with that enterprise." He looked as if saying that gave him physical pain.

"Was . . . was that what you came for?"

"In no small part," he said. "I'm just a simple merchant, selling goods that are perhaps too exotic a luxury to be lucrative. But I took the venture of preparing a small sample of my wares, to present as a gift. I offer this with no expectations or conditions." He held out the case to her.

He kept the case held out for a period of time that turned awkward—just holding it for her to take without any change in his expression. Perhaps this was a Poasian method of presenting a gift.

"Thank you," Raych said, taking it from him. She wasn't sure what else to do. "I'm afraid I'm not too familiar with Poasian spices or how they might be used."

He nodded. "While they have proven popular to some circles of Druth culture, knowledge of their potential is still quite limited." He made a strange tapping gesture on his ear. "I know someone you might ask. Your brother-in-law."

Raych felt her blood chill. "Asti, why—"

"Asti Rynax has very broad knowledge of many subjects. For example, this one—" He pointed to one jar in the case. "That one is *rijetzh*. I believe he knows exactly how he could use that."

Raych wanted to run upstairs and lock herself in the safe room, but her feet wouldn't move. "Why—" Her voice deserted her for a moment. Clearing her throat. "Why would Asti . . ."

"Be of serenity, Missus Rynax," Nafath said, taking a few steps away from her. "This is nothing more than a simple gift from one local business to another. We should all do such things from time to time. For the sake of the neighborhood." He said this last part with a strange emphasis that she didn't quite understand, but he gave her a nod as if they were in complete covenant with each other.

"But—"

He was opening the door. "Simply tell your husband's brother what I brought you, and who brought it. And do that as soon as you possibly can. I am *certain* he will appreciate it."

He touched his neck while bowing his head, and went out into the street.

Raych ran over and latched the door, and then threw the secret double-bolt. Then she went to the back alley door and did the same. Leaving the box of Poasian spices on the kneading counter, she went up to the apartment to lie in the bed with Corsi. She didn't need to do anything else until her husband came home, and no saint or prophet could make her do otherwise.

Chapter 24

"HOW'S THE FOOT?" ASTI asked Verci as he adjusted the walking brace in the back of the carriage as it rumbled its way east. Asti and Helene were both in their full regalia as a pair of nobles, though there still was a certain shabbiness to their finery. Asti had insisted that it was fine—they were playing the role of low-in-the-family nobility, pretending that they weren't out of money. Both of their disguises were excellent, though. Almer had done some treatment to their hair to give them both the same light-brown shade, and with Pilsen's makeup, they really did look like siblings. Helene was quite cross about Almer's chemicals in her hair, especially when he told her that it would grow out in time.

"Tolerable," Verci said. The brace was doing its job, so the pain was now a dull ache. Constant, but bearable. Verci had a small vial of Almer's pain reliever with his gear, but he had already resolved not to take any of it. Pain with clarity of thought was far preferable to a cloud of bliss.

Verci wondered if Asti felt the same about clarity of thought, or what that even meant for his brother. Two months ago, Asti had said he was on the verge of snapping completely. Verci had feared that he would have to put Asti in Haltom Asylum, spending the rest of his days in a strapper-coat to stop him from tearing his eyes out.

Asti didn't use the word "mission" much, but it was clear to Verci that all of this—going after the Andrendon Project or whatever was behind the fire—was the anchor holding Asti's sanity in place. Verci wanted to get these people, bring justice to them since they would never be brought to it—but he didn't need it.

He just needed to keep his family safe.

That included Asti, and his wits. If this gig was what Asti needed, Verci would dive into the blazes and beat every sinner there for his brother.

"And you?" Verci asked. "You're ready for this?"

"My mouth is still stinging from the *chr'dach*."

"Be serious," Verci said.

"I know. I've got a cork on my skull right now," Asti said.

"Does that mean you won't try and kill this Liora woman on sight?" Helene asked.

"I'm pretty sure I won't," Asti said. "But that's because . . ." He looked out the carriage window for a moment.

"Because what?" Verci asked.

"Killing her won't solve anything," Asti said. "It's not like it would bring me peace."

"Is peace an option for you?" Verci asked.

"Can we not get too heavy here?" Helene asked. "I've got enough to worry about right now. Like how I'm going to walk while wearing all this around my legs."

"We didn't make women's fashion," Asti said.

"These noblewomen never needed to do anything serious," Helene said. "How did this dress get worse since the Emporium gig?"

"Vellun made some adjustments," Verci said. Vellun, for a naive, pretty boy with a seemingly empty head, had a decent set of skills when it came to the prep for this gig. Verci had to admit that they probably wouldn't have pulled off the disguises if it wasn't for that kid.

Of course, it still remained to be seen if they did pull it off.

"You're still armed, though," Asti said.

Helene pulled up a bustle of fabric to show a hip-hanger crossbow and a few bolts strapped to her bare leg. "I don't know how I'll get to it in a pinch, but I have it. You've got your knives?"

"Four," Asti said.

"Next time we do some sewage like this, I'm dressing as a man," Helene said. "I don't care, that's what I'm doing."

"I've got your other two crossbows hidden in the seat down here."

"You've got them already loaded and prepped?" Helene asked.

"Yes, even though I've told you—"

"I know, it's bad for the cords—"

"We're out of money, so we can't—"

"Hey!" Asti snapped. "Come on, we're coming up on the entryway."

"Fine," Helene said. Using her noble accent—or a best approximation, which came off as over-enunciating every word, she said, "There will be food at this, yes? Because I am starving."

"It's a feast," Asti said. "Though I believe the whole hiding game thing happens before we eat, and if everything goes smoothly—"

"We'll be flying down the road before it actually comes to eating," Helene said.

"I should get hidden," Verci said, opening up the panel in the seat. "This is it."

"Drive forward," Asti said, looking at him and Helene. "Especially if something goes wrong with me."

Verci was half into the secret compartment. "What's going to go wrong with you?"

"Let's not underestimate Liora," Asti said. "There's still one big mystery hanging over all of this."

Helene nodded. "Why she wants to use us at all for this."

"There's fire coming, and I'm going to take it," Asti said. "I need you two to be ready to sweep up the ashes."

"I'll tell you what I'm going to sweep up, boys," Helene said. "No matter what else we find, what else happens, we need to walk out of here with a few more crowns in our pockets. We've already been through too much fire to have nothing but ashes and dust."

"We'll get the Old Lady, get our money," Asti said.

"Before I go in," Verci said. "Things go wrong, no safehouse, no stable . . ."

"First meet point is the safehouse in Colton. Then we all go to the bunker of the bakery," Asti said. He shrugged with acquiescence. "It'll do for tonight."

Verci nodded. Asti had accepted his point—Josie wouldn't come for them. Not tonight, at least. "See you in a bit." He dropped into the secret compartment and closed it shut.

The carriage came to a stop. "Invitations?" a grumbly voice asked.

"Here's at it, old top," Asti said in his noble voice. "Cansling and Jennidine Onterren of Greckinvale."

"Thank you, my Lord," the grumbly voice said. He gave some instructions to Almer, up in the driver's seat. The carriage rolled forward again.

"Really," Helene said. "What sort of name is Jennidine?"

"Yours," Asti said, maintaining character. The carriage came to a stop again. "Get it straight, because here we go."

The carriage doors were opened, and Asti and Helene got out. After a moment, the carriage slowly rolled away. They were in, and Verci was on the grounds as well.

So far, all to the plan.

Asti had to admit, despite her protests, Helene was walking like a woman right out of a noble finishing school. Her accent was a bit spotty, but she had gotten at least that part right.

"It's the shoes," Helene whispered to him as they went through the grand hallway toward the ballroom. "You either walk the right way in these things or fall on your face."

"Fascinating, Jennidine," he said. Hopefully that would be enough to keep her in character. He could see her eyes had gone wide at the level of opulence on display here:

silver and gold sconces, gilded portraits—thousands upon thousands of crowns.

"Quite a bit of opportunity, brother Cansling," Helene said.

"Put a button on your mouth, sister," Asti said. They reached the entrance to the ballroom, presenting their invitation card to the steward at the door—namely, Win in his role as Mister Ungar. He had a brief moment of surprise at seeing the two of them, but covered it well enough. He had been expecting them, after all.

"The Honorable Cansling and Jennidine Onterren of Greckinvale," he announced to the room. Asti gave Win a nod of approval, and Win returned it—all very appropriate for their roles. Win also gave Asti a subtle signal with his hands, with his thumb crossed under two fingers. Confirmed—Win got Asti's note, and he and Julien were briefed on the plan.

All good so far.

The ballroom was now lit up with hundreds of candles, and the room was filled with nobility and other swells, dressed in their finest. Asti spotted a handful of faces he knew by reputation, including a few in military dress uniform. Musicians—a traditional string quintet—were in the far corner playing a lively traditional piece that some were dancing to in the center of the ballroom. The dance was a regimented bit of steps that seemed far more work than fun. Asti never quire understood the appeal of such things.

The crowd largely took no note of their entrance, save a woman in a purple dress whose attention fixed on Helene. Helene didn't seem to notice, and before Asti could ask her, someone else stepped up to them.

"What ho, Greckinvale?" Lord Henterman approached, dressed in a resplendent red suit of Turjin silk with hasps made of silver and walrus ivory. He really was a face of teeth and emptiness. "You must be these splendid cousins I have heard my dear Ana go on and on about. Nathaniel Henterman." He put out an open arm to Asti.

The urge to pull out a knife and plunge it into Henterman's heart surged through Asti's skull. He beat it down. This was not the moment.

"Cansling," Asti said. "Truly a pleasure to finally meet the man who captured Phidie's heart." If Liora was going by "Anaphide" here, by Saint Senea, Asti would make a meal out of that.

"And you must be Jennidine," he said to Helene, kissing her on both cheeks. Helene was clearly not quite ready for that greeting.

"A pleasure," she said, her voice cracking a bit. "We are ever so grateful for your hospitality."

"But of course," Henterman said. "When Ana said you were in Maradaine and she had to have you come, of course, I could not deny her. My doors are open, as is my spirit. It is a blessed day."

"A blessed day of a blessed saint," Asti said.

"Indeed," Henterman said. "Ho, Canderell! Bring those here."

Mister Canderell was carrying a tray of drinks—deep red in glass tumblers. "My Lord, I was to be delivering these—"

"Sorry, nonsense, these are my Lady's dear cousins, and we must not let them remain parched a moment longer." He took two drinks from the tray and handed them to Asti and Helene. "You'll forgive Canderell, he's something of a stickler for proper methods."

"Of course," Asti said.

"My Lords, I must continue on," Canderell said.

That was one test passed. Canderell had looked right at Asti and showed so sign that he had seen "Mister Crile." Not even a hint of recognition.

"This is not wine, my Lord," Helene said. "I presume this is your own special recipe for the sainted day?"

"Red wine for the bloody feast is far too . . . simple," Henterman said. "I had blood oranges shipped up from the Acserian coast, and their juice is mixed with Fuergan sloeberry liquor of the Astev family, and a little something special I've bought from Ravi Kenorax. Taste it."

Asti sipped at the drink, which was absurdly sweet. Almost sickly so.

"Isn't it divine?" Henterman asked.

"Saintly," Asti said.

Helene didn't seem to mind the sweetness, as she finished her drink in almost a single gulp.

"That, my Lord, is quite something," she said. Her demeanor was far more Maradaine Westside than Patyma Finishing School.

"Indeed," Henterman said, putting on an even larger and more soulless smile. "Ah, and here is my Ana."

Liora glided over to Lord Henterman, a stunning figure in her red dress, matching his outfit perfectly. She somehow made even a ridiculous high, white-haired wig look elegant. Asti was a bit amazed at how easily he could be of two minds about her. The beautiful, charming, and talented woman whom he had worked with—and even loved, if he was being honest with himself—was on full display, and he couldn't help but be taken in a bit by that. She was an astounding woman, and he couldn't deny the draw, the attraction.

But at the same time, he wanted to rip her throat out. Even if everything she claimed was true, she had been given orders to betray him . . . he didn't care. They had worked next to each other, in complete rhythm with each other, and she still had it in her to cross him as thoroughly as that.

"The"—mumble—*"thanks you for the sacrifice."* Those last words she had said to him still danced on the edge of his memory—something he knew was in his grasp if he could just reach it.

He shook it away. Focus on the gig. Smile and nod.

"Why, Nathan, I see you've already met my dear ones. Cansy, Jenny, darlings, it's been too long."

"Too long," Helene said, this time prepared for the kiss on the cheek coming from Liora. "But I had no intention of missing you tonight."

"Oh, I'm certain you didn't, dear," Liora said.

"How was your journey to Maradaine?" Henterman asked. "Uneventful?"

"Blissfully so," Asti said. "I've been quite fortunate by getting nothing but boring stories."

"Fortunate, indeed. Surely Ana told you of our ordeal right after the wedding."

"It is funny, my Lord—"

"Nathan."

Asti took the cue. "It's quite funny, Nathan. In her letters she danced around the subject, mentioning that it was quite the trial, but neglected to ever get to particulars."

Henterman gave a sly grin to Liora. "And here I thought these cousins were your dearest confidantes."

"But they are," Liora said, crooking her arm into Asti's. "However, some stories are best told face to face."

"Of course, darling," Henterman said. "You two aren't going to keep her to yourselves all night, are you?"

"By no means," Asti said. "But you'll forgive us in advance?"

"Absolutely!" he said gregariously. "This is a night of joy and celebration. And you need a new drink, Jennidine."

"I would not object, my Lord."

A man came over to Henterman—not dressed like a butler or other servant, but he had a regard of deference that implied he was in service to Lord Henterman. "My Lord, the Baron you wanted a private word with? He is ready."

"Thank you, Ender," Henterman said. "Forgive me, darling. Duty calls." He kissed Liora on the cheek.

"Not too long, I would hope?"

"Of course not," Henterman said. "We'll be doing the Hide shortly. I can't miss that."

He went off with Ender up the stairs.

"He's such a boy sometimes," Liora said. She turned back to Asti and Helene. "Don't you two look . . . rustic."

"Well, Greckinvale is on the outskirts," Asti said.

"We don't live the tony life of Maradaine there," Helene added.

"A word like 'tony' ruins your disguise, dear. This is what you have to work with, Cansy?"

"She's got my back," Asti said. "That's the part that matters."

"Yes, you and trust are challenging friends. Fair enough."

"He's going up to the office right now," Asti said. "Will that be an issue?"

"It shouldn't. He'll be down to play Saint Jontlen, he is so eager for that. It boggles me."

"I imagine you're easily boggled," Helene said.

Liora narrowed her eyes at Helene. "Don't think I don't know nine different ways to kill you and make it look like a tragic accident."

Helene shrugged. "When I come for you, darling, you'll never see it coming." She pointed to a table at the far end. "There's something involving bread and hot cheese over there, I'm going to look into it."

Asti saw that as Helene went off, her attention was still trained on him and Liora, keeping her line of sight clear. She knew her job, and that included burying a crossbow bolt in Liora's chest if anything went wrong.

The band changed songs to something a bit more up-tempo.

"A *carendatta*," Liora said brightly. "You remember this one in New Acoria?"

"Don't start to—"

She took his hand, which stirred an instinct in him, but for once, not a violent one. For just a moment, her hand in his felt natural and normal. For a moment, he felt like he could be normal as well.

"Dance it with me," she said. "For the memory."

They went out to the center of the floor, engaging in the dance. The steps were easy enough, and the *carendatta* was one of the few of these formal dances that didn't involve a ring of eight or more and a constant switching of partners. Even in these prescribed steps and staid structures of propriety, the *carendatta* was filled with underlying intimacy, a simmering heat between the dancers. Especially since the two of them had their eyes locked on each other the whole time.

In her eyes, he saw the deceptive, murderous traitor who had destroyed him. And even still, he could get lost in those eyes.

"You still have it, Asti Rynax," she whispered.

Too many eyes were on them, too much attention. The revelers would mark both him and Liora, and if they remained the most interesting thing in the ballroom, that attention would hold through the Hide. That was the last thing he needed.

Fortunately, the thing that he wanted as the most interesting thing in the room suddenly walked through the ballroom doors, right on schedule.

"Lord and Lady Intiara of Upper Edelvale," Win called out, with Vellun and Mila coming down the steps. Win coughed for a moment, and then announced the person right behind Vellun and Mila. Ken, with his hair in tight braids and wearing a modified version of a Druth gentleman's dinner suit that showed his bare arms. Arms that were covered in scars and elaborate tattoos.

"And the honorable Natkel-cha of Paht'Kira."

Nobody's eyes were on Asti now.

"And the honorable Natkel-cha of Paht'Kira."

It hadn't escaped Mila's notice that no one paid much attention when she and Vellun were announced, despite the fact that she looked spectacular in this dress. If every gig could involve some sort of regal ball, she would be perfectly content. It beat the blazes out of flower girls and street rattery. This was nothing like anything she had ever seen in her life. The ballroom was filled to the walls with beautifully dressed people in splendid coats with embroidered epaulets and pearl-laden dresses and opulence that took Mila's breath away. Paintings and sculpture and silver and so much raw wealth she almost wanted to cry. This was how the nobility lived, while plain folk in North Seleth and farther west were scraping by, half-starved.

It was no wonder that they ignored her and Vellun. These people had seen plenty of girls in pretty dresses.

But once Kennith came in, that all changed. Heads—especially those with pale-powdered faces and wearing curled white-hair wigs—downright spun when Win announced that Ch'omik name.

A young couple approached with an eager air. "Did he come here with you?" the woman asked. Her dress was possibly the most scandalous thing Mila had ever seen outside of the Birdie Basement, with a display of cleavage so profound a man could get lost within it.

"Yes, he did," Vellun said proudly. "I've been deeply

privileged to have him as a traveling companion for many months."

"You've been to Ch'omikTaa?" the woman purred out. "I am just fascinated by the eastern world."

"Ch'omikTaa and the Jelidan cities, which I would never had survived without Natkel-cha. A gift from the saints, he was."

Kennith strode over to them as if each step he made carried a portentous weight. "This is the celebration of the blood god?" he asked, putting on an accent that Mila assumed to be Ch'omik. She had no idea if it was properly authentic.

"Blood god?" the cleavaged woman asked. "No, it's Saint Jontlen, who is the bloody saint."

"But it is a fighting spirit that you worship." Kennith said this with confidence. Mila was amazed—this was a performance on the same level as Pilsen at his best, and she had no idea that Kennith had been capable of such things. She always had the impression he rejected anything Ch'omik, save the *chr'dach*. But in this moment, he was reveling in the role. "This seems like a coddled place for such a sacred ceremony."

"It's hardly sacred," the woman said.

"Just a bit of silly fun," her companion added.

Kennith looked to Vellun. "You told me this honored the blood spirit of your people."

"It does," Vellun said. "In its own way." He turned to the couple. "Baron Restick Intiara, and my wife Chelianne."

"Charmed," the woman said. "Lady Elisvea of Tiber, and my intended Thorton."

"A pleasure," Thorton said. Mila noted that his accent was far from the noble one she had been learning to fake. Perhaps Lady Elisvea had intentions outside her class.

"I'm sorry to be so brazen," Lady Elisvea said to Kennith. "But can I see your arms?"

Kennith presented them to her. Fortunately they were quite well muscled, presumably from his machine work and caring for his horses. But the woman wasn't asking for that, though she touched Ken's arm with a sensual reverence. She was examining the series of intricate scars and tattoos that Kennith had put on with help from Almer and Mister Gin. Mila hoped they had made them well enough to withstand the close scrutiny the woman was giving.

A few other swells had approached, one in a military dress uniform. "So, chap, those tell your story, your rank, and what have you."

Kennith turned to him, with a glower that could melt iron. He pointed to the markings on his right forearm. "Cha. From the House Taqhna of Paht'Kira."

"And what brought you to Paht'Kira, old bean?" another of them asked Vellun.

"Well, it's quite a tale . . ." Vellun launched into a yarn that was detailed and elaborate, involving a failure of fortune from his father, a merchant venture, and a shipwreck on the Ch'omik coast.

Mila used that opportunity to wander away from Vellun and Kennith while several people gave them their complete attention. She scanned the room. Asti was on the ballroom floor, dancing with a woman—an absolute treasure of a woman. Not just beautiful, but graceful and fluid.

This had to be Liora Rand. In a few moments, Mila could tell this woman was every bit as shrewd and dangerous as Asti had made her out to be. Every movement she made was deliberate and perfect. Her attention was on Asti, but yet she seemed to take in every part of the room as well.

But she didn't give Mila any special notice as she made her way over to the table where servants were pouring drinks—strange blood-red drinks that didn't look anything like wine.

"Careful there, it's very sweet."

Helene, holding up a glass, staying in character.

"I appreciate it," Mila said, taking one of the drinks. She took a sip and found it shockingly sweet, even sickly so. It was not unlike licking pine needles dipped in honey, but with the added kick of Doctor Gelson's breath. Mila nodded to Helene and held onto the drink, with no intention of having any more of it.

That was all the acknowledgment needed. Mila sometimes wondered if she should learn all the strange codes and signals that Asti and Verci shared, but most of the time it seemed like the Rynaxes were just showing off or something. Mila was pretty confident in her ability to get what she needed to know off a look from Helene. Things were going fine. Save for herself and Helene, and a woman in a purple dress who was stalking the drinks table, everyone's attention seemed to be on themselves or Kennith. Helene slipped away from the table—she had handed off her duty of "eyes on Asti and Liora" to Mila, and she was going to her next task: making contact with Julien.

The music ended, though only Asti and Liora were still dancing at all. Almost the entire room was listening to Vellun and Kennith. One person wasn't, though—he was the one who had signaled to the musicians to end. He went over to Asti and Liora.

"Well then, we've gotten quite a commotion in my absence, no?" he asked.

"Indeed," Asti said. "It's a bit vulgar, if you ask me. You think these people had never seen a foreigner before."

"Yes," the man said. "Did you catch the name of that man with him, darling?"

"Lord Intiara," Liora said. "You know him?"

This man must be Lord Henterman. And it was obvious that Liora noted everything that happened. Mila looked at this young lord. He was a handsome enough man, but he looked devoid of any sense of guile. Or soul. The man seemed so jovially empty, Mila could scarcely believe he could be behind the fiery murder of all the people on Holver Alley. When she saw Mendel Tyne—when she killed him—she saw a man who ruled by petty fear, who held most other people in contempt. That man wouldn't care who died at his word. She couldn't quite see that in Lord Henterman's face. There was almost nothing there at all.

"Not off the top of my head, but there are a handful of people that Ender sent invitations to who are up-and-comers of note. I imagine this Intiara is one of them." He shrugged, as if complete strangers arriving at the party was to be expected. That wasn't something Mila was about to complain about.

"He does know best," Liora said.

"That would be your man there," Asti asked, nodding in

the direction of the stairs. Mila couldn't quite see up there from her position. "Not part of your household staff?"

"No, no, he's my attaché and secretary. Indispensable, that man. But come now, before we lose the crowd to this Ch'omik. The footmen will be bringing out the feast, and then we'll be doing the Hide."

"Joyous!" Liora said. "I plan on hiding very well, my love."

"We'll still strive to find you, dearest."

Henterman walked toward the double doors on the far side, which servants were opening up as tables and trays were brought in. As soon as he had turned away, Liora's face changed slightly, showing just a hint of disgust at the man whom she called husband.

Asti gave Mila the slightest of signals with his eyes, pointing her toward the stairs. He probably wanted her to note this Ender, the attaché. Made sense. If he was Henterman's right-hand man, he would have plenty of information about whatever deals Henterman was involved in. Maybe Ender would prove an easier target than Henterman himself, and through him, they could find out what they needed to know about the fire, and what was behind it all.

Mila moved her way through the ballroom to get a better look at this Ender. As soon as she was in view, she gasped and almost dropped her glass. She was able to hold herself together, keeping the glass in hand and her mouth silent. There was no need to make a spectacle of herself, drawing every eye in the room on her, especially "Ender". That would be disastrous. The last thing she needed was to have him make note of her, and recognize her as easily as she did him. Even in the smart suit, the crisp jacket, the face was one Mila wouldn't forget.

"Ender" was none other than Treggin.

Chapter 25

THE DISTRACTION WAS CERTAINLY doing its job. Kennith put on an excellent performance. Helene had to give him full credit, she had no idea he had that in him. What had he said when Asti suggested he play an actual Ch'omik warrior lord? "I had heard enough stories from my grandfather to fake it well enough for a bunch of noble swells."

The people seemed to buy it. The eyes that weren't still on Asti and Liora were on Kennith and Vellun. So no one was marking Helene. Most importantly, Liora wasn't paying any attention to her. Which gave her the chance to slip down a corridor to find the kitchens, find Julien. She had gotten enough of that oversweet swill on her breath that she could fake a tipsy wander if anyone caught her.

She only got two steps to the hallway when a lady in a sleek purple dress placed herself in front of Helene. "Well, hello again."

Helene put on the best ladylike smile she could manage. "Hello yourself. You'll forgive me—"

"Worry not, I already have," the lady said, giving something of a bemused smirk. "I wouldn't have expected to run into you here, however."

"Well, this is the event, isn't it?" Helene said, giving that "noble titter" Pilsen had taught her. She wished he was in here right now. "I mean, a real Ch'omik warrior? Very exciting."

"Oh, him? Fraud. But you know that."

"I what?"

The lady in the purple dress took Helene's hand and pulled her into the hallway. "You really do need to work on your facade, girl," she said. "Of course I already knew you don't belong here."

"Whatever do you mean?" Helene asked. She made a point of hitting every consonant the way she was supposed to, which probably made her sound like a lunatic.

"Darling," the woman said calmly. "Clearly you don't recall. I forget that my memory is uncommon. We've met. Two months ago, in Carol Woods."

"Why . . . why . . . no, you must be . . ." Helene's memory sparked. When was she in Carol Woods? When she was testing out her first Verci Rynax crossbow, hunting rabbits. When she was interrupted by that bounty hunter.

That rather posh bounty hunter.

"You're a fake too!" Helene exclaimed, perhaps a little too excitedly. She had definitely lost any trace of her regal affect.

"I wouldn't go that far." She extended her hand to Helene. "Lady Melania Landron of Canthen Hall."

"But you're—" Helene looked around, making sure none of the other guests were paying them any mind. "You're a bounty hunter."

"A girl can be two things."

"All right," Helene said cautiously. "So . . . what do you want?"

"Well, I wanted to not be bored to tears, but Lord Henterman and this party were determined to do otherwise. You can imagine my joy in spotting you here."

Helene shook her head. "Wait, no. We met for a minute. How could you—"

"So what are you hunting today, girl?"

"Helene." Helene cursed to herself. Why had she said her name?

Lady Melania paused. "Is that who you're hunting, or your name?"

"My name," Helene said, regretting saying it as soon as it came out. "I'm not hunting anyone. Exactly."

"But you're clearly up to some shenanigans, for a west Maradaine girl who's a crack shot with a crossbow to be at a lord's shindig like this."

Helene wasn't sure if that was some sort of threat to expose her, or an offer to join her.

"So what do you want?"

Lady Melania patted her on the arm. "Helene, darling, don't worry. I'm hardly interested in snuffing the lamp on your plans, unless they interfere with my own. I was just thrilled, because your presence means at least *something* exciting might happen now."

"Your own? A bounty on one of the swells here?"

"That would be fun, wouldn't it?" Lady Melania sighed. "Though it would be dreadfully easy to take one of them down. Wouldn't even have to take off my shoes." She extended her foot for Helene to appraise. "You like?"

"I suppose," Helene said. They were perfectly nice shoes, if she were the sort to be interested in shoes. "I'd kill to have my boots on and this frippery off."

"Saints hear you on that, darling. This costume is a necessity of event." She poked her head out of the hallway to look at the ballroom. "Am I spoiling some timing?"

"Not yet," Helene said.

"But soon, yes. Then I won't dally. Are you hunting someone called Crenaxin? Sometimes called 'The Fervent Fire' or some such nonsense. The rumors on him are rather sketchy, to be honest."

That was new to Helene. "Sounds Kell or Racquin."

"Yes, probably," Lady Melania said. "I'm guessing that's a no."

"Never heard of him—it is a him?"

"I had presumed, but you have a point. I don't know exactly what I'm looking for, but if I see him, well . . ."

"Can't help you."

"I understand," Lady Melania said. "I think I quite like you, Helene. You have your crossbow on you?"

"These layers of petticoat can hide a lot," Helene said.

"Capital. Well, you probably have some mischief to be about. You need any assistance, give a whistle. I don't think my information tying this Crenaxin fellow to Henterman was meaningful. Now I'm simply bored. I'd leave, but appearances and family name must be preserved. Saints help me."

She looked out into the ballroom again. "Oh, Nathaniel is having the bloody foods wheeled out. He'll be starting the Hide soon. I swear to the saints, he is such a *boy*."

"The Hide?" Helene asked. She had lost sight of Asti, as well as Mila. Hopefully they still had sight of each other. She needed to find Julien. He was here in the house somewhere. That was first. He should be somewhere in the kitchens.

"Ah, your timing. I've delayed you too much. Be about it."

"Do you know how to get to the kitchens?"

Lady Melania pointed to one of the doorways across the ballroom. "Through there, left down the hallway, around the corner and then the second door on the left. Stairway will lead you down."

"How did you—"

"Because, dear, I remember everything." She sighed wistfully. "Everything." She went out into the ballroom, spinning on her heel as she walked to look back at Helene. "Truly, whistle. You'd be doing me the favor."

"All right," Helene said, and went out the other way.

"Ladies and gentles, friends all!" Lord Henterman called out to the room. "The time has come to begin our official festivities."

Mila moved herself back, so she couldn't be seen by Treggin at the top of the staircase. How was he here? How could Treggin have embedded himself as Lord Henterman's personal attaché?

She must have it backward. Henterman was working some plan in North Seleth—this Andrendon business—so "Treggin" was probably the act that Ender put on to gain influence over the neighborhood. To what end, Mila had no clue, but she was going to find out, and before that bastard could use his magical-glass blade on her again.

Lord Henterman went on. "I acknowledge, this is a bit of a foolish tradition, and I am grateful to all of you for putting up with it, and me. But if you know me, you know I relish every holy day and strive to celebrate and honor every saint in the canon."

"Tell me, Nathaniel," someone in the crowd called out. "Are we just going to Hide, or do your 'guards' hunt for us?"

"And how bloody are you going to be?" someone else shouted.

"Oh, these are lovely questions," Lord Henterman said. "Almost the entire household is open for you to hide in, and I expect you to make it a challenge to find you all. The guards *will* be looking, friends. Hopefully, Saint Jontlen will save you."

Asti and Liora weren't quite in her line of sight. She needed to get Asti to see her, let him know about Treggin. But she had no way of approaching him without making a spectacle, certainly not without blowing her cover with Liora. And that would get Treggin's attention, and blow everything. She could tell Helene, and then send her over to Asti. That would work.

Helene was nowhere to be seen.

She'd have to get a message to Asti without coming close to him.

This would be a moment where knowing those blinking codes or hand signals would be useful.

Maybe she could use Ken or Vellun. No, even with Henterman speaking, they had a crowd around them.

It was on her. She couldn't tell anyone, and she didn't dare let Treggin out of her sight, or let him notice her. So she needed to get him. Maybe, if she could grab him, get him to talk . . .

He was a blasted mage. Her best shot was to get a drop on him and put him down before he knew what was happening.

Mila eased her way over to the other staircase. People would be scattering in a moment, based on the rules of this game. Absurdities—rich swells and officers, adults all, playing some child's game. She was probably the youngest person in the room, and she thought it was the stupidest thing she had ever heard of.

"But first," Lord Henterman announced, "We must drop the darkness upon us all. So I—or my 'guards'—don't see where you all go."

So the lights were going to go out. That could help.

Mila had reached the landing of the staircase on the left. Treggin was still up at the top of the right-side staircase, his attention on Lord Henterman. Asti and Liora were by Lord Henterman, Liora playing the part of a doting wife. She had the most beatific, loving expression. Mila marveled at her performance. No wonder Asti was so apprehensive of her. She had beauty and skill, and from Helene's description of the brief fight at the safehouse, she was deadly.

Asti's focus was on Liora. His face was unreadable—no emotion, just intensity. So much so, there was no chance at all Mila could get his attention right now. Lord Henterman was continuing to natter on. Mila crept up the stairs as quietly and unobtrusively as she could. As long as Treggin didn't notice her, that was all that mattered.

She reached the top of the stairs before she realized she had absolutely no way to get to the knife she had strapped to her leg, not without upending herself and lifting her petticoats over her head. Again, nothing she could do without making a spectacle of herself. Why didn't she have a rope on her? Stupid fancy dress, that a girl couldn't use a rope belt with. Totally impractical.

"So, now!" Henterman shouted. "Footmen and butlers, if you would? Snuff out the lamps!"

The order was obeyed rather efficiently, and darkness hit the room in a flash. Shouts of glee amongst the swells down below as they all went scampering in every direction. Footsteps pounded up the stairs in a rush—probably Asti and Liora, heading to where they could get into the study.

Was it possible that Henterman suspected them? Did he have Treggin up there to protect the study? If so, Asti wasn't ready to fight a mage. Treggin had to be taken out of the situation, now.

It was far too dark to see much of anything, but her eyes

were adjusting quickly and she could see the shape of Treggin's body. Good enough for what she needed. At this point, there was no need to worry about spectacle.

She ran at Treggin with everything she had, throwing her body into him. He yelped in surprise as she slammed her shoulder into his chest. Before he could do anything, her momentum sent the two of them over the railing, falling toward the ballroom floor.

Chapter 26

AS SOON AS THE darkness hit, Liora had grabbed Asti's hand and pulled him up the stairway, past folks who were squealing and yelping in the blackness. Asti had seen Mila in the corner of his eye, slipping up the stairway to place herself on the second floor. That was a good instinct, but he wondered why she had taken that initiative. It seemed like her attention was elsewhere.

He didn't have time to figure that out. People were already shouting and hollering, and the whole Hide was well underway. Liora was dragging him up the next set of stairs to her personal quarters.

As soon as they were in, she slammed the doors and threw a latch.

"Oh, thank the saints we're done with that charade," Liora said, tearing off her dress. "I'm ready to scream just being around that man."

"Not a happy marriage?" Asti said, taking off the jacket and waistcoat.

"Ugh," she said. "If all goes well, I can slip off into the night and not give this place another thought." Down to her stockings and skivs, she went into the wardrobe. "Come on."

Asti went in, checking that he could get at his knives in a pinch. Right now, things were going smoothly. Liora was . . . what she had always been. Engaging, on point, effective. His desire to slit her throat had diminished significantly over the evening.

"Bet you wished you had some decent boots right now, instead of those fancy shoes," she said. She was putting on her gear from Intelligence.

"We don't have a lot of time," Asti said. "Shouldn't we be about it?"

"Right," she said. She kicked the rug back, revealing the trapdoor. "Let's get at it."

Asti knelt, ready to open it. "Wait, you want me to go first?"

"Nervous it's a trap, Rynax?" she asked. "If I wanted to trap you, I wouldn't have gone this far for it."

"I was thinking you wanted me trapped instead of you."

"Oh, of course," she said. She strode over, opening up the trapdoor. Nothing clicked or released, not to Asti's ear. "You saying you couldn't beat that?"

"You got the wrong Rynax for clever traps," Asti said.

"Yes, your brother is the master. If I could have used him tonight, I would have. Let's move."

Asti dropped through the trapdoor, into a crawlspace. Liora came down, carrying a small lamp.

"You expected this was going to go straight in?" she asked, clearly seeing the disappointment in his face. The space was barely large enough for them to crawl through, wood flooring and ceiling. "You never did see my bath chamber, did you?"

"No," Asti said.

"This is so they could put in the piping for my water closet and bath. The handyman has to be able to get at it to fix it, after all. If you hadn't lost your temper on the sight of me. . . ."

"Can you hush up? What's the idea?"

Liora put on that devious smile of hers. "The plan is, we've got to get through the ceiling. So how do we do that quickly?"

"Quickly is easy," Asti said. That scenario went through

his brain several times, most of which involved using Liora's head as a battering ram. "But quietly is crucial as well."

"So what should we do to get in there?"

"Let me think." The beast had its own ideas, and none of them were helpful.

"Don't waste time pontificating it. Nathan's 'men' will start the search soon."

"And he probably will make sure you're found, right." Time was too short, and he was doing this gig far too blind.

Liora was blinding him. He still didn't know what she wanted or why she was using him, not yet. She had an angle here, and he was still stumbling about in her net.

He needed to think like Verci—he was the one who could solve this, he'd be carrying the tools he needed to do it. Asti didn't have any tools. He was useless, he was failing, he wasn't going to do anything to save his neighborhood, his family. He had pulled Verci back into all of this for no damn reason. This was—

"Asti!"

He snapped out of his thoughts. Liora was glaring at him. Think like Verci.

"All right," he said. "Sorry, I had presumed you had scouted this part out, but I guess it was too much to expect you to be a professional about this sort of thing."

"This sort of thing?"

"You're an excellent spy, Liora. But you don't think like a thief."

"What does that mean?"

"That you didn't have a plan for this point—you just counted on me to have one." He started a series of light raps on the floor paneling of the crawl space. As he guessed, the wood they were on was light, and it was bolstered in key spots. That meant there were weak spots, and they were easy to suss out. A few more light knocks showed him the place. Plan. A bad one, but it would probably work. "I've got quickly, but not quietly. You have a rope?"

"What am I, an amateur?" she asked. She pulled one out from her small bag.

"Tie it around those pipes, and then come over to me." She did so. "Now what?"

He wrapped the rope around his waist and hips several times. Not much slack. Didn't want that.

"Now what, Asti?" she pressed.

He grabbed her and held her body close to his. She thrashed and grabbed his throat, stirring the beast on its chain. He held it tight as he looked her in the eye.

"Trust me," he said.

He rolled across the crawlspace floor, keeping her body tight and close on him. He rolled so he was holding her on top of him, her weight pressing on his chest.

"This is not—" she started.

"Wait."

The crawlspace floor creaked, and then cracked, and then broke beneath them. They fell through the hole, and as the busted pieces of ceiling crashed onto the office desk below, Asti and Liora dangled a few feet above it.

"That was definitely not quiet," he said.

She looked at him with bright eyes, a bright joyful smile. She grabbed his face and kissed him, hard and rough, and then dropped onto the desk.

Mila had braced herself for the hard crash onto the ballroom floor, hoping that she'd at least have Treggin's body to break her fall. Instead she felt a warm blast of air, and for a moment she found herself hovering a few feet from the floor. That moment did not last long, and Treggin's eyes met hers in the darkness. With an almost feral growl, he punched her in the teeth and knocked her off him. She fell to the floor, Treggin still floating above her. He righted himself, and as soon as he put his feet to the floor, he broke into a run down one of the back hallways.

"What's the commotion?" someone called. "Is everyone fine?"

People were in a state, running in every direction, shouting. Playing the game. Mila had no time for that or letting any of them get in her way. She pulled herself to her feet and gave chase.

The shoes she was wearing were absolutely terrible for running through the hallways here. She nearly tripped and fell several times, skidding and colliding with a random servant at one point.

"Where did he go?" she yelled at the woman she had run into.

"Who, my Lady?"

"No man came barreling through here?" What was the name Lord Henterman had used? "Ender?"

"Mister Ender? Was that who that was?"

"Yes!" Mila shouted. She took the moment to kick the useless shoes off.

"I think he went down the stairs to the kitchen, my Lady, but—"

"That way?" Mila asked, running down the corridor to the stairs.

A wave of something that looked like flaming ice came roaring up the stairs right when Mila rounded the corner. She dropped flat as soon as she saw it, and the blast barely went over her head.

"You stupid girl!" he snarled at her from the bottom of the stairs.

Mila sprung up and bounded down the stairs, resisting the urge to leap while howling out a battle cry at Treggin as she fell onto him. Was this how Asti felt all the time?

It was good she hadn't gone full bore at him—when she reached the bottom, he had formed those prismatic blades of broken reality in both hands. He swung them at her, but she darted back out of his reach, sliding past him to the other side of the downstairs hallway. She stumbled and fell backward, crashing against the opposite wall.

"I don't know why you keep showing up, Miss Bessie. Especially here," he said. "But I'm ending you." He brought up those impossible magical blades and swung them down on her.

Before he hit her, a crossbow bolt hit him in the arm, and the blades fizzled and vanished as he cried out.

Mila didn't waste time, driving her foot into his knee. He dropped to the floor.

Helene was there, her crossbow reloaded and trained on him. "Down, son."

"You foolish girls," he hissed.

"Who is this guy?" she asked Mila. "Why did you—"

"It's Treggin," Mila said. "And he's—"

"Mage," Treggin said. With a wave of his hands, Mila and Helene went flying down the hallway, smashing into the kitchen walls. The servants and cooks all screamed.

Mila couldn't breathe, couldn't force her lungs to draw in air. She collapsed to the ground, trying to gasp for breath.

Helene seemed a bit better. "Mention that first," she gasped. She drew up her crossbow and fired.

Treggin stalked down the hallway, brushing the crossbow bolt aside with a wave of his hands. "You must be Kesser," he said brusquely. "And here I thought Poller was exaggerating."

Helene had gotten to her feet, raising up her fists. "You want a fight, boy?"

"I don't know how or why you two are here," he said. "But I'm not interested in finding out."

Mila managed to stand, to breathe, to draw out her knife. "We're interested in finding out about you, Treggin."

"Not today," he said. Both hands erupted into sparks, and the lightning grew into long lashes, which he swung out at Mila and Helene, raking across their bodies. Mila screamed; she was on fire, every inch of her body. It was the most horrific pain she had ever felt. Treggin laughed. "Today you'll only—"

He was interrupted by a great clanging sound.

"Not today."

The pain and fire ended, and Mila's vision cleared. She saw the massive form of Julien standing over Treggin's senseless form, wielding a giant stew pot in one hand.

"Jules," Helene whispered. "I found you."

He dropped the pot and scooped her up. "You thought you'd save me, hmm?"

"I had a notion," she said. Julien pulled Mila to her feet. The pain had ended, but the echoes of it still filled her body. Her heart fluttered like a moth, and she could only manage shallow breaths.

"This wasn't the plan," he said.

"No," Mila said, trying to bear her own weight. Her legs felt like they were made from Kimber's peach preserves.

"But hopefully we made enough commotion that no one will be paying attention to Asti."

"Are we sure there aren't any traps or alarms?" Asti asked as she climbed off the desk.

"No," she said. "Not that alarms really matter after that."

"Depends on what else is in here." He untied himself and dropped onto the desk. "Not that we should be spending much time in here."

"Then stop wasting it."

She went straight for the portrait on the far side of the wall, taking it down to reveal a lockbox embedded in the wall.

"You seem to know what you're going for," Asti said. He went through the drawers of the desk. Account books, ledgers. He started pulling them out.

"I had something of a plan, yes," she said.

"I'm certain," he said. "I'm still waiting."

She started working on the lockbox. "Waiting for what?"

"The drop of the feather, as it were."

She chuckled. "Ah. Right, of course. Waiting for the sudden, inevitable betrayal."

Thumbing through the ledgers—a lot of information on accounts and finances. Nothing that specifically said Andrendon, not that he saw. He took off his suit coat and removed the knapsack that was hidden underneath. He put the paperwork in it and kept digging through the drawers.

"You're not looking for money," she said.

"Sure I am."

"Someone looking for money would be far more interested in this lockbox."

"And someone looking for information of collusion or treason would be interested in these ledgers and journals." Asti put a journal and more papers in the sack. No need to look right now—take it all, get away, sort through it later. Saint Senea, watching over the Righteous Outlaws, would hopefully guide him to what he needed. The rest of the saints could fret over the absolute mess they had made. There was nothing subtle or quiet about this gig. They might still get away with a strong lead and no direct chase, but there was no chance that Henterman wouldn't know what happened tonight.

"Just once," Dad would say back in the day, "I want a gig where you slip in, steal something, and your marks don't know anything happened for months."

Tonight was not that night.

"That depends on the nature of the treason, my dear," Liora said. With a flick of her wrist, she opened up the lockbox. "I still have the touch."

The lockbox revealed a tiny, ugly statue—green jade with six arms.

"The blazes is that?" Asti asked.

She gingerly removed it from the box. "I'm given to understand it's an sacred idol to a forbidden religion."

"It's a *tazendifol*."

Asti looked up to see Lord Henterman standing in the doorway, at least half a dozen armed men behind him.

"Nathan," Liora said sweetly. "You're supposed to be playing your hiding game."

"Yes, of course. I had hoped, ever so hoped, that my instincts were wrong. But as soon as he arrived, I knew you were some kind of charlatan." He looked over to Asti. "So, you're the, what . . . lover? You're certain not a cousin, with the looks you were giving her earlier. Not even in the northern archduchies."

"An old friend is all," Asti said. He slid the last journal into the knapsack.

"Why don't you both put everything down," Henterman said. "And then these boys will see you out."

"Nathaniel," Liora said in her sweetest honey tone. She moved closer without getting herself in arm's reach of him. "I know you're probably cross, but I can explain everything to you. This man—this man here has blackmailed me to help him."

"Really?" Henterman asked. "How did he?"

"Saints, Nathan, use your eyes. You don't even recognize the handyman who tried to kill me the other day?"

"What?" He moved a bit closer to Asti. "Hands away

from the desk and that sack, hmm? And what is that stench?"

Asti raised his hands up. A scent to make the saints cry had hit the room. That meant at least one thing was probably going to plan. He just had to buy some time. "How about you get your hands away from the west side, huh?"

"West side of what?" Henterman asked. He peered closely. "Well, I'll be damned and blazed. You do look like that Crile fellow."

"The West side of Maradaine, you clod," Asti said. "The Andrendon Project?"

Henterman just gave him a blank look.

Now Asti wanted to kill him. "The Creston Group? You and your cronies buying up land in North Seleth, murdering people for it!"

"I—what?" He looked back at Liora. "You're telling me he ensorcelled you, when he's clearly quite addled in the skull."

"Oh, you have no idea," Asti said.

"I have no idea what you're on about. I do know that you will leave the idol and the papers alone, and these men will then thrash you quite liberally. Perhaps you'll live."

A bird cry pierced the air outside the window. That was all Asti needed. He grabbed the knapsack and hurled it at the glass. It shattered the window, falling to the ground below.

"Now, that was silly," Henterman said. "We'll just go fetch it. After the thrashing."

He snapped his fingers, and four of the men moved in on Liora, grabbing her wrists. She didn't make any attempt to resist immediately.

"Come on, lad," Henterman said to Asti as the other men started moving around the desk. "You're stuck in here with at least eight of us. You've hardly a chance."

"I kind of like those odds," Asti said, pulling out two knives. These guards didn't worry him. Even the beast wasn't pulling at the chain right now. "Let me show you something about thrashing."

Liora spun, and pulled the two men holding her wrists

into each other. As soon as they collided, they let go of her, and she bounded onto the desk and grabbed the rope. Asti took the cue from her and jumped up to the rope as well.

"Get them!" Henterman shouted.

She and Asti were back up through the hole in the ceiling before anyone could even grab them, and moving back through the crawlspace.

"Was this your plan?" Asti asked her.

"Not entirely—I was hoping to have a few more minutes to get some distance, but we'll make do."

They emerged from the trapdoor into the wardrobe. They could hear plenty of shouting—Henterman's guards were coming up, as well as Henterman giving instructions to go up to the Lady's quarters.

"All this for a silly idol," he muttered. "I hope that's the proof you need."

"It's definitely what I need," she said, admiring the ugly thing for a moment. She went over to her rack of clothing and pulled out a satchel. She was the very image of complete calm, despite the urgency of the situation.

"Well, what do you suggest now?" Asti asked. He had hoped for something better than "fight their way out."

"Now?" She looked up at him, absolutely no tension or stress in her body at all. She gave a slight smile and said, "I'm going to leave, and you're going to cover my escape."

"Why the blazes do you think that?" he shouted. He didn't understand why Liora was standing there so calmly. Then she looked over at him, her cool, gray eyes locking onto his.

"Asti," she said in a clear, sedate voice. "Nine. Saint Crellick. Nine. Serve the Brotherhood."

And then, in an instant, the beast awoke, and the chain was gone.

Everything went red.

Chapter 27

IN THE COVER OF darkness, Verci and Almer had slipped around the grounds—or as much as Verci could "slip" anywhere with a cane and a braced foot—to the study window, while Pilsen stayed with the carriages. There were several other drivers from other nobles, and a handful of armed grounds men there. Normally they would have had a sharp eye all over the grounds, but Pilsen was engaging them with an epic, fascinating tale of daring and adventure that kept their attention. There was even a song.

"That's the window," Verci said as they approached.

"And that is definitely bileworth," Almer said, looking at the plants growing up the side of the wall.

"And you have an idea for that?"

Almer reached into his satchel and pulled out the dead-hand device Verci had given him for the meeting with Liora. "This thing of yours is pretty blazing clever," he said, pouring a couple of liquids in the top of it. "I've got a dozen different ideas how to use it. Some of them even properly medicinal." He pushed it toward the wall and pulled Verci back.

"Now?" Verci asked.

Pilsen handed a kerchief to Verci. "Try not to breathe anything for a minute."

Thick yellow smoke poured out of the device, hiding the wall—and the bileworth—from sight completely for a moment. The smell of it hit Verci like a punch in the gut, and before he could cover his face with the kerchief, there was a second wave of newer, viler stench.

"What is that?" he asked Almer, holding in the contents of his stomach by pure force of will.

Almer was holding a scarf over his face. "That's a pretty toxic smoke, is what it is. And when it hit the bileworth . . . woo." He started hacking up a storm, pulling Verci a few more steps back as he did. As his coughing subsided he added, "I wasn't quite prepared for that."

"There's no way this isn't noticed inside the household," Verci said. His eyes were starting to burn as well, so he took a set of goggles out of his pouch and put them on. He had brought them in case circumstances forced him to swim in the lake—unlikely, but he preferred to be prepared. He was certainly glad he had them now.

"Is this why you say a gig is 'skunked'?"

"I will hurt you, Almer."

The smoke started to fade away and drift off toward the tiny lake in the center of the houses. The bileworth had blackened, turning into shriveled strands of nothing.

"I'm just saying, I've been subjected to all sorts of horrible smells since working with you boys."

"Which you're the source of half the time," Verci said. The path to the window above was clear, and there were a few lamplights shining. "Let's see if this works."

He reached into his satchel and pulled out the modified crossbow he had made, with a grappling claw and pulley at the front of its shot. He aimed it at the eave above the window and fired it.

The claw latched on. Verci tested the hold—strong enough to take his weight—tied on one end of the rope around his belt. "You can manage on your own if there's trouble?" he asked Almer.

Almer pulled a bunch of vials out of his own pack. "I throw these and run like a sinner. And you're on your own if I have to."

"Fair enough," Verci said. He strapped his cane to his back and started the climb—his broken foot screaming at him. If it wasn't for that, he probably could manage without the rope. At least he had the option to balance out his short-coming with his gear. He just wished he didn't have to do this with additional difficulty.

"Wasn't there a signal?" Almer whispered from below.

Right. He needed to let Asti know he was getting in position. He made the bird call and kept climbing.

Just before he reached the window, something came smashing out of it, plummeting to the ground below.

Verci's heart stopped cold for a minute, looking down to Almer. Bit too dark to see clearly what it was.

"What the blazes?" he whispered down to Almer.

"It's Asti's pack!"

"Just the pack?"

"Loaded with papers."

Verci made a quick assessment. Asti wouldn't do that unless there was trouble—the kind of trouble that meant getting the papers out of the place was more important than getting himself out. Which probably meant he needed rescuing.

"Take it and run if I'm not back in two clicks," Verci said.

Verci pulled himself up to the window—just in time to see Asti's feet slip through a hole in the ceiling, and a few of Henterman's guards start to climb up the rope behind him. A decked-out swell—surely, Henterman himself—shouted some orders to his men, who ran out of the room.

Henterman stalked over to an open lockbox in the far wall. He scowled at the empty box, and slammed it shut.

Asti was up a level, and he needed help. Verci climbed up to the next window.

This was a grand bay window—a huge amount of glass, giving Verci a glorious view of the wardrobe and bedroom of Lady Henterman.

At least three guards were dead on the floor, and Asti was in a mad, furious fight with five more who had come into the bedroom. He was—Verci had never seen anything like it. He had never seen a man fight like that, not even

Asti. Every move was perfect, like a dance where only Asti knew the steps, and everyone else was struggling to keep death at bay.

Everyone but Liora, who was sitting calmly on the bed, changing her shoes.

Asti killed two more guards, nothing but empty rage in his eyes. Liora calmly stood up, taking a bag with her.

Verci didn't know what was wrong with Asti, but he was sure it involved this horrible woman.

He pulled himself up a bit higher, pulled out his walking stick and smashed the window.

That, at least, startled her.

"Oh, the brother," she said. "I should have expected."

Verci bounded into the room, landing on only his good foot. "The blazes is this?"

"This? This is me leaving." She gave the hole in the window an intrigued regard. "You've given me a new option, though."

"Asti, what's going on?"

Asti gave no indication that he heard Verci, instead continuing on with the business of murdering guards.

"Work it out yourself, Verci dear. I'll be off."

She went to the window. Verci brought his walking stick into her chest. She caught it with one hand with an almost callous disregard.

"You're not leaving," he said.

"This is dreadfully boring," she said. Turning to Asti she said, "Kill him, Asti."

Asti had just gutted the last guard present, and without missing a beat, he leaped onto Verci with both knives. Verci barely had time to get the cane up to block Asti. The pure force of the savage attack sent Verci to the floor, where he struggled to hold back the knives.

"It's been a pleasure, gentlemen," Liora said, going out the window.

"Asti," Verci hissed out. "It's me."

Asti paid him no mind, his eyes were empty. Instead he kept trying to bring the knives down into Verci's chest. Verci held him off for a moment, but he couldn't keep it up too long.

"I don't want to—" was all Verci said before one slash sliced his arm. He cried out, and instinctively brought the stick up into Asti's jaw. That gave Verci the opportunity to push him off and roll up onto his feet. His broken foot screamed out, and Verci felt one of the springs on the brace snap. He couldn't put any weight on it now, and balanced on just the good foot.

Asti came back at him, furiously, with his knives. This time, Verci stayed on the ready, blocking the attacks with the cane.

"Wake the blazes up, Asti," Verci shouted.

Asti gave no sign of awareness—it was like he had become a mindless machine, his brain a gearbox that was just winding through its cycle. And that cycle was bringing the knives closer to Verci's throat, and he wasn't fast enough to hold Asti off for much longer. He certainly couldn't run.

He could release the spring knife on the cane. That and a quick twist would drive it into Asti's neck. That would end it quick.

Even with the cold steel of Asti's knives bearing down on him, staring at his brother's empty, soulless eyes, he couldn't bring himself to do that.

"Look at me, brother," he pleaded.

"You aren't going anywhere, Anaphide, or whatever your name is." A man in a bright red suit—presumably Lord Henterman—came striding into the room, but the look on his face showed that he expected to see a completely different scene than several guards dead on the floor.

Asti suddenly broke his attack on Verci and launched at Lord Henterman. The nobleman didn't have a chance to react before Asti was on him, the knife just half an inch from his throat.

And then something in Asti snapped. In a moment, he went from an empty stare to a frightened animal. Hands shaking, he stepped away from Henterman, staring back and forth between him and Verci. Panic and fear in his eyes, Asti dove out the window.

"What—what the blazes is happening?" Henterman bellowed.

Verci couldn't run, and he probably couldn't fight. Only one option left.

"Lord Henterman, sir," Verci said, bowing his head as he regained his composure. "Captain Krennick Trent, Druth Intelligence."

"What?" Henterman stared about in disbelief. "Why . . . how?"

"I deeply apologize, my Lord," Verci said. "I had tracked a pair of rogue agents engaged in an infiltration of you and your home. I had hoped to extract them without incident, but. . . ."

"But clearly that failed, Mister Trent!" Henterman snapped at him, gesturing at the dead guards. "We are quite neck deep in 'incident'!"

"Indeed we are, my Lord," Verci said, limping over to the man. That required no show. His foot was in agony, and the rest of his body was no better. "Especially since one of these rogue agents was your wife."

"My—she was—"

"She was—had been, rather—one of ours. Liora Rand, now disavowed. I'm afraid I'm not cleared to tell you more than that right now." Verci was glad he could wrap this con up in some truth. "That other man was her former partner in the service."

"Ha!" Henterman shook his head and went to sit in a chair. "You know, I had . . . do not think me a bag of rocks, Captain. I knew something was not quite right with my wife, that she wasn't what she said she was. And that 'cousin' of hers! But I can't imagine!" He sputtered a bit more.

"I understand, sir."

"The sister!" Henterman shouted, jumping to his feet. "She must have been in on it as well!" He charged off. Verci struggled to keep up. If Helene was still in the house—and Verci had no reason to suspect she wasn't—it was going to be challenging to get her out safely. And given how badly things were going, Verci was not about to abandon anyone.

"My Lord," Verci said, doing his best to navigate the stairs with his foot and cane. "This is a sensitive operation in which I have embedded a few operatives in tonight's festivities."

Henterman turned on him, stopping in the middle of the stairs. "You're telling me that Druth Intelligence *infiltrated my party*? And left me unawares?"

"I do not have the words to properly apologize," Verci said. "We were still trying to ascertain their goals. We have very little idea why they targeted you." Verci decided, if he had gone this far, he might as well take a chance. "Something to do with an Andrendon Project."

Henterman's eyes went wide. "Yes. That little man mentioned such a thing, with real ... vehemence. I've not heard of such a thing—although, come to think of it ..."

He was lost in thought for a moment.

"Anything you know may be of aid, my Lord," Verci said.

"There is something vaguely familiar about the name. I've put some of my holdings in investments—projects of improvements, industry, or infrastructure around the city." He lowered his voice conspiratorially. "I'll confess, I'm not sure what it all is about, but I'll gladly put my name on a bridge or park or such. There certainly *could* be an Andrendon or such among them. You'd have to ask my man Ender about it."

"And he is where?"

"That, Captain, is an excellent question."

Helene's head was starting to clear—that was some powerful hoodoo Treggin had hit her with. If it hadn't been for Julie, she'd—

She didn't want to think about it.

She looked around. The kitchens had cleared out, probably in the commotion.

"We need to move," she said. Treggin was still a lump of nothing on the ground. "We need to get him in one of the carriages."

"Him, who?" Helene looked up. Standing in the hallway entrance was Win. "What have you done to Mister Ender?"

"He was hurting them," Julien said simply.

"And he's a mage," Helene said. "We have questions for him."

"Why, for the saint's sake?" Win asked. "There's much commotion all around the house, and if anyone but me—"

"Win," Mila said sharply. She looked like she could barely stand, pale as curdled milk, but she also looked like she was willing to fight every armed man in the house if she had to. "This is Treggin. He's directly involved with everything happening in our neighborhood."

"How, what . . ." Win started. "Fine, it doesn't matter. We need to get you all out of here."

"Not until we know what he's doing," Helene said.

"If you want to question him, then do it somewhere else," Win said. "The only reason there are no guards here is because of Asti's mess upstairs."

"Then let's get him and us out of here," Mila said.

Julien scooped up Treggin's body. "Looks like this job is done," he said with a resigned sigh.

"Sorry," Helene said. "We'll—we'll figure something out later. All right?"

"Just go!" Win said. "I'll—I'll think of something."

As they raced behind the house up to the carriage house, Mila grabbed hold of Helene's hand. She didn't seem like she could keep up. Helene wasn't going to leave her behind this time.

"Why isn't Win coming?" she asked.

"He's covering our escape," Helene said, hoping that was true. "We'll see him later."

At the carriage house, a dozen drivers were abuzz. The action in the house hadn't seemed to have reached here— instead, it was the action of Pilsen Gin, who was up on a platform, downright shouting and getting all the attention.

"And bring the lightning! Bring the storm! For my sword will hold back those as well! My kingdom shall be mine, and brook no invaders!" He seemed—altered. Helene couldn't tell if he was drunk, or so deep into his performance he didn't know where he was. But there was no sense that he was playing, no spark in his eye. He didn't even seem to note their arrival.

"What is he doing?" Julien asked.

"I think it's *Maradaine the First*," Mila said. "Verci said it was his triumph on the stage."

"It's *The Autumn of Corringshire*," Helene said. That had been Grandmother's favorite. "Let's get to the carriage, and get out, before those folks realize we're carrying a body."

Almer came running up, out of breath, carrying a sack, his head bleeding. Helene grabbed him and pulled him behind the carriage, out of sight of the drivers and guards watching Pilsen.

"What happened to you?" Helene asked.

Almer looked stunned for a moment. "The woman came out of the window. She clobbered me. Asti followed, growling at her. And Verci was inside. I—I had this sack that Asti threw out."

Helene glanced at the bag, full of documents. Probably no money. Blast and blazes. "And we need to get that out of here. Julien, pull Pilsen out of there, take that carriage."

"Hel!" Mila said. "Asti and Verci both!"

Julien was at the carriage, having loaded Treggin's inert body into it. He was now helping Pilsen, despite the protests of the other drivers. Pilsen was also protesting, that he shouldn't be taken away from his crowd. Something was far from right with him.

"All right, we need . . ." Helene faltered. "We need to . . ."

She wanted to help Verci, but there wasn't much she could do if he was inside the house and caught. And if Asti was chasing Liora, he'd . . . he'd probably need help. Mila was in poor shape, as was Almer and Pilsen. And she wanted Julien far away from Liora Rand.

It fell on her. Asti had told her, she had to step up.

"Julien!" she said. "Give me The Action and the Rainmaker."

Julien tossed the crossbows to her.

"Get them all out of here," she told Mila. "Almer's hurt, Pilsen's . . . I don't even know. Take charge."

"But—"

"Go!"

Mila jumped up on the carriage, snapping the reins. Helene was surprised she even knew how to do that.

Helene checked the Rainmaker. Loaded, ready, over-cranked to the fourth stop.

Out in the yard, an animalistic roar cut through the air. If Helene didn't recognize the voice, she would have thought it was one of those great wildcats she'd heard about.

Asti was out there, like a beast on the hunt. She raced out of the carriage house to the main grounds, and almost collided with someone.

"Look at you." Lady Melania, standing in her way with a bemused look on her face. "I did say to whistle if you had something fun to do."

Helene had no time or interest in banter. If this woman wanted to help, Helene wasn't about to pass it up. She handed The Action to her. "Then come along, your Lady-ship. I've got people to save."

Asti remembered everything.

In the wardrobe, his mind had suddenly opened up, locks to doors he didn't even know were in his skull popped loose.

He remembered what Liora had said on Haptur months ago.

"The Brotherhood thanks you for the sacrifice."

He had no idea what that meant, but he would know. After he slit Liora open and danced in her blood.

He remembered the rest. Being powerless, unable to stop himself as he nearly drove his knives into Verci's heart. Like a passenger in his own skull. It was only when he saw Henterman, tried to kill him that . . . something snapped, and he was himself again.

Or as much himself as he ever could be.

He barely realized that Almer was still on the ground as he dropped down the rope, his attention entirely on Liora. She was running toward the lake. Perhaps she had a plan in that direction—a boat, swim away.

Didn't matter. She wasn't going to make it.

He charged at her, not even realizing that he was howl-ing as he ran. She stopped in her run, turning on one heel and planting a foot in his chest.

"You stupid man," she snarled.

"What did you—" he said, swiping at her with his knife. She blocked him easily, and jammed an elbow into his nose.

"You could have just killed a bunch of guards and gone home," she said, launching a mighty punch at his chest. He blocked that, tried to slice her arm, but she twisted out of the way.

"I'm still in a killing mood," Asti said.

"That's sweet. Verci wasn't enough for you?"

That made the beast take hold for just a moment, a lashing blow of pure rage into her face. She grinned and wiped the blood away as she darted back.

"He's better than you give him credit for," Asti said.

"He lived? Pity."

"You won't."

He threw one knife, which she caught—but he was expecting that. He dashed in, ready to slice her belly open. She nimbly avoided him.

"Asti, dear, I could play this game all night," she said, slipping away from his blows again. "But I don't have the time to waste."

She reached into her coat and threw three darts. Asti dodged two, but the third hit him in the arm.

And then the arm went numb, followed shortly by the rest of his body. He fell down to the ground, unable to move anything but his eyes.

"Oh, Asti," she said, fingering his knife. "I really did want to keep you around as a useful tool. But I think you and yours are going to be too much trouble."

Chapter 28

HELENE RAN IN THE direction of the howls. Guards were now shouting from the house, dogs barking. Time was not on her side.

Off by the lake, she saw two figures fighting. Even in the dim of the moonlight, she could tell it was Asti and Liora. They were furious in the fight, absolutely savage.

Then Asti fell. Liora was on top of him.

No time to get any closer. She brought up the Rainmaker to her sight.

"You're too far, dear," Lady Melania said.

Liora brought up a knife.

"Not with this old girl," Helene said. Time to see what this sort of overcrank could do to a person.

Liora in her sights, Helene took the shot.

The bolt hit Liora in the arm. It didn't just hit, it tore through, taking flesh with it. Liora's scream pierced through the night, like nothing Helene had ever heard before. Looking through the scope, Helene saw that her arm was hanging limp at the shoulder, as if nothing but pure willpower kept it from falling off. Liora held onto it, and started limping away.

"Well done," Lady Melania whispered.

"Aiming for her body," Helene said.

They ran over to Asti, whose whole body was trembling.

"Asti," Helene said, kneeling next to him. "What's wrong?"

"He—he—he—" was all he managed to say.

"I've got you," she said. She looked around. She didn't see where Liora had gone.

"Do you see her?" she asked Lady Melania.

"No, too dark. Though there's a lovely trail of blood. I'm amazed the poor girl didn't pass out." She ran toward the lake.

"Hel—" Asti still was in tremors. He managed to reach up to her face.

"You're all right," Helene said.

"Cr—crew?" He was fighting just to speak.

"Mila got most of them out already. With those papers."

"G—g—good."

"And Treggin."

He just looked confused.

"Verci. I almost—"

Helene nodded. "Let me get you safe, and then I'll find him." She hauled him up to his feet.

Lady Melania came back. "She had a boat at the ready. And used it one-handed." She held up The Action, now unloaded. "Afraid I don't have your aim."

"Who is this?" Asti asked.

"A strange friend," Helene said. "She's—helping."

"Yes, and the fun is going to turn to not fun rather shortly," she said. "I think I should unceremoniously throw the two of you in the back of my carriage. Guards and dogs are all about, and that's going to be a nuisance." She got on Asti's other side. "Let's be about it, then."

"Why is she helping us?" Asti wheezed out as they reached the carriage house.

"We don't have time for a complicated answer," she said as she opened her carriage door, giving a nod to her driver. "The short answer is, I realized you and your friends were planning on doing something awful to Nathaniel Henterman." She pushed them both inside. "And I approve." She shut them in.

Asti was still breathing shallow. "Are we safe?"

"I think so," Helene said. She said it with much more confidence than she felt.

Asti nodded. That seemed to be all he could physically manage for the moment. And then his head went down, tears flowing out of his eyes.

"Hey, hey, Rynax," she said sharply. "No crying on the job."

That didn't stop him at all. If anything, it opened up the river.

"Hey," she said. "Verci's going to be fine, I'm sure."

"But I'm not," Asti said. "I don't know if I ever will be."

Verci had found himself in the last place he would have thought he'd end up this night—sitting in Lord Henterman's lounge and being handed a drink by the man himself. He had been quietly escorted there, to not disturb what remained of the party.

"I appreciate your discretion, Lord Henterman."

"Well, I understand that the services, including you boys in Intelligence, do what you must to protect Druthal." He pointed to the portrait on the wall. "My grandfather served in the War. An officer, one of the last ones at Khol Taia."

Verci knew he should have known what Khol Taia was, but he never remembered the history lessons.

"He must have been a good man."

"I suppose, died when I was a tot." He shook his head and took his own drink. "I suppose I'm still at a loss. Tonight has been a lot to take in."

"Your wife was betraying you," Verci said.

"Yes, well . . . I suspected that was coming. But I did not expect it to quite take this form."

"Can you give me any details of what she did, what your suspicions were?"

"Well, a man just knows, doesn't he?" He sipped at his drink. "She seduced me in a whirlwind, and I embraced the impulse. She has that effect, you know? But once the bracelets were on our wrists, that dried up."

Verci felt some sympathy for the man—he was definitely a victim at the end of this night, and Verci had some certainty he had nothing intentional to do with tragedies in

North Seleth. He had likely invested in whatever the Andrendon Project was—there was probably a mountain of proof behind that. But he was hardly the architect of anything nefarious.

Simply put, Lord Henterman seemed far too frivolous to be the mastermind they were seeking.

The lounge doors opened, and a butler walked in. Win Greenfield, to be specific.

"Ah, Ungar, good man. All handled?"

He nodded. "I've . . . discreetly—let the guests who were working with the captain here know that their mission is over, and invited them to leave."

"Excellent," Henterman said. He got to his feet. "And have the guards caught her Ladyship or her accomplices?"

"I'm afraid there've not been any reports of anyone being caught, my Lord." Win threw a pointed look at Verci.

"Damn and blazes," Henterman said. He finished his drink and put it down. "I'll be a laughingstock, it's true."

"No, sir," Win said. "We'll clean up the study, and deal with any scandal."

"Good man, Ungar," he said. He sighed. "Captain, I presume I'm keeping you."

"Yes," Verci said, getting to his feet. "I—and the service—appreciate your cooperation."

"Glad to give it," Henterman said. "Ungar, see the captain out."

"Of course, sir," Win said, opening the door. "Captain, if you will."

Win stayed in character until they got out of the house to the driveway. It was at that point that he finally started laughing. "Captain?"

"I had to think of something," Verci said. "And I'm quite amazed he bought it."

"I think . . ." Win held his thought for a moment. "His life was just shattered. I understand what that's like. He was ready to accept any rope someone threw to him."

"I actually told him the truth, at least about his wife."

"Hmm," Win said, nodding. "So, I told Kennith and . . . what's that young man's name?"

"Vellun."

"I told them to go and wait for you about two blocks away on Flynn."

"You're going to make me walk two blocks to the carriage on this foot?"

Win smiled, almost solemnly. "I've heard the reports from the folks looking about the grounds. No sign of anyone else. There is, apparently, a fair amount of blood on the lawn near the boathouse. I do know that Julien slipped off with Helene and Mila."

"Which is for the best. So we're clear?" They had reached the gate, still hanging a few paces away so that they were out of earshot of the gatekeepers.

"To the best of my knowledge, you and I are the last ones on the grounds, yes." Win looked down at the ground. "Helene and Mila said that Mister Ender—the Lord's attaché—was actually someone named Treggin? They took him with them."

"Treggin was here? So is he—"

"The one behind all this? Perhaps. Or he is at least in league with those who are. I decided that merited further investigation." He reached into his coat pocket and pulled out some papers. "While the rest of the household was in disarray, I cracked into Mister Ender's office and his own documents. It's a little beyond me, but there are numerous references to the Andrendon Project in there. Perhaps you and Asti will find it useful."

Verci took the papers. "Well done, Win. We'll make a thief out of you yet."

Win chuckled ruefully. "Perhaps you boys could. But . . . that was never a life I was meant for, Verci. I came along with you because . . . well, because Win Greenfield was a man who had nothing left in his life. He needed . . . he needed something to do to fix himself. But the man that I was . . . he died in that fire with his wife and daughters."

"What are you saying, Win?"

"I'm saying . . ." He looked back over to the house. "I need to keep being Mister Ungar."

Verci looked over to the house, and then back in Win's eyes. It made perfect sense, in a strange way. "Who am I going to look up to, then, Win?"

"You never needed me for that, Verci," Win said. "Look, say goodbye to Asti and the others for me, but . . . this here, this is the closest I've been to happy in some time."

Verci nodded. "You deserve that, Win." Verci took his hand. "You take care of yourself."

"You too," Win said. "And your family. Never forget, they are the most important thing you have."

Win made his way back to Lord Henterman's house, and Verci went off into the night, limping his way to the carriage.

Vellun and Kennith were waiting right where they were supposed to be, neither of them looking sure of what had happened.

"Look, I know our job was to be a distraction," Kennith said. "But a little bit of guidance would have been good."

"Saints, Kennith, I'm not sure what happened." Verci climbed up into the cab. "I presume he's driving and you're staying here."

Kennith slipped into the accent. "Unless you want a Ch'omik warrior driving through the city."

"I think you've had enough attention for a bit."

Kennith shrugged. "I do have some people in the Hodge, if I had to go there."

"Let's figure that out tomorrow," Verci said. "According to Win, all of our people managed to get off the grounds. Or are hiding well." Though for all Verci knew, Asti was dead at the bottom of the lake.

"And Win?" Kennith asked.

"Win is going to stay."

Kennith didn't seem surprised, but appeared disappointed. "If that's what he wants. So what do we do?"

"Vellun!" Verci said, tapping on the roof of the carriage. "Bring us around to the Colton neighborhood safehouse." That was the meet point they had agreed on. Vellun drove them over, to find the other carriage parked in the street, with Mila pacing around out in front of the house stoop. Almer was up on the carriage driver's seat, and Julien sat on the walkway.

"Asti? Helene?" she asked when she saw them.

"Haven't seen them," Verci said. "I thought Helene was with you."

"She went back for you and Asti," Mila said.

"I think—I'm sure they got off the property." He tried to make that sound confident. If Helene and Asti were together, that improved both their odds. Unless Liora Rand had killed them both.

Another carriage pulled up—a rather fancy, well-appointed one. The door opened and a woman in an impressive purple gown stepped out.

"Well, this isn't conspicuous in the slightest. I haven't met you yet. You must be Verci."

"That's—"

She stepped aside to show Asti and Helene in the back of her carriage. Asti looked like he had been bleached, wrung, and left in the sun, and Helene was holding his head in an uncharacteristically tender way.

"These are yours, yes?"

"Yes," Verci said. Helene helped Asti out of the cab. Asti came over and draped his arms around Verci, and despite himself, Verci flinched for a moment.

"I'm so sorry," Asti said. "You don't—what she did to me—"

"I think I understand," Verci said. "How much do you remember?"

Asti pulled away, his eyes filled with fear. "All of it. And I wasn't . . ."

"Nothing happened," Verci said. "You get me? Jobs done, no one skunked or pinched."

"Well, this is touching," the noblewoman said. She looked to Helene, who was embracing Julien. "It was glorious fun. Call on me if you're ever in Canthen. Ta, now." She swept up into her carriage, and with a whistle to her driver, went off.

"Who the blazes was that?" Verci asked.

"That was Lady Melania of Canthen," Helene said. "A friend I made in the woods a few months ago."

"I don't even want to know," Verci said.

Helene held up the Rainmaker. "You should see what this beauty does to someone's arm when it's overcranked to four."

"Was it gruesome?" Mila asked.

"Was it Liora?" Almer added.

"Yes to both," Helene said.

"So she's not about to hunt us down right now?" Mila asked.

"No, I think she found me most disarming."

"Shot it clean off?" Verci asked.

Helene frowned a bit. "Not quite. But I'd bet she'll lose it in a day or two, once the gang sets in. More painful that way."

"Stop," Asti said. "I'm sorry, tonight was a disaster, and it's all my fault. I never should have—"

"It wasn't a complete disaster," Verci said. He held up the papers Win gave him. "Documents that mention Andrendon."

Almer held up the bag. "Plus the ones you got."

Mila went over to the carriage, opening the door, revealing two sleeping men. One was Pilsen, and the other Verci didn't recognize.

"Is that Lord Henterman's aide?" Asti asked.

"Yes," Mila said. "It's also Treggin."

She had a self-satisfied smirk on her face, and Verci thought she'd earned it. He couldn't say much to that, and Asti was stunned silent for a minute.

"Near as I could tell from interviewing Henterman," Verci said. "His aide was behind any investments he made."

"How did you—" Asti started. And then he looked to Mila. "And how—"

"Look," Mila said, closing the carriage. "We should get out of the street but quick. We look like trouble, and when he wakes up, he *is* a mage."

"Right," Asti said. "Load up, and let's get out of here while we can."

"Where to now?" Verci asked.

"The only place we've got," Asti said, clutching Verci's hand. "The bakery."

"Home," Verci said.

Chapter 29

MILA DIDN'T KNOW WHY they were going to the bakery to question Treggin. It seemed like a stupid plan to her, but she also acknowledged they didn't have anywhere else.

"But why is the bakery safer than the warehouse?" she asked Asti as their carriages trundled west through the quiet streets. He insisted on riding with her in the carriage Treggin was trussed up in. She rode with him, Vellun driving. Everyone else was in the other carriage.

"It's really not," he said. "But—look, Verci is on target about the Old Lady. And she—she's got a style. She doesn't want us dead, or she would have killed us this morning."

He sounded like he wasn't mad at her anymore. Mila said as much.

"No, I am. Quite. But at the same time . . . I only have so much anger to spread around. On a night like this . . . Josie isn't at the top of my list. But here's the thing with her, and I'm chuffed at myself for not really thinking about it. You've got to trust her to be Josie, and part of that is not trusting her."

"That doesn't make a lick of sense."

He nodded. "All right, listen. I know the past few weeks, I've been focused entirely on who did this to us. The folks behind Andrendon. And you've had your eye on the neighborhood."

"Not entirely." She had definitely failed her boys, especially the twins.

"More than me," he told her. He prodded Treggin with his foot. "Blazes, I saw this guy at the party, and I had no idea. This guy took over half the Seleth gangs and crews, and I didn't even know who he was."

"That's hardly your fault."

"Is it? Point is, I missed him, and I missed Josie, and that's because I didn't have an eye on what was really happening in the neighborhood. If I did, I would have realized that she was doing what she always does."

"Which is?"

"Looking out for her power and comfort." He sighed and leaned back. "She wasn't in this for the same reasons as we were. She wanted her position back as the crime queen of Seleth. Tyne, and the gangs working with Treggin, had chipped away at that. She needed—"

"She needed the money," Mila said. "And didn't care about screwing us over."

"Like I said, trust that you can't trust her. Damn, even Dad would tell us that about her. I knew that even when I was one of her thugs. I had blinded myself to it, because . . ."

"Because you've got a lot going on in your skull," she said. Something had snapped or turned in there during the mission. "Liora did something, didn't she?"

"Yeah." He stayed quiet for a while. "I don't quite have it all sussed out yet. Tonight has been horrifying, but . . . there's clarity in that horror. And I think that's all I can really ask for right now."

Their carriage pulled up to the alley next to the bakery, and Asti pulled Treggin out with Mila's help. Vellun stayed parked at the alley entrance until they brought Treggin to the false backhouse that led to one of the tunnels to the basement bunker.

The bunker was not unoccupied. Verci's wife was down

there with the baby asleep in her arms. She had brought quite a few things down—blankets, clothes, food, other supplies. Mila started tying Treggin to a chair while Asti went to her.

"What are you doing down here?" he asked her.

"I'm not blasted well staying anywhere else when I'm alone in here," she said. "Where's Verci? Is he all right?"

"He's fine," Asti said. "He should be coming with everyone else in a few minutes."

"Who is that guy?" she asked.

"This is Treggin," Mila said. "Or Ender. He was somehow both the new gang boss here and the assistant to Lord Henterman."

Raych looked at the two of them. "So, that clinches it, right? He's the connection between everything?"

"Maybe," Asti said. "We're going to have to ask him some questions, though. And that's going to be ugly."

"Right." Raych took Mila's hand. "Why don't we go upstairs."

"I can handle the ugly, Missus Rynax," Mila said.

"I can't. And I don't want to go alone."

"Then stay until the rest get here," Asti said. "We can wait." He opened up the man's shirt, revealing a tattoo of a bird on fire.

"What's that?"

"A mark of his Mage Circle, I imagine. I really don't know which one that one's for. But he's definitely circled."

"And saints know we can't wake him up until we've figured out how to make him not magic us all to death," Mila said. "I imagine those ropes won't make a difference."

"No," Asti said.

Mila saw that he was thinking, and being a bit too silent about it. "And what might?"

He scratched at his chin. "Mage shackles would, but I doubt the constables would lend them."

"What about that stuff Almer made to dose the mage in the Emporium?"

"From what you all said, it didn't last very long. And too much might make him too cloudy-headed to answer us. We need his magic disabled while keeping his head clear."

"Anything else we could give him? There must be some trick you know."

Asti shrugged. "A few options we don't have. Some metals, salt mixtures, spices, but . . ."

Raych's eyes went wide. "Spices!" She turned hard at Asti. "That Poasian, Mister Nafath, he came here and gave me a bunch of spices."

"Nafath came to you?" Asti looked quite troubled by that. "And he gave you spices? Just came up and gave them to you?"

She nodded. "And he said to tell you that one of them was *rijetzh*. He made it very clear to tell you about that one."

Asti looked very confused for a moment. "*Rijetzh*. That's—that's exactly what we need. Natural magic inhibitor, though dangerous in the long term. Poasians use it on their imprisoned mages the way we give saltpeter to prisoners so they don't roll each other."

"I didn't need to hear that," Mila said.

Raych came over with a case. "It's this one."

Asti picked up the jar. "Why did he—" He paused in thought for a moment. "He's been trying to give me a spice jar for days now. I ignored it, but that's a conversation to have with Nafath later." He asked Raych for a jar of preserves and went to work.

While Asti mixed up the spice and the preserves in a bowl, the rest of the crew arrived. Verci kissed his wife, and everyone else fell into chairs and cots. Julien carried Pilsen, who was now asleep, and put him on a cot.

"We need to do this bit now?" Helene asked as Asti started to force the preserves into Treggin's mouth.

"It's not like we want to hold onto him for an extended period," Verci said.

"Definitely not," Raych said. She put the baby down on the bedding, and went over to Verci, wrapping her arms around him. "But let's get it done."

"You're staying?" Mila asked. Maybe more people here steeled her courage.

"Warn me if you're going to get gruesome."

"You hear that, Helene?" Asti said.

"It was one time."

"You must have clocked him good," Asti said as he held up Treggin's head, pouring water in his mouth.

"He was hurting Helene," Julien said simply.

Asti frowned. "I'm just hoping you didn't crack his brains completely."

"Speaking of." Mila wasn't sure if she should say something, but enough had happened in the past few days that she couldn't pretend it wasn't happening. "I think Pilsen's brains aren't what they were. He was . . . definitely not on task tonight."

"Good thing he didn't have a crucial task," Asti said, signaling to Almer to do something to wake Treggin. "I've noticed. Either his age is taking its toll, or he's playing us."

"If he is, he's playing me as well," Vellun said. "I've—this is why I've been trying to help you all out. It's been going on for a while. When he first worked with you all, it was like it brought him back into sharp form. But after that—he's been covering. I don't—" Vellun shook his head.

"We'll deal with that," Verci said. "For now . . . let's talk to this guy."

Almer waved something noxious in front of Treggin's nose, and the man jolted awake. He looked around startled for a moment, and then his eyes focused on Mila. "You! Oh, you're about to—"

His brow creased, and he looked around confused.

"Something not working, Treggin?" Mila asked. "So sorry."

"Since we have you," Asti said, pulling up a chair to sit in front of Treggin. "Maybe you'd like to talk a bit about what's been going on."

Treggin nodded. "So you're the Rynaxes. Oh, Poller was so worked up about you two. 'Have to watch the Rynaxes. Have to stay on them.' I'll admit I thought very little of him."

"Still do?" Asti asked.

"I'm not unimpressed," Treggin said. "I'll confess, I had no inkling you would track things to Henterman's household."

"Let's talk about that, Treggin—is that a good enough name for you? Or is it Ender?"

"Treggin is fine," he said.

"So," Asti said. "Draw some lines for me. North Seleth. Lord Henterman. Andrendon. And you, apparently, in the middle."

"Oh, you know about Andrendon," Treggin said. "In that case, what else do I need to say?"

"You're behind it."

"Me?" Treggin said with a bit of a laugh. "I'm quite flattered you would think so."

"You expect me to believe that?"

"Please, Mister Rynax," he said quite calmly. "I had jobs to do. Funnel funds from Henterman. Rile up the street factions."

"All right, who gave you those jobs? And why you?"

"I can't tell you."

Asti pulled a blade out. "Raych, this might be your gruesome moment."

"Hurt me if you will, but I can't," Treggin said. "You can't pull out of me what I don't know." He signaled down to the tattoo on his chest. "Firewing mage. We're largely a mercenary Circle, mages for hire. Whoever hired out the job did it through the Circle, and I was assigned through them."

"Then give me names of your superiors."

"Give up my fellows, Mister Rynax? That isn't what Circles do."

"Fine," Asti said. He brought the blade to Treggin's face. Raych gasped and turned around, and then screamed.

"Mister Rynax, put the blade down."

That came from someone else entirely, standing in the door. Someone Mila had never seen before.

Verci had never seen his brother surrender anything so quickly before in his life. The knife was on the ground and Asti's hands were in the air before Verci even knew what was happening.

Seven people—all in dark clothes—had come in from every direction. At least one from a door Verci didn't even know was there. And none of the usual alarms had gone off. What happened to the janglewires in the sewers?

Helene was bringing up her crossbow when Asti hissed at her. "Drop it!"

"You would be wise to listen to him, Miss Kesser," the man who had spoken said. Verci thought he looked familiar.

"These guys ain't sticks," Helene said.

"No, they're rutting Druth Intelligence," Asti said. He turned to the man who had spoken. "You come to finish the job that Liora couldn't, Major?"

Now Verci recognized the face. This was the man who had helped him onto the tickwagon the other day. "Major Grieson?"

"Major rutting Grieson," Asti confirmed.

"Asti, it's good to see you," Major Grieson said calmly. He wasn't armed—at least not obviously so—but the other six were ready with crossbows, short swords at their hips, and who knew what else. Verci didn't see a way for them to fight their way out of here.

"Don't give me that," Asti said. "You're the one who washed me out."

"And look what you've done. Restarted criminal enterprises, terrorized a member of the peerage, left a trail of bodies all over Maradaine."

Raych's whole body was trembling as she clutched tighter to Verci. "Are we being arrested?"

"These people don't arrest anyone," Asti said. "Do you, Major? It's either throw them in a hole or kill them outright."

"If it comes to that," Major Grieson said.

"You don't want us dead," Asti said. "Else you and your boys here would have mowed us down as you came in. So you want something."

Grieson pointed to Treggin. "This man is a person of interest for us. We'd prefer to take him alive to question."

"Oh, and what about what I prefer?" Treggin asked.

Grieson snapped his fingers, and one of the agents cracked a vial in his gloved hand, and waved it in front of

Treggin's face. Treggin's eyes rolled back and he slumped down, insensate. Almer let out a low, respectful whistle.

"We were questioning him," Mila said. "You could wait your turn."

Grieson laughed a little. "I like you, Miss Kendish. You've got the same spirit we saw in Asti five years ago."

"Leave her be," Asti said. "Now that you've knocked him out, what, you want us to give him to you, and you'll just walk away?"

"Something like that," Grieson said. "And then I would encourage you—all of you—to forget about your other enterprises and go back to living lives of honest decency." He turned to Verci. "That is what you want, isn't it Mister Rynax? Missus Rynax?"

"Yes," Raych whispered. She was still shivering, terrified. With good cause.

"And I'm prepared to be magnanimous about that," Grieson said, waving to his men to lower their weapons. "Case in point, Mister Rill is currently being pursued by local Constabulary—though of course, that's certainly a case of mistaken identity. I know they think all Ch'omiks look alike."

"And?" Asti asked, looking over at Kennith.

"And that problem can just vanish."

Asti seemed to take this in. "Go on."

"I don't see Missus Holt here, but I imagine she—"

"I don't care what she wants," Asti snapped.

Grieson nodded, looking around. "Yes, of course. Clearly some files need to be updated. But perhaps Mister Cort would like his Guild certification reinstated."

"And?" Helene asked.

"Don't be greedy, Miss Kesser," he said.

"I'm not," she said. "Clearly you could kill us all, or put us in a hole and throw away the hole. But you want to make a deal. So what else is on the table?"

"And what do you want, Miss Kesser? A payout? Your own little cheese and charcuterie shop to run with your cousin?"

"Really?" Julien asked.

Helene held up a hand to Jules. "Maybe."

"And you, Mister Rynax?" Major Grieson turned to

Verci. "There's an empty shop just a few doors down from here. A perfectly good location for the Rynax Gadgeterium. We could arrange ownership transfer, even use your current property and debt as collateral for it, so it feels like something legitimate."

That rang some janglebells in Verci's head. "And we would want to get rid of the current property, right?"

"I would think it was the proverbial Chain of Saint Deshar on your necks."

Asti gave Verci a signal. *Play along.*

"Right," Verci said, squeezing Raych's hand. "And what about the bakery?"

Realization clicked on Grieson's face. "Ah, of course. I can't guarantee anything there, but I can at least . . . negotiate the safety of this business."

"That's all nice," Asti said. "But why would you bother?"

Grieson turned back to Asti. "Because, you see, Asti . . . you've fallen into some troubling business, though I know that it was for good reasons. You and your associates don't deserve Quarrygate . . . or worse, Fort Olesson. After all, impersonating an Intelligence officer is a Crime Against the Crown." He said this looking at Verci with a hint of threat in his eyes.

"They don't," Asti said. "Whatever horror show you have planned for me, let them all lead clean, happy lives."

"Horror show?" Grieson said. "Asti. I want you to enjoy your retirement. You've been through too much at the hands of the Poasians."

Here Asti half sprang on Grieson. "Right? Thanks to you all selling me out to them."

"That was Liora, Asti. You know that."

"She told me it was orders. She told me it came from Major Chellick, verification Six-five-six-nine-one-two-nine. Authorization by Standing Order Nineteen."

This seemed to give Grieson pause. "She told you this when?"

"Two days ago."

Now Grieson sprang, grabbing Asti by the collar. All his men brought up their weapons in a snap. "You spoke to Liora Rand two days ago. In Maradaine?"

"Of course, she—" Asti's eyes went wide. "You didn't know?"

"Where?"

Asti backed off a little. "You didn't know that Liora was Lady Henterman? She said she was running a Black Rat op on Henterman."

Grieson gave a whistle to his men and signaled them all to leave, pointing to Treggin. They scooped him up and took him off, leaving Grieson alone with the crew. He sat down in a chair and indicated for Asti and the rest to do the same.

"You're going to debrief me on everything that happened with the Henterman house—tonight and the lead-up. Everything with Liora. And then you will all keep your traps shut and forget you ever heard the name Henterman."

"Why?" Asti asked.

"You're questioning this?"

"Gifts from Kierans, as the saying goes. You could just kill us."

"Trust that it doesn't suit my needs," Grieson said. "And I can suit yours as well."

"And we get our deals?" Helene asked.

"You want the cheese shop?"

"Rent free," Helene said.

Grieson nodded. "And Misters Gin and Colsh?" Gin was still asleep, and Vellun had been quiet this whole time. For a moment, he looked like a lost lamb, eyes wide. Then in an instant, everything in his face turned canny and clever.

"We need the deed for the West Birch Stage, an enterprise set up in the name of the West Birch Players, with a fully funded honorarium for a troupe of players to put on six shows a year, including commissioning new plays."

That made Grieson blink. "Done. And you, Miss Kendish?"

"I'm not sure," Mila said.

Asti spoke up. "RCM. She starts in the autumn."

"What?" Mila asked.

"I can't do RCM," Grieson said, as if this was the thing that was a step too far. "I can manage University of Maradaine."

Asti nodded in acceptance.

"Wait, you're sending me to college?" Mila asked. "I didn't even go to regular school."

"You've got the brains for it," Asti said. "If you want it."

For a moment she looked like Asti had told her she could fly if she flapped her arms. Then, quietly, "Blazes, yes, I want it."

"Fine, done," Grieson said. "Now talk. And remember that I'll know if you leave anything out. I know your blasted tells."

Asti nodded and started the story. Occasionally Helene or Mila interrupted with some detail he didn't have, but for the most part, he led the narrative. When Asti talked about the small statue Liora stole, that triggered a memory in Verci, and he could see Helene and the rest had the same reaction. Helene even grabbed Julien to stop him from speaking.

Then Asti talked about what happened in the wardrobe. His voice cracked as he described, in detail, how Liora put him under her control with a few words.

"Did you know about that?" Asti asked Grieson hotly.

Grieson nodded. "When you came back from Levtha, our own telepaths checked you out. They said—they suspected there was some sort of trigger embedded in your mind, but damaged somehow. They weren't sure it could work. But we knew it was too much of a risk to keep you in the service."

"Why didn't they fix it? I know the service has—what did you call them—psychic surgeons? Why didn't you fix me?"

"Asti," Major Grieson almost reached out, but then pulled back. "They said your mind was too damaged, and what remained from the Poasian's botched job was too fragile to further work on. They said—" He faltered.

"What did they say?" Verci spoke because he saw that Asti couldn't right now.

"They said they were amazed he could function at all." Grieson turned back to Asti. "I know you've got a caged beast in there. According to my experts, that's all you should be. Yet you—the real you, Asti Rynax—prevailed. We don't even know how."

"Lucky me," Asti said. "Are we done?"

"We're done," Grieson said, getting up. "I'll honor it all. One more thing, though—"

"Yes, we'll stay quiet," Asti said. "Don't worry."

"Not that." Grieson looked at all of them. "Liora Rand is an Enemy of the Throne. If you ever see her again, kill her on sight."

"I would have done that anyway," Asti said. "Why tell me that?"

Grieson leaned in and whispered something to Asti, and then saluted them all, and left.

As soon as he was gone, Raych collapsed into a chair, weeping.

"Are you all right?" Verci asked her.

"Not really," she said. She looked over to Asti. "This means you're done, right? This madness, all of you? No more gigs, no more nights like this. You're done."

Asti was staring off into the air, and when he spoke, it was flat and emotionless. "You heard the man. We'll get the Gadgeterium. We'll all get what we need. Straight, honest lives."

"Good," she said.

Helene spoke up. "We're not going to talk about how that tiny statue she stole sounded a lot like the big one we stole right after the fire?"

"It does?" Asti asked.

"You never saw it," Verci said. "But, yeah, it did."

Asti was still disaffected. "And we never knew who we were stealing it from or for."

"The Old Lady would know," Kennith said.

"Are you going to ask her?" Helene asked.

"It doesn't matter," Asti said. "We don't know. And we're not going to be able to do anything about it now."

Asti was definitely in no state to continue right now. Verci needed to pull everyone off of this. "Nothing we can do about that now. Let it drop, we'll figure out if it's important later."

"As for tonight?" Helene asked. "We don't exactly have our cushy 'honest lives' deals yet."

"Sleep, all," Asti said. "I presume down here is fine for everyone?"

All nodded, and started settling in. With everyone's attention elsewhere, Verci came over to his brother.

"What did he tell you there?"

Asti smirked, and looked about the room for a moment. "He said that Liora was honest about one thing: Intelligence is full of rats. Including her. The only person he's confident isn't . . . is me."

Chapter 30

THE SAFEHOUSE WAS ONE of many hidden through-out Maradaine, every one of them a real sanctuary where she could hide out for days, weeks even, stocked with food, water, medical supplies, and anything else she might need.

Liora Rand was not wanting for a place to hole up and lick her wounds.

As wounds went, she had a real beauty. Liora had her share of scars, and had taken plenty of beatings, but she had never been shot with a crossbow bolt that went clean through her arm. This was a new kind of pain. It was only the makeshift tourniquet and unflinching force of will that let her get this far, instead of passing out in the boat.

She worked her way inside and threw all the latches and alarm bells, as best she could with just her right arm. Not that she expected company, but she had already underestimated Rynax and his people. No need to be lazy. She sat down at the worktable where the medical supplies were, lighting a lamp and setting what she needed on the table.

Before she went any further, she reached into the jacket's inner pocket and took the ugly idol out. Horrible little thing. Acserian, Nathan had thought. She knew better.

She couldn't possibly get her jacket and blouse off with her left arm in the state it was in. Blazes, the jacket and blouse might have been the only things keeping the arm attached. Didn't matter. She found a knife and sliced the cloth, peeling the garments off her.

That was a mistake. That hurt almost as bad as the shot. There were quite a few doses of *doph* in her kits, but she couldn't take those, not yet. As much as she wanted to drink them all, sail into oblivion, that wasn't an option right now. Bear the pain. For a bit longer.

She craned her neck to get a good look at the wound but it was too hard. Taking a mirror out of the kit, she held it up and looked around.

It looked like a huge mass of flesh had been torn out, almost to the bone. An inch to her right, it might have taken her arm off completely. As it was, it was a miracle she hadn't bled to death.

If she had been anyone else, she'd probably have to re-sign herself to never using her left arm again. But she was Liora Rand, and she had resources that almost no one in Maradaine had. She just had to handle it until she could get to them.

Using her good arm, she cleaned and bandaged the wound as best she could, and wrapped it up. Slinging her left arm, she made her way to the water closet to wash the rest of herself. Time to scrub Lady Henterman away.

"You've had something of a day, haven't you?"

Liora had been startled by the voice, even though she knew exactly who it was.

"You have anything better to do but skulk after me, Major?" Liora asked, peeling off the rest of her outfit.

Major Silla Altarn, looking crisp in her proper Intelligence Uniform, sighed as she came over to the door of the water closet. She had been sitting on the bed as if she had spent the whole night there, waiting patiently. "I have many better things to do. But you've made something of a mess."

"A mess?" Liora said. "I did what you asked, and it was time for Lady Henterman to vanish, anyway."

"Did you?"

"Got that monstrosity," she said, pointing to the idol on the table.

"And?" Major Altarn asked.

"Yes."

"Yes, what?"

Blazes, this woman was a stickler for specifics. "I have his seed growing inside me. Are you happy?"

"No, I'm not. Your exit was noisy. People took notice."

"Only Asti Rynax—"

"There are people who still regard Rynax as credible. And his brother—resourceful bastard."

"What did he do?"

"Pretended to be one of us. Mentioned you by name. That was a tie we didn't need Henterman—or anyone else on the list—to know."

"Not my worry. I'm going to move on, yes?"

"If anyone starts digging, there's a limit to how much I can shield you—"

"You're a bloody mage, Altarn," Liora said. "I'm confident that you—"

Liora suddenly found her whole body pinned against the wall. Altarn still stood on the other side of the room, holding up just two glowing fingers.

"And I'm your superior officer," Altarn said, moving in with an angry scowl.

"That doesn't count if I'm not really in Intelligence," Liora said. "You can't pull rank on me when we're committing treason."

"Your arm is a mess," Altarn said, stepping away. With a wave of her hand, Liora was released from the wall.

"I noticed. I need to see Crenaxin."

"I'm aware, I'll arrange it. Can't have you going on your next mission not looking your best."

"Thank you," Liora said. "Sooner would be nice."

"I'm sure. But first, we should take care of the precious gift inside you," Altarn said, placing her hand on Liora's waist.

Liora shuddered a little bit. "We need to see him first? He's a creepy bastard—"

"Respect, Liora," Altarn said. "You know how he is about respect."

"Fine," Liora said. "Lord Sirath is a creepy bastard."

"That he is," Altarn said. "But he serves the interests of the Brotherhood, and so will you."

There was nothing Asti wanted more than a simple quiet life of boring predictability. Tonight at Kimber's, the menu was the same as it was every Lemes in the summertime: roast ham with a honey glaze and Jaconvale mustard, roast potatoes and other root vegetables, bread, cheese, and fresh butter. Asti found her consistency to be very comforting. If you knew the day of the week and the season, you knew what Kimber was serving.

That consistency was the anchor Asti needed in his life, which was why he had decided to pay a month's rent for his room at her pub, and actually stay there. He needed a place that was actually his. Saints knew that Verci and Raych didn't need him underfoot all the time.

Kimber watched with a warm regard. It was a quiet afternoon in the taproom—the front window still just patched with a wooden board. Asti told her he would help her fix it.

"It's a little unnerving, you watching me eat."

"I didn't think you were easily unnerved."

"Rather easily," Asti said. "I just hide it well."

"Doc Gelson wanted me to ask you about that boy from the other night. He made arrangements for a proper interment in the field by Saint Bridget's."

"He's paying for it?" Asti asked.

She nodded. "I'm helping as well. I thought, maybe . . ."

"Absolutely, I'll help," Asti said. That boy was killed on his watch. Paying for a decent headstone was the absolute least he could do. "Whatever he needs."

"We don't know what the marker should say."

"Jede," Asti said. He had no idea about a family name. He thought about what ought to be added, what he would put if it was Verci. "Beloved brother."

Verci came in and sat down with him, now having gotten

quite skilled with moving on his crutches. No special brace or cane now. Asti wondered if that was a message.

"You hungry?" Kimber asked.

"Just a beer," Verci said.

She went off to fetch it.

"So how are things panning out?" Asti asked.

"So far, Grieson's promises are holding. We were delivered the new papers of debt, with a new payment schedule. And the debt is to a Keller Cove firm. Nothing with Colevar and Associates."

"Which means they might be free to do what they want with the land," Asti said. "Making Almer the only holdout on the alley."

"Almer said he got a letter of reappointment from the Guild. Vellun and Pilsen are doing well, their deals are rolling in."

"And Pilsen?"

Verci shrugged. "Vellun says he's better, but I wouldn't put it past either of them to play some sort of long game, even with each other."

Helene and Mila came in and joined them next.

"The strangest thing just happened," Helene said.

"You mean, besides opening a cheese shop on Kenner?"

"No. You know that Lieutenant Covrane?"

Verci nodded cautiously.

"Just bumped into him, and he asked if he could call on me later this week."

"Is this what being legitimate feels like?" Mila asked.

"Get used to it," Verci said.

Asti sighed. "Yeah, about that. We're here for a reason."

Verci narrowed his eyes. "We're not going to do—"

"Not do, no." He nodded over to the door. "But we've got some business to finish. So we got called to a parlay."

"By who?" Mila asked.

The door opened, and Enanger Lesk strolled in, oozing confidence, carrying a satchel, with a familiar-looking young man at his side. They came right over, and Lesk put the satchel on the ground and signaled Kimber for a beer.

"Thought you were in Quarrygate," Helene said flatly.

"Served my time," Lesk said. "Came out to a very

different situation here. You kids are thinking you're big dogs, did some serious scratch."

"What are we talking to him for?" Verci said.

"Who even is this guy?" Mila asked, her attention on the boy he was with.

"Enanger Lesk," Helene said. "He's the one—"

"Who led Poller and the rest, right," Mila said. Gears were turning in her head, clearly. "So why are you with him, Conor?" Now Asti placed the kid, one of her Bessie's Boys.

"Why wouldn't I be?" Conor sneered. "Where were you?"

"I was dealing with things."

"Getting Jede killed, the rest of us in Gorminhut. Tarvis told us."

"Where's Tarvis?"

"He's alive, if you cared."

"Settle, lad," Lesk said. "Him and the rest of the boys are all just fine, miss. Don't you worry."

"Want to tell us what this is about?" Asti asked.

Nange pushed the satchel over with his foot. "That is from the Old Lady."

"You're with the Old Lady now?" Asti asked.

"Yeah. Like I said, a lot has happened. Poller tried to run things on his own, and got tied up with that Treggin character, who apparently vanished after his boys cracked some skulls around town. And you all cracked some skulls back. Now, we don't want there to be a war here, since everything's settled. So that there, that's four thousand crowns."

Verci was on target about Josie. Waited a few days, now the offer. The only real surprise was Lesk and the kid as the messengers. But that was probably part of her message.

"Four?" Helene almost shouted. She glanced over at Kimber, who was hanging back from the table. The last time Nange was in here, he was threatening her, and Asti thoroughly thrashed him for it. Helene lowered her voice. "She took over a hundred from us, and she's thinking four is a peace offering?"

"I don't know about that. I just know, she wants to bring back some order to the streets of this neighborhood."

Asti gave Helene a signal to let it lie for the moment,

which she took begrudgingly. He pressed on Nange. "So let me guess the rest. Now you and yours—including the Scratch Cats and the Crease Knockers—you'll run the streets of North Seleth under Josie?"

"*Under* her. Let's be clear about that. We've been brought to heel. And if you all are going to stay out of things, all the better."

"And what's North Seleth under Josie going to look like now?" Verci asked.

"Same as it used to. The neighborhood how it was. Ain't nobody gonna make any more plays on it." Nange was talking real calm and sensible. He hadn't even used one insult yet. Josie had certainly gotten to him. "And nothing like that fire will happen again. She's made deals with the Street Barons, even Mister Gemmen. No one's going to dare now."

So that explained where the money went. Lining the pockets of the north side crime lords. Bending her knee to them so they'd give her the queendom down here.

"So all we need to do is just take this and stay out of it," Asti said.

"Didn't you want to?" Nange asked. "All of you?"

"Sure," Asti said. "No war from us." He knew Verci would agree, and gave Helene and Mila a glance to follow along.

Nange offered his hand, which no one took. He seemed to accept that, and got up from the table.

"Always a pleasure, Rynax," he said with a mock salute. He walked away, and Conor took a moment to spit on the floor at Mila's feet. They both left the pub. Once they were out the door, Kimber let out a heavy breath and brought drinks over to the table. "Tell me that isn't going to be a regular thing," she said.

"It's not," Asti said. "Don't worry about him."

Kimber nodded and left.

Mila grabbed Verci's beer and drank deeply from it. "I didn't deserve that."

"Let it lie," Helene said. "Those boys didn't deserve you."

"So, is that it?" Verci asked, taking his drink back from Mila. "A little extra cash, a clean deal?"

"Yeah," Asti said. "If that's what you want."

"We said we'd live clean. Honest. Give Corsi a chance."

Helene nodded, and Asti wanted to do the same. He wanted it to be that easy. He knew it wasn't going to be, and he could see on Mila's face that she was thinking the same thing.

"I kind of did something," Mila said.

"What did you do?" Verci asked.

"I dressed up like a clerk, went to the city records office, and asked some questions. Dug through some files."

"Why the saints did you do that?" Verci asked.

Asti knew. He and Mila had already gone through the papers they had stolen from Henterman and Treggin, even if no one else cared. Whatever Andrendon was, it was buried in a mess of bureaucracy and legalities. Someone very clever had made sure that Henterman had no idea what he was supposed to be funding. Neither did Treggin.

"What did you learn?" Asti asked.

"Nothing more about Andrendon. But that new house on Holver Alley? That's a Mage Circle's chapterhouse."

"That reporter suggested something like that," Verci said.

"And you know whose house it is? Firewings."

Helene gasped. "Treggin was a Firewing, right?"

"Exactly. So I did some scouting."

"Mila," Verci chided. "We said we were going to—"

"I watched the blasted house," Mila said firmly. "And you know who I saw going in and out? That guy. Lesk."

"That doesn't—" Verci started.

"A lot." She said it with finality. Whatever choice he made, or whatever Verci did, her arrow had already been fired. She would do it all alone if she had to.

"Asti," Verci said firmly, probably because he knew exactly what Asti was thinking. "We need to be done with this. This whole deal is a rabbit warren we can't get lost in."

"You're right about that," Asti said.

"What are you suggesting?" Helene asked, though her face told him she was already with him.

"I mean, we go on like we talked about. Clean, honest lives."

"Good," Verci said.

"But with our blasted eyes and ears open," Asti said. "Because there's a whole spiderweb between Andrendon, the Firewings, Lesk, and saints know what else. Maybe even the Old Lady now. We're going to untangle that web, however long it takes. But we won't put a toe off the line. We want them to think we've let it go."

Verci looked both relieved and nervous. "And then what?"

"And then, when we're ready—when we know what's what—that's when we make them all pay."

APPENDIX

A Brief History of Druth Influence
in the Napolic Islands

It is unclear exactly when civilization first came to the Napolic Islands—the chain of tropical islands halfway across the Tesolic Ocean—though it is believed that refugees and exiles from the Futralian Empire (ancient Acserians) fled to the largest island (Napoli) when their reign fell to invading Kierans in 850 BFE. Over the centuries, the Kierans, Acserians, and eventually the Druth would come to "the edge of the world", establishing trading outposts and influencing the local islanders with colonies or missions. However, their influence rarely expanded past the large island.

The first major change of Druth involvement came in 852 FE after the fall of the Acorian Republic (in northeastern Druthal, what would later become the Archduchy of Acora). Thousands of Acorians, including their ruling elite, fled in ships through the Gulf of Waisholm and down the western coast of Druthal, making landfall on the northern part of the big island, in the territory of the Hakohi people. The Acorians made a peaceful agreement with the Hakohi, and founded the city of New Acoria. New Acoria became a thriving community that stood as the pinnacle of peace and advancement in Napoli.

Over the centuries, trade routes were established between New Acoria and the Druth kingdoms, as well as it being a favored stop for ships from the Near East and Tyzanian nations.

In the late eleventh century Druthal had been re-united and had begun a campaign of significant invest-ment in the Napolic Islands, establishing colonies in the other islands, and claiming sovereignty over the local people. By 1150 they had claimed five small islands in the northwestern region of the island chain, naming them Halitar, Falsham, Fendrick, Bintral, and Santral. Cities like New Maradaine, New Lacanja, and New Marikar were all founded.

At the same time Poasia had taken an interest in the Napolic Islands, coming from the Far West and staging per-sonnel and resources on southwestern islands. In 1150 they began a war with the Druth Colonies by brutally attacking the outpost of New Fencal on Santral: thousands of Poasian troops against a few hundred civilians protected by a mere twenty pikemen and archers[*]. Only a handful of people es-caped to warn the other colonies.

For the next fifty years the war between Druthal and Poasia raged on, with the Napolic Islands as the main bat-tleground. Rarely did the war touch the mainland of ei-ther nation[†]; instead the main cost was to the lands and people native to the islands. It wasn't until 1199, when Druth morale and Poasian resources had been strained to the breaking point, that both parties agreed to meet for an accord mediated by the Tsouljans and Lyranans. The final agreement gave three islands each to Druthal and Poasia, Poasia taking the islands that had been Bintral and Santral.

The Druth people who had remained on those two is-lands fled, some of them taking native spouses and children with them back to the other colonies or Druthal itself.

The colonies of Halitar, Falsham, and Fendrick remain

---

[*] Despite their defeat, the last stand of these soldiers became ro-mantic legend and a rallying cry to the Druth people, immortalized in works like the song "Twenty Druth Men" and the opera *Sand and Blood*.
[†] Druth forces occupied the Poasian city of Khol Taia for three years, from 1158 to 1161, and in the 1190s the Poasians razed the city of Corvia, and had a handful of minor incursions along the Maradinic and Sauriyan coasts.

intact in 1215, now militarized city-states ruled by Viceroy-Commanders, under the sovereignty of the Druth Throne and Parliament. While they mostly function as watchposts for Poasian treachery, they are also vibrant communities with well-established trade routes with the Druth mainland and the rest of the modern world.

Don't miss any of the exciting novels of
Marshall Ryan Maresca

MARADAINE

"Smart, fast, and engaging fantasy crime in the mold of Brent Weeks and Harry Harrison. Just perfect."
    –Kat Richardson, national bestselling author of *Revenant*

THE THORN OF DENTONHILL   978-0-7564-1026-1
THE ALCHEMY OF CHAOS   978-0-7564-1169-5
THE IMPOSTERS OF AVENTIL   978-0-7564-1262-3

THE MARADAINE CONSTABULARY

"The perfect combination of urban fantasy, magic, and mystery."
    –*Kings River Life Magazine*

A MURDER OF MAGES   978-0-7564-1027-8
AN IMPORT OF INTRIGUE   978-0-7564-1173-2

THE STREETS OF MARADAINE

"Think *Ocean's 11* set in Maradaine, complete with magic, violence, and plenty of double dealing."   –Bibliosanctum

THE HOLVER ALLEY CREW   978-0-7564-1260-9
LADY HENTERMAN'S WARDROBE   978-0-7564-1264-7

To Order Call: 1-800-788-6262
www.dawbooks.com

DAW 213

Necromancer is such an ugly word
...but it's a title Eric Carter is stuck with.

He sees ghosts, talks to the dead. He's turned it into a lucrative career putting troublesome spirits to rest, sometimes taking on even more dangerous things. For a fee, of course.

When he left L.A. fifteen years ago he thought he'd never go back. Too many bad memories. Too many people trying to kill him.

But now his sister's been brutally murdered and Carter wants to find out why.

Was it the gangster looking to settle a score? The ghost of a mage he killed the night he left town? Maybe it's the patron saint of violent death herself, Santa Muerte, who's taken an unusually keen interest in him.

Carter's going to find out who did it and he's going to make them pay.

As long as they don't kill him first.

Dead Things
by Stephen Blackmoore
978-0-7564-0774-2

DAW 210

Kari Sperring

Living with Ghosts

978-0-7564-0675-2

Finalist for the Crawford Award for First Novel

A Tiptree Award Honor Book

Locus Recommended First Novel

"This is an enthralling fantasy that contains horror elements interwoven into the story line. This reviewer predicts Kari Sperring will have quite a future as a renowned fantasist."
—*Midwest Book Review*

"A satisfying blend of well-developed characters and intriguing worldbuilding. The richly realized Renaissance style city is a perfect backdrop for the blend of ghostly magic and intrigue. The characters are wonderfully flawed, complex and multi-dimensional. Highly recommended!"
—*Patricia Bray, author of The Sword of Change Trilogy*

And now available:

The Grass King's Concubine

978-0-7564-0755-1

To Order Call: 1-800-788-6262
www.dawbooks.com

DAW 206

Jacey Bedford
The Rowankind Series

"A finely crafted and well-researched plunge into
swashbuckling, sorcery, shape-shifting, and the Fae!"
>—Elizabeth Ann Scarborough,
>author of *The Healer's War*

"Bedford crafts emotionally complex relationships
and interesting secondary characters while carefully
building an innovative yet familiar world."
>—*RT Reviews*

"Swashbuckling adventure collides with mystical
mayhem on land and at sea in this rousing historical
fantasy series...set in a magic-infused England in
1800." >—*Publishers Weekly*

Winterwood
978-0-7564-1015-5

Silverwolf
978-0-7564-1191-6

To Order Call: 1-800-788-6262
www.dawbooks.com

DAW 199